I0602670

Legacy

CARRIE ANN RYAN

NEW YORK TIMES BESTSELLING AUTHOR

LEGACY

ASHFORD CREEK
BOOK ONE

CARRIE ANN RYAN

LEGACY

Legacy
An Ashford Creek Series
By: Carrie Ann Ryan
© 2026 Carrie Ann Ryan

Cover Art by Y'all that Graphic

This book is a work of fiction. Names, characters, places, and incidents either are products of the author's imagination or are used fictitiously. Any resemblance to actual events, locales or persons, living or dead, is entirely coincidental.
No part of this book can be reproduced in any form or by electronic or mechanical means including information storage and retrieval systems, without the express written permission of the author. The only exception is by a reviewer who may quote short excerpts in a review.

All content warnings are listed on the book page for this book on my website.

NO AI TRAINING: Without in any way limiting the author's [and publisher's] exclusive rights under copyright, any use of this publication to "train" generative artificial intelligence (AI) technologies to generate text is expressly prohibited. The author reserves all rights to license uses of this work for generative AI training and development of machine learning language models.

For the ones who are lost.
I see you.
We see you.
Keep fighting.

PRAISE FOR CARRIE ANN RYAN

"Count on Carrie Ann Ryan for emotional, sexy, character driven stories that capture your heart!" – Carly Phillips, NY Times bestselling author

"Carrie Ann Ryan's romances are my newest addiction! The emotion in her books captures me from the very beginning. The hope and healing hold me close until the end. These love stories will simply sweep you away." ~ NYT Bestselling Author Deveny Perry

"Carrie Ann Ryan writes the perfect balance of sweet and heat ensuring every story feeds the soul." - Audrey Carlan, #1 New York Times Bestselling Author

"Carrie Ann Ryan never fails to draw readers in with passion, raw sensuality, and characters that pop off the page. Any book by Carrie Ann is an absolute treat." – New York Times Bestselling Author J. Kenner

"Carrie Ann Ryan knows how to pull your heartstrings and make your pulse pound! Her wonderful Redwood Pack series will draw you in and keep you reading long into the night. I can't wait to see what comes next with the new generation, the Talons. Keep them coming, Carrie Ann!" –Lara Adrian, New York Times bestselling author of CRAVE THE NIGHT

"With snarky humor, sizzling love scenes, and brilliant, imaginative worldbuilding, The Dante's Circle series reads as if Carrie Ann Ryan peeked at my personal wish list!" – NYT Bestselling Author, Larissa Ione

"Carrie Ann Ryan writes sexy shifters in a world full of passionate happily-ever-afters." – *New York Times* Bestselling Author Vivian Arend

"Carrie Ann's books are sexy with characters you can't help but love from page one. They are heat and heart blended to perfection." *New York Times* Bestselling Author Jayne Rylon

Carrie Ann Ryan's books are wickedly funny and deliciously hot, with plenty of twists to keep you guessing. They'll keep you up all night!" USA Today Bestselling Author Cari Quinn

"Once again, Carrie Ann Ryan knocks the Dante's Circle series out of the park. The queen of hot, sexy, enthralling paranormal romance, Carrie Ann is an author not to miss!" *New York Times* bestselling Author Marie Harte

Careless is the prequel to the Ashford Creek series. While you don't need to read it before Legacy, and can find it on it's own as a free thank you, I'm including it just in case. This way you don't miss a thing, in case you didn't pick up the prequel before this.

Thank you so much for reading and I cannot wait for you to join the Ashford Creek family!

—— ~CARRIE ANN

CARELESS

CARELESS

An Ashford Creek Prequel

CHAPTER 1

Felicity

"Happy birthday!"

I grinned at my four friends who I'd dragged up to my small town from college. The crew not only knew how to plan an event, but they were also a fearsome foursome of joy, exuberance, and abundance.

Lauren, Laura, Laurelin, and Laurel had been best friends since grade school. They'd all lived in the same suburb of Denver, gone to the same schools, lived within the same group of neighborhoods—even though they'd moved a couple of times throughout their lives—and went to Denver State University. They'd split dorm rooms, and when it had come to renting a house for their junior and senior years, they'd all lived together. And somehow, I had been enveloped in their L-named arms when I'd been on the hunt for an off-campus room.

Sadly, as my parents had named me Felicity, and I didn't quite fit in name-wise—or in many aspects other-wise—but I loved these girls. They treated me nicely and reminded me I wasn't alone even though I was technically a small-town girl, complete with Journey's musical lyrics.

"Thank you!" I said as we each held up our shot glass of tequila, tapped it on the bar top, and slugged it back.

The burn was like nothing else I'd had in my life. It felt as if a clawed hand scraped down my throat, set it on fire, and told me *that trash* was the most amazing and delicate taste that would send me over the edge.

I choked, throat burning, before I bit into the lime that Laura handed me.

"You were supposed to lick the salt first, silly," Laurelin teased.

Eyes watering, I blinked a few times and set the shot glass down on the bar top. The bartender with familiar eyes just raised a brow at me, and I ignored him.

Of course, I was going to ignore him tonight.

Rune would never let me hear the end of it. After all, he was my big brother. At least one of them. In a world of over-protectiveness, I had two big brothers. While Atlas was out on the road, playing for the Portland Gliders and kicking ass as a goalie in the NHL, Rune had stayed behind in our small town of Ashford Creek because he loved the place. Or so he said.

And I stood here in Summit Grill, his bar and grill—the only true one in all of Ashford Creek—and nodded in thanks as he handed over a glass of water.

"Oh, thank you," Laurel purred as she fluttered her eyelashes at my big brother.

I gagged again, but this time, it wasn't over the drinks. "Hey, remember what I said. No hitting on my brother," I said with a laugh and choked once again since the burn of tequila wouldn't go away. "How do people drink this?" I asked before chugging half of my water.

It was my twenty-first birthday tonight, and while I was going to drink to my heart's content because that's just what you did and I didn't mind following some traditions, I wasn't going to be an idiot and end up with alcohol poisoning. Hence why I knew exactly how many drinks I was going to have. I marked each shot or cocktail with a Sharpie on my arm and was required to have one glass of water per drink.

The four Ls didn't follow my mantra, but Rune wouldn't serve me in his bar if I didn't. And while he was grumpy, kind of mean, and way too overprotective, he was right.

"Oh, I forgot he was your brother," Laurel said with a soft laugh, still fluttering those eyelashes. She was probably going to blink out her contacts soon if she didn't stop.

"There's my baby girl."

Head slightly spinning, chest warm, and throat finally hydrated, I looked over and held back a groan—even though a smile crept over my face.

Gwen Carter, with all her gorgeous honey-blonde hair, threw herself at me and hugged me tightly. Jackson Carter followed behind and picked us both up as if we weighed nothing and as if the man wasn't in his fifties.

"Mom. Dad. You're here!" I quickly glanced down at my arm, grateful I was only on drink two of the night. Dad set us both down and kissed the top of my head. I didn't miss the look, that glance between the four Ls. Maybe they weren't as close to their parents, but I was. I loved them. I wasn't exactly embarrassed by them.

"I didn't know you guys were going to be here tonight," I said, and didn't miss the rough chuckle Rune gave from behind the bar.

"Like these two would miss their baby girl out in the world, able to drink legally. When their son owns this bar? No. I don't know why you're surprised."

I barely resisted the temptation to flip him off. It didn't matter that I was now twenty-one—my parents would kick my butt if I flipped him off or cursed at him. I may be an adult who was now two legal drinks into my night, but I was still the baby girl, and there were rules in Ashford Creek.

I put on a bright smile, hoping the cracks didn't show

at the edges, and gestured to the four Ls. "Mom, Dad, this is Lauren, Laura, Laurelin, and Laura."

"It's so nice to meet you," my mom said as she leaned forward and hugged each and every one of them.

They hugged her back, looking surprised, and yet each melted into my mother's embrace. That was my mom—sweet, slightly terrifying if somebody hurt one of her cubs, and the mom's mom. After all, I knew that each of my friends had their own mother issues, but I actually liked my parents.

Shocking.

"The next round is on us," my dad said as he gestured towards Rune.

"You don't have to do that, Dad," I said as I wrapped my arm around his waist.

"Just one because I'm old, and I'm joining you guys."

"Every time you call yourself old, you're calling me old, darling, as we're the same age," Mom teased.

"No, no, you stopped aging at twenty-eight. I know the rules."

I smiled at their banter as they kept going, and Rune made a round of drinks for everyone. This time, not tequila.

"And water for you," Rune said as he gestured towards my second glass.

"Of course. Thank you, everybody," I said as we each clinked glasses and, this time, slowly sipped our drinks.

The music blared a country tune that was easy to

dance to, and by drink four, my parents were gone, Rune wasn't behind the bar anymore, as he owned the place, so he didn't always have to work there, and the four Ls and I were on the dance floor, trying to pick up the line-dancing moves.

"How are you so good at this?" Lauren asked with a little annoyance in her tone.

"I don't know. I just follow what the person in front of me is doing," I said, gesturing to the gorgeous redhead in front of me. I didn't know her name, and that surprised me. Ashford Creek wasn't exactly a tourist town. Yes, people came up here and stayed during the summer months, as well as stayed here if they wanted to ski at the resort a little bit away. We were cheaper than the major resort town next door, and that meant they could save money and only had to deal with a drive that, thankfully, the town had leaned into. We had a bus line, an entire community line of vehicles to get people to that tourist destination.

But on a Wednesday night at my brother's place, I wasn't used to seeing strangers.

Then again, I hadn't been home in a while.

I came for the holidays, of course, but it was few and far between because I still worked down in Denver. My parents and Rune came to visit often, as did Atlas when he wasn't on the road. Hockey season was always weird to me because even when he wasn't playing, he was still training and conditioning. My brother worked harder than anybody I knew, and I was sad that he couldn't be here.

Just then, Laurelin sucked in a breath, and the hairs on the back of my neck stood on end.

I turned, and there he was.

The man of my dreams. *My hero.*

I held back a snort at that.

Callum Ashford wasn't my hero. Okay, maybe he was. He had been a teenager when I had been a little younger, as I was an 'oops' baby, and he'd saved me after I'd fallen off my bike.

He'd put the Band-Aid on my knee, kissed the top of it, and told me I was going to be okay.

All I had to do was smile and let others I could trust know I was hurting, and they would take care of it. But I wasn't a little girl anymore, and Callum had grown into those wide shoulders of his.

"Oh my God, you did not tell me that Ashford Creek made men like that," Laura whispered.

"They sure do," I mumbled.

"Between your brother and whoever that bearded man is, I am in love."

Jealousy zinged up my spine, but I told myself it was fine. I wasn't going to act on it. Callum knew who I was, of course. Because I was Rune and Atlas's little sister. Although I hadn't truly seen him in years. He'd left town when he was seventeen and come back to town right when I had left for college. So I had known him when we'd both been kids, and now we were both adults, and he looked far better than any dream I had made up of him.

"Ashford," an old man called out, and Callum raised a brow.

"Are you talking to me or one of the other Ashfords?" he asked dryly.

"Wait, is his name the same as the town? Is his family royalty or something?" Laurelin whispered, slightly tipsy on her feet.

I handed her my water, but she ignored it, going for her vodka Red Bull.

Shrugging, I chugged the rest of my water and picked up my own vodka Red Bull. This was drink five. Or six. Had I labeled that on my arm? I was fine. Right? Oh no. Time for more water.

"The Ashfords, years ago, developed this town, but it was like his great-great-grandpa or something. Or great-great-great. How many greats did I say?" I asked, blinking as the girls laughed.

At the sound of our laughter, Callum looked over at us, and I froze like a deer in headlights. Bambi, scared in the meadow and unsure of what to do with wobbly legs. But then he lifted his chin, and I waved at him, smiling.

Maybe I wasn't Bambi. Maybe I was the skunk who could learn to flirt and wave. I just hoped I wasn't the little rabbit, who spoke too much and slipped over their own feet. No, that sounded more like me.

"You know him?" one of the Ls whispered. I couldn't tell which one was which. That was probably an issue that I would deal with later.

"Yes, I know everyone who grew up in Ashford Creek. We're a small town. And he's friends with Rune and Atlas."

"Oh," two of them said at the same time, their voices breathy.

I just shook my head and smiled as Callum walked over.

"Here he comes. How do I look?" Laurelin asked, sliding her hands down her tiny, red dress.

Jealousy bit at me, and I pushed away that irritation. No, I wasn't going to let that have any hold over me. After all, the girls wouldn't be back, most likely, and it wasn't like Callum was for me.

"Happy birthday, Felicity," he whisper-growled, and my knees nearly went weak.

"Thanks, Callum. Buy me a drink?" I asked, trying to act like an adult. Because I was one. Damn it. "Or I'll buy you one."

He looked down at my nearly full drink and winked. "I'll buy you a soda, little flower."

One of the girls sighed behind me, and I blushed. "How about another time then? It's my twenty-first birthday, after all? I'm legal."

Something went over Callum's eyes, but I couldn't tell what it was. Instead, he nodded. "Another time. Though you're in Denver now, right? Not up in Ashford Creek that often."

"You never know. I could come home. I love home."

He shook his head. "There's so much more out there than Ashford Creek, little flower. You should go out and see it." And with that, he lifted his chin at the other girls and made his way back to the bar and Rune.

"I have so many questions," Laura whispered, and I just grinned before draining the rest of my drink.

"Brother's best friend and all that," I said with a shrug.

"Well, he's not my brother's best friend, so maybe I have a chance," Laurel slurred.

"Didn't you just try to hit on my brother?" I asked with a bite.

"Maybe. But it's Ashford Creek. There's nobody else here. It's a small town on a mountaintop. With nothing."

"Hey, it's my small town."

"That's right," Laurelin said as she wrapped her arm around my shoulders. "Be nice."

"I'm mean when I drink, I'm sorry."

"Forgiven. But you owe me a drink."

"Like you're paying for a single drink tonight," Laura whispered, and the four of us laughed, walking back out on the dance floor.

We danced for another hour, and I tried to keep up with my water, but I was dizzy. By the time I was back at my brother's house, tucked into his guest room with all of my friends, I was nauseous, regretting that last drink, and ignoring the roll of Rune's eyes.

"You're lucky I love you and you're staying here. Mom and Dad might not have been too happy about you drinking as much as you did."

I smiled brightly, my head pounding only slightly. "I didn't mean to. They were free."

"We'll teach you how to take care of yourself better next time, okay?" He leaned forward and kissed my forehead before making his way out of the guest room. I blinked a couple of times, wondering if I saw another shadow beside him. But it was such a *wide* shadow. Was it Callum? No. It wouldn't be Callum. He was just the man of my dreams.

I let out a sad sigh, curling into my blankets. Rune had two double beds in his guest room, so the girls and I were sharing, with one of them on the floor on an air mattress.

We could have stayed at my parents' house, but Rune had known we would be out late, so we'd stayed here. My family was amazing.

And considering what I knew the Ashfords had gone through, I was grateful for the home I grew up in. Part of me wondered if I would come back. If this would be my home. I ignored that part as dizziness took over, and I scrambled to the bathroom.

It turned out that having my brother hold my hair as I emptied the contents of my stomach wasn't the greatest way to celebrate my twenty-first birthday. Especially when I knew for a fact that it was Callum leaning against the doorway, holding my water glass.

"Happy birthday," I whispered to myself.

"We'll take care of you, little flower. Don't worry."

And while I believed him, I couldn't believe I was once again careless.

With my night, with what I had drank, and with my feelings for him.

CHAPTER 2

Callum

"Seriously, is there a reason we're at your house and not the Summit Grill?" Teagan asked as she leaned against my kitchen island.

I rolled my eyes at my younger sister but couldn't help the twitch of my lips. "Just because you have a crush on Rune doesn't mean we should be spending all our time at his place." Beer sprayed over the edge of the counter, and I glared. "Seriously? You're an adult. In your thirties. Clean up after yourself."

My sister snarled. "Fuck you, I'm thirty. And what the hell? I do not have a crush on Rune."

"Wait, who has a crush on Rune?" Finnian asked as he strolled into the kitchen, his twin Sterling at his side.

"Teagan," I said as if it were true. It wasn't, but I enjoyed fucking with my sister. If I could continue to keep the light on a fake crush when it came to my sister and my best friend, I could ignore the actual feelings going on deep inside me.

Very deep. So deep, I was going to suppress them slightly more so I wouldn't have to think about them again.

See? Perfection. I wasn't thinking about Rune's little sister's curvy body and the fact that she could fit against me perfectly. And the way that she giggled and pressed her finger to my chest, batting her eyelashes.

That was little Felicity Carter. Yes, she was twenty-one now. Yes, the last time I had really hung out with her at any point, we had both been children, but I was still too damn old for her.

I'd lived lifetimes since then, and I was an old bastard for even thinking about her that way.

It hadn't stopped me from fucking my soaked-up fist in the shower after I had come home from the bar that night, but that was my own problem. I was going to hell, but at least I could get myself off before I got there.

"Excuse me," Teagan said, snapping her fingers in front of me. "Listen to me."

"What?" I snapped. My lips still twitched, however, thinking of Rune and Teagan and the fact that there would be zero chance of anything happening between them.

"I do not have a crush on Rune. And if you tell him I do, and he tries to give me a wedgie again like we're kids, I'm going to kick your ass. You may be the Ashford Creek NFL legend, but I can still kick your ass."

My younger brothers just laughed, Finnian full-out body quaking, as Sterling just shook his head, his rough chuckle filling the kitchen.

Bodhi finally walked in at that moment, looked at the group of us, and sighed before going to the fridge and pulling out a beer. "Do I want to know?"

"Callum has something up his ass and is fucking with Teagan by saying she wants Rune," Sterling explained.

"What's new?" Bodhi growled before he leaned against the counter. He folded his arms over his chest and glared.

It was a nice glare compared to his normal death one, so I figured he was in a better mood than usual. The fact that he'd even shown up to family dinner was proof that maybe he wasn't such a badger afraid to leave is den.

Although maybe I was just like him.

No, I wasn't. I was worse. I was like the other one. The other man that I saw whenever I looked down at my hands. Because they weren't my hands. They were my father's hands.

And maybe that was enough beer for me. Even though it was damn good beer.

"I'm just fucking with you," I said after a moment, having ignored the way that my siblings—minus Bodhi—snapped at each other good-naturedly.

Teagan tilted her head as she studied my face as if trying to figure out why I kept fucking with her. I probably should be more careful since she always saw far too much. "I feel like I need to punch Rune in the stomach just in case."

I rolled my eyes. "Maybe. But I do know that you could take Rune."

"Damn straight." Teagan beamed. "And with the way that Briar is being all mama bear, our baby sister could probably take him too."

That made me grin as the others tried to decide who could kick Rune's ass. To be honest, none of us could. Well, maybe a few friends who were out of town and still playing in their professional sports. I was long since retired and couldn't take a beating like I used to.

Which was why it was probably a good thing that I was staying away from Felicity. Because Rune could kick my ass. He ran the bar and grill in town, the only place that stayed open until two o'clock these days. Every once in a while, another bar would open, but it wouldn't last long against Rune's clientele.

Because it wasn't as if he let any shadowy figures walk through the doors. No, he took care of his people, and that was why he was my best friend. But that also meant that Rune had to kick out anybody who fucked with him.

Hence, the guy who probably had to walk sideways through the doorway.

"How is Briar? All she does is text me back. Somebody's too busy to answer an actual phone call," Finnian said as he grinned.

"Well, it's because you keep bothering her." Sterling stole a chip from the bowl in front of him, and I pushed it toward him.

"Everybody start helping with dinner. We're having fajitas, and I've sliced most of the veggies. Bodhi, you want to go check the grill?"

"On it." He looked over his shoulder before he walked out to the deck. "And I talked with Briar this morning. She, the husband, and the most precious baby girl out there are staying in Texas for a bit. We'll get her to family dinner soon."

I met Teagan's gaze, and she was the one who shook her head.

"No, we'll go down there. It would be easier than her coming up to Ashford Creek."

Bodhi nodded tightly, a knowing look on his face. Because Bodhi wouldn't be leaving town. He either came to my place or hid up in his cabin in the woods. There were good reasons for that, and frankly, I didn't blame him.

But Briar wouldn't be coming up to Ashford Creek anytime soon if she was staying and being super careful.

She was not only a Grammy Award-winning

songwriter; she was married to one of the hottest rock stars on the planet at the moment. They were new parents, newlyweds, and out on a world tour. They didn't need to come back to a town full of shadows and secrets. Secrets I was going to fucking uncover if it was the last thing I did.

Though the rest of my family didn't need to know that.

However, as soon as Briar stepped foot into Ashford Creek, not only would the town jump on her, wanting to know more about her life, about why she had run away from town, but the one person that I continually tried to protect her from would show up.

And I'd be damned if that man ruined anything else in our lives.

"Are the kids with Promise?" Sterling asked, taking a sip of his beer.

Finnian nodded. "It's her night," he answered, speaking of his ex-girlfriend.

Finnian and Promise had been high school sweethearts and ended up with twin daughters. They weren't together anymore and were figuring out co-parenting better than I thought they could.

I wasn't sure how they had ended up being nearly best friends out of it all, but maybe when you loved somebody, that's what you did. You found out that maybe you didn't love somebody the right way, and you wanted to protect your kids.

Both Promise and Finnian were finishing their college degrees, parenting the twins, and each living with family. Promise with her parents, and Finnian with me for now. There was no way that we'd ever let the twins near their grandfather. I suppressed a shudder at that.

No, the world would do better if Matthew Ashford never stepped foot in Ashford Creek or in this world again. But he was the town drunk for a reason. And he would find a way to embarrass us all at any moment now.

No wonder Briar never wanted to come back.

Finnian pulled out his phone and, instead of helping cook, showed off the latest pictures he'd taken of the girls.

I rolled my eyes and went back to chopping, knowing that I was damn lucky to have all of my kids under my roof.

I might be their eldest brother, but I pretty much raised the twins and Briar. It wasn't as if my father was doing it.

After Mom had died, leaving seven kids behind, Teagan had stepped in, taking over that mothering role even though she had been far too young. It had killed me trying to help out, knowing that Teagan was putting her own feelings and future aside to make sure that the youngest could survive. I had put all of my effort into not only helping the younger kids but getting that scholarship. And when I'd gotten into college on a full-ride and ended up in the NFL—albeit a late-round draft pick, I had made enough money to buy the house we stood in, start my own business, and ensure that the rest of the family never had to go into debt to pay for school and could get out of Matthew Ashford's home.

"You know, I think this is the best IPA you've made," Sterling said, and I nodded tightly.

"I'm just glad that you're old enough to drink it now," I said dryly.

"I prefer the Pilsner." Teagan shrugged. "I'm not an IPA person, sorry. I don't like to chew my beer."

"Please do not get her started on IPAs," Finnian said with a dramatic sigh. "Do you know what your yearly special is going to be yet?"

I did, but I wasn't about to tell them. They wouldn't mean to, but they would tell one person, and then they would tell another, and suddenly Ashford Brews would make not only the local paper but the next town over, and my secrets would be out.

We were a decent business for the town, and my two years in the NFL had made sure that I at least had an entryway into this random life of mine. Maybe if I hadn't gotten hurt, things would've been different, but I was home, making this work.

I might surround myself with shadows and secrets in Ashford Creek, but I knew I was running away from them too.

For a damn reason.

But it wasn't as if I was going to let my family deal with those problems. They dealt with enough as it was.

"Here, I'll finish up the guacamole," Teagan said as she rubbed her shoulder against my upper arm.

"I forgot how short you were," I said, trying to push the darkness from my mind.

She rolled her eyes. "I'm taller than Briar."

"Well, she's not here, is she?" Teagan's eyes filled, and I cursed. "What? What did I say?"

"Just thinking about who else isn't here." She looked across my open-concept kitchen into the dining room, and I sighed.

Malcolm. That's who wasn't here.

Bodhi's twin brother, the rock star of the family, literally. A drummer prodigy who had made us all so fucking proud. I still couldn't quite believe that it had been over three years now. Three years since Malcolm had died in a bus crash while he was on tour. A bus crash that had nearly taken Briar out along the way.

Briar had come back to Ashford Creek to heal and had ended up needing her future husband more than she needed us, and I understood that.

We Ashfords knew how to remind others of their own darkness.

"I love you, Teagan," I said as I wrapped my arm around her shoulders.

"Love you too, you oaf."

"Why am I an oaf?"

"Because I don't have a crush on Rune."

"The more you say it, the more I feel like it's real," Finnian teased.

"I'm going to throw this avocado seed at you."

"If you do, then you have to clean up the mess," Sterling said as he took the plate of lettuce and tomatoes from me. "Go sit. We'll handle this."

I sighed. "Okay, but don't you dare get out the yellow cheese. You know the rules. No yellow cheese when we make Tex-Mex in this house."

We grumbled about it, but I just laughed, taking a seat at the long table that I had pried out of Bodhi's hands when he had finished making it.

"I do like family dinners," Finnian said after a while. My belly was full, and I had another beer in my hand. I'd only had two, but I wasn't planning on anymore. I did not need to get drunk tonight, not when I knew one of Dad's old friends had spotted him in town. Somebody needed to be alert.

"You only like it because you didn't have to pay for it." Teagan shook her head, a smile playing on her face.

Finnian gave a mock gasp. "Hey, I'm a single father of two. I need to save money."

Teagan rolled her eyes and I sat back and watched the show. "You say that as if Promise isn't the best ex-girlfriend in the world who co-parents with you in an organized way to the point that it scares me."

My brother shrugged before digging into his food. "True, I love Promise, and I'm so glad she's my daughters' mother. But I'm also relieved that we figured out this whole co-parenting thing after a rough patch."

"Is she going to open that bed and breakfast when she gets through college?" Teagan asked.

Finnian nodded. "That's the plan. There used to be one up Heritage Street, and I know she's is+ looking at the deeds now along with her family's help."

"That would be a great place for it. And you'd help her fix it up, right?" Teagan asked as she played with the rest of her food.

There was something going on in my little sister's head, and I would figure it out. I would figure it out with all of them. I just hated the fact that I couldn't fix everything for them.

"That's the plan. Once I finish this program, I have to go through an apprenticeship. But I'm going to end up with all of my certifications. The town needs my special hands," he said as he wiggled his fingers.

"More like spirit fingers," Sterling teased under his breath, and I growled as Finnian lifted a chip to throw it across the table.

"We are not children, no food fights in my fucking house."

"Yes, Daddy," Finnian said with a roll of his eyes.

How the nicest and yet most sarcastic one of us ended up a father of two, I would never know. Because the man was one of the best fathers I'd ever seen. He didn't have a blueprint for it, though, considering our father, so I was just damn happy that Finnian was figuring it out.

"So, did you see who's back in town for the week?" Finnian asked again, and I tried not to look too alert. After all, my brother was talking to Sterling and Bodhi, not me.

"I cannot believe that Felicity's already twenty-one. Wasn't she just in braces?"

"You say that as if you aren't only eighteen months or so older than her," Teagan said dryly.

"And those eighteen months count. We've seen worlds since then." Finnian rolled his shoulders back, looking like the pompous jackass he sometimes pretended to be.

"She's almost done with college. What do you think she's going to do after that?" Teagan asked.

Finnian took a big bite of his food and thankfully swallowed before answering. "No clue. Though with Rune here, and her parents, she might want to come back."

"Why would she come back to Ashford Creek?" I asked, my voice low. "There's nothing for her here."

Bodhi gave me a look that I couldn't read, or rather, I didn't want to read, so I ignored him.

"There's plenty in Ashford Creek and we're growing yearly," Sterling said with a shrug.

"We might not be the center family anymore, with the town mayor in our pocket or growing the town's population and lines, but the town itself is cleaning up and getting a good reputation. Your brewery's helping with that. With the addition of the bar and grill room put in, and maybe this bed and breakfast, we're kicking ass." Teagan shrugged as if she hadn't tried to cement our family into this town once again.

"Not to mention your gift shop," Finnian said with a grin.

"It's not my gift shop. I only manage it," Teagan said as she continued not to eat her food. What the hell was going on with her?

"I'm thinking about maybe coming back to town after I finish culinary school," Sterling blurted.

I blinked and set my fork down. "What? Why?"

"The town could use a higher-end restaurant. You know, for the tourists that don't want to stay in the resort town. Summit Grill is great, as are the diner and bakery..."

"The bakery's shit, and we all know it," Bodhi grumbled but didn't elaborate.

Nobody needed to. Not with the owner and the way she constantly annoyed the fuck out of everybody in town. And frankly, her baked goods didn't rise to the occasion. I could not believe I just said that own pun in my head, and I was grateful I hadn't said it aloud. Finnian would never let me live it down.

I leaned forward, focusing on my brother's words. "Restaurants are hard to maintain. It's not just knowing how to cook."

Sterling nodded, and I was grateful that he had taken my words at face value and not heard any underlining rudeness. Because I believed in all of my siblings. The fact that any of us had lofty dreams to begin with surprised me, considering how we had grown up.

"I have plans. I promise. I'm not going to throw all of my savings into a restaurant and bail right out the gate. I'm going to learn along the way and then come back to town after school and get it done. The town needs it."

"Well, I run more than two businesses at this point, so I don't mind helping with whatever you need," Teagan said with a grin.

I nodded. "You run part of my brewery, Bodhi's business, and you pretty much do everything for the fucking gift shop, even though the owners treat you like shit. And I know that you help Rune out sometimes."

"While you're crushing on him," Finnian teased and ducked when Teagan threw her chip.

"Seriously?" I snapped.

Teagan glared at each of us. "I'll clean it up."

Wincing, I squeezed her shoulder. "No, I'll clean it up. I started the Rune thing. I'm sorry."

Teagan raised a brow, and I probably shouldn't have offered to help clean that up. Because that meant she would wonder why I had pushed the whole Rune thing.

I was going to hell.

Again.

"Either way, if you come up with a business plan, we'll look at it."

I still had a shit ton of money because I had friends

who knew how to invest, and I wanted my siblings to succeed. Even if I knew they wouldn't take my money at face value. No, they'd fight to pay me back. And that's why I was so damn glad I had raised my kids better than my dad had tried to raise us all.

By the time we were finished cleaning up, my phone buzzed, and I looked down at the readout.

Rune: Can you go and check Felicity? She had a hangover all day, despite how much water she had. I need to head to Summit Grill, and I don't like the fact that she's alone.

My dick perked up at the idea of seeing Felicity, and I needed to tone it down.

What the hell was wrong with me? I was over a decade older than her. I was a lecher. A crude old man.

Not really. But enough.

Me: Sure. Anything for the kiddo.

Rune: I can't believe she's twenty-one now. She's an old lady.

Me: Don't let her hear you calling her old.

Rune: Truth.

"Everything okay?" Teagan asked, a frown on her face. "We were going to make dessert and play video games until we decide that we've kicked your ass long enough."

I rolled my eyes. "I need to check something out for Rune real quick, but I'll be right back."

"Leave a love letter from Teagan!" Finnian called out, and I threw my head back and laughed as Teagan ran out of the room and jumped on Finnian's back. They wrestled to the ground, and Sterling threw his elbows in, protecting his twin and his sister at the same time.

My family was full of menaces.

"What's really going on?" Bodhi asked, his voice low.

I swallowed hard, not wanting to worry my brother for no reason. "Felicity was hungover from her birthday, and Rune wants me to make sure that she's doing fine. He doesn't like leaving her alone, and her parents are out of town."

"She's staying with Rune, then? Interesting." Bodhi took another sip of an Ashford brew, and I shook my head.

"Rune's my best friend."

"Yes. He is."

And with that subtle remark, Bodhi turned on his heel and went to end the play-fight in the living room.

I grabbed my keys and phone and told myself that I was doing this because my best friend needed help.

Not that I wanted to make sure that Felicity was okay.

I was a damn idiot.

By the time I got to Rune's house, I told myself I would be five minutes and then go home. There was no reason to stay.

I needed to stop thinking about Felicity as a woman. She just needed to be a blob. A blur, if you will. Because my dick got hard whenever I thought of her, and that was fucking ridiculous.

I knocked on the door, confusing myself since I

usually just walked right in. But now Felicity was here, and that felt wrong somehow.

She opened the door quickly, her eyes bright. She didn't look like she had a hangover. No, she didn't look sick at all.

Instead, she looked like my worst nightmare.

Tiny shorts that barely covered her ass, and I was pretty sure I could nearly see her pussy. An even tinier T-shirt that showed every inch of her boobs, as well as her hard nipples since she wasn't wearing a bra, and pink toenail polish.

That's all she wore.

Dear God, this was my test. This was my battlefield. My testament.

And I was going to fail it all.

"Callum! I didn't know you were coming over. I was just getting in the shower, and I'm grateful that I heard you knock on the door before I did."

Felicity. In the shower. Soapy.

There was no way I was going to be able to hide my hard-on for much longer.

I cleared my throat. "Rune wanted me to check on you. Make sure you weren't hungover."

Felicity rolled her eyes. "I'm fine. The four Ls left, and I think he wants to just make sure that the house didn't get completely destroyed when he was gone. But you can tell Mr. All-High-and-Mighty that I cleaned up after them, and the house is spotless. I'm going to shower, make some soup, and go to bed early. Yes, I had a headache this morning, but I'm fine. He kept me properly hydrated. And oh, you're still standing on the porch. You should come in."

There was no way in hell I was going inside if she was going to shower. *No way in hell.*

"No, it's fine. I was just checking since he asked. I got to go back to the house. The family's there."

"You drove all the way out here on family dinner night just to check on me?" The confusion etched on her face would've been cute if I wasn't so careless with everything that I did these days.

"Rune asked. He's my best friend." If I kept repeating that, it would help me remember. Why were her shorts so tiny?

She blinked at me and smiled. "Yeah, he is. Well, I'm going to bed early, and the four Ls are at the hotel now. They wanted a bit of mountain city life before they headed back to school. But we have dinner plans tomorrow if you want to come by and visit."

"I have work. Lock the door behind me. And don't open doors for random men anymore." The growl in my voice bit, and when Felicity's face paled, I could have kicked myself. But if I made her not like me, it would make this whole thing easier. Instead, I turned on my heels and went back to my truck, grateful when I saw her close the door behind me.

I was just like my father. Careless. Cruel. Careless with

my feelings, careless with whatever the hell was going on with my dick and its reaction to Felicity.

And if I didn't rein it in, I was careless with my anger too.

I wasn't going to become my father.

And that meant I had to try harder to stay away from Felicity.

CHAPTER 3

Felicity

Wat had just happened? Seriously. What the hell had just happened?

Why had Callum Ashford been at my door after dinner just to check on me? He could have called. Could have texted. Could have done anything. Instead, he showed up.

I frowned, tapping my foot against the carpet. Maybe he had only done it because, once again, he needed to take care of Rune's baby sister. But I wasn't a baby. Though, with the way that Rune treated me, maybe everybody was always going to think that.

I pulled my hair out of its bun and made my way to the shower. I hadn't been lying. I was going to shower and then cuddle up into a blanket with a book. There wasn't much out there that could compete with how amazing that idea was.

My phone buzzed, and I looked down at it, a bright smile on my face.

I answered, the video call coming in brightly, and the background sounds a little obnoxious. My brother's smiling face, including a lovely black eye and a cut on his chin, filled the screen.

"Atlas! What the hell happened? Are you okay?"

In answer, my brother glared. "What the hell are you wearing? Are you out in public in that? Go put some clothes on."

"If you're really going to talk about what I'm wearing, let's talk about the girl that was sitting on your lap in that photo that just hit the internet. Huh? What was she wearing? And frankly, I'm glad she was wearing that. Because she's allowed to wear whatever the fuck she wants. She's an adult. At least, I hope to hell she was over eighteen. So if she's an adult, she could do whatever she wants, and you can't judge. I'm not going to judge her. So step off."

Atlas merely blinked at me. "The circular reasoning of that, in which how I'm suddenly a bad guy and creeper, confuses me. And I don't know who that girl was."

I rolled my eyes as he flipped me off. Yay for big brothers. "You have so many women on your lap that you don't even know who she was?"

"No. She just showed up at the restaurant we were at. It wasn't even a dive bar or anything. She showed up and ended up on my lap. I tried to shove her off and then realized shoving off somebody so they hit the floor was probably not the best idea, so I put my hand around her waist to help her stand up. She giggled, said it was for a dare, then kissed my cheek. That was it."

"Oh, brother of mine. What are we going to do with you?"

"She didn't find out, did she?" he asked, his voice low.

I winced, knowing show *she* was. It seemed that whenever anybody tried to leave Ashford Creek, you couldn't truly do so. The past was always there to bite you in the ass. Or at least haunt you when you weren't expecting it.

"Probably. She does have a phone with social media on it. And knowing the town busybody baker, it's probably going to be in the town bulletin."

"Fuck. I'm not an asshole."

"I know you aren't. You're my favorite big brother who happens to play hockey."

"I'm your only big brother who happens to play hockey. And seriously, what are you wearing?"

"I'm wearing random clothes that I left here last time I was staying at Rune's because I was just cleaning up after the four Ls."

Atlas cringed. "Are they still there?"

"You don't need to keep the disgust in your voice when you talk about my friends from college."

"I do when they treat you like shit."

"They don't," I argued for what felt like the twentieth time.

"They use you."

"What could they possibly use me for? It's not like they're using me to get to you or Rune. You guys wouldn't touch my friends like that." Atlas's jaw tightened, and I gasped. "Which one?"

"None of them. But each of them has come onto me. It was awkward as hell. And I didn't like it. Despite what the press says, I don't like it when women constantly fawn over me. I'm not a lecher."

"I'm going to write that on your tombstone," I grumbled. Of course, the four Ls had hit on Atlas. They were doing so with Rune and Callum the night before. I hadn't missed it when Laurel had sidled up to Rune and rubbed her body all over him. Then Laura had tried to do the same to Callum. It had taken all within me not to pull them by their hair and scream about how Ashford Creek was mine.

I wasn't too territorial about my brother because, hello, he was an adult who could do what he wanted with his dick. And frankly, I shouldn't be territorial at all when it came to Callum.

He wasn't mine.

"Did they really hit on you?"

"It doesn't matter. They're your friends, and I'll be better about them. I'm sorry that I'm an asshole. I'm just tired. We lost."

The dejection in his voice slapped me, and I cursed once again.

"I wasn't checking the scores. I was too busy cleaning up all the vomit, and well, I'm sorry, big brother. I'm sure you kicked ass."

He snorted, though the humor had long since fled his expression. "I let two in during the last period, so not too great. Coach wants to kick my ass."

"Are you in trouble?"

"No, maybe. We have a young D-line, and they're having issues, so I'm having to step up. It's just, well...it's work. I'm one of the old men on this team, and it takes me longer to recover." He pointed at his black eye. "This was from an elbow in the locker room."

I burst out laughing, even though I hated seeing Atlas hurt. "Are you serious?"

"Yes, because I'm an idiot. Or these young kids are idiots. I didn't realize how young they were. A couple are younger than you. Infants."

I scrunched up my nose. "I really would appreciate it if everybody would stop calling me young and infantile. I'm an adult. A woman. About to graduate college and get a full-time job. Maybe even get my own place."

"Why would you need your own place? You could live

with Rune or Mom and Dad. Hell, live in my empty house that I have up there, and I only stay at when I'm in town."

I resisted the urge to roll my eyes because he was just never going to get it. That I was an adult. With fully functional feelings that sometimes needed space. It wasn't like I was going to go out and buy a place of my own and go into crippling debt without thinking about it, but it would be nice to think that maybe they would assume I wouldn't be alone. Or I would want to step out on my own.

But I didn't say any of that. It would just be talking to empty space at this point, when I knew everybody had their own words.

"Enough about me. Are you really okay? Did you put ice on that?"

"I did. Don't worry. I'm taking care of myself. I just wanted to see how you were after that lovely twenty-first birthday. How much of that puke was yours?"

"I made it into the toilet and only did so because of the sugar. But I'm fine because I drank water. That's what happens when you have a brother who owns a bar and grill, and his best friend owns a brewery. They make sure you're fully hydrated. I had to pee like one hundred times, but I digress."

"Too much information, little sister." He paused. "Wait. The four Ls made you clean up after them?"

"They were guests."

"So were you. And they're fucking adults too. I don't understand kids these days."

I truly didn't want to think of the four Ls at the moment. Not that we weren't friends, but because Atlas always got grumpy. "And on that note. I need to go shower. I feel gross, and I just want to go to bed."

His brows rose. "It's six thirty in the evening. I guess when you said you were an old lady, you meant it."

I rolled my eyes. "Have fun. Don't end up on the front page of the gossip column when I'm not looking."

"You know I will. I can't help it." He let out a sigh.

Poor guy. "I love you."

"You too, kiddo."

I said my goodbyes and went to take a shower. I was a little tired from cleaning up after the girls. They had cleaned up most of the things on their own. But any vomit that had been in the bathroom had made them feel queasy. I hadn't minded cleaning up after a hard night. After all, a job was a job. I'd worked in offices and retail all during college, and the four Ls hadn't. My parents had a steady income and had been able to send me to a nice college, but I still needed to work for room and board.

I didn't mind that I was a different socioeconomic level than my friends. I only minded that they dared put their hands on Callum. No, I wasn't going to think about that. No, no, no, no.

I was just stepping into the shower when my phone buzzed again.

Thankfully, it wasn't a video call, so I answered.

"Hey, Lauren. Everything okay?"

"Everything's great!" she practically squealed, the sound of music blaring through speakers likely behind her.

"It sounds like you guys are having fun," I teased as I shook my head. I put my face under the spray, careful not to get my hair wet, as I quickly began to wash.

"What's up?" I asked, wondering why she was calling me tonight.

"Go get that little black dress on and come meet us."

"I told you that I'm staying in tonight."

"No, you aren't. I've got you a date."

I sputtered, practically drowning myself in the shower. I quickly turned it off, ignoring the soap underneath my arms. "What?" I snapped as I put the phone to my ear. "I have a date?"

"Yes. We're going on a cinco date. I don't know if that's a thing because I don't know how to say double date or triple date. That makes no sense. But there are five guys and only four of us. And while Laurel wouldn't mind taking two home with her, the other guy wasn't feeling it. However, we showed him photos of you, and he's super excited to meet you."

I groaned. "Are you serious right now? I can't believe you just set me up with a random stranger."

"It's a blind date. And all of his friends vouched for him." Friends that they had literally just met. "And everyone seems like nice guys. Don't worry, we're all going to be together and have dinner. You don't even have to drink since I know you're going to have to drive home tonight. Just have fun. You deserve to have fun. This is your whole birthday weekend. We have to go back to school and finals and all that horrible stuff later. But Bradley's here now."

Bradley. Well, I wasn't going to let his name give me pause. Just because he had a douchey name, according to my brothers, didn't mean he was going to be a douche. After all, between my brothers and the Ashfords, we had ridiculous names. I was used to names that weren't exactly of the social club set.

"Where are we going, and what time do I need to be there?"

I listened as she explained everything, knowing I was going with the punches and doing what they wanted yet again. However, maybe spending the night after my twenty-first birthday at my brother's home alone while reading a book wasn't exactly the way to spend it. I was in college. I was supposed to have fun. And I would.

I'd be sober tonight because I was driving, and I wasn't an idiot. And I'd go dancing. Or whatever this cinco date was.

I only had fifteen minutes to get ready, and thankfully, my hair was already done. I'd put it back up in a bun when I'd gotten in the shower, so now I let the long dark blonde strands fall down my back in somewhat curls. I plugged in the curling iron, set it to as high as it could go, and quickly redid my makeup. It took me eight minutes to do my makeup, lotion up, and reshave my legs, not because I was planning on getting some tonight. No thank you very much. But because I was going to wear that little black dress. Instead of the strappy high heels, I went with wedges because I didn't know exactly where we would end up, but I was going to have fun. The four Ls would all be there, so it wasn't like I was going to be alone with some guy. And I needed to get over whatever crush I had on Callum. He was never going to see me as anything but little Felicity. And I needed to get over him.

With two minutes to spare, I got into my car and headed out to the park near the resort less than an hour away. There was a little restaurant there that had music and dancing, and I was excited now. I had left a note for Rune, and I wasn't going to be a little old lady.

I turned up the music, sang along, and finally felt as if maybe this birthday weekend wasn't so fuddy-duddy, as Atlas would say.

I pulled into the parking lot and was grateful I'd found a spot since this place seemed to be the center of attention for the night.

"You're here!" Laurelin said as she threw up her hands. Then she practically jumped on top of me, and I was grateful that I could catch her without breaking an ankle.

"Hey there. Have you had any water?"

"I'm making sure she drinks water," a tall man with a deep voice said behind her. "I'm Chad."

"I'm Hansen," another man said.

They all introduced themselves, and I knew I was never going to be able to figure out who was who. Each of them had the exact same color hair, haircut, and country club set. One of them had a dimple in his chin, and the other had darker eyes, but frankly, they all looked as if they could just step off an influencer's photograph page and call it a day.

"Felicity, this is Bradley," Laura said as she fluttered her eyelashes.

"Bradley's about to go to law school, and he's a Pisces."

"Gemini, actually," Bradley said with a laugh. He looked at me then, his blue eyes bright, and blond hair that curled right at the edges since it looked like it was a little too long.

I swallowed hard and tried not to feel too awkward, though I knew it was most likely a lost cause. "It's nice to meet you too. I am sorry if you guys were waiting on me."

"No, we were just having fun. Let's go dancing." Laura winked at me and gave me a hug. "I'm sober. I'm making sure that the girls aren't having too much fun. But we're glad you're here. It's your birthday weekend."

"I'm glad I'm here too." I squeezed her hand and then let Bradley lead me to the dance floor.

The music buzzed through my system, as did the Red

Bull that I drank. I was grateful that nobody was pushing alcohol on me because I just wanted to have fun tonight. Bradley was nice, a good dancer, and when I needed water, he led me to the station. I wasn't about to let him give me an open container. My parents and brothers had taught me better than that.

He leaned down, his breath warm on my neck, and I shifted away slightly, needing space. "So, what are you going to school for?"

"Business and accounting. Honestly, I'm really good with numbers, and I've been working with the town bookkeeper and accountant whenever I come to visit my hometown. I like it."

"That's all you want to do?"

I did not like his tone, but maybe some people didn't get it. Not everybody needed to be an astronaut or doctor or lawyer. "I like it. And some months will be harder than others, but it has weekends off. Meaning I can have a life outside of work."

"Well, that's a good ambition, then. I don't know if my dad ever found that balance with being a lawyer and all. But I enjoy school so far. I'm excited for law school in the fall."

"I almost looked into law school, but I think I like my path more for me. I don't think I have it in me."

"Not everybody does."

I gritted my teeth and told myself that he didn't mean that as a push at me. I was just oversensitive.

When the couples began to break from each other, taking walks near the small lake, Bradley lifted his chin and gestured towards the path.

"You want to take a walk? It's lit. You'll be safe."

I blinked at him, taking a look around to confirm what he'd said. "Okay. Since the others will be around too. I am a little warm."

"Then don't worry, I've got you, Felicity."

We walked down the path some more, and when he took my hand, I didn't pull away. After a couple of those false steps and conversation, he asked genuine questions and seemed to like hearing about Ashford Creek. I didn't mention my brother's name since he had said he was a hockey fan, but when I mentioned the town, his eyes widened.

"Wait, I know that name. Isn't Callum Ashford from there? The tight end that only made it two years before some dumb ass broke his femur? That break was so bad it still makes the rounds when the talk about shit injuries."

I winced. "Yes, he's from there. A family friend, actually."

"No shit? He was amazing. Probably could have made more than a few bucks if he stayed in. But bad break and all. Literally."

"He's doing good for himself now, though."

"Yeah. But whatever he does now probably pales in comparison to being an NFL star. Just imagine it."

I wasn't sure I wanted to. Or could. That part of

Callum's life seemed so far off in the past, it didn't even seem like the same Callum I knew.

When we made our way to a bench underneath a large tree, he gestured towards it. "Want to take a seat? Get to know one another?"

My hair stood on the back of my neck, and I shook my head. "Maybe we should be getting back. We're a little far."

"Oh, Felicity. Just take a seat. You'll be safe."

He kept saying that, but I felt anything but safe.

So when he tugged on my wrist, I pulled back. "No. I want to go back."

"Just a small town girl, after all? What the fuck, Felicity? You're walking out with me all alone and aren't going to let me touch you? Stupid bitch."

And then he pushed towards me, gripping the end of my skirt. I punched out, my fist connecting with his nose.

"Bitch!"

I turned to run, and he tugged on my hair. When he pulled me back to him, I stomped on his inset with my shoes, and he grunted before I elbowed him in the gut. Between my brothers and *Miss Congeniality*, I'd learned a few things. And yet, as my pulse raced and bile filled my throat, it didn't feel like enough.

I ran then, my heels digging into the dirt. And then I left them behind, knowing I could run faster barefoot.

"Felicity!" he screamed.

But I kept going, except I had no idea where I was.

This path didn't look familiar, and I couldn't see the others. Pulse racing, I ran off the path, through a copse of trees, and sat behind a bush, pulling out my phone.

I couldn't think, couldn't breathe, I could barely press my thumb against the screen, trying to dial.

And as soon as he answered, I let out a choking sob.

"Callum. I need you."

CHAPTER 4

Callum

"*Callum. I need you.*"

Her words kept echoing in my head as I gripped the steering wheel and sped down the back roads. If a cop tried to pull me over right now, he'd have to chase me to the lake. There was no way I was going to stop on my way to Felicity's side.

"Just stay where you are. I'm going to find you."

"I don't hear him anymore," she whispered, her voice soft.

She'd sounded strong yet terrified when she'd first called, but now her voice kept getting quieter, and I wasn't sure it was from wanting to hide from that man. No, it sounded worse.

"Just stay where you are," I repeated, my pulse racing. "I'm almost there."

"I know you are. I'm okay. I'm okay."

"Yes, you are, little flower. I'm almost there."

"I should tell my friends where I am."

"You can text them, but don't get off the line. I want to hear your voice, Felicity. Got me?"

"Okay. I trust you."

It was like a kick in the heart, and I swallowed hard. "I'm almost there."

My tires squealed as I turned into the parking lot, and I jumped out of the car just as I turned off the engine.

"Callum?"

I looked up to see one of the Ls. I had no idea which one it was and stomped towards them. "Where the fuck is Felicity?" I growled, even though I knew she could hear me on the other line.

The girl's eyes widened. "She was out with a guy. Bradley. On a date. Why are you here? Jealous much?"

I glared at her and one of the other girls, who seemed to be worse for wear. "Where. Is. She?"

She lifted her chin. "I'm not going to let her get hurt. If you go and chase her, I'll—"

"You fucking let her get hurt by going out alone with that asshole. He's lucky I haven't found him yet."

The girl's eyes widened as the other girl wobbled near

her. "Oh my God. She was out by the lake. That way. I didn't know. I swear I didn't know."

"We'll talk about this later." I turned and ran down the path, keeping my phone to my ear as I heard Felicity's soft breath against the receiver. "Do you hear anything?"

"No. I should just get up and come to you. I'm sure he's not out there anymore."

My stomach clenched, thinking about what could happen. "No, I'll be right there."

I ran down the path, searching for the group of trees that she said she'd hidden in, but it was dark and everything looked the same. Fuck. I was going to have to have her make a noise, but I had no idea where this douchebag was.

"Callum, is that you?"

I paused where I was, searching, but I couldn't find her.

"There you are!" a voice growled on the line, and I ran. Full speed.

I didn't know what the hell I would come upon, but I knew if that kid touched her, I'd end him. I wouldn't care that it would be my father's hands once again beating someone to near death. I'd do it.

Nobody touched Felicity.

Felicity screamed, and there was a sound of skin against skin as somebody slapped another person, and I had to hope she was fighting.

I couldn't think about anything else.

I turned the corner and finally caught sight of the two of them. Felicity kicked out and ran as the guy chased after her. I moved quickly, heart thudding.

The moonlight danced over her skin as she ran barefoot. Her face was pale.

"Whore!" the kid called behind her.

She ran past me, skidding to a stop, but I kept moving toward the kid who only had a few moments left to breathe. I'd kill him.

"Fucking bitch," the kid snarled before glaring at me. "She's a tease. Calling her daddy out to save her? What the fuck. She was asking for it, man."

My fist connected with the kid's nose, the crunching sound satisfying. Of course, it looked as if Felicity had already broken it before I got to it, and when the kid wailed, I didn't care. I just hit him again.

"You little bastard. You put your hands on her. You're lucky I don't kill you." Another fist to the jaw. The kid tried to kick back, but I pinned him to the ground.

"My father's going to end you." Funny thing to say through the blood pouring from his mouth.

I snarled, leaning over him. "Your father can try, but if I bury your body right now, nobody's going to miss you."

Finally, alarm hit his eyes, and I spread my hand around the kid's throat. For a moment, it looked like my father's hands on my throat, a flash of memory, the feel of strength around my neck as I tried to gasp for breath. That burning in my lungs when I nearly passed out.

But no, this wasn't then. No, this was a little boy who had wanted to have something he couldn't. To forcibly take it.

"Do you want me to end you?"

"No, no," he rasped.

A hand on my shoulder, and I froze.

"I'm okay, don't kill him."

I swallowed hard, trying to find some semblance of control. "You like this kid enough for him to live?"

She squeezed my shoulder again. "I don't want you to get in trouble. He's worthless. I'm fine."

I caught a quick glance at her face, the paleness there, the sight of blood on her lip. Then, looked down at her feet—torn up and bloody from running in the forest barefoot. I turned back to the little creep. "You come at her again, you touch her again, you even think about her again, I'll kill you."

And that wasn't an empty threat. I'd do it.

"You're insane. Both of you are insane. It was just a little ass. What the hell's wrong with you?"

I squeezed a little harder around his neck, and the kid finally seemed to get it.

"Callum."

The fear in her voice was mixed with worry, and I finally let out a breath. I released my hold and stood up, not bothering to be careful where I kicked.

"What the hell?" a few voices said behind us, and I turned to see an entire group of people moving.

I pulled Felicity into my arms and ran my hands up and down her skin. "What hurts?"

"I'm fine," she whispered, but her teeth chattered.

I cursed again and just held her close.

"Felicity!" one of the Ls said, probably Laura or Lauren. I didn't fucking care.

"I'm fine," Felicity whispered against my chest as I just crushed her to me.

"What the hell did you do to him?" another kid asked, his polo askew.

"He attacked me," Felicity said as she pulled away from me slightly. But I wasn't about to let her go. "And he wouldn't take no for an answer."

The guys looked at her for a moment, and I was worried that they were going to stand up for their friend, but instead, two of them just sighed, and another lowered his head while the fourth came forward. My hand fisted at my side, and I glared at him.

The other kid held up both of his hands and shook his head. "I don't want any trouble. But we'll take him from here."

"Oh? You're just going to take him away, and we're not going to press charges? I don't fucking think so," one of the Ls said, chin raised. She surprised me, and from the way Felicity stiffened, it surprised her as well. Why the hell was she even hanging out with these girls?

"Stupid bitch," the boy growled beneath us, and I looked down at him, narrowing my gaze. He shut up.

Felicity tugged on my shirt, once again bringing my attention to her. "I don't want to press charges. I just want to go home. Please, can I just go home?"

"What if *I* want to press charges?" the little weasel snarled.

"Shut up," the other kid said. "We'll take care of this. He's not going to be a problem." He turned to Felicity, gaze narrowed. "If you want to press charges, we'll vouch for you. He's a little dick weasel."

"Then why the hell did you want him to go on a date with her?" one of the girls asked, and thankfully, she looked sober.

The other kid's cheeks pinked. "His dad works with my dad. I knew he was an idiot, but I didn't realize the rumors were true, and he was actually a creep too."

"Are you kidding me?" Felicity asked as she slid her hand into mine, taking a step away from me. I didn't let go, but I knew I probably should. "That's why you thought it'd be okay for him to take me out alone? What the hell is wrong with you?" She looked between all of them, shaking her head. "What's wrong with all of you?" Her knees nearly buckled, and I wrapped my arm around her waist.

"Take care of him." I lifted my chin at the piece of shit struggling to stand. "I'm taking Felicity home." I stared at the sober girl. "You good to drive?"

She nodded, eyes wide. "Yes. I'm good. Felicity?"

"I'm fine, Laura. I'm fine."

I didn't think that was quite the truth, but I wasn't about to let go of her. Everything moved quickly after that. The guys half-dragged, half-fireman carried the idiot away, and I lifted Felicity into my arms.

"Callum," she gasped as she wrapped her arms around my neck.

"You don't have any shoes on." I paused. "Where are they?"

"I kicked them off when I was running. I was wearing wedges, and it was harder to move with them on."

"Good girl." I struggled with my control once more. "The guy looked like he had a beating or two before I got to him." My jaw tensed, and it took all within me not to go back and kill the kid. That was the anger that ran through my veins. The carelessness. The Ashford.

And I wouldn't let Felicity see any more of it.

"My father and brothers taught me to defend myself. I didn't think I'd ever have to use it."

I cursed under my breath. "Let's get you home."

"Thank you for coming for me," she said, nestling her head underneath my neck.

"I'll always be there for you, Felicity. Always."

And as I got her into my truck, and headed back to Ashford Creek, I had to wonder to myself why exactly she had called me instead of her brothers, instead of anyone else. But I didn't want to think about that, nor did I didn't want to focus on the fact that I was damn glad she had.

The next morning, jaw tight after a sleepless night, I answered the door.

Felicity stood there, face clear of makeup, her hair flowing around her shoulders. She had on an old sweatshirt of one of her brothers and jeans with a hole in the knee. She wore tennis shoes and a cross-body bag, looking so different than she had the night before.

There was a slight bruise on her chin, and I wanted to go back and find that little asshole to teach him another lesson he'd probably forget.

"Rune said you slept well. That's good," I said before she could speak.

I'd called her brother as soon as I dropped her off, and the man had run back home, letting his team take care of the bar. Rune had given me one questioning glance before focusing on his baby sister.

"Thank you for taking care of my sister," he'd whispered to me, and I nodded tightly, not knowing what to say. Because I was a fucking bastard when it came to Felicity Carter. And no one else needed to know that.

"I'm okay. The girls all called to apologize, and I will have to go back and talk to them since I still have a couple more weeks as their roommate, but I'm okay."

I wasn't about to touch that since I didn't understand why she hung out with them to begin with. "You're not going to press charges?"

She shook her head, hands in front of her. "I just don't want to think about it. Okay? Nothing happened."

I raised a brow but took a step back. "It's getting colder out there. You shouldn't be standing on the porch."

And I shouldn't be letting her inside.

Her shoulders sagged in relief as she stepped forward.

I closed the door behind her and raised a brow. "You should be at home resting. Or going back to school."

"I will. I promise. I just wanted to say thank you. For being there. For dropping everything and coming to me. I don't know why I called you first... I just knew you would be there."

She shrugged as if it meant nothing, and I couldn't let it mean anything. Because if I let her call me again, to reach out, it would be too much. She would see too much. I needed to nip this in the bud right then and there.

"Don't think of me as a white knight," I snapped, and her eyes widened.

"Callum."

"No. I'll break you just like I nearly broke him. You get that, don't you? Don't be careless with your life. Because I'm not always going to be there to save you." I knew the words were cruel, but I needed to push her away. Needed to get that look out of her eyes. Because I recognized that look. It was the same look I wanted to feel. And damn that. Damn whatever the hell mounted between us.

"I don't need you to save me."

I raised a brow. "You called me. And yes, you do

need me to save you, little flower. You're a kid. You're fucking Bambi." Cruel words, and yet she didn't back down.

Instead, she did the worst thing possible. She stepped forward, put her hand on my chest, went to her tiptoes, and pressed her lips to mine.

I cursed and knew I should push her away.

But I didn't.

Instead, I broke.

I wrapped my hand around the side of her neck, my thumb below her chin, my fingers digging into her flesh, as I crushed my mouth to hers, kissing her harder. She moaned, a little gasp of surprise, as my tongue flicked along hers. The kiss went on and on, exploring, deepening, and it took all within me not to lift her up by those hips of hers, press her against the back of the door, pull down those jeans, and slide my cock right into that tight pussy.

But she was already bruised, already hurting, and already scared.

And I wasn't that man.

Abruptly, I pulled away and pushed at her side slightly.

She staggered back, and I nearly reached out for her. Regret shamed me, but I didn't touch her again. Instead, I stood there, chest heaving, as she stared up at me, looking like fucking sweet with her eyes wide and her lips swollen.

"I'm not a good man, Felicity. Just stay away. It'll be good for both of us."

And then I stomped out the back door, leaving her alone in my house, and knowing that the taste of her would be forever branded into my lips.

I was a careless man, and I did not deserve Felicity Carter.

And that would be the last time I let myself break.

LEGACY

LEGACY

LEGACY

With one scowl, I fell just that much harder for Callum Ashford—NFL star turned small town brewer. He's not only older, but he's my brother's best friend. Two very important reasons I should stay away.

Only two years ago, after the worst night of my life, he kissed me and I can't keep him off my mind.

When the only house available to rent in town happens to be the one across the street from him, the close proximity does its work.

We can't keep our hands off each other. Yet as the heat rises, so do feelings. He might want me, but he wants peace more.

There's a darkness within him I know he fights. Just as there are secrets his family needs to uncover. But when the danger comes full force, it won't be from the obvious corner. No, we both have our pasts we chose to hide.

And our fears.

Yet when I break, he catches me.

And I hope I have the strength to do the same.

Legacy is an age gap, best friend's little sister, small town romance and the first in the Ashford Creek series featuring Callum and Felicity. Each one can be read as a complete standalone. A HEA is guaranteed!

CHAPTER I

Callum

Ashford Creek. Home of small town lore, single dads, a bakery that judged you, a brewery owned by a former NFL linebacker, a couple of restaurants without a rivalry, family drama, secrets, and most likely a murderer.

And why the hell did I continue to live in a town that my family had not only founded long ago but tried to destroy multiple times? I'd run from what crawled beneath and moved out of town. Gone to college, played a sport to the best of my abilities, had a career in which thousands upon thousands of people knew my name.

Found a life.

Lost that life.

Then, I moved back to this hellhole known as Ashford Creek.

Yay.

"What's crawled up your butt?"

I narrowed my gaze at my best friend Rune before going back to pull the tap. A customer needed a beer, a shit beer since it wasn't one of mine, but the customer was always right. At least, that's what they told me.

"Nothing," I finally answered, since Rune wasn't about to let me off with just a glare. The man was damn persuasive and annoyed the hell out of you until he got the answers he wanted.

That was probably why we were still best friends after all these years, despite the fact I'd lived far from the area for over a decade, and why he was such a damn good bartender. It didn't matter that he owned the bar and grill. He was at his best when he was behind the bar, watching over the town residents and making sure we stopped fucking things up. We weren't always great at it, but Rune did his best.

I much preferred my brewery. Yes, we served beer behind the bar and some small eats, but we weren't open as late as the Summit Grill, nor were we open every day for the public. The scent of scarcity made reservations a top hit, and we sold more beer because of it. People would line up for hours for just a taste of the latest small batch in whatever four packs we sold that month.

I didn't need to be behind the bar in order to get my job done. The fact that I was behind the bar today just to help Rune notwithstanding.

Rune finally shoved my shoulder, lifting his brow as the light above us glinted off his septum ring. "I totally believe that 'nothing' you just said. Seriously, what's going on with you?"

I shrugged. "Not a damn thing. I'm just being myself. I'm sorry that I'm too much of an asshole for you right now."

Rune rolled his eyes. "Well, now that you mention it, you're always an asshole, so you looking like you want to stab my customers is pretty much on brand for you. However, if you could *stop* looking like you want to stab my customers, that would be wonderful."

"He looks like that when he walks into Ashy Buns, so I assume it's just his face."

I turned and looked at the familiar voice and did my best not to roll my eyes. Fiona, said owner of Ashy Buns, loved to get under my skin. First off, who the hell named a bakery Ashy Buns? It made no sense, and frankly, it felt rude. She hated her job, hated her bakery, and hated the town. Sure, I might complain about the town, and I might hate some people within the town for good reasons, but I didn't actually hate Ashford Creek. I was just an asshole sometimes.

Fiona, however, was just completely ridiculous. Her icy blonde hair was pulled back into a tight bun on the top of her head, and she had this new cat eye makeup thing going on that I didn't understand. She glared at me as she pointed to the wine behind me.

"Can I get you something, Fiona?"

"You can get me a few things, Callum," she purred. "In fact, why don't you get out from behind that bar, and we finish what we should have after high school?"

I resisted the urge to look over at Rune, who snickered behind me. Asshole. Fiona and I had never dated. Not in high school, and sure as hell not when I'd come back home. She'd always wanted to date the quarterback of the football team, and since Rune had turned her down, she'd tried for the tight end. I'd run faster away from her than I had on the field, and she'd never truly forgiven me. Even when I'd been playing in the NFL, she'd tried to find a way to hit on me and treat me like shit at the same time. I never quite understood her. Nor did I feel the need to any longer.

"Fiona, what do you want to drink?"

The edge in my voice was not lost on her, and her gaze narrowed. "Are you really going to let this man continue to work here?" the woman asked as if she hadn't just been hitting on me.

"Sure. I'm good like that. What do you want, Fiona?" Rune said, this time his voice was not as sweet.

The bakery owner rolled her eyes. "Chardonnay. The buttery kind, not the kind that tastes like olive juice. You would think you would learn by now."

I pasted on a grin, poured her a Chardonnay, being sure to fill up the proper amount and not giving a single drop extra like I might have with nearly anyone else in town, and handed it over. "Are you opening a tab?"

"Maybe. It depends on what I have going on later."

This time, Rune just threw his head back and laughed, and I flipped him off.

"Let me ring you up," I said dryly in answer.

There was just something diabolical about that woman, and one day, I hoped she would eventually just close up that bakery of hers like she kept promising and go away. Of course, she wasn't the only person in Ashford Creek I would wish would go away, but I just needed to get over it.

By the time she went back to her table, my head ached, and I knew I was done for the night.

"Stop glaring at me," Rune said after a moment. "You're all done for the night. Now we can get on to being customers and let my staff do what they're supposed to."

"It's about damn time," I snarled, though I smiled as I said it.

I did like helping out Rune. He helped me out at the brewery all the time. He was my best friend, and we'd been friends since we were kids. Between him and his brother Atlas, we'd run Ashford Creek scared when we'd been kids. My brothers Bodhi and Malcolm had joined us, as well as a couple of other town mainstays like Kellan and Thatcher. We'd been a menace on our small town, and I knew our reputation still tended to be a little loud for some of the town's residents.

Rune merely winked at me, and I quickly filled one more order before heading to the corner booth where our group had slowly been assembling.

Ashford Creek wasn't that small of a town. There were smaller up in the Colorado Rockies. But it wasn't a huge suburb of Denver or even a town that had multiple schools or versions of stores, either. We had one florist. One bakery, one high-end restaurant. One bar and grill. One brewery. There wasn't too much competition for each place, and that meant we all thrived, but it also meant that places like Ashy Buns didn't try to do any better.

Many people moved away from Ashford Creek once they finished school. There wasn't a university or community college here, and though some people did their courses online, most went down to Denver for school. There were countless colleges and community colleges there, and our small high school worked hard with a few of them to make sure our students got the right degrees and trade opportunities.

So, while we were still a small town, the fact that we even had a fire station, police station, and more than one building as a school for all of our kids, I considered us a decently sized town. Then again, I had lived in multiple major cities in my twenties, so perhaps I was a little skewed.

I'd even lived in LA when I had played for the LA Ruins, and that was pretty much as big as you got. Ashford Creek felt like sometimes it was smaller than a few of the neighborhoods a couple of my fellow players lived in. So maybe I was just a little off. I'd only been back in town for a few years once everything had crumbled, and my family had needed me.

"It's about damn time," Kellan said, lifting his chin at me and taking a sip.

Kellan was the main general physician in town. He could have gone anywhere and found his specialty as a doctor. He could have been a neurosurgeon with how brilliant he was, but he'd come back to Ashford Creek after he had finished school and, instead of specializing, wanted to be the doctor the town needed. When our older doctor had finally retired, the gaping hole in medical services in Ashford Creek had been evident, and Kellan had taken their place. All while single-parenting three boys. How he found the time to come out tonight surprised me, but I knew he had a fantastic support system with his family—let alone the people in this room.

"I'm surprised you're even here," I said as I shoved him into the center of the booth. He rolled his eyes but scooted in a bit so I could have space at the end.

"My parents kicked me out." The other man ran his hands over his face. He looked like he needed a nap or a vacation, not a night out at Summit Grill without his kids, but I wasn't in charge.

I rolled my eyes. "You're in your thirties, Kellan."

He smiled, his eyes brightening. "They stole my kids and decided that I needed time out of the house. I assumed that my time off would mean I would finally be able to sleep, but what is sleep?"

Thatcher snorted as he took a seat on the other side of the booth. "Tell me about it. My parents are currently watching my three kids, and instead of napping or doing the countless things I need to do around the house, like work on the fucking staircase that is about to crumble at any moment, I'm here with you idiots." He held up his drink. "Cheers."

I rolled my eyes. "How am I surrounded by so many single dads?"

"Because Ashford Creek seems to be a small town of single dads," Bodhi put in as he sank into the back of the booth. My brother glared as he said it, and I could have kicked myself for even mentioning it.

Only Bodhi was the one who had spoken, so I wasn't going to elaborate. After all, Bodhi might've never been a single dad, but he had been a father. I wasn't sure if Bodhi even considered himself one anymore, not since the worst had happened. I wasn't about to ask him, though. He wouldn't have answered anyway.

"I thought Finnian and Sterling were coming." Changing the subject seemed to be the best route, and I leaned forward.

"The twins are out doing their thing," Rune said as he took a seat next to me, shoving me further into the booth.

"What does that mean?" I asked.

"It's Finnian's night with the kids, and Sterling's working. He needs to be working tonight, considering he owns that fancy-ass restaurant and is a damn good cook," Rune answered.

I nodded, wondering why they hadn't texted me. Then I remembered that my siblings were all in their twenties and thirties, and they didn't have to tell me where they were at all times. Of course, as those thoughts slid through my mind, my sister Teagan walked into Summit Grill, lifted her chin in hello, and then went off to the corner with a couple of her friends.

"I see Teagan's here," Callum said.

Rune followed my gaze and narrowed his eyes as he counted the crew. He liked to keep an eye on the people in his circle, for sure. "Is it nice to have most of your chicks under one roof?"

I rolled my eyes. "If you ever say that around Teagan, make sure I'm there. Because I really want to be there when she tears your balls off."

"Your sister scares me," Rune said with a mock shudder.

"We've taught her well then," Bodhi put in and then went back to his normal glare.

I rolled my eyes and sat back as everybody talked about their weeks. We didn't have a lot of time these days to get together like this. When we did, we usually ended up at my brewery or Summit Grill because Rune and I barely took nights off.

The fact that our friends could even take time off from their busy lives to hang out with us was a testament to planning and pure exhaustion. Let alone the support systems that let the single dads in the group have a night out.

Pulling Bodhi down from the mountains and into town was like pulling teeth, and I had a feeling the only reason that my brother was even here was that he needed to sell a few of his pieces at the shop Teagan worked at. And rather than going back up to his cabin and ignoring the rest of the world like he was prone to do, he decided to kill two birds with one stone and hang out with us.

That meant he would have a respite from us kicking his ass at his cabin and just pulling him down into civilization sometime soon.

"Wait, they're having prom?" Rune asked, and I leaned forward, finally listening to Callum and Thatcher's conversation.

"Yes. Junior prom. Which makes no sense to me because my children are still infants," Thatcher said as he growled into his beer.

I snorted. "Your twins are fifteen. I don't think they're infants," I said with a laugh.

Thatcher flipped me off. "Fuck you."

"I only have one fifteen-year-old, and they're already

talking about this prom as if it's the be-all-end-all. Thank God the thirteen-year-old isn't old enough to be invited." Kellan took a sip of his beer, his shoulders finally relaxing.

"How are we old enough to have kids in their teens?" Rune asked with a sigh. "Weren't we just dealing with prom at Ashford High?"

"We're old. Crotchety old men." Of course, as soon as I said the word, the door opened, and the true reason I was a crotchety old man walked through the doorway.

She'd pulled her honey-blonde hair back from her face in a crown braid but let the rest of her hair flow down her back. She had on this lacy, flowy top and tight jeans with holes at the knees. She wore these platform wedge heels and a tiny little crossbody bag that separated her breasts in just the right way.

I was going to hell for whatever thoughts happened to cross my mind when it came to Felicity Carter, but I had known that for more than deemed right.

After all, my best friend's little sister was now in her early twenties and all woman.

And I knew exactly what she tasted like.

I quickly drained my beer, adjusted myself in my jeans, and stomped towards the bar.

"You're not going to get anything for us!" Rune called out before the rest of the table laughed, and I ignored them.

The bartender handed me another drink, and I

gestured towards the rest of the table. "Another round for them. I'll carry them back over with me."

"No worries, I got you," one of Rune's people said with a grin.

"We don't mind walking to go help out the boss. Keeps him on our good side."

I snorted. "I didn't know Rune had a good side."

"Amen," they said, and I shook my head, gulping more of my beer.

Felicity and a couple of people I didn't recognize moved over to where Teagan was, and the girls laughed, the noise of the whole room intensifying with the frequency of their voices.

A couple of tourists moved in on them and pulled Felicity and one of her friends out onto the dance floor. I fisted my hand at my side, taking another drink. I didn't need to do anything. She wasn't my sister. Wasn't my woman. And she was far too young for me.

But as the asshole grabbed her hips and moved her so he was practically grinding on her, my feet were moving before I thought better of it. Felicity laughed and shoved the guy back.

He held up both hands, grinned innocently, and went to dance with someone else. I didn't even realize I was standing next to her, worrying, until she looked up at me.

"Callum. Something I can do for you?"

"You're going to let some boy paw you like that?" I growled.

Her eyes widened, even after her cheeks pinked. "Maybe. You have a problem with that?"

"You know damn well that I do," I whispered, keeping my voice low so no one would overhear.

She tried to look over my shoulder, but she was so small that she couldn't even do so on her tiptoes. She was too small, too delicate. I'd break her, and we both knew it. The fact that my hands ached to reach out and grab her hips, to pull her closer to me, nearly broke me.

But this was Rune and Atlas' little sister. Off-limits didn't even begin to cover it.

She was more than a decade younger than me, and it didn't matter that we hadn't known each other as kids. All that mattered was that she couldn't be mine.

"Callum. Stop looking at me like that. I'm fine. I'm not drinking. And you need to stop worrying about me."

"I'm always going to worry about you. You're a little Carter."

Her eyes narrowed. "Really? That's what you're going with. Why don't you go hang out with my brother and all your friends and think about being old men or whatever the hell you keep thinking that you are? I'm going to go back with my friends and enjoy myself. That's what you told me to do all those years ago, right? Enjoy myself? Alone? It's what I'm good at, after all."

"Atlas is going to be here next week." I changed the subject quickly. I did not want to think about what happened two years ago. The way she had felt under me, the way her heart had beat so rapidly against my chest. I didn't want to think about her curves, the feel of her breasts against my chest. I didn't want to think about the fact that I'd nearly bent her over, spread her legs, and tasted that liquid honey between them.

No, I wasn't going to think about that.

From the way that her eyes narrowed, I had a feeling she knew exactly where my mind had drifted.

"I do know he'll be here. I miss my brother, so it'll be nice to have him home for a little bit, even though I know he has to go right back on the road. He's my big brother, just like Rune is. You aren't, Callum. Stop acting like it."

"We both know that I don't treat you like my little sister."

She threw her head back and laughed, making her breasts jiggle. Fuck. "Oh, shove off, Callum. You have no idea what you even want."

Well, she was right about that.

"Boy, what the hell are you doing with that little girl?" a familiar voice slurred, and Felicity's face paled. Without thinking, I shoved her behind me and glared at the old man.

"What are you doing here?" I asked my father.

His bloodshot eyes tried to blink rapidly, but instead, he just stared at me, wavering on his feet. "If you want that cat to scratch your itch, I'd look another direction. Young pussy ain't what it once was."

I didn't even realize I was moving until my hand was

around my old man's throat, shoving him against the wall.

"You talk about her again, and I'll kill you."

"Just like you think I killed your ma?" Matthew Ashford growled, his voice barely above a whisper.

Though the entire bar had gone silent, with the way that we were positioned, nobody had heard our conversation yet. Only Felicity had heard the cruel words my father had spoken. Frankly, I was grateful for that. My father was already the town drunk. I needed to ensure that his words wouldn't paint Felicity in any light that could harm her.

When a small hand pressed against my back, I froze. "Callum. It's okay."

I didn't turn to her, afraid if I did, my father would see too much. "Go back to your table. I've got this."

"Callum."

"Felicity. For once, just do what I fucking say."

Her hand dropped, and I hated myself, but I needed her away from him. Needed her away from me. Because as I looked down at the hand around my father's throat, I didn't see my own. No, I saw his. I saw the hands that had beaten me within an inch of my life when I was a kid. The hands that had wrapped around my sister's throat. The hands that had shoved my mother out of the car one too many times.

The hands that had never been stopped because nobody had been brave enough to stop him.

"Callum, head back. Let me handle this." Then Rune was there, and I forced myself to stand back, letting my best friend take care of him.

"You're not always going to have your friends around you, boy," Dad slurred once again.

"You're a weak, old man. Go hide and do what you're best at," I snapped.

"Well, don't do what you're best at because we both know *that* will end well." Dad pointedly looked over in Felicity's direction, but I didn't follow his gaze. Instead, I stood there, hands fisted as Rune and Thatcher dragged my father out of the bar. Somebody started the music again, and eventually, the crowd went back to normal. After all, this was nothing new.

The town drunk and embarrassment. The sons of Ashford had decided to make a scene. Shocking.

"Callum?"

I turned to see my sister standing there, Teagan's eyes full of sorrow. "He's gone. He's not going to hurt you."

"I'm not worried about that. Dad doesn't matter, and we both know it. Are you okay?"

I reached out and pulled my sister towards me, needing that touch. I was the eldest of us all. The oldest brother of seven siblings. The twins were the youngest, with Finnian and Sterling coming in late and as a surprise. Mal and Bodhi had been the older twins, and when Mal died, our family had shattered once again, leaving behind Bodhi, a twin without his other half.

But below me in age had been the girls. Teagan and Briar. Briar had found a way out of town, with a family and a life out on the road as a songwriter with one of the biggest bands in the world. She had finally found a way to health and happiness.

But Teagan was the one I was closest to. Even more so than Bodhi. Because we'd been in the family of horrors for the longest. And while I'd been the one to protect my family from my father's hands and words, Teagan had been the one to nurture the rest.

I rubbed my cheek on the top of her hair and let out a breath. "Sorry for making a scene."

She patted my back quickly before taking a step away. She never truly liked being touched. "You didn't make the scene. Dad did as always. Do you want to talk about it?"

"Nothing new to talk about. Go hang out with your friends. I'm going for a walk."

"Don't find him and try to fuck him up or anything," she said dryly.

I snorted. "Dad's the type who would try to sue me for something like that. Not that he has money for a lawyer."

"But he has a big mouth and a bigger attitude. Just let him drink himself into an early grave."

"Not early enough." And with that, she gave me a sad smile and walked away.

I just waved at the others at my booth, knowing I wasn't in the mood to deal with anyone any longer. My friends would understand. When my gaze shot past

Felicity, I met her stare and did the one thing I was good at.

I walked away.

Because I was not going to stand there and turn into the man who destroyed everything. I wasn't going to be the man who had tried to raise me.

Though, as I looked down at my hands, I figured maybe I was already on that path.

After all, violence had been the first thing to hit me. The first thing to come to my mind when my father had said those words. That's why I would push Felicity away. Not because she was too young. Not because she was my best friend's little sister.

No. Because I knew if I wasn't careful, I would become my father. And Felicity would be the one to pay the price.

CHAPTER 2

Felicity

"It's your turn."

"No, it's your turn." I folded my arms over my chest and tapped my foot. "I went last time. You had to go pick up the pies. I'm not walking in there and dealing with that woman."

"You won't get eye-fucked or yelled at or sneered at or maybe all three at once." Rune shook his head as he wiped down the counter of the bar. "Excuse me, I may not get eye-fucked—because that's totally something I want to think about in terms of my brother—" I ignored Rune's chuckle and continued. "But I still have to deal with her. She's meaner to women than she is to men. Yet walking into Ashy Buns is a rite of passage for holidays and events for our family. Why can't Mom just bake her own pies?"

That time, Rune threw his head back and laughed, and I winced, hoping that Mom wasn't anywhere near. "Do you remember the last time she tried?" Rune asked, his voice tinged with humor.

Memories of that evening haunted me, and I nearly went queasy once again. "Yes. And Thatcher had a great time making sure that all of our smoke alarms were ready to go for the next time she tried to bake." The idea that the current fire captain was on call for my mother's baking was a mix of humor and cringe for sure. I shook my head, remembering the smoke and burned blueberry smell, even though my mother had been trying to bake cherry pies.

My mother was an amazing cook. She could also bake cookies, cupcakes, and breads. But she could not bake a pie or cake to save her life. I didn't know why cupcakes were so easy for her and not pies or tarts or even a full cake, but that was my mother.

"Why didn't you bake one for the family dinner, then?" Rune asked.

"Because I got Mother's baking gene," I said dryly. "You're the one who can cook."

My brother smirked. "Maybe, but I don't do pies. Just go to Ashy Buns and pick up our order. Please?"

"I'm making Atlas do it next time. No matter if he's

out of town or not. I'm going to force him to drive here, so he has to deal with that woman."

Rune chuckled. "Deal. I'm sure he will legit get on a plane, maybe even one of his friends' private planes, and get his ass over here just to deal with *that* woman."

"Do I want to know who *that* woman is?" a stranger asked, and my cheeks heated.

"Sorry. I just realized that we are in a public space talking about this."

The woman waved her hand at me. "Oh, don't worry. Although you just said the name Ashy Buns, right?"

I cringed. "I'm sorry if you're a tourist to our lovely and welcoming town, and I'm being a terrible introduction to Ashford Creek. We really are nice people. I promise."

"Is that our new slogan? Trying to placate people?" Rune asked, his voice vacant of emotion.

"No, really, I went in there for a coffee this morning, and a woman with blonde hair and a pinched expression raked me over the coals when I asked if they had any caramel flavoring. I mean, it was on the board, and I thought I could ask for it, but no. Apparently, caramel flavoring was only for special customers." The woman rolled her eyes as Rune chuckled, and I shook my head, trying not to laugh. "I'm Keely, by the way. And I just moved to town, so I really hope that Ashy Buns isn't the full introduction of Ashford Creek."

"I am so sorry about that. I don't know what is up

with her or why she hates people so much. But nobody's been able to pry that stick out of her butt since before I was born," I said after a moment, then I held out my hand. "I'm Felicity. This is my brother Rune." I gestured towards my brother, wondering why he was so growly today.

Rune just lifted his chin. "Welcome to Ashford Creek. We don't usually get transplants that move here without knowing the lay of the land."

Keely beamed at the dryness of his tone. "I wouldn't think so. You aren't completely on I-70. You have to go through a couple of back roads to get here, but there was an opening for a job, and I needed one. So it all worked out."

"Where are you working?" I asked. I leaned against the bar, ignoring my brother's pointed looks. Yes, I needed to go pick up the pies so we could make it to family dinner, but I would deal with that later. Any time I could avoid Ashy Buns was a legitimate use of time.

Keely practically bounced in her seat. "I just got a job at High Country Bed and Breakfast. They were looking for a chef, and I had the experience, and frankly, working at a small-town bed-and-breakfast is seriously the dream. I thought I would have to wait years and save up and build one of my own at some point. But Promise needed a chef since her old one moved away, and here I am."

My eyes widened. "Oh, I love that place. And Promise is amazing."

"You know her?" Keely asked before she shook her head, laughing. "Of course you do. It's Ashford Creek. I will learn this small-town thing eventually."

"Honestly, I'm surprised we haven't heard through the grapevine that you were hired," Rune said, his brows furrowed. "When did you move here?"

"Technically, today's my first full day in town." Keely blushed. "I start work tomorrow, or at least prep, to make sure that I can fit into what the old chef needs and find my own way. But Promise is fantastic, and the kitchen staff already looks welcoming. Which is always scary when you show up as a head chef to a former chef's staff. Not that you need to know all that information. Sorry, I ramble when I'm nervous."

"There's no need to be nervous," I said as I patted her hand. "Welcome to Ashford Creek. And I know Promise has been on the hunt for help for a while now. She's fantastic."

Keely's eyes filled with tears, and I nearly did the same. "She really is. I don't know how she's been doing all of that on her own, and I know she's a single mom. She must not sleep."

I shook my head, thinking of the twin girls I adored and didn't see often enough these days. "I don't think she sleeps, and thankfully, our town is a decent community, and we all help where we can. Plus, while she is a single mom, she doesn't have the twins every evening. So it works out, and she gets to have that thing called sleep."

"She mentioned her ex is in the picture. I don't know if I could be that cool with an ex. But then again, with children in the picture, it makes sense. Plus, she must have liked the guy at some point. He couldn't be all that bad."

"He's our friend, just like Promise is, so it works," Rune finally put in.

Keely blushed. "And look at me, stepping into gossip and being a dork. I am sorry. Anyway, thanks for the welcome, and thank you for the fantastic chicken strips." She pointed at her empty basket.

Rune snorted. "You can probably hook up something better than fried food."

"Maybe. But chicken strips and onion rings while sitting at a bar and having a nice beer before I head back to my house to go unpack are actually some of the best things in the world. And if I'm not mistaken, these are freshly battered, aren't they?"

My brother merely shrugged. "Maybe. Not everything comes from a box."

"See? Perfection. And I've never heard of this beer before. I'm going to have to see if I can find it in the store."

Rune shook his head. "It's a local brewery, and they may have it sometimes in the main grocery, but it's hard to come by unless you go to the brewery itself. It's just down the street."

My heart raced, thinking about that brewery owner, and I nearly kicked myself. Why was I bothering to think about Callum again? It wasn't as if he liked me. He just liked ordering me around.

He didn't actually see me as a woman.

"Oh. Really? I love that. I'll have to see how that all works."

"Felicity here can probably help you with that."

I froze, wondering exactly what Rune meant by that. Because I wanted to see Callum? Because I wanted to go to the brewery?

But when I looked into his eyes, I realized he had a whole other reason for pushing me in this direction.

Because I needed friends.

I would've felt ridiculous and embarrassed that my brother was trying to set me up on a friend date, but frankly, he wasn't wrong.

"Let's exchange numbers, and I will totally take you to the brewery."

"That's wonderful. I'm so glad that I came in here." Felicity rattled off her number, and we quickly exchanged them, and I smiled.

"I'm glad you did too. And now I have to go into the belly of the beast."

"Goddess speed," Felicity teased, and Rune saluted me.

I waved at them, nodding at a few other people that I knew from town, and made my way to the bakery. Seriously, who the hell named a bakery Ashy Buns? Maybe it was just because it mirrored her soul. Ashy, like the devil's wasteland.

I was going to have to remember that so I could tell Rune later. He would laugh.

Maybe.

I turned into the bakery, ignoring the high-pitched bell as I walked inside. There were a few people milling about, enjoying late afternoon coffees and pastries, and of course, the owner was behind the counter. She couldn't be in the back, making a glorious pie. It galled me that this woman with such a bitter attitude could make the sweetest and most delicate pastries and pies I'd ever eaten.

Maybe she pushed out all of her sweetness and gentleness into her baked goods, and it only left her brittle edges behind.

There were a couple of people I didn't recognize at the counter, and Fiona gave them a bright smile that didn't quite reach her eyes as she handed over their pastries after they paid.

I moved forward, heart in hand, praying that she was in a better mood than usual.

"Felicity Carter. It's about time you showed up. I was about to sell your pies."

"I didn't realize that you were closing so early. Or that times were tough. I'm so sorry about that. Here, let me help you with your burden."

Okay, maybe I was a bitch right back to her. But she

started it. And the only reason I didn't mind talking back to her was that she would never sully her baked goods by taking revenge on anybody by hurting her pies. She may spit in our faces, but she would never do so to anything she cooked. She had standards.

"Are they ready now? If you need more time, let me know. You are busy." I looked around the mostly empty bakery. "I wouldn't want to take too much of your time."

"Such a snarky little Carter like usual. You're as bad as the Ashfords."

"Well, good to know some things haven't changed."

That voice sizzled down my spine, even as the hairs on the back of my neck stood on end. Callum must have put his hand over the bell as he walked in since he hated the damn thing as much as I did. Only I couldn't reach it, and that galled.

"Oh, Callum. I didn't see you there. Is there anything I can get you? Something sweet on your mind?"

I barely resisted the urge to put my finger down my throat and gag. I seriously did not understand this woman. "Pies, Fiona?" I asked, doing my best to sound nonchalant and not as if the very idea of Callum behind me made me want to jump over something or jump him. Either or, at this point.

"Oh. Sure. I'll get that for you."

I had a feeling she only wanted me out of the way, which was fine. It wasn't as if I was an obstacle for her. No, Fiona could do that all on her own.

"Pies for dinner tonight?" Callum asked, and I finally turned, trying to catch my breath.

Why did this man change everything for me? Why could I not just breathe? But no, he always made things difficult.

"Family dinner. You know how it is."

He nodded, his eyes looking off into the distance. I could have kicked myself. The anniversary of Malcolm's death had just passed, and I had no idea how to help him with that. His little brother was gone, and though it had been years, the wound still felt fresh.

There was nothing I could do other than be there for him, but it wasn't as if he would let me be there for him. There were rules, after all.

"There you go, and I added a couple of extra cookies for your mom. Tell her hi from me."

I raised a brow at her but didn't say a thing. We had already paid up and would be square. Instead, I just moved past Callum, trying to once again get my bearings. It was hard to when it came to him. So damn hard.

I hadn't realized he was following me until he touched my elbow, and I nearly dropped the pies.

"Here, let me help with that."

"I've got it. I'm parked right down there, and I'm heading to my parents' house. You don't need to take care of me, Callum."

I hadn't meant for the sharp bite in my words, but then again, I couldn't help it when it came to him. He was trying to help me. But not out of the goodness of his heart, not out of the sweetness of just being a good man. No, it was because he constantly tried to put me in the role of best friend's little sister. Too young, too naïve. Not his.

But I could still remember that night. Then the next morning. When everything had changed. Not only had my life been rocked, but the idea that someone could want to hurt me like that boy had tried all those years ago, and then the idea that I could still remember Callum's taste, was what echoed in my memories day in and day out.

And it killed me. Because he wasn't mine. He would never be. And I needed to grow up and get over him. Not that the man would ever make it easy.

Callum held up both hands, eyes wide. "What's your problem?"

"I don't have a problem, Callum. And I'm really independent and can handle holding a couple of boxes on my own."

"I was just trying to help."

"I think you've done enough, then."

"What the hell's wrong with you?"

"Nothing's wrong with me. Nothing's ever been wrong with me. You are the one who always saw faults."

"I have no idea what the hell you're talking about right now. Let me help you because I know opening your car door is going to be difficult."

"Then I'll drop the pies."

"It doesn't make any sense. Why would you do that to spite yourself?"

"I'm careful. I'm an adult. I can do little things like holding boxes of pies by myself, Callum. You don't need to keep rushing out to save me."

When his eyes widened fractionally, I thought maybe he got it. Yet, I needed to make sure. "I don't need another big brother. I don't need you to constantly act all growly around me and try to help. In fact, I'm moving on. So just let me be." I whirled on my feet, nearly dropping the pies again, and stomped towards my car.

Well, that would show him. Speaking out of turn and flailing like a little girl, all while saying I was getting over him. Because when had I ever been under him? No, he had never known the full extent of my crush. And yet, I was pretty sure I'd just blurted it.

I was an idiot.

I did indeed get the pies into my SUV without dropping anything, though it had been a little precarious.

I was so stupid when it came to Callum Ashford. I always had been. My palms were freaking sweaty at this point, and I blamed him. Or rather, my reaction to him. I just needed to get over him and whatever crush might be annoying me at the time and move on. Just like I had told him. To his face. Like an idiot.

I groaned and tried not to lean my head against the steering wheel since I was still driving. By the time I pulled into my mother's driveway and parked behind her car, I was finally breathing a bit more and feeling as though I wasn't fully losing my mind.

I didn't even have to open my door before my dad was there, a grin on his face.

"There's my baby girl."

I laughed, unbuckled my seatbelt, and threw myself into Jackson Carter's arms. At fifty-five, he was robust, strong, and looked nowhere near his age. I was an 'oops' baby, to say the least, but I was fine with that. My two older brothers were far older than me, and yet, it hadn't mattered. I'd come along, and they'd treated me like their little doll. Maybe an action figure, if I was honest. Both Atlas and Rune had carried me around on their shoulders and showed me off to the world. Then they'd all gone off to college, Callum and the rest included, leaving me behind. That's when my parents and I truly bonded. When it felt as though I was an only child, waiting for my big brothers to return.

My dad's hugs were an example of exactly the type of guy he was. They were real hugs. You could divulge all of your secrets and know you were safe in his arms as he held you. He squeezed me once and kissed the top of my head.

"It's been far too long."

I smiled despite my nerves from before. "It's been forty-eight hours."

"Far too long. My baby chick lives so close, and yet, I never see her."

I grinned and pointed towards the right wing of the house.

"I live with you. I haven't seen you in forty-eight hours because you went on a fishing trip, and the timing interfered with my work hours. I'm sorry you don't see me often enough."

"You'd think I would since we share a roof. Now, do I see some of Fiona's pies there?"

I grimaced and gestured towards my passenger seat. "There they are for you. And I didn't drop one."

He raised a brow. "I wouldn't think you would have. Something you should tell me?"

I pressed my lips together and shook my head. "Nope. Other than next time, Atlas gets the pies."

My dad threw his head back and laughed. "Deal. There's a reason your mother and I do not go into that shop."

"Are we bad-mouthing Fiona again?" my mother called from the doorway, and I rolled my eyes.

"Always."

"Well, come on in. Rune should be here soon. I folded your laundry for you if that was okay. Since I already know where everything is, I just set it aside. Though I did leave your delicates alone. I know we have boundaries."

I laughed. I couldn't help myself. Boundaries? My parents didn't know them. Yes, they were the best parents you could ever have in the world, and I loved them dearly, but I truly needed to find an apartment of my own. I had been saving for it since college, but when I had moved out of the four Ls' place and moved back to Ashford Creek to work at my favorite bookkeeping place, I'd stayed in my old childhood room at first, and then it had just turned into nearly a year of it. We each took turns grocery shopping, we all had chores, and I cooked dinner two nights a week. It was like living with the best roommates in the world. But they were still my parents.

There was only so much one could do with that. No wonder I didn't date.

Okay, it wasn't just that. It was the giant elephant in the room, aka, my brother's best friend, but I wasn't going to mention that.

"Is everything okay, baby?" my mom asked as she patted my cheek. I leaned into her touch and sighed.

"Everything's great. I think I made a new friend."

"I was the one who made sure they exchanged numbers," Rune said as he walked up the pathway, four-pack of beer in hand. "Callum's on his way too, by the way. I cornered him outside of his brewery and forced him to eat with us. He was going to microwave something. How wrong is that?"

"Of course, Callum's always welcome. He's like an honorary son. I'll go set another place at the table."

"Don't worry, I'll go do that," I said quickly as I moved past her, heart racing.

This was good. Dinner with Callum was a normal thing. Ever since I had moved back, Callum at the dinner table had been an unwelcome reminder of the fact that we were in certain roles, and I needed to get over whatever crush I had. I needed to forget the kiss that had changed my life. Maybe it was earth-shattering and life-changing, but it couldn't keep me where I was at. Only if I let it.

So I would have dinner with Callum. And my family. And I'd make a new friend soon with Keely. And I would find my own place. Or at least where I could find myself in Ashford Creek. It was time for me to get past whatever was blocking me.

Even if that block happened to be named Callum Ashford.

CHAPTER 3

Felicity

I remembered this taste. The way his hand had slid along the back of my neck, squeezing ever so slightly. I remembered the way his tongue had slid against mine, the resting, exploring, demanding. I remembered it all. And I craved it all.

"That's a good girl. Now spread your legs for me."

I groaned, letting my knees fall to the side, baring myself to him.

He licked his lips, then ran his hands through that thick beard of his. "Look at you. So sweet, all swollen for me. Have you been touching yourself?"

"Always," I breathed.

The man in front of me just grinned, then reached down to slide his fingers through my wet folds. My hips shot up off the bed as he speared me with one finger, that thick digit achingly perfect. "So tight. This pussy will be mine. Do you understand that?"

"It's always been yours," I teased.

He chuckled, sliding his finger in and out of me. "Well then. Let's make sure that's the case." He stood back, and I immediately felt the absence of his touch.

I groaned, reaching for him, but he slid through my fingers like smoke. I tried to focus on his face, but there was nothing, just a shadow.

"Callum?"

"You know I'm not for you, little flower. You're too sweet. Too innocent. Too pure."

My chest seized. "You don't know that. I'm nothing like that. Why are you acting like this?"

"Because I know the truth. You're never going to be mine. We both know this. Now, why don't you go back to school like a good little girl, and I'll go find someone who can take me."

Then Callum Ashford wrapped his arms around Fiona, and they both moaned into one another. He picked her up at the waist, set her on the bakery counter, and slid deep inside her. Eyes wide, I watched as he fucked her on the bakery counter, his fingers still wet from my cunt.

My eyes shot open, and I sat straight up on the bed, chest heaving.

"What is wrong with you?" I asked before I rubbed my hands over my face.

I looked down at myself and realized that I had shoved my panties off in my sleep, and they were bunched at my ankles, with my blanket in disarray along my lap, and I was pretty sure I hadn't even gotten off in my sleep.

No, even Dream Callum decided I wasn't for him.

And while I knew with one hundred percent certainty that he would never be with Fiona, the fact that it was her in my dreams just made the entire thing a nightmare.

I shuddered, kicked off my panties, and got out of bed. I tossed my pajama bottoms that had fallen on the floor, as well as my panties, into the hamper and then stripped my sheets. I might as well make my bed and be the good little flower that I was and do a whole spring cleaning.

I could already hear my parents out in the kitchen, getting ready for their day, and I was grateful that I'd had the fan on full blast so they wouldn't have been able to hear me in case I had moaned in my sleep. I knew that I had an issue. A big issue. And I needed to move out of this house. The fact that I was over here having sex dreams about my brother's best friend while my parents were on the other side of the house just told me that it was time for me to put one step forward and use my savings account for good.

While I could use a roommate, finding a roommate in Ashford Creek was easier said than done. All of my friends from school had either moved on or gotten married and stayed, so I couldn't find someone here for that. However, I had a good job, a decent savings account since I was blessed with a family that had helped me throughout school, and determination.

I rolled my shoulders back, knowing that that stupid sex dream was just a reaction to my own epidemic.

I was only slightly lonely. I needed to settle down in my hometown, make friends, find someone that was mine, and move on with my life.

I could do all of that. I knew it. I wasn't that socially stunted.

But I also knew if I didn't get started soon, I would just be stuck in this house until I was thirty, and nobody would see me for who I was.

I didn't want to be the baby Carter sister anymore. I had a college degree and a full-time job. It was time for me to finally move out of my parents' home.

Despite the fact that I knew both of my parents would rather I stay their little girl forever. They liked me as their roommate; I knew that. We were a good team and made things work. But I truly needed a different way to work on things.

I tossed everything into the corner and jumped into the shower so I could get ready for the day. I had a full plate, including an orientation, a new client, and lunch with a friend.

Look at me, making friends.

I showered quickly, not bothering to wash my hair since it wasn't wash day, and got ready while humming to myself, trying to formulate a plan for the rest of the month. I loved living with my parents. I loved being near my family, although Atlas needed to visit more. I just needed some space of my own. A girl didn't ask for much.

With a laugh, I pulled on cute slacks and a flowy blouse since we weren't too formal at work and dropped everything off into the washer.

"Is that my baby girl I hear!?"

"That's me! I have a little bit till I have to head into work, so I'm going to wash my sheets on the quick cycle."

"Do it on permanent press and hot. I'll slide it into the dryer and into your room later. Coming home to a bed you have to make is probably the worst thing ever."

I rolled my eyes. "It's really okay. I can handle it."

"That's what roommates are for." Mom leaned down and kissed my cheek, and that sliver of guilt crept in. Because I did my parents' laundry when I could as well. It was just easy to put a few of their things into my load. We really were a good team.

But I needed space. And I wasn't quite sure how to continue to broach that subject.

So I didn't. Yet.

"Seriously, stop stressing. You're on dinner duty tonight anyway." Dad kissed the top of my head, and I rolled my eyes. "Fine. Thank you. I'll go fix the washer." I set the correct cycle and quickly picked up my favorite bread to make toast and cut up an avocado and tomato.

"I can make you a decent breakfast."

I pointed down at the two vegetables with my knife. "This is healthy. I'm doing just fine, Mom. Please stop. I lived on my own for four years and did just fine."

My mom pursed her lips. "I just don't like thinking about you and those girls."

I cringed. "They weren't that bad."

"They were," Dad added. "They were rude, and didn't clean up after themselves, and expected you to do a lot more for them than they ever did for you."

And they didn't even know the extent of everything that the 4Ls, my former roommates from college, had done. I held back a shiver because my parents could always read my mind these days and smiled. Laura, Laurelin, Lauren, and Laurel had been my roommates in college. However, the girls had grown up together, had attended preschool through high school together, and were each other's dorm mates. When they had moved off campus and needed a fifth roommate, I'd joined in. As a Felicity, I hadn't met the qualifications of becoming a fifth L, but I had still been their friend.

And they had just been dumb girls the one night I truly needed them. However, they'd also stood up for me when I needed them as well. So, maybe, they hadn't been all that bad.

But it had been nearly two years since the end of

college, and we didn't speak often, other than every once in a while, opening up a group chat.

And if my dad had anything to say about that, it would remain that way.

"Anyway, I have to finish getting ready for work."

"How is Gregory doing?" Mom asked, speaking of my boss.

My smile widened. "As ornery as ever. I adore him. I'm just happy that he had space for me at his shop."

"You are a brilliant bookkeeper and accountant. Of course, he had space for you," Mom put in.

"And that man should have retired twenty years ago. You're probably making sure that his place doesn't go under."

They weren't exactly wrong there, but I wasn't going to put down my boss. I remember when I had been a little girl, and he had given me lemon drop candies when I had walked by. He had always been so brilliant and bright in my life that it was an honor to be able to come back and work for him.

And yes, he was past ready to retire, but it wasn't as if me taking over for him fully was a done deal. I still had a lot to learn, and that's why I did not want to be late.

I ate quickly, listened to my parents as they spoke about their upcoming days, and drained my coffee.

"I'll be home to make dinner. Don't worry. And I'm going to continue to look for apartments."

"Felicity, you don't need to do that."

My dad put up his hand as Mom tried to add to her statement, and he sighed. "I'll help you look as well. Ashford Creek is a nice town, but there are some seedy areas."

I resisted the urge to roll my eyes because it was true. Every single town had its gray spots, but it was a good town. I just needed to find a place I could afford.

I kissed both of their cheeks, put my dishes in the dishwasher, and went to brush my teeth.

By the time I made it to work, I was vibrating for my second cup of coffee, and instead of going to the coffee shop to get a fun latte, I drank the drip coffee from the office. I tried to save money where I could. And I had a lunch date.

"Oh, Felicity, can you look at this folder?" Gregory Teller asked, and I moved my way over to the seventy-three-year-old bookkeeper and accountant of Ashford Creek. He may be in his seventies, but his mind was just as sharp as ever. He had begun to crouch ever so slightly and continued to try to roll his shoulders back, and he didn't move quite as sprightly as he once had, but he still ran the quarterly and holiday 5Ks in town. If I could be half as in shape as he was at his age, I would be one happy camper.

"How can I help?" I asked as I went to his side of the desk.

He hunched over a folder, a frown on his face. "I'm having trouble with this one account. Nothing is adding up. I know that they're not money laundering or anything, but I always want to double-check things."

My brows shot up, and I looked down at the Ashy Buns folder. I tried not to smirk, considering that meant I would be a little too callous when it came to that woman. Still though. Having Fiona go to jail for money laundering would be quite nice. No, that would be a little too much. Sure, she was rude, and yes, she had infiltrated my sex dream with Callum, but she wasn't evil. At least, I didn't think so.

"I'll take a look. Is there anything specific you want me to look for?"

"I took a few notes for you. Take your time, and maybe get it back to me by Friday?"

"I can totally do that."

"You're heading out with Keely for lunch today, right?" he asked, and I grinned.

"I am. But do you want me to cancel, though? Do you need me for something?"

He waved me off. "It's good you're getting out there. You young people need to get out and enjoy life. Not everything is about the numbers. I know. Shocking that I just said those words. But it's true."

I smiled. "I will get my work done, don't worry. We're only heading to Summit Grill together for lunch."

"Oh? Going to hang out with your brother? I thought maybe you would go for The Range."

The Range was a higher-end restaurant on the north

end of town that was run and operated by Finnian Ashford, Callum's youngest brother. "I think that's a little too fancy for a lunch date."

"You never know. You young people always surprise me these days."

"Keely is just a friend. At least I hope she'll be a friend. She seems nice and new."

"And she runs the restaurant at Hill Country Bed and Breakfast. Perhaps you'll end up there for lunch for another lunch date."

"They're not serving lunch right now, but I know it's something that Promise wants to add. Maybe that's what Keely's here for."

"Well, as we do their books, we'll be able to tell them exactly what timing is good for them money-wise. Now, I need to head to my doctor's appointment."

I stiffened. "Is everything okay?"

"I'm seventy-three. Nothing's exactly okay. But I'm just fine. It's a normal appointment. I promise." He patted my cheek like he had when I was a little kid and went to pick up his cane. "I will see you after your lunch. You text me if you need anything."

"Because you're so fancy with the texts these days," I teased.

"I may be old, but I'm up with the youths and their technology."

I threw my head back and laughed, and he skipped out of the office, not leaning on his cane at all.

I seriously loved that man.

I worked for a couple more hours, and then it was finally time for lunch with Keely. I put on a little lip gloss, fluffed my hair, and then realized that it felt like I was getting ready for a date.

I used to be great at making friends. It had just been long enough that I wasn't quite good at it yet. But I would learn. Right?

It didn't help that my brother and all of his friends and most of the people that I knew around town were just a little bit older than me. Usually, it wouldn't matter, but many of them were single parents or happily married parents as well. Meaning they were in different stages of their lives than I was. While that really didn't bother me, in some aspects, though, it meant that finding time to hang out or interests that we could both have didn't always work out.

And Keely was new in town, meaning she wouldn't have all of the cute yet annoying and invasive stories from my youth because I was the oops baby, the youngest, and had always traveled behind my brothers, wanting to be part of the group.

So, this was just for me.

I practically skipped into Summit Grill, belatedly realizing that if I wanted to have something just for me, maybe I shouldn't have lunch at my brother's place of business, but thankfully he wasn't behind the bar.

I spotted Keely already at a table, and I moved towards her with a bright smile on my face.

"Hi! I'm sorry I'm late."

Keely looked up, a wide grin on her face. "Oh no, I'm early. You're right on time." She stood up and hugged me, and I quickly hugged her back, immediately feeling at ease.

"I just got us waters. I wasn't sure what to get. Your brother is in the back, and he glared at me for a minute. So I assume that means he's in a good mood."

I rolled my eyes. "Who knows with that man. He's always grouchy. Atlas is the one that isn't quite as grouchy. But that's not saying much."

"Atlas is the goalie in the NHL, right?" she asked, and I tensed.

"Yes. He plays for the Portland Gliders."

Keely smiled, pushing her hair back from her face. "He's amazing. I'm a hockey fan. I can't help it. But don't worry, I am not usually a hockey *player* fan, if that makes sense."

"I have no idea what that means," I said with a laugh.

"Meaning, he does great at his job, but I'm not going to fan girl. Nor will I ask you for details about your brother. Because that just seems weird. And now I've made things awkward."

"Not at all. Honestly, that makes me feel better. You have no idea how many people would come up to me in college just to try to be my friend so they could get to know Atlas. Atlas doesn't even live in the same state. Or the same time zone, for that matter."

"Well, they're just rude. I may not have any famous siblings, but I do know how not to be a jerk. At least, I hope so." Her cheeks pinked, and I grinned.

"Same here, at least, not to be the jerk part."

"Well, that sounds like a perfect way to begin a friendship. I'm so glad that you weren't scared away from when I first said hello that first day. I'm so awkward sometimes when I'm nervous, and I still can't believe I moved to a small town in the middle of nowhere."

"Well, I'm glad you're here. I may have been born here, but most of my friends ended up not coming back after college. Which sucks."

"And making friends as adults is so hard. When you don't have kids, and when you work in an isolated place, sometimes you don't have time to make friends."

"Exactly."

"Exactly what?"

I blinked and looked up at Bodhi Ashford and grinned. A couple of years younger than Callum, he looked just like his brother. But his beard was a little bit darker, his eyes a little more jaded. And considering everything he had gone through, I didn't blame him.

A couple of regulars glared at Bodhi's back, stood up from the bar, and walked out. I narrowed my gaze, opened my mouth to say something, and he held up his hand.

"They weren't that quiet. Don't worry about it," he whispered.

Keely frowned at me, but I wasn't sure what I was supposed to say. It wasn't my story, and frankly, Bodhi had to deal with enough as it was in this small town. No wonder the man preferred to stay up in his cabin.

I cleared my throat and put on a bright smile that I knew didn't quite reach my eyes. "Bodhi, Thatcher, this is Keely. She's new to town."

Bodhi lifted his chin, and Thatcher smiled.

Thatcher was around Callum's age, if I remembered correctly, and the fire captain for the entire town. I still couldn't quite believe that he had gone up the ladder, pun intended, so quickly, but he was damn good at his job. He also was raising three kids on his own, so the fact that he was out here at lunch, even in his uniform, surprised me. Though the kids were at school at the moment and for all I knew, he was done with his shift.

"Keely. Welcome. I hear you're working with Promise?"

Keely's eyes widened. "I am. I guess the small-town rules really do apply here."

Bodhi just snorted, but Thatcher continued to grin.

"Yes, and you've just been featured in the Ashford Gazette."

I cursed under my breath as Keely paled. "What does that mean?"

"It means that our lovely small town wanted to

announce that you're here," Bodhi growled. "They do love their gossip." Bodhi tilted his chin at me. "It's good to see you, Squirt."

I narrowed my gaze. "You only call me Squirt when you're trying to annoy me."

"Is it working?"

My lips twitched, but Bodhi just smiled, and I would take him making fun of me until the end of my days for that smile. Considering those smiles were few and far between.

Thatcher grinned, his eyes dancing, as he looked between Keely and me. "It's good to meet you, Keely, and good to have you home, Felicity. I know you're an adult now with actual money and a full-time job, but if you ever find yourself in the mood to deal with two fifteen-year-olds and a seven-year-old for an overnight, we'd love to have you back."

"I can probably make it work in an emergency. I do love your kids."

"And they've missed you. Welcome to town, Keely."

And with that Thatcher went to the corner to have lunch with Bodhi, and Keely just shook her head. "I'm never going to remember everybody's names."

"It's really okay."

"Thatcher has three kids? And two of them are fifteen? He doesn't look old enough to have a fifteen-year-old, let alone two."

I shrugged. "It's a long story. And yes, he does. A few

of my brother's friends are all single dads here. So there are lots of children around. Meaning I had tons of babysitting money growing up."

"And I take it the mom's not in the picture?"

I winced, grateful that she was whispering. "No. His parents help him out, though. They sort of have to with his hours."

"I noticed the badge. Fire captain? That's a lot of responsibility. And well, a man in uniform." She wiggled her brows, and I knew she was trying to lighten the mood, and I was grateful for it.

"I said something along those lines to my brothers once, and they promised to lock me in the closet."

"I guess dating in a town where everybody knows you as the Carter little sister isn't easy."

I rolled my eyes. "You have no idea. But I'm trying. In fact, I'm going to do this thing called online dating."

Keely shuttered. "I used to do that in my old town, and it sucks. However, if you're going to try, let me know, and I can help you. At least to wade through the initial parts. And to be your backup. You know, the person to call you during the first course for help?"

"Deal."

I grinned and sat back as our waitress came and we ordered our lunch. People in town came by to say hello, and I introduced them to Keely. Apparently, the Gazette hadn't been too thorough in their introduction of her, and so everybody was curious. Keely took it in stride and was still bubbly and happy by the end of our lunch.

"When you're ready to online date, let me know, and I will help you through the app."

"I have no idea what I'm doing, so yes, I'm going to need your help."

"We can work on your profile tomorrow if you want?"

"Done."

We said our goodbyes, and I headed my way back to the office. Gregory should be back, and I had a few things to do before I called it a day and began my apartment search.

I turned the corner and ran into a full body. The man gripped my arms, and I looked up and froze.

"Well, hello there, little girl."

I swallowed hard and pulled away from Matthew Ashford, Callum's father. "Excuse me. I didn't see you there."

"Too high and mighty to look where you were going. Such a Carter way. You guys were nothing when my family built this town. But then again, you're still nothing." The whiskey on his breath filled the space between us, and I tried not to retch. I pushed past him, ignoring him and making my way to the office.

That man had always startled me. It never quite clicked in my mind that he was the father of some of the kindest and most driven people in town. But you couldn't choose who your parents were. I was so damn lucky, and I knew it. But the Ashfords hadn't been.

I got to my office, sat down at my desk, and let out a breath. Gregory had worked at this office for years on his own. And it wasn't lost on me that one of the last people to sit at this desk and work alongside him was Matthew Ashford's first wife. Eve Ashford.

She'd had the same job as me when she wasn't at home raising Callum and the rest of his siblings. Eve Ashford had once sat at this desk. Had once worked her hands until they ached in order to keep her babies fed. All while Matthew Ashford had been the town drunk. And then she'd died. I hadn't even known her.

All I knew was the town lore.

That Matthew Ashford had killed his wife and gotten away with it.

And now I sat at her desk.

And dreamed about her son.

CHAPTER 4

Callum

Teagan frowned as she went through her notebook, a question forming behind her eyes. I leaned forward and rubbed the lines in between her brows. "Stop frowning. You're going to end up with tan lines there."

I should have expected the punch, even though it was gentle because we didn't hit each other hard as siblings. But I still let out a gasp and laughed. "Ouch."

"Be nice to me. I'm going through your calendar for you. You're lucky that I love you and will do this. If anything, you should hire Felicity. I know that you used to use Gregory, but he got a little behind since the old man should have retired years ago. But now that Felicity is working for the company, they're all caught up and doing great things for the books. My shop uses them. The bed and breakfast uses them. You should too."

I wasn't about to touch that concept with a ten-foot pole. There was no way I was going to hire Felicity to work on my books. That meant I would have to be near her. Talk to her. And keep her from my mind.

What I needed to do was get laid.

Getting laid in a small town wasn't always easy. Mostly because I didn't want anything permanent, and I didn't like gossip. However, we had enough people coming in as tourists to the brewery, the bed and breakfast, and through town for outdoor activities and skiing that I could usually find someone. Something that didn't need to last more than a night or two and where we both walked away getting exactly what we wanted.

I should just do that and not think about Felicity Carter.

Except every time I left the damn house, I either saw her or someone mentioned her. There was no escaping her.

And it was my own damn fault.

"You're doing such a great job. Why would I hire someone outside the family?"

"I thought the Carters were family," she said as she marked up another line on her notebook. "I am going to see if I can get Bodhi to hire Felicity too. Because I'm a decent manager, but his artwork is getting enough traction out there that I feel like I need somebody who's an actual accountant for some things. There are only so many things I can do when it comes to taxes. I'm sure that I'm losing you guys money."

"Without your organizational skills, every single one of us Ashfords would be fucked over. You know that."

"I do not." She laughed, shaking her head. "You have a business manager and financial advisor when it comes to all your earnings from the NFL, but for the brewery? You rely on me. That's silly."

"It's family. I told you when I came back to town that I was going to make sure that our family figured things out on our own and grew closer. That we would walk away from whatever the hell that old man wanted us to do. So here I am, making that happen."

Compassion covered her face. She reached out and patted my hand. "And you're doing a damn good job about it."

"That was a little patronizing."

"Maybe. But look at this brewery. Ashford Brews is hitting all the blogs and influencers out there. Every time that you do a four-pack line, it takes hours to get to the line. And you haven't even announced what the yearly brew is going to be. Your IPA, Pilsner, and Ale are flying off the shelves locally, and I know a few national chains have already contracted you."

I snorted. "I'm not selling. We're good the way we are. If I sell, they're just going to water it down, put on a different label, or skyrocket the price where it makes no sense. I don't want to build another brewery or figure out how to keep my secret recipes secret from the man." I rolled my eyes. "I like what we're doing."

"And you're doing it well. But you need another accountant."

"I don't know how I feel about you trying to fire me," I said dryly.

"What? When you first started, Georgia was the one who handled the paperwork. She was great at it. I just came in when I could." She paused and winced. "Sorry. Didn't mean to bring her up."

I shrugged. That pain was an old ache that would always be there. "Georgia's been gone for ten years now." I paused, shaking my head. "Still can't believe it's been ten years."

"Time moves abnormally slow, and yet so fast sometimes it scares me."

"I know for a fact that I wouldn't have been able to open up this brewery or be where we are without Georgia being there at the beginning. I just hate that she didn't make it to see where we are now."

Getting married at twenty-two, right when you were drafted into the NFL, might seem ridiculous to some people. But Georgia and I had gotten along, and I loved her. *I loved her.* I loved the way that she made me laugh and that she centered me. Starting off as a rookie on one of the best teams in the NFL, where we made it to the AFC

Championship both years I was in, meant the pressure on my shoulders had increased with each passing moment. But Georgia had been steadfast. We'd been the same age, wanted the same things, and when I'd broken my leg in two places and lost whatever dreams I'd thought I'd be able to have, she hadn't walked away. Instead, she'd picked up the pieces and helped me figure out what to do with the rest of our lives without even taking a moment to crash out on her own.

We'd only been married three years, and then she died. She died and left an already broken man behind.

My family hadn't even truly had a chance to get to know her, and the town had pretty much forgotten her. After all, I hadn't moved back to Ashford Creek until right before she had died, and that was only to start the brewery. I'd been locked in my own world, in the cabin, just like Bodhi was now.

"I really don't mind you mentioning Georgia, you know. Not many people do."

"Our family's really good about not mentioning things that hurt." Teagan began to draw little doodles on the corner of her notebook, a frown etched on her face again. "We barely talk about Malcolm. Or Mom. We sure as hell don't talk about Bodhi."

"He doesn't want us to. And even though it might be good for him, it's not our place yet."

She looked up at me then, sighing. "When is it our place?"

"I don't know, Teagan. I don't know."

She let out a shaky breath, then rolled her shoulders back.

"Anyway. Let's get everything set up for the next big event, and then I want to try a beer."

"Didn't you used to say you were a wine girl?" I tried to lighten my voice because I knew there were reasons our family didn't talk about things. The more we did, the more it hurt. And talking about the fact that our mom was dead, and our dad was probably the one who had murdered her, wouldn't bring Mom back. It would only bring more resentment because the cops hadn't been able to do anything. Just like we didn't talk about the fact that our stepmother had walked away from us and had never come back. Was she dead? We would never know. And deep down in my heart, I had a feeling that my dad had something to do with it, but nobody could prove it, and so here we were, pretending the Ashfords weren't the town messes and my dad wasn't the town drunk.

"You're thinking about Dad again."

I blinked at Teagan's words. "What?"

"You're thinking about Dad. And since you are, you're going to get tan lines in between your brows from frowning like that."

I barely resisted the urge to rub my forehead to check if those lines were indeed carved into my skin. "Fuck you. Come on, I'll go get you that beer. We have family dinner tonight anyway."

"Oh, yay," Teagan said dryly, and I threw a balled-up piece of paper at her.

"You're the one who wants to continue to have family dinners in such abundance. We could just go to any one of the siblings' places. But no, you like it at my house."

"You have the bigger house. You can fit all of us. And you're closest to Bodhi, so we can drag him down."

"One day we should just show up at his cabin and annoy the fuck out of him."

"He would probably shoot us and ask questions later," she added, and I wasn't quite sure she was kidding.

I shook my head as we headed to the tasting room. There were a few people milling about, but the big rush wouldn't happen until later. I nodded at a few locals and went to pull a draft for Teagan.

"Are you going to tell me what the new one is?" she asked, kind of fluttering her eyelashes.

"You don't want to be my bookkeeper anymore, so maybe I won't tell you."

"I'm just saying Felicity would be better at it."

"Felicity would be better at what?" Rune asked as he walked into the tasting room, a pile of large and smaller boxes in his hands.

Teagan leaned forward to help with the smaller box on top of Rune's pile. "I think that Callum over here should hire Felicity to work on the books. It just makes more sense."

"You should. And if you don't, I'll feel like you don't trust my baby sister, and then we're going to have words."

Trusting his little sister wasn't the problem. And he was going to have words with me if he ever knew what ran through my mind. Or the fact that I knew exactly what she tasted like.

I cleared my throat. "What are you bringing me?"

Rune rolled his eyes. "An empty box or four. I'm here to buy more."

"More empty boxes?" Teagan asked, her tone so polite that I just snorted.

"I need a couple more packs. People are in the mood for bottles rather than just on draft. Which is ridiculous because everything tastes better on draft."

"Fuck yeah," a customer said as he lifted his glass.

I tilted my chin at him in thanks, then looked over at my team member. We had a limit on how many drinks a person could have, and while I didn't think this person had reached it yet, they were a little too bleary-eyed for my liking.

The team member immediately went to smile and chat with the other group, and I looked back at my best friend.

"When did I last give you stock?" I asked while running my hand through my beard.

"You would know that if you looked at this notebook. And I don't know, maybe hire a bookkeeper who knows what they're doing?"

I sighed. "You aren't going to let this go, are you?"

"I'm not. And it's not because I'm tired of this or anything. It's because I think you could really use someone with more expertise. You're getting bigger, Callum. And while you're not expanding to a worldwide business, you are expanding some of your reach. And I think they could help."

"I'll think about it. Okay, Rune, I'll stock you up. You know you could have sent anybody to us or even texted, and we would have brought something over."

My best friend shrugged. "Felicity and her friend got off work and are sitting at the bar, looking at dating apps. According to them, I was being an asshole and was asked to leave them alone. They could have done this at Keely's house or even at Felicity's, though my parents are there, and my mom and dad probably would have wanted to give their opinion on whatever guy they're swiping left or right for." He rolled his eyes. "Don't understand why Felicity needs to date, anyway. She's perfectly fine joining a convent."

When the washcloth hit the ground with a splat, I swallowed hard, ignoring the odd looks on Teagan and Rune's faces, and reached down to pick it up. I didn't even realize that I had squeezed it so hard that my knuckles had turned white.

I cleared my throat, trying to sound nonchalant. Perhaps he'd think I'd sound like a concerned big brother.

Even though any feelings I had toward his little sister were anything but brotherly. "Felicity's dating?"

"Trying."

I met his gaze, and we both remembered a previous date of hers. Her parents didn't know, but Rune and Atlas knew exactly what had happened with Bradley, the douchebag we hadn't heard from since the night he had attacked her. He was lucky to be breathing, but then again, I was glad I wasn't in jail for murdering the kid. For a little while, we'd been afraid that he'd reach out to his parents and try to get me arrested for beating the shit out of him or even come at Felicity for breaking his nose, but he'd kept quiet. And according to Felicity, his friends had ensured that. I didn't know what to think exactly about that other than the fact that I was glad Bradley was out of her life forever.

But that didn't mean I wanted her to date.

Though if she was dating, that meant she wasn't dating me, and I wouldn't have to think about her anymore.

I didn't know what was wrong with me.

Or rather, I knew everything was wrong with me.

"It's good she's getting out there. Dating is hard in a small town. Especially when everybody knows your secrets." Teagan scowled. "Believe me. Nobody will ever let me forget the fact that I came to Christmas with a boyfriend once, and then by graduation, I didn't have him anymore. They love to throw that in my face."

"You know, I can still fly to England and kick his ass for you if you want," I said, speaking of Teagan's ex-boyfriend. A guy who I'd liked. Then he'd broken her heart, and I hadn't been able to say a damn thing.

"I'm over him. Promise. But I'm not over the gossip. So she's online dating? Good for her. It scares me, and I never want to touch an app again, but if she has a friend helping her, I'm sure she can figure it out."

"And what if it's some creep?"

"Then she can take care of herself. And if she can't, between the Ashfords and the Carters, she has like fourteen big brothers who aren't going to let anyone touch her. No wonder she needs to go to an app and find a stranger. I can't even date here without you guys growling all over me, and I'm not the younger one."

"You say that as if I've scared away all of your boyfriends," I said dryly.

"You threatened to put my prom date in a trunk," Teagan said, her brows raised.

"He had his hands on your ass, you tried to push him away, and he wouldn't listen.

"He was just joking." She rolled her eyes. "We were doing a bit."

"I didn't know it at the time, and then I realized later you guys were enacting a movie scene, but still, he's lucky I didn't put him in that trunk."

"Oh yes. I remember that. And then, didn't Atlas punch the guy later?" Rune asked, a frown on his face. I quickly went to help him fill out his order and listened to a few staff members as they worked with our customers.

"Yes, but that was because of a sports thing. Not me. I like sports. I was decent at sports. I will never understand men in sports, though." Teagan rolled her eyes.

"What's there to understand? We like ball. We kick ball. We throw ball. We catch ball." I shrugged, and Rune threw his head back and laughed.

"Please say that to Atlas and Gray when he comes back to town."

I laughed, thinking of the fact that both played hockey. Gray was a friend of my younger brothers and on a different professional hockey team than Atlas. I was decent on skates, but nowhere like my brother. I preferred to keep my feet on the ground and a ball in my hand. Hockey had never made much sense to me.

"Anyway, I'm going to bug my sister about whoever she dates next. It's fun. And Atlas isn't here to do it, so I have to help."

"And such a good brother you are," I said dryly.

"And such a big brother you are," Teagan said dryly.

"It's what I do. Oh, I forgot. Do you think you can watch Thatcher's kids tomorrow?" Rune asked, and I frowned.

"Me or Teagan?" I asked.

"Either one. His parents are out of town on a well-deserved vacation, and his sitter decided to go on a tour with one of her favorite bands. Meaning Thatcher's going to need another nanny."

"Yeah, I can help. And I'll help find a nanny too. I know Thatcher's been working his ass off trying to make sure that the kids have steady people in their lives, but I can't believe the way that his recent nannies have been behaving."

"Like the one that hit on him?" I asked, rolling my eyes. "She was like twenty."

"The age gap really wasn't the problem since the person was an adult. It was the fact that she wouldn't take no for an answer and wasn't even taking care of the kids." Rune shook his head. "Honestly, I think he and Kellan should just pool their houses together and get somebody that can watch all six kids."

"I don't know if I would say having one person to watch two middle schoolers and four teenagers is a good idea," I said with a laugh. Although I couldn't help but wonder if Rune had been serious about the whole age gap thing. No, I wasn't going to think about that. I couldn't.

"Honestly, the two should work together."

I nodded at Teagan's words. "They used to when the kids were younger. But with all of the different activities that teenagers have these days, it's kind of hard to make it work, especially when you're the town doctor and the fire captain. It's not like you have decent hours."

"We'll help out. All of us. But I'm just glad that Promise and Finnian figured out childcare for their girls."

My younger brother, Finnian, had four-year-old twins with Promise. Though the two weren't together anymore, they had a great co-parenting plan. They even lived next door to each other to ensure that the girls could feel like they were home and not shuffled around. Between Promise's parents and all of the Ashford siblings, we made sure those kids were taken care of.

"Okay, here's the beer that you need, and how about at dinner tonight Teagan and I will try to work up a flow chart or spreadsheet or something for all of our friends with kids? That way, we can figure out childcare."

"You're a good man, Callum Ashford," Rune said with a smile, and I did not want to correct him.

I wasn't a good man. I couldn't be a good man.

If my friends and family needed me, I was there.

But I was keeping secrets. Secrets that would probably ruin my friendship with the man in front of me.

So I would do what I could to help the others, but honestly, there was no helping myself.

CHAPTER 5

Felicity

So, were there no available apartments in Ashford Creek? It didn't make any sense that every single place to live would be full at this point. There had to be people moving out or new buildings being put in. Yes, the town wasn't that big, but it wasn't a postage stamp in the mountains.

I rubbed my temples, annoyed with myself for continuing to get my hopes up.

Not only had the last apartment I had looked at been a bust, but the first date I had gone on with a tourist on a dating app had walked into the bakery, taken one look at me, laughed, and walked right out.

I really should have been slightly offended at that, but at that point, I didn't have the energy. I was too busy trying to run out of the place before Fiona came out from the back and noticed. It was only some luck that she hadn't been out front when I had been sitting in my little seat, waiting for this stranger to show up. Of course, she had video cameras all over the place and probably rewatched it in glee, waiting for the perfect moment to jump out of the shadows and terrorize me with it.

I'd gone from a wonderful day at work, a fantastic lunch with my parents, to an apartment filled with cockroaches, trash, and some form of white substance I never wanted to think about again. I'd known that it was going to take forever for me to find a place. I just hadn't realized it would be so fraught with ridiculousness. All I wanted was to cement myself in town, grow roots, and maybe, just maybe, move on. It was just hard to do that when everything felt as if it were pushing against me.

Maybe I was being slightly dramatic, but my date had laughed at me.

"Doing okay, Felicity?" I looked up at Gregory Teller and smiled. He leaned against the doorway, his white hair fluffy since he needed a haircut, and the lines around his eyes and mouth deepened as he smiled at me.

"Just frustrated. I can't find a place to live."

"I'm sure your parents would love to have you stay with them. After all, you don't need to quit having a multi-generational home just because you've grown up."

"That is very true. But I'd like to try this part of my own independence. It's just finding something in my budget and available in town is oddly difficult."

"The town council is very particular about what buildings are allowed to be built on town grounds. So, it does limit the full population potential. Not to mention all the short-term rental properties out there for tourists. It's ruining the housing market."

"Don't even get me started. Don't even get my mother started. She could probably stand on that chair right over there and have an entire speech ready for you. She hates short-term rentals. It ruins neighborhoods."

"And it's even worse in larger cities. I do know that our town council's working on limiting those. So hopefully, that won't be an issue soon."

I had been hearing that concept for a while now. And while that would be lovely, it wasn't going to help me at this moment. Not that I was going to say that.

"Anyway, my break is over now, so it's back to this notebook." I gestured towards the notebook and stack of folders for a local company and grinned. "Was there something you needed?"

"Yes, actually, I do have a favor to ask." I set my pen down and stood up.

"Is everything okay?"

There was something in his eyes I couldn't quite read, and I moved forward. "Did the doctor call with your test results?"

"Everything's fine. Like usual. Do not worry about me. I would love for you to add a new client to your roster. One that is solely yours because I failed them in the past."

I frowned, confused. "You failed them? That doesn't sound like you."

He let out a breath and patted my hand. "Sascha passed just weeks after they first opened their business, and well, I couldn't add them to my roster like I wanted. They slid through the cracks."

My heart hurt thinking about his late wife. She had been such a kind woman to me when I was younger. And though I hadn't known her well, I knew Gregory missed her something fierce.

"That's understandable. Especially since you rarely hire anyone to help you."

"The best person, other than you, of course, that I've ever worked with was Eve Ashford." He sighed again, his expression falling. "That's why the fact that I failed her son like I did just pains me. However, I'm pretty sure Teagan finally convinced Callum to come in and request a little more help for Ashford Brews. They would be a great asset and client for us, and I truly hope that you can take them on."

I froze, my throat parched at even thinking about working with Callum. But that was a silly reaction, considering I didn't even like Callum that way anymore. It was a silly crush that was now gone forever. Just like in the memory of that kiss. And we were friends. He was

136

Rune's and Atlas's friend. Meaning I could work with him. As a professional.

"Of course. Should I call him up?"

"No need, he's right here. Callum, son, come on back to the office. Felicity will get you set straight away."

My eyes widened, my palms going damp. "Oh. Now?"

I swore my voice squeaked, and I quickly wiped my palms on my linen pants. "Okay, well. I mean. Sure. This time works."

Gregory moved back and to the side of the doorway as Callum moved forward. He had on dark jeans that molded to his thighs, a black Henley, and his leather jacket that had seen better days. It was chilly out for an April afternoon, and I couldn't help but remember the time that he draped that jacket around my shoulders one day when we were outside, watching one of Thatcher's kids in a soccer game. It had just been a kind gesture, one that had made me swoon. Thatcher's daughter had fluttered her eyelashes at me, and I had rolled my eyes at her. Teenage girls saw everything, and I was grateful that she only teased me, not knowing my true feelings.

"Thanks for taking me on. Teagan is great at what she does, but she fired me."

My eyes widened. "Really? What did you do?"

"He's too successful. He needs an accountant." Mr. Gregory raised his brow.

"Between Teagan and my financial advisor, I've made everything work, and my original staff from back when I was in the NFL still does my personal taxes, but the company taxes and bookkeeping needs someone else. So what do you say? Want to help a guy out?"

"I'd love to." I swallowed hard again. "I mean, it's about time you came to the best." I winked as I said it, and Gregory burst out laughing, but Callum just stared at me, those eyes far too knowing.

"Good. I was worried you wouldn't want to work with me."

"Why wouldn't she? You're family."

Gregory tapped Callum's shoulder and had to reach up to do it since he was huge and took up most of the doorway before the old man and traitor left me alone with Callum, heading back to his office.

"So what is it that you're looking for?" I asked, and when Callum just smirked, I knew that this was probably a recipe for disaster. But it is what I asked for. For him to treat me like a normal human being and not someone who wasn't old enough to know their own ways and choices.

"I don't know if you should phrase it just like that."

"How else shall I phrase it?"

"Felicity."

"Callum," I drew out. "Do you have something in mind with what you need, or do you want to make an appointment? Are you looking for somebody to do the actual bookkeeping and payroll? Or just your taxes."

"Everything. Teagan literally fired me."

I held back the twitch of my lips. Barely. "Well, she handles so many others, and I know she was just doing it because she's your sister. She manages a business, a very good business in town. I don't know how she has time to deal with the rest of you."

"She said pretty much the same thing. Plus, she's spending a lot of time helping Kellan and Thatcher with childcare."

I winced as I gestured toward my desk. "Come take a seat. I've been working with Teagan on that too. I really hope that they find someone soon. I know that they were deciding to go in together on that."

"Honestly, with the teens being old enough, it makes sense. They just need someone to help organize their lives in a spreadsheet sense. The guys don't have easy work hours."

"Pretty much. They're meeting a new woman named Tess today. She's new to town and needs a job."

"Well, that's helpful. Though I hope she doesn't take any nice apartment that I need," I added, the words slipping out before I meant them to.

"House hunting, little flower?"

"I am. And you shouldn't call me that when you're in my place of business. I'm the one that's about to know all your secrets."

His face closed, and I could have kicked myself. "You don't want to know all of my secrets, Felicity."

"I just meant the work ones. Promise. Anyway, I hope

this Tess works out. And she finds a lovely apartment on her own."

"I'm pretty sure she already has a place to stay. And is looking for employment. I also know that Thatcher and the rest will get a background check, and they'll be off to the races. I just hope that this person stays long enough."

"Considering how many people that they've gone through because people that they hire are so unreliable? I agree."

"Anyway, let me know when you find a place. I'll help you move your shit."

"I have more than just shit," I teased. "But thank you. I'm sure if you hadn't offered, Rune would force you anyway."

"That is true. And your mom will have a complete spreadsheet of exactly where things should go, and your dad will order us around according to how your mom orders him. I know the rules."

"My parents are pretty amazing that way."

"I was so jealous as a kid, but I'm glad that you guys had them."

It occurred to me once again that Callum was sitting in the office that his mother had worked in. But it had been over two decades since that moment. Would Callum even think about that? Would it matter?

He was right. I didn't know his secrets, though part of me craved to.

And that part of me needed to shut the hell up.

"Anyway, let's get started on your paperwork."

"Yippee."

"Excuse me, but my mother taught me spreadsheets for a reason."

His lips quirked. "Whatever you say, little flower."

And this time, I didn't correct him. Even though I should have.

L ater that afternoon, I swiped the correct way and was headed to the Flicked Bean, the local coffee shop that made headlines when our town council had approved the name without knowing what it meant.

They made fantastic coffee, and I always held back a giggle whenever I came through the doors.

It was a typical Colorado coffee shop, complete with comfy chairs, oversized mugs, and multiple baristas with nose piercings, full tattoos, and amazing hair.

I loved it.

A late evening coffee and Danish was probably going to be an awkward date, but Landon seemed really nice online, and I wanted to be in a public place. My phone buzzed, and I smiled at the screen.

Keely: Are you sure you don't want me to come down there?

Me: I'm going to stay in the coffee shop where everyone can see me. Don't worry!

Keely: I'll always worry. It's something you'll learn about me. LOL

Me: I already love it.

Keely: Tell me how it goes and good luck! Hopefully, it's better than the last one. And the one who ghosted me. Now, back to work! Promise and I are going to add a lunch menu soon!

Me: Crossing my fingers on both!

"Hey Felicity, what can I get you?" Lorenzo said from the counter, and I grinned.

"Maybe just a vanilla latte? I'll figure out if I want a snack soon."

"Date?" he asked, wiggling that pierced brow.

"Yes. From an app. So if you could just ensure this guy doesn't drag me out the back door, that would be wonderful."

"I hate the fact that you're only kidding there, but not really kidding. Don't worry, we've got you."

He pressed his right fist into his left palm and glared.

"I love you, Lorenzo."

"I love you too. And if I loved women that way, we could just go and get married and run off and not have to deal with apps."

"Those are the dreams," I teased.

I took a seat in the back corner so I could watch the door and see if a curly-haired blond walked towards me. The last time I had been on a date with a blond man had ended in one of the worst evenings of my life, but then I remembered I had fought back, and I hadn't been alone in the end.

I didn't think about Bradley often, and I wasn't planning to tonight. Right now was a late coffee date, and it was going to go wonderfully.

When Landon walked towards me and looked exactly like his profile picture, I smiled and stood up. "Hi there. I'm Felicity."

"Hi Felicity, I'm Landon. I'm so glad that you look like your profile photo."

I laughed softly. "I was just thinking the same thing."

"Felicity, babe, have your coffee here." Lorenzo gave Landon the once-over and then smiled at me. "Anything else?"

"I'm sorry, I already ordered. I'm a regular here."

"I like it. I'll take a flat white, and what do you say to sharing a cheese Danish?"

My stomach rumbled because I wanted my own Danish, but I'd share one. Why not?

"Sounds good."

"On it. I've got you." Lorenzo winked, and Landon and I went to our seats.

"So..." Landon said and didn't continue.

"So... how long are you in town for?" I asked, feeling awkward.

"A couple of days. Not too long. I'm a business analyst. And I'm on a break just to see the mountains. Get that mountain air. You know?"

"I do know. I love it here for that reason."

The bell over the door jingled again, and a familiar, far too built, far too alluring presence walked in, and Callum strolled towards the counter. He gave me one look and glared over at Landon before turning to Lorenzo.

"I'm here for Teagan's order. Because apparently, she needs caffeine after five pm."

Lorenzo laughed. "Okay, old man. I guess once you reach a certain age, caffeine is a problem."

"You're lucky I like you, Lorenzo." Callum shook his head, his lips twitching.

"Felicity. Did you hear what I was saying? Do you know him?"

I whirled towards Landon, nearly spilling my drink. "Oh, sorry. Got distracted. Long day. I'm sorry."

"Oh." Landon frowned and looked over at Callum before turning back to me.

Landon was slender, probably far slenderer than any man I'd ever dated, a runner's build, if anything. He had long, curly blond hair but had pulled it back into a pony-tail. He had one of those soul patches and wore suspenders. I didn't mind the look, considering all my friends dressed however they wanted. But he did not give off the same aura as Callum.

That was probably why I had swiped the way I had.

"Anyway. I've been married for about four years now, and when I go to different towns, my wife and I like it when I hook up with someone. That way, she can watch over the stream, and we can spice up our marriage."

I finally clued in to what he was saying and continued to blink. "Excuse me?"

That time, my voice had gone high pitched.

"What? I thought I was pretty clear in my texts to you, right? This is just for the evening?"

"No. That's not at all what you said."

He frowned, looked at his phone, and his eyes widened. "Oh shit. I told that to someone else. You. Well. I mean. Same goes. You know?"

"I think I'm going to go now. Excuse me." I stood up, coffee sloshing over the rim. Landon stood up quickly and looked down at the coffee now staining his pants.

"Are you fucking kidding me? Just because you're not into an open relationship doesn't mean you had to burn me."

"Something wrong here?" Callum asked as he strolled over, that glare on his face too alluring. Damn that man.

"Nothing. Landon was just leaving."

"I thought you were? But you know what, maybe I don't understand small-town girls. My wife and I can find someone else." He gave a two-finger salute, didn't bother to get his drink or pay for it, and just walked out.

I looked around the other tables, filled with people I knew, and glared up at Callum.

"If you say a word to my brother about this."

"About what? The fact that you just went on a date

with a married man who was looking for a third for the evening?"

"Dating is hard. And apparently, I don't know what all of the acronyms mean on apps. Or maybe I do, and he lied. Either way. I'm going to go eat that entire Danish and then head home. To live with my parents. Because there's no other place I can live."

"I might have a line on something for you," Callum said softly.

I turned my gaze up to him. "Really? You're not just saying that because I've had a bad night?"

"Oh, you've had a bad night. Hilarious. And by the way, you do realize that one of the busboys at Summit Grill is over in the corner, right? He's going to tell Rune."

Before I could glare at the kid, he was already out the door, probably to be the town crier of my bad date.

"Yeah. At least this beats the whole laughing-at-me thing."

"What?" Callum asked.

I waved him off. "Anyway. I'd love to hear about the whole house thing, and I will. But I'm going to eat this Danish and cry."

"Felicity. Don't cry. He's not worth it. No man is worth your tears." Callum took my chin and met my gaze. "Nobody is worth your tears," he repeated.

I swallowed hard and took a step back, forcing him to let me go.

"You're right. But some days are just worth a Danish."

"It's on the house," Lorenzo whispered, and that time I nearly did cry. Instead, I took my Danish, went back to my table, and calmly had myself a solo date.

That was all I was good for at this moment. And I ignored Callum's pitying gaze until he finally left with his sister's coffee, and I could finally breathe. Getting over Callum Ashford was going to be harder than I thought.

CHAPTER 6

Callum

Though Ashford Brews wasn't a multinational corporation, at any moment in time, we had at least three or four things happening at once.

Today, we were in the malting and milling stages of our IPA, where we would spend enough time that my eyes would begin to cross. The large steel barrels took up a majority of the room, and I was grateful that we'd expanded our warehouse in the past couple of years. At the moment, though, our grains were being germinated and would soon dry so that way they could activate the enzymes that would convert any starch into sugar. Then, it would be milled so we could get to the next stage, mashing.

When I had gone to school for business, I'd had a few friends in the chemistry department, mostly because they were helping me pass gen-chem, and they'd had home brews in their bathrooms. It seemed to be the thing of the moment for many a Colorado college kid—to try to figure out how to make their own beer. There'd been a few explosions, the taste of vinegar that could coat your tongue and never let you go, and enough bad beers that I'm surprised none of us had ended up in the hospital. But I had fallen in love with the concept of making beer and trying to figure out the perfect recipe. While I wasn't in business with any others, those initial friends that I had worked with still received a few of the profits. Not much, since I'd worked with so many to figure out my own taste and recipe, but enough that it was a thank you.

And every single one of them had tried to return the money at first.

Ashford Brews was proprietary in their recipes, but I could say thank you to those who had gotten me where I was.

This was the legacy that I wanted my family to have. The legacy of innovation, progress, and damn good beer. And between the rest of my family pursuing their own avenues of their legacy, one day, when people thought of the Ashfords of Ashford Creek, they wouldn't think of the failed dynasty. They'd see what happened with this generation.

Finnian's girls, as well as Briar's daughter, would have a nest egg for them when they were ready. They would have a sturdy foundation of family lore that had nothing to do with their grandfather.

That bitter taste coated my tongue again because, no, I did not want to think of my father. He had never met Briar's daughter and had only accidentally met the twins a couple of times.

If I had any say in it, they'd never meet the dumbass again, but that Ashford continued to creep around town, loitering.

And no matter how many times I cornered him, no matter how many times I worked with the sheriff and other avenues, they couldn't figure out where our stepmother had gone and couldn't pin him for my own mother's death.

Eve Ashford had been an amazing mother. The light in her eyes had died over time, and I had even seen that as a young kid, but she'd raised her children with as much love as she could before she passed. Sterling and Finnian had been babies when Mom had died. They didn't even remember her face, didn't remember her laugh. Didn't remember the fact that she had held them both close to her heart, humming sweet lullabies to keep them content.

When Julie had married my dad, she'd come in and taken over. She had been a sweet woman but without a spine. Maybe that's what my dad had been looking for. She'd helped raise the younger kids to the best of her ability, but Teagan and I had done *our best* to make sure that we were the ones the youngest looked up to.

But Julie had been the first one to give Malcolm drumsticks and to lead him down the road that would eventually make him an international rock star behind his kit.

Part of me wondered if Malcolm and our mother, wherever you ended up after you died, were singing and playing along together. And maybe Julie was with them, watching the man, the boy she had helped raise, become a talented musician.

Julie had run away after five years with us. Fourteen years ago.

Dad had said she had taken all her things and left us because she couldn't handle us anymore.

I wasn't sure I believed that.

But what else was I supposed to think?

That Dad found a way to kill both of them? He'd gotten away with it the first time, and maybe he'd truly gotten away with it the second time too.

Because there was no evidence of what had happened to our mother. She'd slipped and fell and drowned in the river. And any bruises on her body could have come from the fall, and any older bruises hadn't led to her death.

I frowned at the next barrel, watching the wort boil as it sterilized everything inside, and wondered how much death a family could take.

Malcolm was gone. Both of the mothers were gone. And my wife had followed.

No wonder I was tired.

Or that could be the fact that I had barely slept the night before, thanks to dreams of Felicity that continued to haunt me.

"So, is this when you add the hops?" Bodhi asked as he came forward, a frown on his face.

I was surprised to see him out and about, but considering the anniversary was coming up, I probably should have expected it. Bodhi would either spend time with us, hiding from the rest of the town, or wallow in a bottle in his cabin. I was grateful he had chosen this avenue, at least for the day.

"Yep. We want a little bitterness and that aroma as well as flavor. When we hit the fermentation phase, we add yeast, and then we can get our alcohol from that."

"Because it can convert sugar into alcohol and carbon dioxide. I remember the notes last time."

"Good. Then you won't mind coming over to help me figure out if I actually like this new beer for the quarter."

Bodhi shook his head, his lips twitching. "You wouldn't have made it if you didn't like it."

"I've made a few beers that I didn't like. I don't mean to. It just happens."

"I cannot believe you turned into a chemist."

I rolled my eyes. "Don't say that around the smart people who actually understand chemistry. I may have taken a few extra classes when I got back to town, but I'll still never be smart enough to pass a class."

"Thankfully, you had smart friends who carried you along."

I rolled my eyes again as we went to the tasting room. We were in the private section that customers couldn't see. This was where we did our tastings before we went into packaging.

"I went for a red ale this time. A first."

Bodhi's eyes widened. "My favorite."

"Because I do everything for you," I said dryly.

No, somebody else liked red ales, and I hadn't even realized that I was making a beer for her until we were already into the fermentation process. It was probably going to end up shitty.

"Okay, let's go through the process."

"Did somebody say beer?" a familiar voice said, and I turned as Briar ran towards me.

I held out my arms, and she threw herself at me, wrapping her arms around my neck as I twirled.

"I didn't know you were coming." I kissed the top of my sister's head and then looked around for her husband and baby girl.

"Where are they?" I asked, frowning.

"I see how it is. I come all the way to Ashford Creek, and I am pushed aside because you can't find my daughter."

"Maybe I was looking for your husband. I am a fan of Gabriel Wilder."

"Will the drummer do then?" another voice said, and I turned to see Kiera West come into the small room right behind Briar.

"Kiera. Good to see you."

She grinned at me and tilted her head up at Bodhi. That's when I remembered that since Bodhi hadn't come down to Texas at all, this would be the first time the two were meeting.

"Bodhi, this is Kiera West, the drummer for Wilder, and Kiera, this is Bodhi, mine and Briar's brother."

Kiera smiled softly and stared at Bodhi for a moment before my brother's jaw tightened.

"Yes, Mal and I were twins," he bit out.

Kiera's face paled, but she jutted out her chin.

"I know. Hard to miss. Just like it's hard to miss the fact that I'm the one who took Mal's place in the band. Sorry for staring. I was just thinking about how baby Maisie has your nose."

Bodhi's eyes widened.

"No shit?" he asked, turning to Briar.

Briar rolled her eyes. "Yes. Somehow, she has yours and Mal's nose, and then everything else is Gabriel's. I was part of the situation there. I went through labor. But no, Maisie is turning into the best of the Ashfords and the Wilders, and I got none of it."

Kiera wrapped her arm around Briar's shoulders and squeezed. "It's okay. We'll make sure that we don't tell Gabriel that, though. We'll keep teasing him that Maisie looks nothing like him."

I snorted, though Bodhi didn't make a sound.

"I do like doing that. He gets so growly." Briar grinned, and I shook my head at the two of them.

"So, why are you guys here? Not that I don't like seeing you. Because I do."

"We had to come up to Denver for a few things for our management companies, so I figured we'd take the extra couple of hours to drive up to town to see you. I wasn't sure what time I was going to make it, or even if it was going to work, so I didn't warn you. And no, Maisie isn't here. She's at home with her father, meaning I have all the mom guilt. This is the first time I've been away this long, and I'm not doing okay."

"Aw, I'm sorry. Though I do miss my baby niece." I held out my arms again, and Briar sighed but leaned into me.

"And I do realize that I probably shouldn't be back here, and this seems like a workplace or family vibe, so I can head out if you want," Kiera said, pointedly not looking at Bodhi.

"No, it's okay, we're trying a beer. Do you like beer?" I asked, tilting my chin towards the setup.

"I love beer, so I'm in, if you don't mind me crashing."

"It looks like it's going to be a bit full in here. I'll taste it when you're ready to figure out the label, okay?" Bodhi said as he pushed past Kiera, kissed Briar on the top of her head, and headed out of the small tasting room.

Kiera's shoulders fell as she stared between us. "I'm sorry. I didn't mean to annoy him. I mean, I enjoy annoying men most of the time because they get in my space and think I don't know what I'm doing in my job, but I don't think that's what it was."

Briar squeezed Kiera's hand. "It's not you. I promise." My sister met my gaze, and I nodded tightly.

No, we both knew what was going on, and while I didn't fault him for it, I really wished that there was something we could do.

"If you're sure. I feel like I should go apologize."

"Then you'd be apologizing for existing, and for all the times I've met you, that doesn't seem like a you thing."

The drummer's lips twitched. "Very much true. Okay, show me your favorite beer."

"I don't know if it's my favorite yet. It's our first taste. It could be piss water."

"Please, make sure that you put that on the next T-shirt," Briar said with a laugh.

I looked past them through the glass doors, but Bodhi was long gone.

I didn't know how to fix this, but then again, I couldn't fix most things in my family.

After all, what did you say to a man who not only lost his wife and kids but had been blamed for it long enough for the scars to dig deeper than the burn scars that already covered his body?

"And then, the guy comes up to me and says something along the lines of how if I would wear a skirt while behind the kit, maybe more people would take me seriously. But we both know it's so that way he could see what was beneath the skirt. As if that was the only time he was ever going to see pussy in his life."

I threw my head back, laughing at Kiera's expression, and looked over at Briar.

"Please tell me you don't deal with this type of shit on the road too?"

"All the time. Though now it's mostly along the lines of how I slept into my Grammys position because I'm married to Gabriel. It doesn't matter that I had more Grammys than him when we first got together, but whatever. It's all about who you're sleeping with."

"I am having at least four affairs right now." Kiera fluttered her eyelashes. "And nobody will ever know which one is the actual real one."

"I'm sure he really likes that," Briar said, but there was something in her tone that worried me.

Kiera just laughed it off, though her eyes had darkened slightly. "It's fine. This is what happens when you date someone in our business. You deal with the blowback and gossip."

"Sounds like dating someone in a small town," Rune said as he came over with a few more beers. Then he took a seat next to Kiera and grinned.

"Glad you were able to come visit. We have heard all about you from Briar, of course, but it's nice to have you here."

Kiera beamed. "I do like it. I know that small towns aren't all quiet, and yes, there's gossip and everything, but it is so much more peaceful than being on the road."

"Here here," Briar said as her gaze drifted towards the door once again.

"He's banned from coming in here," I whispered, and her shoulders relaxed.

"I hate that you knew what I was thinking."

"I won't let him near you."

We both knew who we were talking about, and from the look on Rune's face, he had heard and understood.

"Briar!" Teagan exclaimed as she came forward, and Briar pushed me out of the booth so she could run into her sister's arms.

"I've missed you," they both said at the same time, and they practically danced in place.

I looked over at Rune, who just rolled his eyes.

"Well, I'm glad that I finally made it in," Finnian said as he came forward, Sterling at his side.

We pulled up another couple of tables, and suddenly, most of the Ashford family was there, though I wished Bodhi had come back after he'd stormed out.

But the rest of my siblings were here, and with Rune seated with us, our family felt nearly complete.

Though we would never be fully complete, not with what we had lost, but we were slowly coming back from that.

And I had to be grateful.

My phone buzzed, and I looked down at it. A sigh escaped my lips.

Bodhi: Tell Kiera I'm sorry I'm an ass.

Me: You should probably do that yourself.

Bodhi: That would mean I would have to text more than you. Just tell her, okay? She didn't deserve that.

My brother was a good guy—he just forgot that sometimes. I would figure out how to tell Kiera, though. She deserved his apology, even if I wasn't sure if she'd accept it. Not that she was mean, but I guess I felt like sometimes she was so kind that I was surprised she made it in her world.

"I'm surprised Thatcher and Kellan aren't here," Finnian said as he leaned forward, grabbing a chip out of Sterling's grip.

Sterling just rolled his eyes, taking another chip.

"Kellan is stuck at the clinic all evening," Rune put in. "He had to switch shifts with someone."

"Thankfully, it seems that their new nanny might actually work out, though, because having to switch like that really messes with the childcare," Finnian put in.

Rune nodded. "Pretty much. And Thatcher's on call all night. I was going to send over a few things to eat for the entire staff because I know with the wildfires going on out west, everybody's on edge."

"You're a good man, Rune," Briar said softly, and Rune just rolled his eyes. "Not really. But I don't mind pretending."

I stretched my back and eased out of the booth.

"Be right back."

"Hey, when you're back there, can you let me know if I need to send someone to go clean up anything? I know my staff is working hard tonight, but we're down a busboy, and they won't let me work to help tonight," Rune put in.

"Because you work too many hours as it is. And don't worry, I'll let you know exactly what I think about the cleanliness of your establishment."

Rune flipped me off, and I laughed, making my way down to the back of the bar and grill where the bank of restrooms was.

The back door was propped open slightly, one of the waitresses out there taking her smoke break, but as I heard a familiar growl of a voice, my hands fisted at my sides, and I moved towards the door.

"Just a couple of dollars. If not, you know, a beer? I'll pay. I promise."

"Mr. Ashford, you're not supposed to be here."

"Leslie, why don't you head on in? I've got this."

The twenty-something looked up at me, and relief spread over her face. "Sorry, Callum," she whispered as she put out her cigarette and skittered behind me.

"I wasn't going to hurt her, boy," my dad slurred, and I shook my head.

"Go home. You know you're not allowed to be here."

"Because your friend is a jackass who is too weak to stand up to you."

"You're kicked out because the last two times you were here, you tried to start a brawl. And you try to steal shit, and you're a drunk who continues to hit on waitresses. Just go home."

Briar walked past. "Did she bring that little brat of hers? Nobody will tell dear old grandpa anything. I haven't even met the little tyke."

My spine stiffened, and I tried not to show any of my anger or fear on my face. Because my dad would latch onto that. He was so damn good at it.

I fisted my hands once again, letting out a breath. Those same hands that looked so much like my father's. But I would not use them to beat the shit out of my father. That's what he wanted. That's what he craved.

"Go home."

"What are you going to do about it? Call one of your little fuck boys to go arrest me again? It's public property back here, and I'm not doing anything. Though, if I had a little incentive, I'd head out."

Out of the corner of my eye, I saw Teagan move in close, doing what she always did—trying to protect the Ashfords. Just like I failed to do.

I scowled, then pulled a couple of twenties out of my wallet. "Go."

If Briar hadn't been in there, maybe I'd have just shoved the man out of the way, but I knew if I gave him at least a couple bucks, Dad would let her breathe. Because that's how it always worked.

He snatched the bills from my hand and walked away, whistling a tune that still haunted me. Because he'd always whistle that after he'd beat the shit out of us.

"Why did you pay him?" Teagan asked, and I couldn't even look back at her.

"Because he would fuck with Briar and the kids."

"I just wish he would go away. Or just die. That's something a daughter should always say about her dad, right?"

I turned, walked through the back door, closed it behind me, and pulled my little sister into my arms.

"He has to die sometime soon. His liver can't hold out that much longer."

"The things we wish for."

Both of us ignored the wetness covering my chest as Teagan cried into my arms. My little sister, the fierce one. The one who didn't cry in front of anyone, still cried in my arms.

And that was just one more reason why my dad needed to go.

And why, if he wasn't careful, I was going to be the one who made it happen.

CHAPTER 7

Felicity

Sometimes, the numbers called to me. Sometimes, the numbers made me want to scream in a corner and pretend that they never existed. Sadly, at this moment, I was worried that this was one of the latter times.

I rubbed my temples and stared at the screen. "You can do this. You are numbers. And numbers are set. You understand how to make this work."

"Talking to yourself again?" I looked up as my boss came in, a small smile playing on his face.

"Yes. I can't get this spreadsheet to work, and it's annoying me."

"Well, back in my day, we used to do everything by hand."

I rolled my eyes at him and his familiar refrain.

"Was it with the chisel, or did you move on to different sorts of clay at that point?" I teased.

"You youngsters. And I'll have you know I am decent at a spreadsheet."

"I do know that. You're the one who taught me to use this program. You're hip with the kids."

"Young lady, the fact that you just said that phrase worries me. Are you no longer hip with the kids?"

"Probably not. I'm no longer a teenager. I don't understand the lingo some of our friends' kids say these days."

"Sadly, it's been years since I understood anything a teenager says to me."

"Anyway, I know I can get these numbers to line up. I'm just missing something."

"Who's it with?"

"You know the account."

He sighed and came over to my desk. "She's just not great at receipts. We both know this."

"How has the bakery gone on this long and missed so much? These are the questions I have."

"Because we don't have another bakery in town. And she's damn good. She's honestly a good baker. She's just not the best businesswoman."

"I'll help her get all of her receipts and spreadsheets in order, but honestly, she should have us doing payroll."

"But that costs a fee, and she's not a person who wants to spend money on that."

"Which makes me sad... But maybe you can work your wiles on her," I said, fluttering my eyelashes.

He barked out a laugh. "We both know that won't work. I lost my wiles long ago."

"Are you putting yourself down again?"

I froze at the sound of Callum's voice, my palms going sweaty. The object of my latest dream strolled behind Gregory and winked at the man. "Are you going to make me growl at you again?"

"No, no. No growling needed. I am going to go back to my desk and get things ready for tomorrow. Felicity, you should take off. You're past your hours."

I blinked, pulling my gaze away from Callum's gray eyes, and swallowed hard.

"What?"

"Darling. You've been working for over nine hours today. You can finish your project tomorrow. Go and live your life. Remember, there is more to life than spreadsheets and working long hours. My wife and I learned that when we needed to, and I want to make sure you know it too."

He nodded at Callum, gave me a wave, and went back to his office, leaving me alone with Callum Ashford. Once again.

"Well, I guess my boss said I'm no longer allowed to work. I'm sorry if you were coming in here to ask about your account. I guess I'll have to work on it tomorrow." I winked as I said it, a smile playing on my face.

Instead of glowering or looking annoyed, Callum just smiled.

He looked way too good with that smile.

"Actually, I am waiting for a phone call from a distributor and figured I'd come down here and show you the place."

I blinked, confused. "What place?"

"The house I found for you? It's not an apartment, but it's a small two-bedroom house, and the owners use it for family members and friends who visit, but they also like to rent it out. They just don't tend to tell people, but it's rentable."

"You found me a house. I thought you were just teasing me before with that."

"I don't tease, Felicity."

Well, that was a lie if I had ever heard it. All he did was tease me. Then again, maybe he didn't realize he was doing it. And I was losing my mind.

Yes, that sounded much more like the case.

"You found me a house."

"I did. Come on, close up your things, and I'll take you to it. It's a short drive."

"How did you know about it? What's the rent? Is there a down payment? What's the cleaning fee? Do I need to have references? There are a lot of questions that you just seem not to even care about right now."

"I have a whole packet in the car for you. I know you and your love of spreadsheets. And I'm not going to take you to a crack house or something. You're Felicity. I'm not going to let anyone hurt you." His eyes narrowed as he said it, and a shiver ran down my spine.

No, I knew Callum would do everything in his power to make sure no one ever hurt me. That was who Callum was. Overprotective, forceful, and powerful.

And every single time somebody in his orbit, namely his family, got hurt, he blamed himself.

Then again, my brothers did the same thing. It was probably why they were such good friends.

I let out a sigh and clicked save on my spreadsheet. "I suppose I'll work on it tomorrow."

"Baker giving you trouble?"

"I'm not telling you what I'm working on. That would be unprofessional."

"Your voices carried when I walked in, and everybody knows that the bakery could go under at any moment because Fiona doesn't know what she's doing."

"I'm not going to say anything," I answered with a wince as I grabbed my bag. "Where are we going?"

"To the house across the street from mine," he said after a moment. "That's how I know about it. The older couple who own it lend it out to their adult children. You remember the Radfords?"

My eyes widened. "I do. They haven't been back in a couple of years, though? I thought they sold that house."

The house right across from Callum's. Oh, that wouldn't be a problem at all. Clearly, it wasn't a problem for him. Meaning I'd have to make sure it wasn't for me. This whole getting over my crush thing really wasn't getting any easier.

"Anyway, the family didn't sell it, and their adult kids don't come here as much. They'd rather stay up at one of the resorts in another town that's close by. They don't really feel the need to stay in their parents' childhood home. I know they're thinking about selling, but they're not ready to yet."

"How do you know all this?" I asked as I walked past him, ignoring that cedar and sandalwood smell that just wafted off of him. Did he bathe in the stuff? No, that wasn't right. Because it wasn't overpowering. It was just tempting. Damn that man.

"I take care of the house when there are no tenants."

"Really?"

"Of course I do. They need help, and I'm there." He gestured to his truck. "Hop in."

"I can drive."

"Just get in the truck, Felicity. I'll bring you back."

I frowned, wondering how many orders I'd have to deal with. Okay then. I could do this. It wasn't weird at all. And yet, I couldn't help but feel weird.

When he opened the door for me, I slid my bag inside and reached up for the handlebar, so I could lift myself up. Instead, Callum took me by the hips and lifted me on his own. I frowned, stiffening, wondering how the hell he had gotten so strong. But then again, he had been a tight end in the NFL. He was the epitome of strength.

I swallowed hard as he sat me down, and I turned to look at him. His eyes had darkened, his pupils dilating.

"You good?" he asked, clearing his throat.

I nodded, my tongue darting out to wet my lips.

When his gaze went to the action, I thought I had to be seeing things.

Instead, he took a step back and closed the door in my face.

I only had moments of reprieve, trying to catch my breath, wondering why I couldn't slow my heart rate when Callum moved around the front of the truck and got in on the driver's side.

"Okay, let's head out."

"I can drive myself."

"You're already in the truck. And this way, I don't have to watch you try to parallel park."

"There is no parallel parking on your road. You're just making fun of the fact that I can't parallel park."

"You ran over Rune's foot," he growled as he started the engine.

My cheeks heated, a blush covering my face.

"I ran over the side of his shoe. And he shouldn't have been standing so close."

"He was on the curb." The dryness in his tone made

me laugh, and his shoulders moved as he chuckled with me.

"It was your first time trying to parallel park, and I know that your dad, the best man that I know, and the voice of assurance and calmness when it comes to being a fire captain and in the face of danger, had been freaking the fuck out with you behind the wheel."

"Thank you," I said as I threw my hands in the air. "Everyone always acts like my dad is the calmest man in the world, and while he can be on most days, he was nowhere near calm when I was learning to drive. And Mom would continue to try to press the imaginary brake, so in the end, it was Atlas who had to teach me how to drive. Well, Atlas and Bodhi."

Callum looked at me then, eyes wide. "Bodhi taught you? I don't remember that."

I shrugged. "He's calm. He always has been. Especially since..." I let my voice trail off, not wanting to comment on why he had changed. And for good reason.

"Yeah. He's always been decently calm. Well, I'm glad he could help you. I was never around when you were dealing with all of that. I don't mind it because I barely remember you when we were younger."

I shoved at his arm, even as he turned the wheel. "Mean."

"I am mean. What can I say? However, I'm glad your family was there for you. And Bodhi."

"You weren't around other than that one weekend of

me learning to drive, and even then, I didn't actually get behind the wheel until I was eighteen." I didn't know why I needed to reiterate that I wasn't that much younger than him.

"I always wondered why you took forever to get your driver's license." I shrugged as he turned down his road. The same road that this house was apparently located.

"Everybody drove me around, and I could walk everywhere in town. It wasn't until I realized that I was going to need to drive in Denver that I got my driver's license. A lot of kids these days wait till they're eighteen."

"I've noticed that. It never made any sense to me. I wanted to be behind the wheel as soon as I possibly could."

"But I was spoiled."

"You are a spoiled brat."

"Rude. I'm allowed to call myself spoiled. You can't call me spoiled or a brat."

"You're a brat, and we both know it," he reiterated as he parked in the driveway of the small two-bedroom house that looked fricking adorable. It had blue shutters, blue trim, and a well-kept lawn and garden.

"You do all this? The maintenance?"

"I don't mind. The family needs help, and they pay me in baked goods. You know, that way I don't always have to go to the bakery."

"You could bake yourself, or really, it doesn't look like

you eat any baked goods." I let my gaze slide over him, and he just met my own, a small smile playing on his face.

"I do work out so I can have cookies. That's how the world works. But come on, let's go see the place."

I hopped out of the truck, doing so quickly so he wouldn't have to come and help me.

I didn't know if I could handle his hands on me again.

Because if he did touch me, I'd want to climb him like a tree, and there was something wrong with that.

I swallowed hard and followed him into the small home. It was older, so not open-concept. The kitchen was disconnected from the living room, and I loved it. My parents had a huge open-concept area, though the dining room was separate, and I appreciated it. There were so many of us that it made sense to have it all connected so everybody in the kitchen, the living room, and the kitchenette could speak.

But here, when it was just going to be me and maybe a couple of friends every once in a while, having the separated spaces worked.

Especially since I only had a couple of pieces of furniture.

"This place is adorable. I love it." I finally opened the packet that had been sitting between us on the truck console, and my eyes widened.

"The rent can't be this cheap. What the hell?"

"I told you, they're friends. They're not going to overcharge you because of the area, and it's normal pricing."

"I can't take this. I'd be taking advantage of them."

"You aren't. This place is empty most of the time. They own the house outright, so they only have utility bills and taxes, and this will cover that. Just take the place, Felicity."

"Callum—"

Before I could say anything, though, the door opened, and two familiar voices hit me.

"Atlas!" I called out as I tossed the folder at Callum and ran towards my brother. Atlas opened his arms, and I threw myself in them, and he twirled me around the living room.

"Pipsqueak. You're here. Look at you, looking at a house like an adult. What the hell, Callum? Why are you encouraging this? She needs to be locked away at my parents' house."

I kissed his chin and then punched him in the gut. Of course, my hand felt as if I had just run it into cement and I growled at him.

"Be nice. Callum's doing a good thing. And I think I'm the one taking advantage of him."

"Oh, really?" Atlas asked, lifting a scarred brow. He had gotten a skate to the face during one game at the beginning of his career, and now his right eyebrow had a scar that apparently drew women in droves. There was even an Instagram account just for his eyebrows.

I would never understand puck bunnies or fans.

However, my brother was here, making fun of me. And that was all that mattered.

"Your sister is going to be safe here. Don't worry. And come on, you didn't want to live with your parents when you were in your twenties."

I turned to Callum and beamed. "See. You understand."

"I mean, if I could lock away my sisters so that way they're safe from men and evil things, I would. But sadly, Teagan can kick my ass, and Briar's already married."

"Okay, I take back my thanks. Jerk."

"What about the utilities?" Rune asked as he began to pace the building. "Has anyone looked at the plumbing? What does the backyard look like? What about maintenance? And there are a few other things that I have questions about."

I snorted. "I have the same questions, but don't worry. I can handle it." I rolled my shoulders back and looked around, wondering why it felt so much smaller in here now that there were three very large men with broad shoulders storming around the place.

"I have everything in this packet, but don't worry, I wouldn't steer her wrong," Callum began...

"Because you always take care of my baby sister. That's what I like." Rune squeezed Callum's shoulder, and I rolled my eyes even as Atlas gave me a look.

I narrowed my gaze at him, daring him to mention my

crush on Callum. Rune might be completely oblivious, but Atlas could always tell. Damn that brother.

"Maybe I should stay here whenever I'm not on the road or at my house in Portland. You have a guest bedroom, right?"

"I won't have a bed in it. It'll be my office. Because I'm going to have an office." I threw my hands up in the air. "I love it. Thank you, Callum."

He just shrugged. "Like I'd let you have a shitty apartment."

"Aw, you like me."

He just let out a grunt and took Rune through the rest of the house.

Atlas stayed back, though, as we looked around the kitchen, and I tried to take note and feel that this home would be mine.

"It's a good place. Better than your place with the four LS."

I nudged Atlas with my shoulder. "It is. I mean, I liked living with them at first, but then they got to be too much, and I didn't realize it until, well, you know."

He wrapped his arm around my shoulder and squeezed. "Yeah. Pretty much. But this place will be good for you. And Callum will be right across the street."

"Another big brother watching over me," I said carefully.

"Yes. That," he said just as carefully.

I never could read Atlas, so I had no idea what he meant.

"Anyway, I'm only in town for a couple of days, and I have to deal with a work function tonight, even if it's online, but dinner tomorrow?"

"Deal," I said softly. "Though I do wonder how you were able to take this time off."

"Things happen. Don't worry."

"Atlas."

"Things happen. Don't worry," he repeated.

"Okay. But I'm always going to worry."

He grinned then. "As will we. Okay, I'm going to take Rune out of here and bug the shit out of him. You let us know if you need any help?"

"Always." I hugged my brother, and he hugged me right back, one of those deep hugs that reminded me that he would always be there to protect me.

Damn that brother of mine.

By the time Atlas had dragged Rune out, I found myself standing hopefully in my new living room alone with Callum, wondering if this was real.

"So what do you think?" he asked softly.

My teeth dug into my bottom lip, and I nodded slowly.

"I love it. It doesn't seem real. But, if you're serious, and if they will actually go for this rent, I'm in."

"Good. You deserve the best, Felicity."

I smiled then, and without thinking, I went to my

tiptoes and pressed my lips to his in thanks. I should have stopped, shouldn't have even been there, but by the time his firm lips were against mine, there was no going back.

I must have let out a little sound because then Callum's arms were around me, one hand digging into my hip, the other around the back of my neck, holding me in place, as his tongue slid against the seam of my lips, and I was lost. He growled into me, taking me, and I let him.

Before I could put my hands on him, to deepen the kiss, to do anything, he pulled back, his chest heaving.

"Okay then."

"Callum," I said, not knowing what I should say.

"Let's get you back to your car. We'll sign the paperwork." He let out a breath, not looking at me. "Okay then."

And then he left me standing there, waiting for me in the truck, and I knew the most awkward ride of my life was about to come.

But I put my hand to my lips and let out of breath.

He kissed me.

He kissed me back.

And he hadn't said sorry.

CHAPTER 8

Callum

The knock on my door didn't surprise me, even though part of me probably should have been. I already had my shoes on, along with worn jeans, an old Henley with paint stains, and my ball cap that I flipped backward so I could look underneath the cabinet. Frankly, I wasn't sure if I even wanted to leave the house. Because I knew once I did, I would be near her. It wasn't as if she wasn't a few hundred feet away from me, anyway. Because I was the damn idiot that was moving Felicity Carter across the street from me. She could walk across the street at any moment in those little pajamas I knew she wore and ask for a cup of sugar.

And I wouldn't give it to her because it wasn't as if I baked.

Damn it, I was an idiot, but it was the perfect place for her, and I could keep an eye on her. Yes, that was the reason. I could keep her safe and keep an eye on her. What other reason could there possibly be for me to want her to be close?

I was going to hell, and we all knew it.

However, the person at the door wasn't who I was going to go help in a moment.

An aggrieved sigh slid through my lips as I opened the door and glared. "What do you want, old man?"

My dad held up his hands, the dark circles under his eyes as evident as always.

"I just want peace."

I snorted. "You don't even know what peace is."

"Fine, I just want to talk. I'm sober. Haven't had a drink in two days."

I narrowed my gaze at him, studying his face. His eyes were clear, and he didn't smell like booze. So maybe the man was telling the truth. He didn't drink every day; it's just on the days that he did, he went overboard and made everyone's life a mess.

"You're not coming inside, old man. What do that you want?"

"Are you sure you really want me outside when I know you're about to have company across the street?" he asked, raising his brow in a way that was so similar to mine that it was once again a shock to the system.

Then his words penetrated, and I stiffened.

"What the fuck are you on about?"

Dad's lips twitched. "You were never a good liar, boy. I know that little girl that you always lust after is moving across the street. Good on you for making sure that happens. You can get that little piece of ass whenever you want."

My hand was around his neck, and his back was against my door without even the next breath passing.

"Watch your mouth. Don't talk about her like that. Don't talk to her at all. In fact, don't even be near her."

"And how are you going to stop that, boy? Look at you, always proving that genes run true." I didn't have my hand tightly around his neck, so he looked down, smiling at the sight of my grip.

"If I let you go, will you leave?"

"No. I need you to listen to me, and if you're going to show how violent you are, how much like *Daddy* you are for the rest of the group while I'm here, you might as well."

With a sigh, I shoved my dad inside the house and closed the door behind me.

"Talk."

"You always were an impatient little bitch."

The problem with my father was that he wanted to talk

shit. But he was no longer bigger than me. He couldn't take me, and we both knew it. Yet we also knew that I wouldn't kill him. Not because it would be a stain on my soul. Or that it would be detrimental to my own life. It was because my family didn't need another murderer in their midst. So my dad couldn't hurt me, but he could hurt the rest of my family. And he was sneaky enough to not use his strength to do it.

"Just spill whatever you need to and get out," I snapped before letting him go. I hated to see my hands on him. Another reflection of exactly who I'd become underneath his not-so-gentle care.

My father just smirked. "I need you to stop bullshitting about what you think I did to your stepmom."

I stiffened, wondering why the hell he would even bring that up. He never talked about my moms. Ever. Because he'd fucking killed them. And yet here he was, bringing her up.

"Why would I do that?" I asked, tilting my head.

"Because you're just reminding the town of what this family is."

"What you've made this family," I corrected.

"Whatever you want to say. I didn't touch that woman."

"We both know that's a lie."

"I didn't kill her."

"And Mom?"

"She slipped and fell. We both know that."

"After you pushed her."

"The cops couldn't prove that, and I've never said those words. So again, baseless accusations get you nowhere."

"You must be sober if you're using words like that."

"I'm much smarter than you give me credit for."

Of that, I had no doubt. He was conniving and cruel but brilliant in some ways. There had to be a reason that so many were drawn to him.

I hated this man with every ounce of my soul, but I needed him out of my house. Just having him breathing the same air as me felt as if it were tainting everything in its path.

"Fine," I lied.

Dad snorted. "You always were a shitty liar. Just be better at it. I would hate for something to happen." His gaze went across the street once again, and it took everything within me not to murder the man.

But I would not become him. No matter how much I ached to do so.

With a sigh, I stomped towards the door and opened it, gesturing for him to leave. "Go. You said your piece."

"Yes, I suppose I did. Have fun. If you know what I mean."

With that, he strolled down to his ancient sedan, got behind the wheel, and sped out of the neighborhood.

Hands on my hips, I was just grateful the man was sober. At least for now. I didn't need him killing anybody on the fucking roads.

Before I could calm down, the moving truck made its way down the street, and I cursed. Well, it seemed the day was just going to be an endless day of what-the-fuck.

I quickly grabbed the box I had been packing, closed the door behind me, and made my way to Felicity's new home. She'd signed on the dotted line, and the owners were damn happy to have her.

They'd watched her grow up from afar, even when I'd been out of town, finding my own way, and were glad she was back.

And now I was going to make sure that she was absolutely safe.

Felicity hopped out of her car since she had been following the truck, and grinned.

"Are you ready? I'm about to use your muscles."

She wore tight jeans with holes at the knees and one at the thigh, double tank tops, and a light jacket, but the effect just made her tits stand out even more. She pulled her hair back from her face, and it was all I could do not to tug on that ponytail, bend her over something, and see exactly how she tasted everywhere.

I was a bad man.

"Let's do it since apparently that's all I'm good for."

She smirked but didn't say a damn thing. Thankfully, Rune came forward and gestured towards the truck.

"Come on, come on, help me get this over with. She has way too much shit for someone who's never lived in a house by herself."

"Excuse me, most of it is books. You know that I love books."

"Of course, it's books. It can't be something like pillows. Why can't you like pillows?" Rune teased.

"Don't worry, darling, we're going to make sure you get tons of throw pillows as well. I want my baby girl to have the best home," Mrs. Carter said. Then she looked at me and beamed. "Callum. My boy." She hugged me tightly, and I kept the box out of reach, using one arm to hug her back. She smelled of cinnamon and Mom, and I loved this woman.

"It's good to see you, Mrs. Carter."

"You know I keep asking you to call me by my first name."

"And you know if I do, your husband will smack me upside the head."

"Damn straight," Mr. Carter said, grinning. He was just as sturdy and wide as he had been as an active fire-fighter, though I knew his joints didn't move exactly the way that they once had. Whenever he met my gaze, though, a shadow always passed his eyes, and I knew what he remembered.

The time he'd been too slow. At least in his mind. The time he hadn't saved them all.

It was the same look that Thatcher gave me and Bodhi or any of the Ashfords when they thought we weren't looking.

I shook that off and gestured us towards the house.

"Let's go."

"How do you already have a box?" Felicity asked, frowning.

Cheeks heating, I cleared my throat. "It's for you. I thought I'd get here early enough to just set it out and misjudged the timing."

Felicity bit her lip. That little worrying action was so damn cute that I wanted to lick the sting and tell her to stop hurting herself. And then maybe let me hurt her just a little, so it felt right.

I swallowed hard, willing my cock not to react. The last thing I needed was to show the rest of the Carters exactly what my dick was up to.

"What is it?" she asked, bouncing on her toes.

"It's nothing really." I opened the box and gestured for her to look, and her eyes widened.

"Callum," she breathed.

"What did he get you? And why didn't he tell me so that way I could sign my name on it?" Rune asked, his voice gruff behind me.

"Well, you were too late, and this is all Callum. Thank you." She went to her toes and kissed my cheek, and I shrugged it off, trying not to act as if anything had reacted.

Especially when her father and brother were standing right next to me. Oh, they weren't glaring at me now, but they would if they knew what went through my mind.

Felicity reached into the box and pulled out the potted plant. "And you really think I can keep this alive?"

"You kept a bunch of daisies alive that one time you tried to save them, remember? You can do it."

"You remember that? You were a kid too."

"Of course I do, Felicity," I whispered before I cleared my throat. "There are also a couple of snacks in there, baked goods that I baked myself, so just know that if they're inedible, deal with it."

She froze and stared at me. "You made me cookies?"

"I burned you cookies."

"You didn't burn me cookies when I moved into my place," Rune grumbled as he opened up the truck door. "Come on, get the presents inside, and then let's get to work. I need your back, Callum."

"On it," I said as I passed her the box. "I'll just give you this."

She stared at me for a moment, her eyes questioning, before she smiled. "Thank you, Callum," she breathed, and I shrugged, hoping she would think nothing of it.

I told myself I wouldn't bake for her. I couldn't bake. But it had been nagging at me, and now here I was, once again doing the thing I shouldn't.

Being far too close.

With a sigh, I went to help Rune pull out an ancient dresser.

"Where did you get this?" I groaned, trying to lift the damn thing with Rune.

"It was in the back barn area where Mom keeps all the little pieces she finds at yard sales and shops. Apparently, she's been planning for this moment longer than we realized," my best friend said dryly.

"Hey, that coffee table in your home is something I found and restored. Don't make fun of me," Mrs. Carter said as she went to her tiptoes and kissed her son's cheek. "I will kick you... lovingly," she teased.

Rune just met my gaze, rolled his eyes, and then we lugged the furniture into the house.

At first, I was afraid it was going to take us all damn day, moving shit around and trying to find a perfect place for it to go, but I should have thought better of it.

Because Felicity loved her spreadsheets and her graphs.

"Okay, that box labeled kitchen goes right here, and this box is labeled living room, so it can go right over there. Don't worry about unpacking everything. I've got it. And I already know where I'm going to donate the rest of the boxes and packing materials. Thank you all. Seriously."

There was no second-guessing where pieces of furniture went, no wondering where the hell that one box should go. She had it in spades, and I had to wonder how she knew how to do all of this. Then again, that was just Felicity. She was damn good at most things she did. It always surprised me that she had so much life experience and could do so much at her age. But then again, she wasn't that much younger than me.

And if I kept telling myself that, maybe it wouldn't make my thoughts so wrong.

Halfway through, Bodhi showed up and dropped off a few things, helping to move around the bigger pieces of furniture. He walked out after a kiss to the top of Felicity's head and a nod at me. He was still in a mood. Then again, I did not blame him.

Right as he was leaving, he bumped into Felicity's friend, Keely, who just smiled at him, and he grunted before heading out again.

"Okay, I hope I didn't offend him. I guess he could have had one of these sandwiches, but he just left."

"It's just the way he is right now. Don't worry, you didn't do anything wrong," I said softly.

Keely smiled. "Okay. Well, I made a bunch of sandwiches and sides to help you through. I have to go back to the bed and breakfast, so I'm sorry I can't help right now. But I will be here to help organize when you unpack fully. Okay?" Keely said as she hugged Felicity tightly.

"You did not have to stop by here with food. But thank you."

"Of course I did. You're my new bestie." She waved at everyone else. "It's nice to see you. And I'm going to be late." She ran out of the house, as bright and sparkly as she had when she walked in, and Rune just shook his head.

"Her and Promise probably click like nobody's business," he said with a laugh.

"I haven't seen Promise in a few weeks, but probably."

Although Promise had once dated my younger brother, and they co-parented their twin girls, it wasn't as if I saw her often. She worked as many hours as I did, many times more, and when she wasn't working, she was with the girls. I did not know how she and Finnian made it work, but the two were the best set of co-parents I had ever seen. And considering many of my friends who had kids were dealing with absolute hell with their exes and other avenues, it was nearly damn perfect.

"Oh my God, I'm in love with this sandwich," Rune said as he groaned into his meal.

I met Felicity's gaze, and we both rolled our eyes. "Do you need a room?" I asked dryly.

"Not any of my rooms. And please, use a plate," she said, gesturing towards the paper plates. "I'll let you use a real plate later. But I want to figure out where everything goes first."

"I would have bet money that you had a list?" I teased.

Felicity blushed. "Maybe. Shush."

I grinned, then took a bite of the sandwich. My knees nearly buckled. "Okay, so it looks like I'll have to go to the bed and breakfast more often. Damn, Keely can cook."

"She made the bread from scratch, and the chicken is perfectly roasted. I just love her food so much," Felicity said, groaning as she ate.

Each groan went right to my dick, and I had to take a deep breath.

"You should have hired her for the bar and grill," Mr. Carter said.

Rune laughed. "Like she'd want to take a step down for a bar and grill."

"Don't cut yourself short. Your bar and grill is wonderful, and it's not some hole-in-the-wall. But honestly, Keely should be either right where she is or working with Sterling." Mrs. Carter smiled at me. "Your brother's restaurant is divine. Mr. Carter and I go there on date nights."

I grinned. "Sterling's baby is The Range. I swear he spends more time there than he does at home."

"He's a high-end chef, and you even saying that around Keely would just make her day. I'm glad that between Sterling, High Country Bed and Breakfast, and Summit Grill, we're really increasing the town's food potential."

"And don't forget Altitude Diner," Mr. Carter put in. "The food there is fantastic. And Ashford Brews has its own little small eats."

I shrugged, finishing my sandwich. "We do okay. Nothing like this. But you're right, we are adding more and more to the town, but not overrunning it. No chains here."

Felicity beamed. "And people keep coming to Teller Accounting and Bookkeeping, and that keeps me happy."

"And that's really all that matters," Rune put in, his lips twitching.

"Damn straight. Now, let's clean up. We have more to do." She clapped her hands twice, and Rune sighed.

"You were always like this, even as a toddler."

Felicity flitted off, running away from her father's glare.

"She used to be so sweet," Mr. Carter said. "What happened?"

"She seems pretty sweet to me," I said without thinking, and Rune raised a brow. "What?"

"Nothing. You were just nice about Felicity. It's worrying."

I ignored him and went back to help move everything in.

By the time we were done, my back ached, and I felt ten years older, but Felicity's home felt like a home.

Her mom and dad left. Her mom said that they wouldn't visit every day, but I knew that was probably a lost cause. Rune had had to head out earlier since he was closing at work for the night, and that left Felicity and me alone, and I knew I should probably step back.

"Thank you so much for coming and helping. You really didn't have to."

I blinked at her. "Of course I did. If anything, I live across the street."

"That is true. And Teagan said she would be here tomorrow with Keely to help out. I love your sister. Plus, she's a force to be reckoned with when it comes to organization. And Thatcher and Kellan sent over gift cards for me to get new sheets and things, and they're so adorable. Every single one of your family members and our friends has sent things to help. And if they can, they're going to come here tomorrow and the next day. I just love it here. It's why I moved back to Ashford Creek."

"It's why I moved back too," I said after a moment. I hadn't even realized we were standing so close until I reached out and pushed her hair back from her face. "Your ponytail's fallen out."

"It's been a long day. I am ready to put my feet up and not move for a while."

"Yeah. Same. I have a long day tomorrow."

"You didn't have to spend your whole day here. You could have gone back to work if you needed to."

"No, I couldn't," I whispered. And then I did the unthinkable. I leaned down and took her lips. She wrapped her hand in my shirt and tugged, so I couldn't help but deepen the kiss. I slid my hands through her hair, tugged the rest of her ponytail out, and tossed the rubber band to the floor. She groaned, lifting her chin, so I nibbled down her neck, biting ever so slightly.

"You taste so fucking good," I moaned against her neck.

"I'm sweaty," she laughed.

"Salty. Mine." I was like a man possessed, licking and sucking, and I hadn't even realized my hand was underneath her shirt, cupping her full and firm breasts until she moaned. Her nipple pebbled through the thin lace beneath my thumb, and I licked my lips, my cock hard, the zipper most likely leaving a scar on my dick.

"I need to stop doing this."

"Don't stop. Please."

"I'm too old for you," I whispered, kissing down the other side of her neck, even as I rolled her nipple through her bra between my thumb and forefinger.

"You're not. I promise."

"Damn it," I growled and then crushed my mouth to hers again.

Her hands went up my shirt, sliding over my sweat-slicked back, and I couldn't help but fit my thigh in between her legs. She moaned, riding my thigh, the seam of her jeans most likely sliding along her clit.

"That's it, ride my thigh," I ordered, and her hips stilled for a moment before she met my gaze.

"Felicity. Ride my thigh," I demanded, and she nodded before rocking her hips. Her eyes rolled as I pressed her to the kitchen island, practically dry-humping her against the tile. I pulled up her shirt slightly, exposing her bra, before I licked over the salty globes of her breasts.

"I have always loved your tits, so full, bigger than my hands. Now I need to know the color of your nipples."

Her eyes widened, and her tongue darted out to lick her lips again.

"Callum."

"I've got you," I whispered. Then I tugged down the lace of her bra, exposing her pretty pink nipples, all hard and tight. "Exactly how I want it."

I leaned down and sucked one nipple into my mouth, knowing I was going to hell.

This was so damn wrong, but I couldn't help it. I had wanted her since the morning after the woods when I'd crushed my mouth to hers that one time and told myself it would be the one and only.

But it couldn't be.

And when her hips began to rock more, and a little distressed sound slid from her mouth, I frowned.

"What is it, little flower?" I whispered.

"I can't, I can't." Her cheeks blushed, and I grinned like a wolf sensing his prey.

"You want to come, and you can't like this?" I asked.

"No. Yes. I don't know."

"I've got you, baby. Don't worry." I took her by her hips and lifted her up so she sat on the edge of the counter.

"Oh."

"Well, what do you think now?" I asked as I ran my finger over the seam of her jeans.

Her eyes widened. "What are you planning?"

"What I'm planning is a one-and-only. Do you get that?" I asked, needing to make this clear.

"Sort of like a welcome-home present?" she asked, her voice shaking.

"Maybe. We can't do this again, Felicity. You know that. You know this is wrong."

"I know you think it's wrong. But okay. If that's what you say."

I wasn't quite sure I believed her, but I couldn't do anything except lean down and take her lips. I undid the button of her jeans, and as she lifted her ass so I could wiggle them down, I groaned at her white lace panties.

"Are you serious right now? White lace?"

"I'm not a virgin if that helps," she said quickly as I tossed her shoes and pants to the side.

I froze, glaring.

"You've let someone else touch you?" I asked, the possessiveness shocking me.

"Seriously? You can get all caveman and growly when you're touching me, but you don't own me."

"Right now, I own this pussy," I said as I slid my thumb over her heat.

Her mouth parted.

"You get me? At this moment, I own this." I cupped her, demanding. "I don't care who you've had in you before. I don't care whatever cock has pressed itself into you like he owned you. He didn't. I do. At this moment, I own you. Once we stop, you're your own person. I don't ever want to be the person who possesses you and thinks he can tell you what to do. But with you in my arms? I'm everything. And you're mine. This pussy is mine. Get me?"

She nodded. "I think I can deal with that. But can I call your dick mine?"

My lips twitched, and I shook my head. "No, little flower. I don't think so." I tugged her panties to the side, exposing her bare pussy, and I groaned.

"Oh damn, Felicity."

"Stop, you're embarrassing me."

"No, don't be embarrassed. Never be embarrassed about how wet you are. How much you want me."

"Maybe it's just how I react to any guy touching me," she teased. I leaned down and bit her inner thigh. She let out a squeak, and I grinned.

"Wrong answer."

"Fine, I'm wet for you. I'm usually always wet for you. Now please, lick my pussy."

"Such a dirty talker. I'm going to have to stuff your mouth with my cock the next time you even try to be snappy."

But I wouldn't. Because this was a one-off, and I wasn't going to let her touch me. I couldn't.

So, instead, I leaned down, spread her thighs, and licked up the crease where her hips met her upper thigh.

Her body shook, and I licked my lips. "So tempting."

I blew cool air over her core, and she shivered, her whole body tensing. Knowing I needed more, I tore at her panties, not able to wait. The ripping sound filled the room, and I shoved her panties off to the side, and before she could say a damn thing, I covered her cunt with my mouth. She was salty and sweet and everything that I craved. My dick ached, and I nearly came in my pants at her first taste. But I couldn't help it. I needed more.

She whispered my name, one hand holding onto the counter for dear life, the other hand sliding through my hair, and I continued to suck and taste and need.

I pierced her with my tongue, probing to find that sweet little spot, and when she nearly shot off the counter, I continued to lick and suck, twisting my lips around her clit. When she finally came, my name on her lips, and her cum all over my chin, I laughed at her, tasting her, needing her. I stood up, ignoring the raging hard-on that threatened to kill me, and licked my lips.

Her gaze went to her wetness on my beard, on my chin, and she blinked.

"Oh."

"You're welcome," I teased.

She rolled her eyes, so I leaned down and nipped at her lip.

"Welcome home," I whispered, kissed her softly, leaving her taste on her lips, adjusted myself, and walked out of the house.

She wasn't for me, and we both knew it, but I also knew I would never have such a sweet taste again as long as I lived.

Because she couldn't be mine.

CHAPTER 9

Felicity

"Wait. He did what?" Keely asked as she popped up from my brand-new-used couch and began to pace. "He just came over, and you ended up coming? Wow. I did not expect that. Callum? Wow."

I ran my hands over my face and let out a groan. "I can't believe I just told you that."

"I thought we were new best friends. I think you should tell me when a very growly, very large, very bearded, very sexy man makes you come with just his tongue out of nowhere." She paused. "It was out of nowhere, right?"

I bit my lip, and Keely took a seat next to me and blinked.

"Tell me everything."

It was the morning after everything had changed. Yet, I wasn't sure precisely everything had changed. After all, I had no idea what the hell I was doing. But once Callum had left me panting and feeling pretty useless on the counter, I'd scrambled and tried to calm myself. Yet the only thing I could possibly do at that moment was continue unpacking. Promise and Keely had shown up soon after, and while I loved Promise, I wasn't sure I could tell her exactly what had happened. After all, it felt weird, considering she used to date Callum's younger brother.

Not that Promise and I weren't friends, because we were, but she'd always been off with Finnian and Sterling, and I'd had my own friends when we were growing up. We were friends now, but slow ones.

Keely and I had just clicked, that moment in Summit Grill, like a bright spot in a somewhat dismal friendship life of mine.

But both women had taken one look at me, at my swollen lips and disheveled hair, and had known something had happened. They just had no idea with who. And both of them were too polite to outright ask. At least at that moment.

We continued to unpack as Keely organized my kitchen, ever the chef, and Promise had figured out the best ways to make what space I had work. After all, she had been in the hospitality business her entire life and now ran the cutest bed and breakfast.

The two women weren't anything alike. With Promise in her business suit attire, having taken off her suit jacket to help me out, and Keely in leggings and a top since she had changed out of her work clothes to come over and help me. Their staff was running the bed and breakfast right now, and I had so many questions about how they were working together as friends, but they were. They just got each other.

Promise looked prim and proper most times, but I knew she was covered in tattoos and had a tiny little nose ring. It was the same nose ring that Finnian once had. They'd gotten them in high school and had caused quite a stir with our classmates—and everyone's parents. I remembered it fondly since I'd nearly done the same thing with them, after all, I was only a grade behind them. Only I'd chickened out in the end.

Perhaps I should get one now. Most of my friends and family had gone down that road long ago. While Finnian had gone on to get a brow ring and, from what I heard, even more piercings, Promise had stuck with the nose, and both of them had ended up the parents of two.

In the end, both of them had helped me organize, and my parents had brought over dinner, aiding me even more.

Then I slept my first night in my new home, knowing Callum was right across the street.

And he hadn't texted. Hadn't come over to borrow a cup of sugar, not that I had a cup of sugar yet. That was on the list.

So when Keely had shown up the next morning, complete with a few kitchen staples, including that sugar, I had blurted out what had happened the day before.

"Tell me everything," Keely repeated.

"Oh, it all started two years ago."

"Two years! You two have been seeing each other for two years? Oh, wait. No. Because you've been going on dates. I'm confusing myself."

"You're confusing me. No, it's not like that. I mean, well, I'm going on dates so I can get over Callum Ashford."

"So you dated both of your brothers' best friend? That is awesome. And amazing and insane."

"We didn't date."

"What did you do? Wait, am I going to need to write this down so I have details later?" she asked, teasing. I knew she was just trying to calm my mind because I had been slightly, okay, overly, panicking before, but still, I had no idea how I'd ended up here.

"Two years ago, on my twenty-first birthday, I was with my college friends. We had decided to come here because I wanted to spend my birthday with my family as well, and my friends had come along."

"The four LS, right?" Keely asked. I had explained to her about my former friends and the fact that none of us talked. It wasn't that things had gone badly; they had just puttered out to the point that I wasn't in their lives anymore. I had been needed for those few moments in time and then tossed aside. Something I had been used to in my friendships. But I wasn't going to allow this to happen with Keely. And maybe even Promise. And, of course, there was Teagan, but Callum's sister scared me.

Okay, scared wasn't the right word. More that she intimidated me.

She was just so put together and knew what the hell she wanted. She ignored the busybody gossips, who loved to talk about the Ashford family. They loved to discuss the downfall of the legacy that came with being an Ashford, and they did everything to put it on the kids' shoulders. Though they weren't kids anymore, and Teagan didn't take any shit.

I loved her for that. But I was a little scared of her.

There were a few other women in town that I had known for a while, and I was trying to grow a friend group with them. After all, there were just so many men in Ashford Creek that sometimes they became overwhelming. I never really noticed as a kid, but the number of single dads in Ashford Creek was pretty much an epidemic.

"Your brain is going off on a tangent again," Keely said dryly.

"I was just thinking about how many single dads we have in town. And that there aren't that many women. Which makes the whole dating tourists thing a little more concrete. Because there are no men to date that aren't related to me or an Ashford," I said with a laugh.

"Oh. I guess that's true. I mean, the single dads things. There are a lot of them. And not all of them are related to you. There was that hot fireman guy, Thatcher, right?"

"No. I mean, there is. But I used to babysit his kids. That would be weird."

"So I guess Dr. Kellan is out." She wiggled her brows.

"Yes. I'm not going to date anybody that I was a nanny for their kids. I mean, I love reading those books, but well, I don't know. I suck at this."

"You don't suck at this, but you are avoiding the whole story." She shook her head. "So two years ago, you came back to town. Did he give you a birthday present that I should know about?"

I shook my head. "No, not that. He didn't even buy me a drink when I asked."

"Jerk."

"He's just grumpy all the time. Which makes sense, considering he usually is the one picking up his dad's messes."

"Mr. Ashford does scare me," Keely whispered.

I stiffened. "Wait. You've met him?"

"A couple of times. He just looms around." She shrugged. "Your brother was actually the one who told me about him, considering I was walking down the street alone when the guy came out of nowhere to be a jerk. But your brother and the fire captain, Thatcher, they physically pushed the guy away."

"Keely! When did this happen?"

She waved me off. "A couple of days ago. It's really not a big deal. I promise. The guy was just drunk. I can deal with drunks. I'm in food service, after all."

"Keely."

"No, it's fine. I promise. Anyway, Callum? He is grumpy for a reason."

I wasn't okay with what she'd said, but clearly, she didn't want to speak about it. For now. "Yes, he *is* grumpy. Family things, and I don't know. When the town gets in a mood, those that aren't the greatest usually decide to pick on the fact that he used to play in the NFL and then was forced out early."

"Wait. He was in the NFL? Did I know this?"

"Yes, I think. No. Well, he was a tight end and played for the LA Ruins for a while. Then he got hurt. He came back and opened up Ashford Brews. But the old biddies and drunks like to remind him that he failed in their eyes."

"Well, fuck them. Getting into any professional sport is difficult and unheard of for most people. The fact that your brother and Callum did it, that's fantastic."

"And Gray is in the NHL too." At her confused look, I continued. "He's a friend of Sterling and Finnian. And I guess, well, the others. The Ashfords all have a big friend group that they slowly collect people in. Like my brothers. And then I sort of latched on."

"And that's how you and Callum come into the picture?"

"I don't think there *is* a me and Callum. I mean, I don't think there can be. Which sucks, but anyway, two years ago, the four LS came, we were all dancing, having fun, got a little drunk, and Callum did nothing."

"And now I'm disappointed."

I shook my head. "The next day, I was planning on staying home and just relaxing, you know, old fuddy-duddy."

"There's nothing old and fuddy-duddy about you," Keely said with a laugh.

"Well, sometimes it feels like it. Anyway, I ended up being dragged out somewhat willingly to a cinco date." I rolled my eyes at the memory. "It just means that the girls met some guys, and there was a free one, and to make the numbers even, I showed up."

"That's always fun. Being the eighth wheel. Or fifteenth wheel."

"I don't know what I was expecting, but I thought maybe I would have a nice time, meet a couple friendly faces, and go home. Only it wasn't like that."

"You don't have to continue if you don't want to," Keely whispered as she gripped my hand. "I know that face."

"No, it's okay. It's just, well, the guy got a little handsy and a little violent, and when I needed help, I called Callum."

"Felicity," she mouthed.

"I'm really okay. I promise. It didn't go far. He didn't even really hurt me. I ended up breaking his nose."

"Damn, girl. I'm proud of that."

"Me too. It scared me, and the first person I called was Callum. Which, in hindsight, was ridiculous because Bodhi lived closer, or I could have even called my parents. My parents would walk through fire for any one of their kids."

"I love your parents."

"I really do too. But I didn't call any of them. I called Callum. And then he rescued me."

"It sounds like you rescued yourself too," Keely reminded me. "Never forget that."

"You're right. I did. And Callum was there, and he beat the shit out of Bradley."

"Of course, his name was Bradley. Fuck him. He better be in jail or something?"

I shook my head. "No, his friends took him away, and I'm pretty sure they aren't friends with him anymore, at least from what I heard. Bradley got the shit beat out of him, and we didn't want charges to be put on Callum because that seemed like what the little twerp would do. Everything just got pushed away, and I didn't think about it."

"That sounds terrifying."

"It was at the time, but Callum picked me up and carried me to the car, and I knew I was safe."

"Aww. That's so sweet."

"And I already had a crush on him. I mean, I have since I was out of high school. A hardcore crush. And it just kept evolving."

"And then he ate you out on your kitchen counter to break the house in. I mean, that's one way for a crush to go."

"Of course, when he kissed me two years ago, too, that sort of surprised me."

"What?" Keely exclaimed. "When did this happen?"

"The next morning. He came to check on me, and we sort of growled at each other because I was scared and pissed off, and he kept treating me like a kid. I'm not a kid. I might be younger than him, but I'm not ridiculously younger. My frontal lobe is developed, I can make my own choices, and well, one thing led to another, and I sort of kissed him."

"Damn, Felicity. Go you."

"It didn't feel like a go-me at the time. I knew I was making a mistake as soon as I did it, but then he gripped my ponytail, and well, it was the hottest kiss I'd ever had in my life. Until yesterday."

"Wow. I mean, just looking at him, he does have that growly dominant thing going on, but wow."

"You have no idea."

Keely visibly shivered and grinned at me. "So, is

anything going to happen? I mean, are you going to tell your brothers? Because I don't know, that seems like a recipe for disaster if you don't."

"I don't even know if anything's happening. He just walked out, and I think it's going to be the only time. But what the hell? That was more than just an accidental kiss."

"Yes, because he just tripped, and his face fell into your vagina."

I burst out laughing. "Oh, yes, that's exactly what happened."

"Just don't use that excuse if your brothers ask."

I groaned into my hands. "Oh my God. I can never tell them."

"Keeping secrets only makes things worse later. You might want to figure out what the hell you and Callum are doing and make sure that your brothers aren't surprised later. Because they are best friends with Callum, and they treat you like you're a precious little princess. All of them do." She paused. "Okay, Callum didn't treat you like a precious little princess when he had his hand around your throat, making out with you, but I digress."

My lips twitch. "No, I wasn't a precious little princess then." I let out a breath. "This is all so messy."

"Small town life. Who knew it would be this kind of messy?"

"I'm just so confused. And now I have to have family dinner and have to act as if nothing has changed."

"Like I said. Messy. But I promise I won't say a thing. Not that I have many people to tell."

"You're making friends. Just like I am. Albeit slowly."

"You have the luxury of being the small-town girl who came home."

"And I'm also the baby sister of the Carter brothers. Meaning, I'll always be that little princess."

Or little flower when it came to Callum. I held back a shudder at that thought.

"Okay, that is true. But I'm the new girl. The random transplant who came to a small town that she didn't know and nobody knows anything about."

"You're mysterious."

Keely snorted. "Not even a little. Although, there is another newbie in town. A nanny."

"Tess?" I ask, speaking of the woman I hadn't met.

"Yes. Her. She seemed really nice, at least, from the two seconds that I saw her at the diner. And she's working for two different families right now, and they haven't fired her yet. So there you go, there's another transplant to town. And I'm already gossiping about it like I'm an Ashford Creek resident. I don't think I like that."

"The gossip? Or the being a resident?"

"The gossip. Because who knows what everyone's saying about me?"

"Well, it doesn't matter what they think. Unless they're lying to your face about it. And now, I don't know if I like this small-town feeling," I said dryly.

"No, continue to like it. I promise it's not terrible. I like it here. Promise is fantastic. And I'm learning all the new businesses and figuring out my routine. I know there's a town meeting coming up, and I have no idea what holiday's coming up next, but there'll probably be a parade, and everything will be cute, and I'm really excited. Just like I'm excited to figure out what the hell you're going to do with Callum."

I cringed. "The problem is, I have no idea what I'm going to do with Callum. Or even if there is anything to do. He's just not doing anything about it."

"Okay then. Then maybe you make the move."

"No. Absolutely not. I already did that once."

"Then talk to him. Talking helps."

"I don't really like that. The whole communication is key thing."

"Because it usually works?" Keely asked with a laugh. Keely's phone buzzed, and she looked down at it and grinned. "And my time is up. I'm working the afternoon and evening shifts at the bed and breakfast because I decided to actually let my team open for me. It's weird. Having a team."

"You're an amazing cook, though, because you made me breakfast," I teased as I looked over at the kitchen.

"And you did the dishes. And that's all that matters.

You've got this, okay? Whatever happens, you got this. Just remember, secrets hurt. And I don't want you to get hurt. You're my friend. I like you. And I'm afraid of this small town without you."

I smiled, and we stood up, hugging. And as I walked her out, I swallowed hard, wondering what the hell I was doing.

I watched as Keely drove away, and my heart thudded when, across the street, the front door opened. Callum stood there, an odd look on his face, and I held up my hand and waved. Like an idiot.

Well, that was brilliant.

His lips quirked into a smile for an instant, and I wanted to walk over there just to talk to him. To see what the hell was going on. But, of course, that never worked out. Instead, two cars pulled down the road and into my driveway.

"There she is, my baby girl. I haven't seen you in forever," my mom called out as she came forward, arms outstretched.

I looked over at Callum before forcing myself to break eye contact and let my mom hug me. "I saw you yesterday. I've only spent one night away."

"You say that, and yet you're my baby girl."

"*Mom*."

"Oh, shush. I just love you. Now, let's get back to unpacking."

I let out a sigh. "I'm nearly done."

"You do realize that we have more stuff for you in the car, right?" my dad asked, giving me an apologetic look.

"Your house is going to be fully decorated at any moment. And if we were allowed to paint, we would be doing that too."

"The owner said she'd be allowed to paint any room she wants," a deep voice said, and I nearly jumped out of my skin.

I looked up at Callum, standing next to my brother, and tried not to look guilty. After all, Callum had just had his face between my thighs less than twenty-four hours ago. Totally normal.

"Wait, you never said that."

"I didn't think it was a problem."

"But we already have the stuff in the house," Rune said as he threw his head back and sighed audibly. "Now I'm going to have to move shit so she can paint."

I pressed my lips together, wondering why my older brother always acted like a toddler when it came to things like that. He acted as if he didn't own a business and wasn't a fully functioning adult who knew what the hell he was doing.

"It's really okay. I don't need to paint."

"Oh, but Felicity, we can totally do that." My mom rubbed her hands together. "Wouldn't that be fun?"

"I'm really okay," I said, looking at the looks of horror on all the men's faces in front of me. "I have enough to decorate for now. And, we all have other things to do other than painting."

"See? I knew my daughter was brilliant." My dad gave me a one-armed hug before he gestured towards his SUV. "Rune, Callum, you want to help me get a few boxes out of the trunk?"

"Boxes?" I asked. "I thought I had everything."

"Well, you needed more frames and things for the walls. And there was that one vase that you liked when we went to that home goods store, and well, you need it."

"Mom. You don't need to buy me everything."

"I don't need to, I want to. Let me spoil you. You're my baby girl."

I wanted to sigh at that, but then my mom reached out and patted Rune's cheek. "Just like you're my baby boy. I don't care if you all are sixty years old, and I'm walking beside you with my little walker. You'll be my babies. Now, help me do the heavy lifting because that is what your strong backs are for." She reached up and squeezed Callum's cheek, and he just grinned down at her, the love in his eyes brilliant.

"Anything for you, Mrs. Carter."

"Stop flirting with my mom," Rune growled, his lips quirked into a smile.

Callum met my gaze for a moment, and I swallowed hard, knowing Keely was right.

Secrets always had a way of biting you in the ass.

The problem was, however, I didn't know if the

secrets were just between myself and the rest of town or if the secret happened to be between Callum and me.

Because I couldn't read his face.

Not entirely.

Yet the desire in those eyes? I couldn't mistake that.

And he didn't look like a man who said it was only going to be one time.

No, he looked like a man on the hunt.

And I was his prey.

And frankly, I didn't feel like I wanted to run.

CHAPTER 10

Felicity

Despite the fact that Ashford Creek tended to know a little bit too much about my personal life and wanted to know everybody's business, I loved this town. I loved the way that they took care of each other. I loved the fact that you were technically never alone, and I just loved that open mountain air.

Settled in the Rocky Mountains, west of Denver, slightly off I-70, Ashford Creek was a typical tourist town, yet not quite touristy. We didn't have the huge ski resorts nor a full national park entrance, but we were close enough to each that we had a decent tourist schedule. People wanted to bike within our parks. They wanted that small-town feel to get fudge and flowers and little gift shop amenities. Tourists kept the town going because mountain towns couldn't last without an influx of people.

And I knew many of the full-timers didn't appreciate that.

Ashford Creek had once been a full grid with north-to-south streets, as well as east-to-west streets.

Then, at some point, a road had been put in to go from the lake in the northeast part of town all the way down to Southwest Creek.

I had no idea when that road had been put in, but it bisected nearly every major road in town. It wasn't Main Street, but it felt close to it.

A creek also bisected the town nearly in half. Main Street was right on the east of it, but Ashford Street was on the left. On the west. The fact that the diagonal street was named Lake Street made no sense to me. You would think the street that bisected all of the northern streets that went to the actual two lakes that surrounded Ashford Creek would be Lake Street, but no. So the eastern lake that didn't feed into Ashford Creek. There were no tributaries that led to it. They were all part of the same mountain range, but still a little different. The Western Lake fed into Ashford Creek, and the forest surrounded everything.

Main Street, east of the central creek, which did indeed lead to Ashford Creek south of us, had many of the main businesses. The bar and grill was up north, where I spent most of my time since Rune owned it. It had once been a different kind of restaurant until he had taken over and rebranded it. Now, it actually had good food, and there weren't fist fights with bikers out in the streets anymore.

Across the creek from the bar and grill was the bakery, which always led to my brother's growling. After all, Fiona enjoyed annoying everybody who came near her. And I knew that probably wasn't the kindest thing to say about her, but it was the truth.

North of the bakery, Sterling had opened his restaurant, The Range. It was the nicest restaurant in town, and there were the usual nice meals that ranged from French to American to fusion. And on Sundays, there was a different focus on a theme that was always a surprise. Well, at least a surprise to me. People made betting games to guess which theme would be next.

Ashford Brews was to the west, closest to the main lake, while the bed and breakfast was a little south of that.

I happened to work slightly south of the bakery, though, across the street, right next to Ashford Creek's outdoor equipment rentals. Which was always helpful for tourists and locals alike because you could rent kayaking equipment, camping equipment, and so much more. And they had an entire business for whitewater rafting and other things you could use on the rivers close by.

Across the street from all of us was the diner, flower shop, gift shop, coffee shop, and ice cream shop. There were plenty more places in town and even more coming, according to our mayor.

And I knew some of the town was excited to have more fresh blood, and the rest wanted the town to stay the same. There was never an in-between.

The schools were to the north and led into the residential areas, and the municipal buildings, firehouse, sheriff's station, and anything else that could possibly be needed for a small town were directly south of that. Homes popped up everywhere, and our tiny town was not quite the one-horse town that it had once been. But I loved it.

It was home.

And yet, right now, the ridiculousness of people's paperwork in this town was driving me batty.

"Gregory, why can't people just remember to sign things that they give us?"

"I'm sure they signed it," my boss and friend said as he came over, a frown on his face. "We went through this a few times with them. How did they keep forgetting?"

I sighed, knowing that he was trying his best, but things just took time. And frankly, knowing that it was frustrating him as much as me made me feel better.

After all, I was exhausted just thinking about all of the other things I had to deal with.

"We can't file these on time until we have it done. I know they filed extensions, and I'm so glad that the main tax season is done, but my word, payroll is never going to happen with a couple of these businesses."

"I know, dear. We're working on it. Some people just aren't the best at keeping up with things."

"Well, I guess that's where I come in. I'll make sure that we keep up with things."

"As long as you don't overwork yourself. You're allowed to have fun, Felicity, dear."

I snorted. "I also have a full-time job with you. I really don't mind doing this extra work."

"Well, I know, and you'll have time, but first, your friends are here."

My heart fluttered, knowing it couldn't be Keely because she was working all day at an event at the bed and breakfast, but maybe it was Callum. We were friends. Of a sort. And I really needed to talk to him.

"Oh, really?" I asked, my heart thudding in my chest.

"You know I'd never lie to you." He winked. "Come say hi to them and actually take your late afternoon off like you should."

"*Them*. Who on earth would be them?"

I frowned, saved my documents, put everything else in the safe place that they needed to be, and headed to the front of our tiny office building.

I froze, confusion settling in when I looked at the two near-strangers in front of me.

"Laurel? Lauren? What are you doing here?"

"Is that any way to say hello to your best friends that

you've ignored for so long?" Laurel said as she threw her arms up and hugged me tightly.

She smelled of over-rich perfume and weed, but I hugged her back tightly.

"I didn't know you'd be here."

Or where she lived. What she did for a living. If she was married. None of that. Because I didn't use social media anymore, and they hadn't reached out beyond the few times the group chat had been used. I had tried at first, even though I still remembered the way both Laurel and Lauren had looked at me when the incident had happened. The other two girls had been kinder, but not them.

Or maybe I was just thinking too much.

"I'm just surprised you're here. It's good to see you." I reached out and hugged Lauren, who just winked at me.

"We're on our way to see a few friends up north, but we stopped by your little town." She looked around my drab yet adorable office building and didn't quite hide her sneer. "I see things are going well with you. I just love that you decided to come back to your small town and stay where things are just good for you. You know? It's good to find where you belong."

"You're right. It is good to find where I belong. What do you guys do now?"

Lauren waved me off. "Oh, you know, this and that."

I snorted. "Okay. That's helpful."

"She's senior ad exec at Harleton and Carlton, while I just got promoted to VP of communication at Franklin's."

"It's just one thing after another. You know. Oh, and..." Laurel held out her hand. The diamond practically had its own zip code.

"Oh, wow. Congratulations."

"Yes, Tyler and I are really excited. He proposed to me when we were in Venice."

"Venice? That sounds like a lovely vacation."

"He takes me anywhere that I want, anywhere that we want." She snorted, and I just blinked at her.

Had she been as bad as before? Probably. But I had been focusing on other things.

And while their titles sounded wonderful, each of them was technically working for their parents and hadn't even applied for jobs once they got out of college. They had just walked into their family careers and called it a day.

And that sounded petty as fuck. And yet, their tones were just as fucking petty. Or maybe I was just tired.

"Anyway," Lauren said as she clapped her hands. "We thought we would take you out to an early dinner. There's a place called The Range? I don't know how good it is, but it seems to be the best place in town. Kind of hard to find a decent restaurant in tiny towns, but that's sort of what you're going for, right? That at-home feeling. I just love it here."

"Yes, I know The Range. And it is wonderful. The head chef is a friend of mine."

"I would think everybody's a friend of yours in town."

I just shook my head. "I really already have plans tonight, but I'm so glad you guys came by to visit."

"Your plans are with us," Laurel said with a laugh. "I mean, what else could you be doing?"

"And on that note, you guys have a wonderful day. I should get back to work here."

"Here? Here." Laurel just kept saying it as if it was going to change where I was at.

"Yes. Here. In a place that I love."

"You're a glorified bookkeeper. I thought you were actually going to do something with your career. You always talked up a big storm, and yet, you're back in Ashford Creek. I just don't understand you, Felicity. We had such high hopes for you."

I blinked at both of them, wondering what the hell was going on.

"Are you guys serious right now?"

"What? Just because it didn't work out with Bradley doesn't mean you can push away all the opportunities we gave you."

My throat went dry, and I wondered how the hell I could have ever been friends with these two.

Bradley.

Why would she even mention that name? I kept wondering why on earth these two were here. Honestly, when these two were together, they brought out the worst in each other because they were bored. They liked to find the worst ways to break others down, and I hadn't caught on until it had nearly been too late.

"Bradley, the guy who tried to attack me?"

"You were just being ridiculous," Lauren said as she waved it off. Waved off my near sexual assault. That is what this girl had just done.

"Get out. Seriously. Just get out."

"Don't be such a bitch," Lauren growled. "Seriously, I don't know what's wrong with you."

"I don't know what's wrong with *you*. I just, wow. I don't understand how you two are like this right now. But I'm not a teenager. I'm not even some college co-ed. I'm an adult with a real-time job. And you guys need to go. Because if you're going to be blaming the victim for shit like this, you can just fucking go."

"We were just trying to do you a favor. Bradley's in town, at his family's estate up north, and we wanted to make sure you were doing fine. You know, making a good impression." Laurel smirked.

"It's time for you two to go," Callum snapped, and I froze, wanting to sink into the floor.

Of course, he was here. Why couldn't the man just be anywhere else? But no, he had to hear. Witnessing my humiliation.

"Oh, I remember you," Laurel whispered as she moved forward as if she didn't have a ring on her finger.

"Out," Callum snapped, that dark energy that always seemed to be right beneath the surface, bubbling.

"Wow. Okay then. I see we're not wanted. But Felicity, if you want to meet up, we'll text you where we're going. Old times' sake." Lauren flipped her hair back and stomped out. Laurel trailing behind her.

I looked up then and realized that Callum wasn't alone.

No, Bodhi stood there, as did Teagan, Thatcher, and Kellan. I had no idea why they were all here, other than, of course, they had to witness my embarrassment.

And that's enough of a soap opera today. Thank you, but I'm done.

"Who were they, and am I allowed to go slash their tires?" Teagan asked.

"No, it's nothing. Seriously. Is there something I can help you with?"

"We have a meeting with Gregory," Thatcher said with a frown. "At least a few of us do."

Kellan, the town doctor and general practitioner, lifted his chin. "You okay?" That deep voice sounded so similar to Callum's, and yet, nothing alike.

Because Callum's did something to me, and Kellan was just a friend.

"Everything's great. And if we could not tell Rune or Atlas about this, that would be amazing. Because I already have enough big brothers in this room."

"We do like looking out for you," Bodhi whispered.

Callum didn't say anything. Instead, he just studied my face, and I wanted to crawl into a hole.

"And on that note, I'm going to go back to work and finish a few things."

"Okay...if you're sure, Felicity," Teagan whispered, worry etched on her face.

"Seriously, it's just silly college drama, and I do not understand why they were even here."

"I can still slash their tires," Teagan teased.

"Maybe I'll take you up on that."

Gregory finally opened his office door and led them in, leaving Callum behind.

"Aren't you going to join them?" I asked as the others filed out, worry still evident on each of their features.

He shook his head. "I was here for you."

At any other time, I would've wanted to hear that. Needed to hear that. Instead, my shoulders just dropped. "What is it, Callum?"

"I was going to bug you to watch that new superhero movie that just came out on streaming. The one I didn't get a chance to see in theaters? You promised you'd watch it with me."

I froze, remembering that vague promise months ago. I'd said it offhand, not taking it seriously, because Callum never watched movies just with me. But here he was, taking pity on me.

"You don't need to do that. The girls didn't really hurt me."

"I didn't hear all of it, but enough that they annoyed the fuck out of me. But I was already coming here to ask you."

"Callum, what is it you want?" I asked, grateful that the other door was closed.

"Felicity."

"No, what is it you want? Because I'm already having a bad day. And I don't think I can handle any more."

"I'm just here to watch a movie with my friend."

A friend. Well, that was better than a friend's little sister. But I couldn't handle it today.

"I have work to do. Maybe another time."

He studied my face, and I wanted to reach out and say yes. That I'd watched that movie, that I could take every part of him that I could get.

But the whole point of my figuring out how to over-come what I once wanted was to move on from Callum.

And that meant I needed to actually start moving on.

"If that's what you want."

"That's exactly what I want."

He didn't say another word. Instead, he turned on his heel and left, leaving me alone with my paperwork. Paperwork I really didn't want to do.

With a sigh, I grabbed my bag and made my way out of my office. The others were still dealing with a committee meeting with Gregory, one that probably had something to do with an upcoming festival that each of them was donating things to. Between time, energy, and materials, the town usually had something to do. The fact that Bodhi was even there meant Teagan had probably dragged him.

And yet, I couldn't really focus on that. No, I could only focus on the fact that today had been a really strange day, and I was exhausted.

I thought about going straight to my car and heading home, but instead, I walked across the small bridge over the creek and to the coffee place. The Flicked Bean was adorable, and I needed that last shot of caffeine, even though it would probably keep me up all night.

I walked past a group of people, trying to keep my eyes ahead, not really paying attention, when the hairs on the back of my neck stood on end.

I turned then and nearly tripped over my own feet.

Because he was there.

Yet another person from my not-so-distant past I hadn't wanted to see.

Landon just smiled, his hair bundled on the top of his head. "Hey, it's you." He had his arms around a tall woman with tattoos down her arms and a broad smile.

I tried my best professional smile since this man literally did nothing but annoy me for my own misguided choices. I didn't need to let him know how bad of a day I was clearly having.

"Oh. Landon. Good to see you."

"Is it? Well. Nice to see you back at the scene of the crime."

"The crime where you tried to ask me out because you were married and wanted extra fun?"

"Yes. I guess so." He nodded toward the woman at his side. "She understands."

I just stared at both of them, wondering how the hell my life had become a circus.

Because, of course, it was.

The next thing I knew, the kid who had pushed me on the sidewalk when I had been in kindergarten, making my dress ride up so everyone saw my peach-colored panties and socks, was going to turn around the corner and remind everyone of the incident.

These are the days of our lives, Felicity, and you are exhausted.

I just rolled my eyes and moved past Landon towards the coffee shop.

Yet when I walked in, I knew my day was only going to get worse.

"And this one time, she totally fell out of the car and went splat right in front of the hottie at the whiteout game. Remember that, L?" Laurel nodded as Lauren beamed as a group of strangers, as well as townspeople, sat in rapture as Lauren and Laurel spoke about things that made zero sense.

And, of course, because my nightmare of an afternoon wasn't over, Fiona stood nearby, coffee in hand, wide-eyed. Well, if this little play didn't make it into the town gazette, I'm sure Fiona would be sure to spread it around town.

And for some reason, two of the Ls were talking shit about me. And I was exhausted.

"Seriously? Why are you bringing that up? I thought you both had places to be."

Laurel beamed at me. "There you are. I thought you were busy? We're just reminiscing about old times. I know that football guy you tutored didn't really work out, but you really only liked him for his beard, right? Like how you used to go on and on about this one bearded hottie from your hometown."

I froze, wanting to crawl into a hole and never come out.

I'd had too much tequila *one* night and had mentioned my crush to one of the Ls. I couldn't even remember which one because they all blurred together even while sober, and yet I had no idea she'd even remembered that conversation.

Laurel smiled that sweet smile I'd fallen for hook, line, and sinker, thinking she was a real friend. "You know, that bearded hottie who seems to think of you as a little sister. Well, it's okay, I understand. Sometimes, you have to make up things so you can fit in. But we're all adults here, right?"

"Young lady, you need to watch your mouth," one of the older ladies from my mom's knitting circle snapped. "I don't know who you are, but in Ashford Creek, we don't take kindly to loose-lipped liars."

Laurel blushed. "I'm not the liar. She's the one who kept talking about her crush on this growly, bearded dude, and yet he never came around. And from what we can see, he's not around now."

"You've been here for like five seconds. What the hell is wrong with you?" I asked. I held up my hand and looked over at Ms. Holly. "I'm sorry for cursing."

"No need to be sorry. I know a bitch when I see one," Ms. Holly said primly, and I nearly gasped as the Ls turned red.

I sighed. "Seriously, it has been a weird day, and I really don't know why you guys are here. And I don't understand what your motivations are. We're not in college. I'm not some gossiping kid. I'm living my life at home. I'm sorry it's not what you think it needs to be, but you clearly didn't know me. Why don't you just leave town and do what you want to do? But this is my town. Talking shit about me and making things up isn't going to help. It isn't going to do anything to help you."

Laurel lifted her chin. "You're the one who made up your mountain man."

"And you two need to get a life."

I closed my eyes, counting to ten, wondering if I was ever going to wake up from this odd nightmare. "Callum. Please."

"Oh, you've got this. But these two need to leave.

Ashford Creek has enough assholes in it. We don't need to add two more."

"Well, I cannot believe you just said that," Lauren snapped.

"You know, I'm pretty much the queen bitch of Ashford Creek, and I'm not even as idiotic as you two. Seriously? Of course, Callum's the hot bearded hottie. The other bearded hotties here are either the other Ashfords or related to her. We've all had crushes on them. It's what we do. But seriously, go home. And grow up." Fiona wiped her hands, winked, and walked past me out of the door.

Mouth agape, I stared after her, hoping I was having an out-of-body experience.

Fiona had just stood up for me. And probably outed my crush to the rest of the world, but seriously. What the hell?

The Ls sneered and walked away without another word, leaving their destruction in their wake, and nothing felt real.

I stared at a few of the town members who had sat in on this odd diatribe and realized that none of them looked happy to be there. Each gave me a pitying look or a confused one. Oh yes, this would make the Gazette. There would be no doubt. A Carter messing up? That was new to them. Because the Carters didn't mess up.

But I'd sure as hell found a way.

I just shook my head, kissed my coffee goodbye, and moved past Callum. I would wake up soon, and this would be over. And I'd wonder what kind of sedative I had accidentally taken before bed.

As I moved down the street, Callum ran up beside me and grabbed my hand. I froze, closing my eyes, wanting this day to be over.

"Not now, Callum. I'm having one of those nightmares where I'm about to stand naked in front of the class to do my book report, and I didn't practice."

"And while that idea is intriguing, come watch a movie with me."

I sighed and turned. "That's what you're going with? A movie."

Though the idea of me naked in front of a class, where he's in it, seemed intriguing to him. Or maybe the lack of a book report was the intriguing part.

"I have no idea what just happened, but you look like you've had a bad day, so let's go watch a movie and eat ice cream."

"Ice cream doesn't solve everything."

"That's not what you said before."

"Is it going to solve the fact that two women that I thought I trusted, who I went to college with, *lived with*, and hung out with for four years, just treated me like a weird hillbilly who doesn't have any motivation and then lied about it? They were gossiping about me as if they knew me, and we clearly didn't know each other. I have no idea what their motivations are other than the fact that they seemed bored. Oh, and is it going to fix the fact that they're on their way to go see Bradley?"

Callum's jaw tensed. "Excuse me?"

I held up my hand, knowing I'd probably said the wrong thing. "Never mind. How about do you think the ice cream's going to fix the fact that the guy that I went on a half date with who tried to add me to his threesome was standing outside of the coffee shop with another date, trying to also treat me like shit? I'm really tired of random people who shouldn't matter to me, kicking me for no good reason."

"Little flower, we're going to go watch that movie, and we're going to go get ice cream. And I'm not taking no for an answer."

"Callum, you don't get to tell me what to do."

And though we were out on the street, in full view of anyone who happened to be looking out, he took a step towards me, so close I could feel the heat of him, and he glared down at me.

He was just so big. And yet, I felt safe with him.

I was a masochist.

"Felicity. Breathe. They don't matter."

"I know they don't. But I don't need your pity."

"I don't feel pity when I look at you, Felicity."

"And what do you feel?"

But he didn't answer.

CHAPTER 11

Callum

I f someone asked me what I was doing, I would tell them I was taking care of a friend. If somebody asked me to tell the truth, I wasn't sure what I would say.

The problem was, I didn't *know* what to say.

I had been going through life pretty well. I'd had a dream career if only for a few moments, and I'd made enough money during those years, however short they were, to sustain the life that I wanted and my family's.

I'd escaped this small town if only for the few years I needed to figure out how to breathe, and that was exactly what I had needed.

I had siblings that annoyed the fuck out of me most times but were pretty great. And I was making it through.

As long as I ignored the grief of not only my mother, stepmother, Mal, and my wife. If I ignored the fact that people never remembered her name. That they barely even knew I had been married, all would be well. If I ignored the fact that I had a craving for someone I shouldn't, I would be fine. I wasn't fine.

So here I was, in my home, with the one person who shouldn't be here.

I wasn't about to let her go across the street.

"I can just go home, you know. I was planning to just take a bath, have a glass of wine, and pretend that today wasn't radically fucking weird."

I raised a brow and gestured toward the kitchen.

"Finnian helped me set up the wine bar in here. Though I'm more of a beer guy. We'll find you some wine."

"You're not going to make a scene about how I'm not old enough to drink?" She slid her hands on her hips.

I just stared at her.

"I was there for your twenty-first birthday. We both know that you're old enough to drink. We both know that you are well past that. Come on, let's get you some wine. You can take it back if you want, but I figured you'd want to watch a movie."

"And how do you figure that? Callum, I do not understand you."

I shrugged. "Just let me take care of you, okay?"

She froze, eyes going wide.

"Why? Why do you want to take care of me?"

"Because it's what I do."

I moved on to the kitchen, knowing she would follow. She was always curious like that.

"I'm not yours to take care of. I'm not one of your siblings, and you don't need to take Atlas's place because he's not here. I have enough big brothers. I don't need you to have some odd sense of responsibility when it comes to me."

"Felicity, we both know I don't think of you as my little sister, so just pick which wine you want."

"Do you have a rosé?" she said after a moment, that resigned sigh of hers too damn cute.

I nodded and pulled one out of my wine fridge.

"Okay. Let's get this ready for you."

"You confuse me."

"Felicity, baby, you confuse me every fucking day. Just call it payback."

Chest rising and falling, she took a step forward as I pulled out her glass.

"I have no idea what that means. One minute, you're kissing me, and the next, you're pushing me away. And then, after that, you have your head between my legs, and I have no idea what the hell I'm supposed to be doing."

"I don't know either, if that helps."

"No. It doesn't help at all."

"Let's just relax. Watch a movie. Ignore those stupid bitches so that way I don't have to go and find them and kick them out of town again."

Felicity's lips twitched. "Honestly, they just looked bored. Like I was fun to kick around for a few moments before they went back to their real lives, or vacation, or whatever. I truly do not understand them."

"I never understood why you were friends with them to begin with."

She let out a sigh and shrugged. "They weren't always like that."

I gave her a look.

"Truly. They had their good moments. At least when the four were together. And Laurelin was always nice."

"One of them wasn't Laurelin?" I asked, and she let out a laugh.

"You do realize they're just jealous, right?" I asked as I pulled out one of my IPAs from the fridge.

"Why?" Felicity's eyes widened. "Why would they be jealous?"

"Because you really don't care what they think. You were always like that. Hell, you were fine just staying at home alone that one night." I cursed. "Well, at least at first."

"I don't want to talk about that night."

I reached forward and pushed her hair back from her face, cupping her cheek. "I don't want to either. But those girls? They're not happy. You can see it all over their faces.

They wanted to come here, make sure that you're just as unhappy, so they can feel better about themselves."

"That's not true."

"It is fucking true. Hell, Felicity. You have a family that supports you, a town that you love, and loves you. You saw all of those people in the Flicked Bean. Even Fiona was nice."

Felicity threw up her free hand. "Oh my God. Right? I mean, Fiona stood up for me. In her own way. Maybe I am in a dream, or this is a sign of an apocalypse."

"You're not in a dream, and this isn't an apocalypse. But it does seem like it sometimes."

"I'm just surprised that she even stood up for me a little bit."

"Maybe she was bored."

"You know, that seems a lot more likely than anything else."

"They're just jealous of you. And they'll skedaddle out of Ashford Creek with their tails between their legs, and you won't have to see them again. You have your own life here. Your own future. You've got this."

"Skedaddle?" Felicity asked, her lips pursed. "Who says that word?"

"I'm an old man. It's what I do."

"We both know you're not that old."

"I'm older than you," I mumbled, gesturing towards the living room. "Go take a seat. We'll find something to watch."

"Why am I here, Callum?"

Why did I like the sound of my name on her lips? She shouldn't be here. She should be at home or with her friends. I shouldn't be anywhere in her vicinity.

Ever since I'd had a taste of her, though, I couldn't walk away. It was so damn stupid. But I craved her. I wanted more. And the part of me that was smart wasn't really listening anymore.

"The honest answer is I don't know," I said after a moment.

"You don't know..." Her voice trailed off.

"No, Felicity. I don't. I haven't known what I'm doing with you for two years. But we're friends." I pause. "We are friends, right?"

"Yes, Callum, we're friends." Her voice was barely above a whisper as she stared down into her wineglass.

I reached forward again and lifted her chin with my finger. When I met that stunning gaze of hers, my heart sped up, my breath catching once again.

"I'm not a good man, Felicity. I've made shit decisions. I've hurt people. I don't always think about the consequences. And part of me wants to keep hurting people." Her mouth opened, and I shook my head. "But I can't stop thinking about you. I know it's wrong. I know your brothers are going to kick my ass. But I want you here. In my house. On my couch. I want to watch a fucking movie. I want to feed you. And I want to touch you. I just want you. Call me insane. But I just want you."

"You want me?"

My lips twitched. "Yes. And I don't talk about my feelings. I don't talk about shit like this." I took a step back and sipped my beer. The hoppy-ness settled on my tongue, and I tried to focus.

"I don't know what I'm doing here. I never know what I'm doing. But I want you."

"You say you don't know what you're doing, but I don't know... it always looks like you know what you're doing."

"And I'm a damn good liar. I know what I like, Felicity."

"And what do you like?" She met my gaze, and I couldn't help but smile. She was so damn strong, so damn fierce, and I knew she sometimes forgot that.

"I like my family. I like to make sure that they're safe. I like working at the brewery. I like creating things. I still like watching football. And I like to fuck."

Her eyes widened.

"What, you don't like me saying I like to fuck?"

"Well, if you're going to say one thing is out of place of the others—"

"I like to fuck. I don't do relationships. Not anymore. And I usually don't fuck townies."

"And that's what I am? A townie."

"No, Felicity. You're my ruination. But I don't fucking care right now."

241

I set the beer bottle down, moved forward, and crushed my mouth to hers.

She let out a little gasp against my mouth, and I groaned. Without looking, I took the wine glass from her hand, set it down on the opposite counter, and moved in.

"You tell me to stop, I'll stop."

"So this is just fucking?" she asked, her eyes wide.

I pressed my forehead to hers, my breath coming in pants. When I slid my hands around her, caging her against the kitchen counter, her throat worked as she swallowed hard.

"I told you. I don't know what I'm doing."

"I don't know if that fills me with joy and reassurance."

"I don't think I'm supposed to reassure you right now. Because I'm not fucking my best friend's little sister right now."

"That's not my only title, you know."

"I do." I moved one hand up to trace my finger along her jawline. Her pupils dilated. My girl liked being touched. Liked being praised. "When it comes to you, I don't think it can just be fucking."

"And that worries you."

"What do you want, little flower?"

"For you to kiss me."

"I can do that. I can always kiss you, Felicity. That's not a problem. What more do you want?"

"I don't know." She pulled away, and I took a step

back, not wanting to completely cage her when she needed that space. I was a bad man, but I wasn't a monster.

"What do you want, Felicity? What do you need, little flower?" I asked, my voice soft.

"I have no idea what I want. And that's the problem. You heard the Ls at the Flicked Bean."

"I don't want to talk about the Ls."

"Well, you heard them. I had a crush on you all of college. I was a full-fledged adult, crushing on an older guy."

"And now?"

"I still want you."

"I've wanted you since I saw you dancing on the dance floor at Summit Grill on your birthday. Your hands were up, your breasts bouncing with each move. You had that little sliver of skin showing between the top of your jeans and the bottom of your shirt. I wanted to lick that skin. Taste your salt. Taste everything. And it took all within me to walk away."

"But why?"

"Why do you think? I'm an old man."

"You aren't. You're in your thirties. I'm in my twenties. I'm an adult. Making my own decisions."

"But you're also their little sister."

"So? Why is that such a big deal?"

"You know why."

She ran her hands over her face. "Okay, that was

stupid. Because yes, I know why. But still. Shouldn't I be a factor on my own merit?"

"And what do you want?"

"I want you to kiss me. I want you to touch me. I just want."

"If I do all that, is that it, then?"

"We both know that we'd hurt each other if it were anything less. Or if it was anything more."

I leaned forward so she would look at me again. I needed to see those eyes.

"Baby, little flower, I'll hurt you. It's what I do."

"You keep saying that, but I've never seen any evidence of the people you hurt."

"That's because people are good at hiding what breaks them the most. And you haven't met the ones I've broken."

And she never would.

"If you kiss me again, I don't want it to be the last time."

"If I kiss you again, it won't be the last."

"You won't hurt me, Callum."

"I will, baby. It's what I do best."

"I think you don't give yourself enough credit."

"I think you don't ask for enough."

Then she went on her tiptoes and pressed her lips to mine.

Groaning, I gave in.

Because I needed her. Craved her.

Not just her taste, but her.

I was going to hell, but I might as well go down in a blaze of glory.

I parted her mouth with my tongue and groaned.

"You taste so good, baby."

"Callum. Please."

"Please, what? Do you want me to kiss you?"

"Yes."

"Do you want me to taste the salt off your skin, kiss those pretty pink nipples, suck on them until they turn a deeper red, and ache from my mouth?"

"Oh."

I narrowed my gaze at her, leaned forward, and bit her lips gently.

She gasped but didn't back away.

"I know you like it when my mouth is on this pretty cunt of yours. Tasting that sweet honey. Have you ever had a man go down on you before? Other than me?"

She nodded, and I growled, squeezing her hip.

"Don't think about them when my mouth is on your pussy. Got that, little flower?"

"But you asked."

"So a man's tasted you, but I'll be the one that you remember."

"I don't think you're going to have a problem with that."

I grinned and slid my hand up her skirt and over her ass. I squeezed one globe, and she shuddered.

"Are you really not a virgin, Felicity? Have you ever had someone's cock sink into this sweet cunt of yours?"

She shook her head, nodded, and frowned. "Those are two different questions with two different answers."

My lips twitched. "You got me there." I moved my hand to get over her, popping her pussy from behind. She gasped, her eyes dilating.

"Are you a virgin, little flower?"

She shook her head. "No. Though I'm not really good at sex."

I growled. "No, those boys who thought they could have you weren't good at sex. Because if you think you're not good? It's on them."

"Callum."

"No. I'm going to show you exactly how good you are. How you can roll your hips. How this sweet cunt can milk my cock. Do you want that, little flower? Do you want to be filled with my cum as I sink into you? Or do you want my cum all over your body, marking it as mine?"

I liked dirty talk. It was one thing that, no matter who I was with, came out of me. But watching Felicity practically melt under my touch as I spoke? I was losing my damn mind.

She needed to know how far I could go, just as I needed to know how far she could go. How far she wanted to go.

I wouldn't hurt her, not like that. But I refused to be the worst.

The thought of some twenty-something college boy touching what was mine made me want to break bones. I was a terrible person. Territorial to the nth degree, but I didn't care.

"I'm going to fuck you, Felicity." She paused at my use of her name. "Do you get that? You'll be mine. For as long as we do this, you'll be mine."

"So it's not an only? Not like you said before."

I sighed, pressing my forehead to hers. "No, Felicity. It won't be an only." I slid my hand again, this time over her panties, between the globes of her ass.

"Have you ever had anyone take you here?"

She froze, shaking her head.

"Good. Then this will be mine."

"Callum, I don't think I'm ready for anal. I'm just saying."

I grinned, loving the fact that she could say the words. That she wasn't scared.

"Baby, not tonight. You have to be prepared for that. Although the idea of me fucking you from behind, sliding into this sweet cunt as you rock a jeweled butt plug in that tight little hole of yours? Damn." I groaned, rocking my hard cock against her stomach. "I'm a bad man."

"You're a bad man who likes to talk, and yet, I still have my clothes on."

"A challenge. I'll take it."

I crushed my mouth to hers then, tugging up her shirt.

Her hands roamed as if she couldn't help but touch me, and I just smiled against her lips, letting her. Maybe next time I'd pin her arms above her head so she couldn't touch, and she'd be all mine, but for now, I'd let her have her fill. She thought she wasn't good at sex? I'd have to just prove her wrong.

I slid my hand underneath her panties, cupping her bare, and she shot off like a rocket, rocking her hips against me.

"You're drenched. Just a few kisses, a bare touch, and you're wet for me."

"It's a problem."

I grinned. "No, baby, I don't think it's a problem."

I looked around the kitchen and frowned. "We sure do like kitchens."

"I don't mind."

"I do. You deserve a bed. At least for what I have planned for you."

Her eyes widened, and in the next breath, I slid my hand from beneath her panties and lifted her into my arms. She wrapped her arms around my neck, and I carried her into the bedroom, nipping at her lips.

I set her gently on the bed, and in quick work, I undid the buttons of her blouse.

She tugged at my belt, and I smiled, sliding it off.

"I need to see you."

"Patience."

She shook her head. "I have zero patience right now."

"Okay, we can work with that."

I stripped her quickly as she pulled on my clothes. It was fast, and we laughed, and I knew that this would be a temptation I wouldn't be able to walk away from. Not without breaking her.

But the recklessness in me didn't care at that moment.

I shoved my jeans down, taking my boxer briefs with them.

My cock sprang free, bouncing against my stomach, as I kicked off my jeans.

Felicity's jaw dropped, and I grinned.

"Take off those panties, and I'll get your bra."

"Um. Um." She licked her lips, her eyes on my cock, and I just grinned.

"Like what you see?"

"You have um. Well. Did that hurt?"

I looked down at the four barbells on my dick and shrugged. "When I first did it? Yeah. It doesn't hurt now. Actually, it feels really good."

"So, it makes you feel good?"

I licked my lips before moving quickly to undo her bra. The straps fell to the side as her breasts fell heavy, her nipples hard points. I leaned forward and pinched her nipple slightly.

A gasp escaped her.

"It was just a pinch and a little sore at first. Just like my nipples."

She looked up then and blinked. "How have I never noticed you have hoops in your nipples?"

"I don't always wear them out like this. Especially if I'm at the lake or something with your family. Don't think everybody in your family needs to see all of my piercings."

"Nobody in my family better see all of your piercings," she said pointedly, staring at my dick once more.

I laughed and ran my hand through her hair.

"They won't. The barbells are going to feel really fucking good inside you. Like an extra ribbed condom."

"And they don't break through the condom?"

I shook my head. "Not the ones I have. Don't worry, I'll keep you safe."

She bit her lip and looked up at me. "I'm on birth control. And well, I'm clean. I just had my physical."

I groaned, fisting myself.

"Felicity, don't tell me things like that."

"What? I want to know what it feels like."

"The thought of having you bare is nearly making me come right now. But fuck. Damn. Okay."

"Okay!"

She looked so damn cute right there, and I couldn't help but shake my head. "Okay. I'm clean too. Promise."

"I trust you."

I held back a groan, wondering why she should. But there was no going back now.

Instead, I leaned forward again and took her lips.

When she reached out and gripped the base of my dick, my hips flexed.

"Felicity."

"What? I just want to feel."

"It's all yours."

She grinned then, exploring my cock, squeezing, her hands go up and down my length. When she tapped the barbells, my dick twitched, and her eyes widened.

"Oh. Well."

"Baby, you're killing me here."

"Sorry," she said but didn't look sorry in the least.

"Can you get blowjobs like this?"

"Yes, you just have to be careful with your teeth. They're far enough back that it's not actually a problem like it would be with a Prince Albert."

"Oh. I'm learning all sorts of new things today."

"My precious little flower. I can teach you so much more. But your mouth is not going on my cock right now."

"Why?" she pouted.

"Because I'd like to be able to last more than thirty seconds."

"Problem because you're an old man?" she teased.

Growling, I took her hair in my fist and tugged her face up to mine. She stood there, my cock against her belly, her nipples against my skin.

"I'll show you what an old man can do."

I bent down and took her mouth. She tasted sweet and like everything I craved.

I didn't know where this was going. Only that it would probably end in disaster. But I knew I needed her. Not just for this. But for so much more. And I had no idea what the hell I was going to do with it.

Her hand slid from my cock to grip my hips as I lowered her to the bed. My mouth slid over her jaw, biting, nibbling, as I worked my way down her body, taking her breasts with my hands.

"I fucking love your tits."

"I thought you were going to fuck them," she teased.

"Another time."

Her eyes widened, and I grinned. Because, damn it, there would be another time. Until this imploded, there would be another time.

I sucked one nipple hard into my mouth, loving the way that she arched against me. And I cupped her breast with my other hand, gently picking the peak, and she moaned.

"So sensitive," I murmured before sliding my beard over her skin, loving the way she shivered. I kissed her other breast, giving it equal attention, before I pulled back, letting go of her nipple with a plop.

"So fucking beautiful. Look at these hard little points."

"Callum. Stop teasing me."

"I've only just begun."

She groaned before cupping her own breasts.

"That's it. Show me what you like."

She met my gaze and nodded, rolling her nipples between her fingers.

I licked my lips before trailing my mouth down her belly, down to the juncture of her thighs. I slid my nose over her mound and blew cool air on her cunt. Her legs fell open, and I looked down at her soft, swollen folds and swallowed hard.

"So fucking wet."

She let out a whimper, and I leaned down, taking her clit into my mouth. She came, in a single instant, she came against my face, her hips rocking. I just moaned, taking her orgasm before spearing her with two fingers.

"Callum!"

"Ride my hand. I want another one out of you."

"I can't. I just did."

"Ride my hand," I ordered, and she rotated her hips as I slid a third finger into her, rubbing that sweet bundle of nerves. She whimpered, nearly at the edge, as I thumbed over her clit. And when she came again, clamping down on my fingers, I lapped at her juices, loving the way they slid down my arm.

When I finally removed my fingers, I met her gaze and slid them into my mouth.

I groaned, that honey-sweet taste mixed with tartness a damn elixir.

"Callum." She blushed, and I shook my head.

"I could taste you forever, Felicity."

I hadn't meant for my breath to go so shallow there,

for my voice to be a whisper. I needed to stay in control. Because if I wasn't careful, I'd fuck things up. Well, I was going to do that anyway, but I'd fuck them up before we even got a chance.

I slid her leg up, gripping her thigh, as I rested her ankle on my shoulder.

"Are you ready for me?" I gripped the base of my cock, tapping the head against her clit. Her eyes widened, and she moaned.

"I've been ready, Callum."

And in that instant, I knew she didn't mean tonight.

We needed to be careful. So fucking careful. But we were being reckless. And I didn't care at that moment.

"Lean up on your forearms so you can look down. I want you to see me enter you. I want you to watch as your pussy swallows up my cock."

Her head fell back slightly as she moaned, but she did as I asked.

And then, knowing I was playing with fire, I pressed the tip of my cock at her entrance. I nearly came right then.

I'd only ever gone without a condom with one person. One person I wasn't even sure Felicity knew about. But I quickly pushed that from my mind. This wasn't breaking a vow. Perhaps a promise to another, but that person wasn't here, nor was the ghost that I did my best to not think about.

Instead, I slowly worked my way in and out of her, watching her face as I slid to the hilt.

"Oh my God, Callum. The piercings. I can feel them."

"Your pussy is so tight. So warm. I'd forgotten what it felt like to go without a condom."

She frowned and then nearly cursed.

Now is not the time to mention exactly who I had been with. Instead, I slid my thumb over her clit, so she rocked against me.

"Look at us. Look how your pussy grips me. I'm so deep inside you right now that I can barely breathe. Are you ready for this?"

"Callum. Please."

I grinned and pulled out. When she whimpered, I licked my lips, leaned down slightly even though her ankle was still at my shoulder, and slammed home.

Her breasts bounced, and her eyes went wide as I moved in and out of her, hard and fast, and she gripped me, meeting me thrust for thrust.

"That's it, Felicity. Take me."

"Harder. Please. I can take it."

"That's my girl."

I let her leg fall before going back and pulling up her knees so I could go deeper. She moaned, reaching for my hair, reaching for anything.

When her nails slid down my back, I knew she would leave marks. And that was exactly what I craved. "Mark me, I'm yours. Right now? I'm yours."

She nodded and then pulled me down so she could take my mouth.

I rolled, needing a moment to breathe, as my cock nearly exploded inside her. But I had to be careful. So fucking careful.

She let out a gasp as she found herself on top of me, my cock buried to the hilt.

"Ride me."

"I thought you were doing the work," she teased.

"I'm going to fuck you hard enough that you'll be catching your breath for a long while now."

"You already are."

And then we moved, with her riding me, sliding up and down my cock in quick succession. Before I could come, I pinched at her nipples, cupping her, and when she came, gripping my cock, I nearly went cross-eyed. Her gaze enraptured me, and I knew I couldn't come while meeting those eyes.

Because if I did, I would break so many promises to myself.

Instead, I slid out of her, ignoring her slight whimper, and positioned us so she faced the headboard, and I kneeled behind her. Before she could say anything, I gripped her hips and buried myself to the hilt.

She groaned, pressing her ass to me as I continued to fuck her, loving the way that she met me thrust for thrust and moved for me.

And when I finally came, she followed me, her body

going limp. We rolled to the side as her entire body shook, and I knew she was coming down from her high. Still deep inside her, my cock twitching, I slid my hand over her hip and squeezed.

"I've got you, Felicity. I've got you."

"So. Good."

My lips hitched, and as I pulled out of her, I couldn't help but sit up and watch as my cum began to slide out of her sweet pussy.

I was never into things like this before. Not really. Yes, I liked it hard. I liked a little pain. I liked giving pain and pleasure. But branding like this? Marking her? No, that was just for Felicity.

I went to grab a towel to clean both of us up, and then held her to me as she slowly calmed her breathing. I kissed the top of her head, letting her rest on top of me, both of us naked, sweat-slicked underneath the blankets, and I knew I was in trouble.

Beyond trouble.

CHAPTER 12

Callum

Water slid down my back, icy cold, as I pulled out of Felicity, my cock spent, still twitching. Cum seeped down her inner thigh, and I slid my hand between her legs, over her swollen folds.

"You good?" I whispered, nibbling at her neck.

Felicity nodded, leaning against me.

"Yes. Though I think my knees are a little shaky."

"Probably not the best thing to happen while we're in your shower." I kissed her shoulder and turned off the water.

Felicity leaned on the shower wall, and I grinned

before realizing that I should probably clean up my girl. She made my brain misfire.

I quickly turned on the water again, ignoring her little squeal, and lathered her up.

Of course, that just made my cock stand at attention, and her nipples pebble, but I only made sure that my girl was clean and taken care of.

I shook my head.

Two weeks.

It had been two weeks of us sneaking around, walking across the street to borrow a cup of sugar.

Two weeks during which I'd been avoiding my best friend.

Because there was no way I could look into Rune's eyes and tell him that I was fucking his baby sister.

Hell, what was worse? Fucking her or catching feelings? Because, at this point, I wasn't sure. Since they both were true.

I shook my head and grabbed one of her fluffy towels.

"This thing is ridiculous. How is this the most lush towel I've ever seen?" I clucked my tongue as I wrapped it around her, and she just smiled up at me, her eyes a little glassy.

"I like comfy things. Can you get me the other towel?"

I frowned, then picked up a microfiber towel that made me want to shiver. I hated the feeling of microfiber.

"What is this for?"

"It keeps my hair healthy. And dries it a little more quickly."

"You have a special towel for hair." I shook my head, then used one of her other ridiculously fluffy towels to wrap around my waist.

"Yes. You've been with women before, right? I mean, I didn't deflower you or something?" she teased.

I rolled my eyes. "No, you didn't deflower my thirty-something-year-old self. But thank you. I have been with women before. I just don't think I ever paid attention to towels."

"Well, you've been missing out. When your hair gets a little longer, you could use mine. I bet Bodhi could borrow it. It would do his hair wonders. Though he does have really soft hair."

"If you could stop talking about my brother's hair when we're both nearly naked, that would be wonderful."

"Jealous?" she teased.

"Yes."

She paused, eyes wide.

"Really? You're not going to cover that up or something?"

"Why?" I shrugged, then reached for my pile of clothes. We'd had sex earlier in the living room and then come to the shower to clean up. Of course, that meant more sex because, hello, it was Felicity. Only, I didn't have any spare clothes here.

Not that I would bring spare clothes here. It was like a punch to the chest, and I let out a breath.

No, I wasn't going to do something silly like move in any part of myself. Not when I was still lying to Rune.

"I'm not going to lie to you."

A small smile played on her face. "Good. Although—"

"I know. I know. I was just thinking about Rune."

"Maybe stop thinking about my brother when we're both nearly naked," she added dryly.

I snorted but continued to dress. I wore jeans and a T-shirt, and my feet were bare since my shoes were at her front door. She'd left a little space for me next to her pile of shoes, but I wasn't sure how I felt about that. Then again, I had her favorite soda and wine at my place, so I guess it wasn't too big of a deal.

Or maybe it was everything.

I folded my arms over my chest as I studied Felicity, wondering what the hell we were doing.

"I don't feel like we're hiding, and yet I know we are."

"It won't be that bad, right? I mean, my parents love you. My brothers love you."

"Until I touch their precious baby sister."

"That never made any sense to me."

"What?" I asked, my gaze on her tits as she slid her bra back on.

She snapped her fingers. "Eyes up here, Callum." Her lips twitched.

"My apologies. Your breasts always distract me."

"Your dick does the same."

"You're welcome."

She just shook her head. "Seriously, though, if you're friends with my brother, that means you respect each other. Meaning you should respect how they treat the women in their lives. So why would your brother have a problem with me? Why would my brother have a problem with you?"

"It's not that simple."

"Enlighten me."

"Because there are just rules. It's not that he thinks I'm a terrible person who's going to throw you away the minute that I get an itch. Because I'm not," I reiterated. "It's just the code."

"The code is stupid."

"Maybe. But there are reasons for that. What if I do hurt you? What if you get tired of this and walk away? Does that mean I can't ever be in a room with you again? That means I'm surely not fucking going to family dinners again. Which I've been avoiding for two weeks. It means that I might not go to the grill, and your brother might not come to the brewery. It means I don't go out to see Atlas play. It means everything. So, you're friends with Teagan and Finnian and Sterling. You hold Briar's kid when she visits. We're all connected like this. So yeah, there was a reason I didn't fucking touch you for two years. And not just because you're younger than me."

Her eyes filled, and I cursed under my breath. I took a

step forward and pulled her to me. I rubbed my chin over her head and let out a breath as she wrapped her arms around my waist.

"I'm sorry. I should have thought more before I touched you."

"I'm glad you touched me. But I guess maybe we should have the talk."

I froze.

"What's the talk for you, Felicity?"

"It's been two weeks, and I can't keep my hands off you."

"It's mutual."

"Okay, it's been two weeks. Do I ignore you when we're together out in public? What are we?"

"I hate that question."

"I know. Because putting labels on things can get weird. Especially when we're figuring things out. But you're right. Everything you just said is right." She pulled away and moved out into the living room area.

I followed, rubbing my hand over my chest.

"This is why I shouldn't have done this."

"But we did. I was a willing participant."

"Fine. But I'm an asshole, you know that, right?"

"Maybe I'm not the nicest person."

My lips twitched. "Felicity. You're like cotton candy."

"Excuse me?"

"Sweet. Melts on your tongue. You're nice, Felicity. There's nothing wrong with that."

"I can be mean."

"If somebody hurts someone you love. But you're nice, and that's fine." I let out a breath. "I'll talk to Rune and Atlas."

"Yeah?"

"I have to. I need to figure out what to say. Atlas is easier because I could just send him a text."

"You're not going to send my brother a text, are you?"

"No. But I could. Atlas would be fine with it."

"Really?"

"It's Atlas. He's a hothead on the ice and sometimes off, but well," I shrugged, "Rune's more protective of you. At least outwardly. Atlas is sneaky about it."

"Tell me about it. The things he used to do when I was younger. Did you know he ran off my middle school boyfriend?"

"What?"

"Yep. Ran off my middle school boyfriend because apparently he didn't like the way the guy looked."

"Well, I trust Atlas."

"Of course, you're on his side. Have you told any of your family?" she asked softly.

"No." Her eyes widened, and I cursed. "Teagan's been out of town. Sterling has been out of town, too, visiting friends in Denver so he can get something special happening with the restaurant. Finnian has been waylaid with the twins getting a cold."

"That was so scary."

One of the twins had ended up with pneumonia, so Finnian and Promise had taken turns spending the night in the hospital with one and at home with the other. The fact that my little nieces were in pain nearly killed me, and I had been there right beside my brother, making sure that he had everything he needed.

"Bringing you up at that moment didn't seem wise."

"That makes sense. But what about Bodhi?"

"Bodhi's dealing with his own things."

Her eyes widened. "The anniversary. Hell. That's why Thatcher—" She shook her head. "And my dad. Crap."

The fire that had killed Bodhi's family had nearly taken out half the mountain. It had been the final fire that Felicity's dad had been captain for, and I knew the man still blamed himself. Just like Thatcher did. He'd been right on the front lines, pulling Bodhi out of the flames, but not able to do anything else.

"It's been an odd two weeks. But it wasn't necessarily all about hiding you. So I don't know what to call you. Okay? I'm not with anyone else."

"Neither am I. Callum, I let you come inside me. There's no one else."

"Damn straight."

I reached into the refrigerator and pulled out two beers. She frowned.

"What are those? Those are your testing bottles."

I smiled softly and handed one to her. "It's our unique batch for the season. Tell me what you think."

"Is this a red ale?" she asked, eyes wide.

"Yeah. Your favorite, right?"

"You remembered." She started to smile. "Did you make this for me?"

I shrugged. "Just take a drink, Felicity."

Her eyes filled with tears, and I nearly cursed. Well, this was going decently. Or not.

She took a sip, her eyes wide. "This is your best to date."

"You're just saying that."

"What are you going to call it? And no, I'm not just saying that."

"I was going to call it just Spring Ale. But I don't know. Maybe Little Flower?"

She rolled her eyes. "Don't do that. And not just because it would just tell the entire world that we're both ridiculous. But it makes the beer sound floral."

"See? I'm having trouble. Maybe just Ashford Red Ale. Go plain."

"We'll think of a good name."

"We?"

"This is my beer, after all." She took another sip and groaned. "So good."

"I'm glad you like it."

"Do you make beers for everybody?"

The worry in her tone made me frown. "My family. Friends. Usually, it's just what I'm in the mood for or what I can figure out a recipe for. You weren't digging my

IPAs, and I know you like red ales. Something we don't always have. So I figured I'd try it."

"Thank you. That means a lot." She went to her tiptoes, pressed her hand to my chest, and kissed me softly.

"Should I be nosy and ask if I'm the first girl you've ever made a beer for, other than your sisters, of course?"

"Actually, the first beer I ever made was for my wife."

Felicity nearly dropped the bottle and stared at me. "You were married?" she blurted out, taking a step back. "How the hell did I not know you were married?"

I frowned and shook my head. "Seriously, how did you not know? It was never a secret."

"I don't know what to think about that. I mean, I know you're a little older than me."

I sighed despite the seriousness of the subject. "Felicity."

"No, you're not that much older than me. And we're friends. Our family is close. How did I not know you were married?"

"It was right after college. When I was in the NFL? Did you not follow me at all then?"

"I was a little busy at the time. And we didn't see each other at all during that time. Which, in retrospect, is a pretty decent idea because it would've been weird considering I was like in high school or something."

I shuddered. "Okay, stop talking about ages like that."

"Exactly. You were married?"

"Yeah. I was."

"And now you're divorced. Right? Oh my God, I'm not sleeping with a married man, am I?"

"Baby." I pulled her beer out of her hand, set it down, and cupped her cheek. "No. You're not sleeping with a married man. But no, I'm not divorced."

"What do you mean? It doesn't make any sense."

"I'm really not good at this." I let out a breath and went to take a step back. Felicity immediately grabbed my hand.

"Talk to me."

"My wife's name was Georgia. Hence the name of the first beer we ever made."

"Oh. I thought it was because of, like, the state or something. Which didn't really make any sense since we live in Colorado, and you were in LA when you were playing in the NFL, but really? You were married. Wait. You said was." Her eyes filled with tears again, and I cursed under my breath. "Oh, Callum. I'm so sorry."

"It was a long time ago."

"Not that long, and it doesn't make grief any easier."

"You're right. It doesn't." I ran my hands over my face and paced the kitchen. "Georgia and I met in college. We got married at twenty-two. She was dead by twenty-five."

"Right when you moved here." Her voice broke.

I nodded. "I've only been back for a few years, Felicity."

Her teeth bit into her lip, and she looked down. "May I ask what happened?"

"She had a brain bleed." I shrugged. That familiar pain long since drilled down into just a sense of grief that ebbed and flowed.

"It came out of nowhere, and her platelets were low for some reason. We'll never figure out why. Maybe if she hadn't had the brain bleed, we would have, or maybe even caught it ahead of time. But we didn't. One moment, she was fine. The other, she was passed out on the kitchen floor."

"You don't have to continue if you don't want to. You've never talked about her before, so if it's too hard..."

"It's not that. I don't talk about her a lot because it's been ten years, Felicity. Ten years where nobody in town really knew her."

"Do my brothers know?"

"They do. But you and I weren't really friends or in each other's realms ten years ago, Felicity. At least, I would hope not."

"True. Okay, I'm so sorry."

"I'm sorry too. I'm sorrier that it didn't take her out right away."

Her eyes widened at the bitterness in my tone, and I continued so she would understand the monster I felt like.

"She didn't die right away. She just fell and didn't wake up. The brain bleed slowly took over. And it was odd watching it over time. Because with each passing moment, when we were in the ICU, life altered. And all I could do was try to figure out the facts."

"What do you mean?"

"At first, they told me that they could fix it. That they just needed to find the right meds, and she would wake up, and we would go from there. And then they had a setback. Then another."

"Oh, Callum."

"And when they did that, they asked me if she had any wishes that needed to be met."

"Like a DNR?"

"Like a DNR. She wanted no extraordinary measures, but she wasn't brain-dead yet."

"Yet."

"So with each passing hour, the nurses and doctors would come in and check her reflexes. They'd roll that little metal spike over the arches of her feet, over her palms.

"The first time, it was her right side. When her right hand no longer responded.

"That's when they told me because they assumed she would wake up, that she would probably have paralysis in that right arm. So I told myself that we would get through. I had the money, and she was so damn strong."

"I don't think I'm sorry really works here. But I'm sorry."

"Me too. But that's not the worst of it."

"You really don't have to continue."

"Yes, I do. Because it wasn't just her right arm. Then, it was her right leg. Her foot was no longer responding. So my mind went to the fact that, at the time, we were living in LA and still trying to figure out where we were going to put this brewery, and we had a two-story house. The main bedroom was upstairs, so I'd have to figure out how we could either move or find a way for her to be down-stairs all the time. Which would devastate her. Then she lost her left hand. So that meant a certain kind of wheel-chair was out, and so many other things that I didn't even understand. Hell, she had sat by my side for the full year that it took me to recover from breaking my leg in two places. I've watched guys that I used to hang out with all the time break down their bodies because they throw themselves at each other for a fucking football game. And I miss football. I loved it. But I'm glad as hell I got out before I did something to hurt my brain."

"I'm glad you did too."

"Because with each passing moment, I got to be a little more selfish when it came to Georgia."

"What do you mean?"

"Because I was so damn afraid I wouldn't be strong enough to help her. Because, by the time we got to her final foot, where there were no reflexes, but her brain still hadn't been declared brain-dead, and her heart was still beating on its own, I had no idea what the hell we were going to do. Because what if she woke up and couldn't talk. Couldn't feed herself, couldn't move. And part of me, just for an instant, thought maybe it would be easier if she didn't wake up. Because I didn't think I was strong enough to help her. And then, an hour later, after the worst thought I'd ever had in my life, the doctor came in and did one final cognitive test. And it was over."

"Callum. You didn't do anything wrong. That was so much to go through in such a short time. Especially since I know you were still healing from your broken leg."

"I don't blame myself that she died. But the monster in me that was relieved for just those moments that she did? That's the part of me that knows I'm no good for you, Felicity. That's the monster. Just like the fact that I beat the shit out of that kid when he hurt you. And I would have killed him too. I wouldn't have felt a single inch of remorse for killing that kid. Just like my dad has not a single inch of remorse for killing my mom. And maybe even killing my stepmom." I held up my hands so she could see the ones that had just held her, that had just left bruises on her hips when I slid into her from behind. "These hands? They're just like my father's. That's what I see when I hold you sometimes. That's why I'm not a good man."

There. It was all out there. All of my truths. Hopefully, all of my secrets.

I reached for my phone, ready to leave, knowing that this was it and it would be for the best, when her phone buzzed.

She frowned at the readout, and I looked up at her.

"What is it?"

"I think it's Kellan. Why would he be calling me? Oh my god. Mom and Dad."

I moved forward as she answered my friend, the town doctor's, call and watched as her knees gave out.

She couldn't speak. She just let out a sob as I put the phone to my ear.

"Kellan? What happened?"

"Callum? Why are you with Felicity? Wait, that doesn't matter. She was his emergency contact. Since his family was here. So I had to tell her first."

"Tell her what?"

"She has to be the one to tell you. I can't right now. Not until I reach the rest of his family."

I paused, my mind going in a thousand different directions before it hit.

"Gregory? Is Gregory Teller okay?"

"I need to call his family first, Callum," Kellan whispered, and I knew. He didn't even have to explain.

"Got it."

"Take care of her, okay? And Callum? You're going to have to explain why you're with Felicity at eleven o'clock at night."

I looked out the window, realized how dark it was, and cursed. But I didn't say a damn thing. I just hung up and leaned down to pick Felicity up into my arms.

"I'm so sorry, baby. Let's call your parents."

"No. Not yet. Just hold me?"

And so I did, as I moved to the couch and settled Felicity in my arms, letting her cry over the loss of her mentor and friend.

And my chest tightened.

Because I'd liked the old man too.

And I didn't want to let Felicity go.

CHAPTER 13

Felicity

L ike all small towns, Ashford Creek had one of
everything.

An ice cream shop.

A bed and breakfast.

An old-school diner.

A bar and grill.

And a cemetery.

There was more than one church, of course, as there
was more than one denomination within town, but even
then, the churches were unique, and some shared the
same building for different services.

But there was only one cemetery.

Gregory Teller had been the town's accountant and bookkeeper for longer than I had been alive. Honestly, he'd been in that position for longer than most people in town had been alive. Even when he had been overwhelmed and dropped a few balls, people had been there to help, and he had ensured the town thrived.

And now he was gone, and I hated myself for feeling relief in this moment. Because all I wanted to do was cry and beg for him to take just one more day off to rest. To enjoy life. To not work until his seventies.

"I would ask if you were doing okay, but we both know that you need time." My mom slid her arm around my waist, and I leaned on her shoulder, my arms crossed in front of me.

"Whenever I would ask why he wouldn't retire, he said he loved what he did. He didn't work every day, but he still went to work. I thought he should be the guy who sat on the front porch with his coffee and newspaper and waved at people as they came by since he still lived right in town. But no, he refused to do that. I just don't understand why. Why would he waste so much time?"

"People find solace in their own actions and their own peace in different ways."

"So he liked working that many hours?"

"He used to work more. And he would always hire those who came with talent." She squeezed my shoulder.

"And those who needed him. But this job was something he loved. He loved numbers, and it gave him access to everybody in town. They could come in and talk about what they were doing, ask advice, and he'd be able to feel as if he were connected to the town as a whole."

"I guess that makes sense. But I don't know. I always thought he would go and find a way to relax more."

"He was able to when you came on. We both know that."

I wiped a tear and let my hand fall back to cross in front of me. "I always felt as if he trusted me every time he gave me more responsibility."

"He trusted you with everything. You know that."

I swallowed hard, my gut aching. The will had already been read, as it had taken a couple of days to get the funeral ready. And our town lawyer had wanted to make sure I understood what was coming my way.

Because he had left the damn company to me. And I had no idea what to do with that.

"When Gregory's wife died, we all mourned Sascha." My mom let out a breath. "She was so sweet and helped him around the office. She wasn't an accountant, but she made sure that he had everything he needed for the business. She ran the church bake sale and, along with the mayor's wife at the time, fixed each bridge in town to ensure we had safe roadways for our children. Martha and Gregory were the ones who opened up the new school so we could split the buildings into three different schools on the north end, albeit smaller buildings, versus having everybody in one place and all of the children stepping all over each other like we had when I was younger. Gregory put so much into this town. And I'm going to miss him."

I swallowed hard, wiping away another tear. "I miss him more and more each day. And I hate that he's gone. I don't know what I'm supposed to do now, Mom."

"You mourn him. You mourn him, and you do what you can to ensure that you allow his legacy to move on."

"And what is his legacy?"

"You baby. You." She kissed my temple, her arm falling away, and I let the cold seep in until two other strong sets of shoulders pinned me in.

"I'm glad you came." I looked up at Atlas, who just smiled at me.

"I'm glad I came too. I loved that old man. You know, he used to give me different sour candies when I would visit, just because he said I had a sour expression on my face."

"You know damn well you put that face on so that way you could get your favorite candy," Rune said dryly. My brother reached up and tugged on his septum piercing slightly, moving it around.

Atlas winced. "Doesn't that hurt?"

Rune rolled his eyes. "I'm just rotating it. It doesn't

hurt. You should get your nose pierced. Join the family lore."

"I would, but then some guy would rip it out by accident, or I'd lose a tooth."

I looked up at my NHL star brother and rolled my eyes. "How you have a full set of teeth, I will never know."

"Maybe if he was a starter and was actually on the ice more, he'd lose some," Rune teased, and I leaned down as the two of them guffawed behind me.

"Boys," my dad warned as he came forward.

Both brothers punched each other's shoulders, and I pressed my lips together, trying not to laugh at one of my dear friend's funerals. Because sometimes it felt as if our family had never been apart, as we fell comfortably into our own positions.

"We weren't doing anything," Atlas said quickly, and Rune nodded.

"You three are ridiculous." My dad clucked his tongue before he leaned down and kissed my forehead.

"I wasn't doing anything," I said softly.

"You encourage them like you always have."

"Well, we're nothing if not on a schedule and routine," Rune said dryly.

"I'm sorry I can't stay for long. I have to head back. We have a game coming up tomorrow that I don't want to be late for, or the coach will chew my ass."

"We'll all be down for the hockey game in Denver. So you better kick their ass," Dad said solemnly.

"Please don't curse at a funeral," Mom said as she came up and leaned against Dad.

Dad just winked.

I loved my family. We had each other no matter what, and I couldn't help but wonder what would happen when I told them my own secret.

Across the way, I looked up and met Callum's eyes. He'd stood by me at the funeral and then at the gravesite. Nobody had thought anything of it. After all, he was a family friend. But I wanted to run into his arms and have him tell me everything would be okay.

Instead, he just stared at me as if memorizing my face, trying to see if anything was wrong.

But *everything* was wrong.

"And it's good to be back home," Atlas said after a moment. "It's been too long." He stiffened at my side at the words, and I looked up at him, worried. Then I followed his gaze and realized exactly why he regretted his words.

Elizabeth stood there, her eyes wide for just a moment before she smiled at me, tearing her gaze from Atlas. In a blink, she turned back to be with Teagan and Bronwyn, another friend and longtime Ashford Creek member. And a stranger stood with them, a woman I didn't know. Maybe she was with Gregory's family, but as one of Kellan's teenagers ran up to her and asked a question, I realized that it had to be Tess, the newcomer to Ashford Creek that I hadn't met yet.

For such a small town, you would think I would have. But then again, if I hadn't been at work or with my family, I'd been with Callum, hiding within our homes because we craved each other.

I needed to get out into town more. To live like I wanted Gregory to live.

Keely wasn't here as she had to be at the bed and breakfast, but Promise had been able to come and stood near Finnian, the two of them speaking in low voices. Thatcher, still in uniform, spoke with Kellan..

The town had shown up for Gregory. Even Gray had come back to town, and I knew he would head back out with Atlas because they each had games on the road soon. But we were all there. The Carters, the Ashfords, and our friends that we had turned into family along the way.

But the man who had trusted me with everything was gone.

And I wasn't sure what I was supposed to do with that.

"You okay?" Rune asked softly, and for a moment, I thought he was speaking to me. But then I realized that Atlas still hadn't moved from his spot.

"What? Yeah. I'm fine. Just thinking about what I need to do before I head out."

I looked at Rune, and neither one of us believed him.

"She's not seeing anyone right now, at least I don't think," Rune whispered, his voice low. Yet it was deep enough that I was afraid it would carry.

If possible, Atlas stiffened even more. "Well, I guess I should go."

"Oh, Atlas. You don't have to go," my mom whispered. "Stay. Let's go get coffee. Before you really have to go on the road."

Atlas gave one last look behind her before facing our mom. "No, I need to head out. I love you. I'm going to miss the old man." He kissed my mother on the cheek, hugged Dad and Rune separately, and then came to me.

"Atlas."

He shook his head. "Be good, little sister. And maybe tell the others?" he asked, that scarred brow raised.

My eyes widened, and I refused to look over at Callum.

"How? I mean. Okay."

"I have the power of observation. And I've been away long enough that I noticed a difference."

"How come you get to be mysterious and talk about things like that, but I don't get to?" I ask, purposely not looking over to our left.

Atlas's jaw tightened. "Because some things are old news. Broken things. But other ones? Others better not break things."

I shook my head, getting what he was saying, even though he was trying to be way too subtle. I kissed his cheek, held him close, and watched as he walked away, noticing I wasn't the only one.

Elizabeth gave me a small smile and then moved on to speak to one of her students.

I let out a breath and turned to my family. "I'm going to go head to the office. If that's okay?"

"You don't need to work today, baby." My mom moved forward, hand outstretched. "Come back with us."

"I just need a few moments to myself. Honestly, I'll meet you back at the house."

There wouldn't be a full wake, as we were all meeting now, but some would visit my parents' home, and I would go with them afterward. I just needed a few moments alone. I looked past my family to where Callum stood with his, and he gave me an imperceptible nod.

Perhaps I didn't need to be truly alone.

I was tired of running, tired of secrets, but this exact moment wasn't necessarily the best timing.

"If you're sure," Rune said, a frown on his face.

I squeezed their hands and then headed out of the cemetery, towards Main Street.

Tourists were still out and about, was well as local residents who hadn't been able to take time off or didn't know Gregory that well. People who hadn't gone to the funeral or maybe hadn't known it was even taking place today.

I nodded at a few of them, and those that I knew either gave me sad smile or reached out to squeeze my hand. Little things that reminded me of why I had moved to Ashford Creek.

Because even though they might not have known Gregory well or at all, they were still grieving for the loss of one of their own.

I turned the corner and took out my small set of keys, staring at them in my hand.

What was I supposed to do now? Take over all of Gregory's clients? Figure out how to take care of the entire town when I couldn't even take care of myself?

A large hand reached out and took the keys from my palm, and I let out a relieved sound, leaning against that strong chest of his.

"You know, I could have been anyone just then."

I shook my head at Callum's deep voice. "I always know it's you."

"I don't know if I should be frightened or not," he said softly as he moved me into the small office.

I let out a deep breath, the tears finally falling as soon as I crossed the threshold. Callum cursed under his breath and pulled me into his arms.

"It's okay, baby. I've got you."

"It's not okay. He kept saying he was fine, even after all of his doctor's visits with Kellan, and yet, he never told me. Never told me that he was sick."

Callum kissed the top of my head and held me close as I cried into his chest, my tears dampening his shirt.

"He was in his seventies, darling. He was always going to have aches and pains. He wanted to be here because he thought of you as a daughter. Wanted to take care of you."

"And I couldn't take care of him."

"He was so proud of you. He would always brag about you whenever he walked into the brewery, you know."

I looked up at him then, frowning. "What?"

"He would come into the brewery once a week and have a single beer and brag about how he poached the smartest person from your entire university program to work in Ashford Creek."

"You never told me that."

He shrugged, pushing a piece of hair behind my ear. "I know a lot of things by working at the brewery or sometimes behind the bar at Summit Grill. He loved you." Callum let out a breath. "Just like I remember him loving my mom. She was another daughter of his, one that he might not have been part of in terms of raising, but one he wanted to help see the world."

My chest tightened, remembering what Callum had said.

Had his father actually killed his mother?

I didn't know. This wasn't the time to ask him, nor did I think he wanted to speak of it. But the town always gossiped about the Ashfords. About their secrets.

How could you not when one of the patriarch's wives had died unexpectedly, and the other had run away, never to be seen again? And between each of the siblings having their own lore, you couldn't help but think of the Ashfords and their legacy.

Callum, the NFL star who'd gotten hurt too young.

Bodhi, the one who everyone had so quickly believed to be a murderer. Teagan, the elder daughter, left behind. Finnian, the one who got his high school girlfriend pregnant and hadn't stayed with her. It didn't matter that they loved each other as friends now because Finnian would always have that scarlet letter, just like Promise. Briar, the daughter who had gotten out and married a rock star.

Sterling, the one who people spoke of but never truly understood.

And Malcolm. The one they lost.

The Ashfords were their own story, their own secret web.

And I wanted to know more.

I just wanted him.

Callum kissed the top of my head as I finally was able to breathe.

"I really just wanted to walk through his office, just for a moment. Then we can head back to my parents' house."

Callum squeezed my hand. "Okay. Do you want me to meet you there?"

I shook my head. "Go with me?" I asked, knowing what I was asking.

He let out a sigh. "I'll tell him. Maybe not today."

I shook my head. "No, today's not the day."

"Are you sure about me? I told you that I'm not the right man for you. And they're going to think that I'm preying on you." His deep voice was practically a growl, shivering down my spine.

"Stop it. My family loves you."

"Your family loves me as your brothers' friend. Not so much the one who's fucking precious Felicity."

"Don't say it like that."

He raised a brow. "It's the truth."

Anger coursed through my veins, and I pushed at him. "If you're going to keep thinking that I'm some precious virginal flower or some shit, just leave. I'm not a piece of property. I'm not perfect. I'm making my own decisions."

"I don't think I'm the right one for you."

I glared at him, my hands fisting at my sides. "Then go. If you're not the right one for me, just go."

"I'm not letting you stay here alone."

"You're not my father."

"No, we both know I'm not."

And there he was, that overprotective asshole that I'd always known. He had tried to keep it in check these last weeks, but he really sucked at it.

I merely shook my head. "I'll meet you at the house. We can keep this secret for a little longer, but then I'm done. Done hiding. It's time to deal with the consequences."

"I won't let them hurt you."

"Callum, they're not going to hurt me."

"No, that'll be me." He leaned down, pressed a hard

kiss to my lips, and left me alone in my office, wondering what the hell I was doing.

I took a few moments, walking through the small rooms that still smelled of Gregory's aftershave.

"Why did you have to go? And why did you think I could do this on my own?" I whispered, another tear tracking down my cheek.

I swallowed hard, knowing I couldn't wallow here for long. Either Callum or my mother would show up, dragging me out. I knew them well enough. With one last look at the office, I locked the door and headed to my car back at the main parking lot.

I frowned, the hairs on the back of my neck standing on end once again. I couldn't tell if anyone was looking at me, but then again, maybe they were just feeling sorry for me after what happened. But no, something was off. I stared down one of the alleys, frowning, before turning back. Strong hands gripped my arms, and I gasped, looking up into familiar eyes, yet ones I did not want to see.

"Hello there, Little Carter."

I tore myself away from Callum's father and lifted my chin. "Mr. Ashford."

"I like the sound of that. Mr. Ashford. Nobody calls me that anymore."

"Sorry for bumping into you. I need to go back to my car."

"He left you alone like this? Not a very protective thing to do."

"I'm just fine. Excuse me."

"Well, if you're sure."

"Felicity? Everything okay here?"

I nearly sagged in relief at the sound of Thatcher's voice and turned to see him and Keely walking towards me.

Keely stared at Callum's father, a frown on her face, before she reached out and took my hand.

"Hey. Glad I caught you. We were heading up to your parents' house."

"Me too. Do you need a ride?"

"I'd love one." She looked over at Thatcher, who was still glaring at Callum's father.

"Mind if I ride with her? I know you're on call tonight."

"No problem. I have a few things to take care of anyway." He looked over at me for a moment. "You good?"

"I'm great. Thank you."

I didn't know exactly what I was saying thank you for, but Callum's father always creeped me out.

No wonder Callum and his siblings did their best to stay away from him.

I took Keely's hand, and we made our way to my car.

"Should I wonder why you two were going to my

parents' house together?" I asked, realizing that I hadn't even known the two hung out.

"Oh, I was walking towards... I was walking in this direction, because I couldn't get my car to start, and Thatcher was just going to drive me. He's a nice guy. But don't worry. Not that nice."

I raised a brow. "Really?"

"You're the one who's dating an older man, not me."

I smiled then, laughter spilling from my lips.

And that was why I loved Ashford Creek. Even with the shadows, my friends could make me laugh.

CHAPTER 14

Callum

"Why did I think that things would be less violent in person? Even after all these years."

My lips twitched as I looked down at Mrs. Carter, speaking through her fingers, as the puck moved around the ice so quickly you could barely keep up with it.

"Come on, Mom, you should be used to the boy aquarium by now. I mean, Atlas has been doing hockey since what, birth?" Felicity teased. She looked past me and winked.

"Boy aquarium?" I growled.

"What?" Felicity asked, fluttering her eyelashes. "It's true. Look at them all out there. Skating around in peak performance, and the boards and glass just make it look like an aquarium. They can even do tricks. Watch, that one can skate backward," she teased.

"Does Atlas know you call it a boy aquarium?" I asked, raising a brow.

Felicity beamed, looking happier than she had in days. I knew there was still grief behind those eyes, and there would be for a long while. Grief didn't go away just because you wanted it to. It ebbed and flowed like waves on the beach but didn't always leave behind ragged tears in the sand. Sometimes, it just reminded you of what you had.

Just like I would always miss Georgia, I would always miss my mother, but I could breathe now. So that was something.

"Yes, I am used to how violent hockey is, and I hate the fact that those pucks are coming at my baby's face." She stood up then, hands outstretched. "Pass! Pass! Come on. Get him!"

I stood up with her and looked down at Felicity, both of us trying not to laugh.

No matter what Gwen Carter said about violence, she would kick anyone's ass who dared to hurt her baby. And by her baby, I meant her six-foot-something, two-hundred-plus-something of muscle, thirty-something-year-old son.

However, Atlas had been at this NHL goalie thing for a while now. I knew he was coming up on his last years because your knees and hips could only last for so long, but Atlas was still enjoying the game.

The Denver Snowcaps came forward, way too close for comfort, but missed the goal right at the end of the second period.

I let out a sigh of relief as Atlas stood up, rolling his shoulders back. He slid up his helmet and guard and just glared at the Colorado forward in front of him.

Words were exchanged, and when the refs pushed them apart, Mr. Carter just mumbled under his breath.

"I realize that Atlas likes a goalie fight, but I really hope one of his enforcers takes care of that asshole."

I grinned and nodded my chin over at Rune, who sat on the other side of Felicity. "Well, at least it's not like we don't like violence on our side," I said dryly.

"Hey, hockey has fights to get rid of the tension and any issues you have. Football is the one where you just run into each other over and over again, land in piles, and then spank each other's asses."

I glared at my best friend. "Really? After all of these years, you still hate football?"

"I don't hate football. I like hockey better. Sue me."

"Hey, are you Callum Ashford? *The* Callum Ashford?" a twenty-something-year-old man said behind me. I turned and nodded. The glare on my face probably should have scared the guy, but he just grinned.

"I knew that was you. Sorry for interrupting, but I just got to say, you were fantastic. And I know if you would've been able to stay for the rest of the season that you guys would've gone all the way to the Super Bowl. Hey, can I have your autograph?"

Felicity reached out and patted my thigh, and I realized that Bodhi hadn't missed the movement. The back of my neck heating, I nodded. "Sure. Why not? Though I'm an old man now, and it's been a while. Don't know if this will get you anything."

"I don't care if it would get me anything. This is going in my collection, man. You were legit. Glad to see you're enjoying yourself, though. Hey, you with Carter's sister? Pretty cool that all you sports guys seem to be friends." The guy looked over at Felicity. "Your brother is a kick-ass goalie. And yes, I say that as a fan of the other team." He winked as I quickly signed whatever flyer he gave me and then narrowed my gaze. "Well, I'm sure we'll kick your ass."

"That's what I like to hear. But we're still going to win."

The guy started talking with his buddies then, and I turned back to the ice, shoulders stiff. "Anyone want a beer? We don't have that much time before the next period starts."

"Dad already went to get some. You were too busy with your fawning fans." Rune continued to glare at me, and I let out a breath. "Oh. Cool. Do you think he can handle it all?"

"Mom went with him," Felicity said, tension in her voice.

"Ah. Well, football is still better."

"Not so much my friend. Watch those hands, friend of mine," Rune growled, and I blinked, realizing that my arm was still behind Felicity's chair.

I shrugged and sank back into the seat. If we were in public, maybe my best friend wouldn't kick my ass.

Maybe.

Felicity just sighed. "Men."

"I thought you liked your boy aquarium," I bit out.

"What? Sweaty guys that are in the best shape of their lives slamming into each other? It's my dream."

"We'll see about that," I grumbled, hoping Rune couldn't hear since the woman next to him kept taking his attention away, thankfully.

By the time the Carters got back with our beers, the last period was ready to go, and we were all set to watch Atlas kick the team's ass.

The Portland Gliders were in the middle of restructuring, and I knew that the backup goalie was right on Atlas's heels, ready to take over. That's what happened when you had new blood in, even though the veteran was still damn good and in his prime. But I had a feeling that the Gliders had a decent chance at the playoffs. And when they finally kicked Denver's ass, 3-1, I was relieved. Though I knew Atlas would probably be pissed as hell that he let that one goal in.

"Lucky shot," Rune grumbled as we all made our way to the side of the arena where they'd let us in as family. Atlas had scored us decent tickets, and if we were in the Portland stadium, sometimes he got us back up into one of the boxes. I didn't mind fitting my large self in one of those tiny chairs near the ice, but sometimes people remembered that I used to have a life outside of Ashford Creek, and it was like a kick in the gut.

I missed playing like I missed so much in my life. I had no idea what my life would've been like if I hadn't gotten hurt. What were you supposed to do with the rest of your life when something that you had worked for and put your blood, sweat, and tears into, was over in an instant?

Felicity rubbed her shoulder against my arm and frowned. "Are you okay?"

"He's just brooding because whenever he comes to a game, he thinks of his glory days as a tight end and remembers that his end isn't that tight anymore." Rune winked as he said it, and one of the women passing by nearly swooned.

I snorted, knowing Rune was doing his best to make me laugh.

"Yep. And I'm all saggy and shit. But it's fine. One day, I'll be as saggy as you, not a single muscle in sight, and I'll learn from you how to make it."

"Asshole," Rune growled, shoving me. I shoved back and pushed Felicity behind me so she wouldn't get hurt.

Of course, we didn't hit each other again because, with one look from Gwen Carter, we froze in our tracks.

"What did I say about fighting?" she asked primly, her eyes dancing with laughter.

"Only on the ice?" Rune asked and ducked as Mr. Carter tried to hit him.

"Boys. All of you. Why is Felicity the only sane one here?"

"Aw, I'm so glad that you think I'm sane."

"She takes turns thinking which one of us is the sane one," Rune said dryly. I laughed as Felicity came around me and shoved at her brother playfully.

"Hooligans. All of you. And I love you all."

Mrs. Carter wrapped her arm around my waist and sighed. "Even you, you big football washout."

I ran my hand over my heart. "Ouch."

"What? One day, I hope to say something similar to my other son. That way, he stops having hockey pucks coming at his face."

"Don't worry, when he finally retires, I'll continue to throw hockey pucks at his face so that way he remembers the good old days," Rune said solemnly, and Mrs. Carter just rolled her eyes.

"Okay, let's get over to the waiting area and get some snacks while we wait for Atlas to shower, go through media, and get through the hordes of women in order to get to us." Mr. Carter rolled his eyes, and I just grinned.

"You really think Atlas is going to choose us over any

of the women waiting for him." I gestured towards the gaggle of puck bunnies, all speaking in rapid tones to each other.

"Hey, eyes over here," Felicity teased.

"I see no one," I growled and winced as Rune continued to glare at me.

Well, hell. This is why Felicity and I usually kept to the houses. We were not good at hiding anything in public. Though I knew Felicity didn't want to hide anymore. I thought maybe we should continue. Because once things were out in the open, everything would explode in our faces, and this would be the end. So maybe this was a good idea. So that way Felicity didn't get hurt any more than possible.

We headed into one of the VIP rooms where Atlas got our passes for, ate snacks, drank a couple more beers, and waited over an hour for Atlas to show himself. When he did, he moved right past the puck bunnies, not even bothering to look, and stomped his way over to us.

"Hey there, grumpy face," Felicity teased as she hugged her brother tightly.

"It was a lucky shot," he growled.

"After how many years on the ice, you're still worried about that one shot? You blocked how many others?"

"It still wasn't a shutout." Atlas turned to the left slightly, his gaze narrowing on a younger guy before his shoulders relaxed, and he smiled over at him.

The guy lifted his chin and went over to talk to a few women I didn't recognize.

And then I understood. That was the backup goalie, the hotshot kid nipping at Atlas's heels. That was the name of the game, but it still sucked.

"Anyway, you going to tell us when you started dating my sister?" Atlas asked, and the room went quiet.

I stood there, hands fisted at my side, glaring at the man. Well fuck.

"Atlas. Really?" Felicity sighed.

"Can you just not be so loud next time?"

Atlas rolled his eyes. "First off, neither one of you is being subtle. I mean, really? Come on."

"Atlas—" I began, but Rune came up and squeezed my shoulder. A little more tightly than he should have, but then again, I was expecting a fist in the face.

"Finally, someone says it. You guys sneaking around has been killing me."

I whirled, staring at my two best friends. "Are you serious right now? You knew?"

"You guys knew?" Felicity asked, her voice going high-pitched.

Thankfully, her parents were on the other side of the room, speaking with another set of parents, and weren't overhearing.

"Of course, we knew. You guys keep giving each other puppy dog looks," Rune growled. "I don't know why you thought you could keep it a secret. Not to mention sneaking off to each other's homes, even though you live across the street, isn't that secretive."

I put my hands over my face and groaned. "Jesus Christ."

"Hey, watch your language," Atlas teased. "You're lucky we're in public, or I'd have to kick your ass. I mean, my baby sister?"

Atlas tilted his head, glaring at me.

I could never tell when Atlas was joking. That was the problem. He was too damn good at hiding his thoughts. Rune, on the other hand, shoved me. Maybe not so gently, but still. "We'll have a talk later."

"Hey. I'm here too. We are both consenting adults, Rune."

"Shush. This isn't about you."

"Don't fucking shush your sister," I growled, keeping my voice low. Because there was no fucking way we were going to make a scene here. I would not embarrass Felicity. But I would kick her brothers' asses for being mean to her. I had depth.

"Oh, standing up for her? Then why was it a secret?" Atlas murmured.

"You guys. There are two of us. Stop glaring at your best friend."

"You hurt her, and I kill you," Rune said simply, narrowing his gaze.

"Sounds about right," I agreed.

"Oh, for fuck's sake," Felicity snapped. "Are you kidding me right now?"

"If he doesn't kill you, I'll find a way. After all, I do skate on sharp blades for a living."

"You do what you have to."

"I'm not mad," Rune continued, his voice low. "Not about this. How can I be? You're my best friend."

My stomach fell out from beneath me, and I swallowed hard. "Rune—"

"No. We'll talk about it later. When we can actually talk." He looked around the room and shrugged. "But secrets? You know we don't do secrets."

"Fuck. I didn't, I mean, I'm sorry."

"Just don't hurt her." Atlas shrugged. "And don't keep a secret. You're not good at it."

And with that, the brothers went off to go speak with their parents, and I stood there, Felicity's hand on my arm, staring and blinking. "What the hell just happened?"

"I have no idea. They knew? Does everyone know?"

I turned then, cupping her cheek, not caring who saw. "I have no clue. But I don't think it's quite over with them."

"Well, at least they didn't punch you."

"I think it's only because we were in public," I said dryly. "Felicity? Are you sure about this? I'm way too fucking old for you."

"Give up. And get over the whole age thing. I'm over it."

"Easy for you to say. I am the old lecher."

"Stop it. You're the one making it weird. And now I have to go face my parents."

I groaned. "I don't want to. Can we just escape?"

Felicity bit her lip and then turned slightly. "You know what? Let's do that." And when she tugged on my hand and practically pulled me out of the room, I threw my head back and laughed.

Oh yes, we were flirting with danger and probably going to end up burning in hell, but it sounded a little fun.

Or maybe, just maybe, the consequences were going to hit later.

Because Rune and Atlas had acted far too calm.

And I had a feeling that soon we'd have to face whatever the hell came at us.

Because not everybody in town was going to be happy. And hell, one day soon, Felicity would wake up and realize exactly what she was doing.

And she'd get out.

As long as I didn't break her first. That's all that mattered.

At least, that's what I told myself.

CHAPTER 15

Callum

When I opened the door, I wasn't surprised to see who was on the other side. I was more surprised that a punch didn't follow the chin-nod period.

"I was expecting you earlier," I said as I took a step back, letting Rune inside.

"Why do you think I'm going to hit you? The fact that you're defiling my innocent baby sister? Or the fact that you kept it secret?"

The bite in his tone had my shoulders relaxing marginally. Mostly because I'd been expecting it far earlier. The fact that Rune and Atlas had been so calm at the game had worried me. But perhaps they'd only acted that way because they had at least some self-control and hadn't wanted to make a damn scene. But now, the only witness would be me.

"I don't defile your sister." I cursed as Rune's eyes narrowed. "To defile her brings on a whole other set of connotations and does nothing but harm Felicity. She's not some piece of property. She's not on this fucking pedestal that is untouched and an object. She's Felicity. She makes her own choices. And for some reason, she chose me. But the secrets? You're welcome to beat the shit out of me for that."

My best friend pinched the bridge of his nose and sighed. "I'd ask if you have a beer, but you always have beer." He held up his hand before I could make it into the kitchen. "But we're heading out to the axe-throwing place that just opened up on the north end of town, and frankly, I probably shouldn't be drinking before throwing axes while I'm next to you."

"I'm glad that you thought ahead." I groaned and leaned against the counter, the weight of reality settling in. "I'm sorry for keeping it a secret."

"Should I ask why you did?" Rune ran his hands through his hair, his tattoos bulging over his muscles.

"I'm not good enough for her. We both know that."

"I think that's bullshit."

My eyes widened. "What?"

"I think it's bullshit. I think my best friend deserves the world. So does my sister. Do I think it's fucking weird?

Yes. But that's because I don't want my sister to be with anyone. I want her to be virginal and in a nunnery."

I snorted. "I think I said something similar about Briar when she met Gabriel."

"And look at her. All married and a mom and seeing the world. Are you that protective of Teagan?"

"Yes. That's why I know I'm no good for your sister."

"Just don't hurt her. I'm not going to ask what your intentions are or what you want. Because I know you guys aren't that far into your relationship. But just be careful. She deserves the world, Callum."

"I know she does. Which is why I don't know what she sees in me."

"I don't know either, with your dirty ass."

"I washed my ass, thank you very much."

"How about hairy ass then?" Rune said with a roll of his eyes.

"That's what waxing is for." I winked. "I just use your waxer. As long as they have enough wax after getting through with you."

"Asshole."

"I'm sure you wax that as well."

We burst out laughing, feeling a little normal for the first time in weeks.

"I'm sorry I lied. And kept it secret. But this small town, man. You know I don't date. You know I don't deal with whatever gossip this town wants."

"So you decided to break that rule and date my sister.

You are dating, right? This isn't just, well, I don't even want to say the words."

"I'm falling for her. And that scares me so fucking much."

"Well, hell." Rune pinched the bridge of his nose. "Did you tell her about Georgia?"

"I did. But for the life of me, I thought she knew about Georgia."

"You don't talk about her at all. I'm pretty sure most of the town doesn't even remember you were married, Callum."

"Well, I'm sure they're going to dig that up and want to talk more about it once everybody figures out that I'm, well, with Felicity."

"Well, you're going to have to deal with the consequences. Because you know this town is not going to withhold judgment. It's what they do. They judge everything."

"As long as they don't fucking hurt Felicity."

"That's what I want to hear. You protect my sister. Because if you hurt her, I'll bury you in the backyard."

"If I hurt her, I'll let you."

"Damn it. You say things like this, and it's why I remember you're my best friend."

"Well, I'm glad somebody still thinks I am."

"Hey, Atlas forgave you right away. I wanted to punch you."

"I'm still waiting for the punch," I said as I grabbed my keys and we headed towards our respective trucks.

"The punch can come any minute."

I nearly ran into Rune as he froze.

"What is it?" I cursed under my breath. "What cat left a fucking dead bird on my porch?"

"I didn't even see that. I'm looking at that," Rune said, and I cursed again.

"Are you fucking kidding me? How long were you in here? Did you see anything when you walked inside?"

"I was inside your house for like five minutes, and I wasn't paying attention to your truck when I walked by. Fuck. Who the hell keyed it?"

"And why would they key the word 'dead'?"

The hairs on the back of my neck stood on end, and I looked around the end of the cul-de-sac into the forest beyond. But I didn't see a thing. Felicity was out with Keely, thank God, so she wouldn't see this. But I pulled out my phone and shook my head.

"It has to be my dad, right? He's such an asshole."

"He needs to leave town or just leave this earth. Nobody fucking wants him here. Hell, Callum. How are you going to fix this?"

"Bodhi will know someone or something. Shit. We're going to be late."

"Well, call the sheriff's station, and I'll wait with you. But maybe we should go inside." Chills slid up my spine, and I nodded. "Yeah, we should."

By the time we dealt with the authorities, and I left my truck right where it was, Rune drove me to the axe-throwing place.

"Okay, I'm going to need to break some shit," I growled.

"Damn straight."

The others were already there by the time we showed up, and at their questioning glances, I explained why we were late. It was a small town, and the report was already filed. They would figure it out soon.

"Are you okay?" Bodhi asked, his voice low. "Did they hurt you or the house or anything?"

I shook my head. "No. Nothing else was out of place."

"There was a dead bird," Rune put in, and Bodhi cursed.

"A *dead* bird?" Thatcher asked, drawing out the word. "I don't like the sound of that. Who did you piss off?"

"Well, I think I'm the only one you've pissed off recently, and I didn't do it," Rune said as he handed me a beer. I tapped mine to his and took a swig.

"What'd you do to piss off Rune?" Thatcher asked. He had his attention on his phone, though, and I knew he was probably texting about his kids. This was his one night off, and I was glad that he was spending it with us. Sterling was working, and if his place wasn't packed, with no reservations, we would have bothered him at the restaurant.

"He's dating my sister," Rune blurted, and I narrowed my gaze at him.

"Really?"

Kellan nearly choked on his beer. "Wait. You're dating Felicity? Little Felicity?"

"She's not little," I snapped.

"Wait, we're allowed to date your sister?" Finnian asked, eyes wide. "I didn't know we were allowed to date sisters."

"Finnian, you're lucky that I'm too far away to hit you," Thatcher snapped.

"Well, it's about time that the rest of the world knows," Bodhi mumbled.

"Wait, you knew?" I asked, blinking.

"Of course, I knew. You two aren't really good at hiding it. You guys go gaga whenever you look at each other. And it's ridiculous."

"That's what I said," Rune put in and took a sip of his beer.

"What the hell? We were never out in public together." I shook my head. "It doesn't matter. Yes, Felicity and I are dating. The rest of the town's going to figure it out soon. So don't give her shit, okay? Be a dick to me, but Felicity doesn't get anything."

"Of course, Felicity doesn't get anything," Finnian said as he bounced on his feet. "She's amazing and way too good for you. And I say this as a brother that loves you."

"Fuck you," I said with a grin. "Seriously, fuck you."

"No, I guess that's what Felicity's doing now," Bodhi said, and from the look on his face, it surprised him. I took a step forward, but it was Rune who smacked him upside the head.

"Really?" He shook his head. "That's my sister you're talking about."

"I'm sorry. I'm sorry. I don't know what came over me." Bodhi rubbed the back of his head, and I nearly smiled because that joke sounded so much like the old Bodhi that I thought it was nearly worth it.

"Well then, this is going to blow up in your face," Thatcher said with a sigh. "Not that I don't love you, but this town is going to eat you alive. And Felicity."

My hands fisted. "They do anything to Felicity, and they have to deal with me."

"And that's why I'm letting this happen," Rune put in as he gestured towards the axes. "Let's get started."

"Letting?" I asked, my eyes narrowed. "Don't let Felicity hear you say that."

"Don't let Felicity hear you say what?" a familiar voice said as I turned around, and the woman that I was trying not to fall for stepped forward. She smiled up at me as the guys behind me all wolf-whistled.

I closed my eyes and counted to ten.

"Nothing. Other than the cat's out of the bag."

"I figured since everybody's staring at me, and well, hi."

"I'm here, too," Keely said as she waved. And Teagan just laughed, shaking her head.

"By the way, you're invited to dinner tomorrow. And I don't think you're allowed to say no, or my mom might actually drag you." Felicity beamed, and I did what I wanted to do the entire time and moved forward to push her hair back from her face. When somebody catcalled, and another person cursed, I ignored them.

"Okay, I guess we're doing this."

"I guess we are. Are you going to kiss me?" she asked, that smile far too sly.

"Maybe."

"Well, you should. Just to annoy the people in the corner glaring that aren't related to me."

With a shake of my head, I leaned forward and brushed my lips along hers.

"Callum Ashford. Really?" a high-pitched voice asked, and I ignored one of the women who had grown up with my mother and leaned back so I could stare into Felicity's eyes.

"You okay?"

"It's going to take some getting used to," Felicity whispered.

"Okay, enough with the moon eyes. Now, I need to throw an axe," Rune spat. "And get your paws off my sister in public."

"But I like his paws on me," Felicity sing-songed.

I groaned. "He's going to throw an axe at me."

"He could try. I'll patch you up." She fluttered her eyelashes, and I merely shook my head.

The Carters were going to be the death of me, but then again, I probably deserved it.

"Okay, enough of this melodrama. I'm ready to throw some axes," Teagan said with a bright grin.

"Hey, I thought this was guys' night," Finnian put in as he came over and hugged his sister.

"There's only one good place to be tonight since the Summit Grill is closed for the evening, so you're stuck with us."

"We need bowling," Finnian said. And I laughed as I took Felicity's hand, and we made our way over to the staging area.

"Is this weird?" she whispered.

"Probably. Let's figure this out. I don't think I've ever gone on a date to throw axes before."

"Oh, so you're finally taking me out on a date?"

I paused. "I've never taken you out on a date. Well, I'm an asshole."

"Well, I've never taken you out on one either. So I guess we're out on our first date."

"I guess we are." I waited as we listened to the safety instructions once again and got to axe throwing.

When Felicity hit the target the first time, I blinked as she threw her now empty hands in the air and did a little butt wiggle.

"Yes. I was so worried I was going to end up hitting the wrong side of the section."

"Please stop wiggling like that while we're in front of your brother," I mumbled, and she laughed.

"I promise. But you have to stop looking all hot and broody."

"I can hear you both," Rune muttered.

"What? Your best friend's hot."

I ran my hands over my face. "Felicity, your brother's going to hurt me."

"I'll protect you. I mean, I know how to throw an axe now."

"Oddly, that doesn't reassure me in the slightest," Rune said with a laugh.

I leaned against the high top and sipped my beer as Felicity ended up perched on the chair next to me. When she leaned against me, I put my arm around her, ignoring the glares and stares from others.

I didn't know what they were thinking, but from some of the narrowed, murderous glances, they weren't happy.

The town's princess with the washed-up football player? Probably not what they had in mind when they thought of Felicity's future.

I paused. Future?

I swallowed hard as Felicity leaned into me, laughing at something Keely said.

Was this a future? Did I want a future with Felicity? These were probably questions I should have asked myself before we went public. But then again, I craved her. I needed her.

Did I love her? I didn't know if I wanted to think those words. Not yet. But I didn't want to hurt her. And that counted for everything.

I pushed all thoughts of what others were doing outside my head and figured their attitudes and opinions didn't matter. It only mattered what Felicity and I were doing. After all, I was going to have to be grilled tomorrow by her parents, and that made my mouth dry enough.

I'd have to tell Felicity about the truck, though, because I didn't want her to worry. But if it was my father, and I knew it had to be, I didn't want her to be scared or get hurt by the asshole.

But I'd protect her. No matter what. Even from my own family. Even from me.

"I'm going to go get you something to eat."

"Okay. Will you get me another water?"

"Of course." I leaned down, brushing my lips against hers once more, and went to get the group a few things to eat.

"So, you and Felicity?"

I looked over at Fiona and sighed. "You got a problem with that?"

"No. You guys are cute. Makes sense."

I blinked, surprised. "I do not understand you, Fiona."

"You're not supposed to. I like the mysterious part.

Just take care of her. She's really nice, and you can be nice, but you are kind of an asshole."

I threw my head back and laughed. "So are you, Fiona."

"I really am, but I like it. Felicity's all sweet and bubblegum, but she has that edge. She's too young for you. But then again, I like older men, and that means you're a little too young for me." She winked. She grabbed her order, and I just shook my head, wondering who the hell that woman was. When she went over to an older man, both of them laughing with each other, I realized that maybe that's what had happened. She'd found someone that could handle her. Because that someone sure as fuck wasn't me.

A familiar man with a man bun glared at me, but I ignored him, figuring he probably just didn't like the fact that I was apparently an old creeper with Felicity. But fuck him. She wanted me just like I wanted her. And I'd be with her.

Even though I had no idea what the hell I was doing.

I grabbed our orders and made my way back to the table. Everybody piled on the burgers and fries, and I pulled away the chicken sandwich as Finnian grabbed for it.

"Get your own chicken sandwich. This is Felicity's."

"Did she order it?" Finnian asked, his eyes dancing with laughter.

"No, but I know what she likes."

"Yes, he does," Felicity teased, her voice sultry.

"Babe. Don't."

"Baby?" Rune growled. "Stop. No pet names. No touching. No knowing exactly what she likes to eat without even asking."

"Earlier she said she was craving a chicken sandwich. Just because I remembered, doesn't make it's magic."

"Exactly. He listens."

"I'm so confused," Thatcher said with a laugh and pulled out his phone. "Hey, you have a second?"

I nodded, having a feeling I knew what this was about. I kissed the top of Felicity's head, ignored the glares from others, even the well-meaning ones, and went over to Thatcher.

"What's up?"

"The chief knew I was out with you tonight and wanted me to keep a lookout."

I froze. "Did they find my dad?"

"He wasn't at his place or at the local haunts. They're looking for him now, but they don't have any evidence as to who it could be. It could have been anyone. Have you pissed anyone else off?"

"I don't know why people would think I would. I haven't done anything out of the ordinary."

Thatcher shook his head. "Other than date Felicity."

"But nobody knew about that until tonight."

"Maybe, maybe not. But in all honesty, this does sound like your dad. I'm sorry."

"No, that's true. My dad, well, you know what my dad is."

"If they could have found any proof, he'd be behind bars," Thatcher said, rubbing his hand over his face.

"I know. I just hate the fact that there's nothing we can do right now."

"It never seems like there is."

"Thanks for letting me know," I said after a moment.

"No problem. By the way, you should tell Felicity. So she can stay on alert."

"I was planning on it. Because I hope to hell that was just a threat for me and not for her."

"Maybe it's just your dad being a drunk. But I'm glad you're going to tell her. Secrets break relationships. Believe me, I know."

I reached out and squeezed my friend's shoulder. "Thanks, buddy."

"No problem. Now I have to go pick up my kids. Having a couple hours just to myself, even while techni-cally on call, was nice. But I can't let Tess have all the teenagers tonight."

"So, she's working out for you?"

"She's a godsend. Between me and Kellan, we're running her ragged with the six kids. But the teenagers are old enough to get themselves around places, so she's helping with our schedule a lot. We're just making sure she actually gets days off too."

"She's a single mom, so that would probably be helpful."

"Have you met her yet?" he asked.

I shook my head. "No, but maybe she should meet Felicity and Keely and the others. Actually settle into town."

"She did throw herself head-first into helping Kellan and me. But she should. Maybe we'll get her to come out to Summit Grill and get to know everyone."

"Sounds like a plan. I'll let Felicity know."

"Look at you, sounding like a couple."

I flipped him off as the other man laughed and headed out.

When I went back over to the group, and Felicity gave me a questioning glance, I leaned down and kissed her temple. "I'll explain afterward. But you do have a mission."

Her eyes widened. "I do?"

"Well, two missions. One involves you being on your knees, but that's for later."

She laughed since Bodhi groaned, having overheard, and I just leaned into her, wondering if this could work.

And hoping to hell I'd find a way to make it happen.

CHAPTER 16

Felicity

I had been on dates before, plenty of them. But I didn't know why I felt so stressed at this point, considering this shouldn't be anything new.

Callum and I had been seeing each other for weeks now. We'd slept together. Our families knew we were together. We'd even been out in public together.

Except now, it wasn't a secret.

I slid my hands over my little black dress, loving the way that it ruffled slightly over the middle of my thighs. The neckline went straight across my collarbones, leaving the long lines of my neck and my shoulders bare. It also dipped low in the back, and I knew that one day soon, I'd finally get my tattoo down my spine, and this dress would showcase it perfectly. I slid my feet into forest green heels, a fun color that had made me smile and would stand out against the black of my dress.

I had put my hair up in a chiffon, one that could easily come out with just one or two pins in strategic places.

I looked like I knew what I was doing. Classier than I felt sometimes.

I wasn't sure why the nerves had settled in so hard. But they were there. And I didn't know when they were going to go away.

My phone buzzed, and I smiled at the readout.

Keely: You've got this. I want to hear all the details later. This is so much better than online dating.

I smiled as I replied.

Me: We can find you a small-town guy. Though most of the men I know are older.

Keely: You don't seem to have a problem with older.

Me: No, I don't. But what about an older single dad? Those are most of the single guys I knew. Other than my brother. Which, I know you don't want to date my brother.

Keely: Well, you're doing the whole brother's best friend thing. I'm not going to do the whole best friend's brother thing. Rune is nice, but no. As for Atlas? He scares me. I will find a nice and calm, maybe, possibly, single dad in Ashford Creek. At some point.

Me: We'll find you somebody. Although, I'm nervous about tonight.

My phone rang this time, and I answered.

"Why are you nervous? This is Callum. You've got this down by now."

"It feels like a first date."

"Why?" She paused, and I heard her snap her fingers. "Oh. Duh. You guys are going out in public. Out to dinner. Where everybody knows you will be dating. It's not just something that people can confuse for two friends going out."

"Ding ding. Why am I so stressed out?"

"Because he matters. Because this matters. But what others think does not. So have fun, enjoy yourself. And ride that hot bearded man. Or at least climb him like a tree."

I burst out laughing. "You're ridiculous."

"I am. Now enjoy yourself. I'm going to go work on these tarts."

"I don't know if you're calling yourself a tart, or me," I teased.

"Haha. We have an event tomorrow, and I really want to make Promise proud. So I'm going to work my ass off on these tarts. They need to settle overnight, so wish me luck."

"Don't work too hard."

"Even if I do, I'll sleep well. Now go get laid."

"You are really the best friend."

"I try. I'm so glad that I picked you up in that bar."

We both laughed and said our goodbyes, and by the time I set my phone down and put my lip gloss on, the doorbell rang. I grabbed my little purse and went to open the door.

My breath caught, and I had a feeling I would swoon. If I did that sort of thing.

Callum stood there, his beard groomed, his hair a little long and bouncy from most likely being on the back of his motorcycle earlier. He had on a black button-up shirt, though he'd rolled the sleeves up to show his forearms. And since I wanted to lick those forearms, I counted that as a win.

He tucked his shirt into black pants, but he still had on his biker boots, and I couldn't help but smile.

"Okay, this is a problem."

I blinked up. "What?" I couldn't help the disappointment that laced my tone.

Callum leaned forward and pinched my chin. "I don't want anyone to see you in that fucking dress."

I grinned. "It's a good dress, isn't it?"

"I want to bend you over and bury my face underneath that dress. I want to lick that pussy, taste every inch of you, and smash my cheeks in between your cheeks. What do you think about that?"

I pressed my thighs together but didn't pull away from his touch. "Oh. Well. That sounds fun."

"You're ridiculous. Now we have to go eat dinner at

my brother's restaurant while I have a hard-on. I can't wait to hear what the town says about this."

"Keely told me to forget what the town thinks."

"So you told Keely about our date tonight?"

I blushed as he took my hand, leading me to his truck which had thankfully been fixed. "Of course I did. She's my best friend. And, well, I'm nervous."

He froze in the act of putting his hands on my hips to lift me into his truck. "Why are you nervous?" he asked, his voice soft.

"Because it's you and me. And this feels different."

He let out a deep breath and pressed his forehead to mine. "It does feel different. A good different, right? We can go back inside. Just have dinner between the two of us. I don't mind never sharing you."

I shook my head. "But I want to claim you in front of the rest of town. Now, who's a neanderthal?"

"Well, I don't mind the claiming. As long as you don't care that I'm going to claim you right back. Because if anybody looks at you with an inch of hunger in their eyes when we're out to dinner tonight, I'll break them."

"No, you won't."

"The fuck I will. I told you, this body is mine. This pussy is mine. When you're with me, you're mine."

"Oh, great, now my panties are wet. I probably should just take them off and leave them here."

I grinned, but he nearly growled.

"Girl, you are testing me." He pressed a hard kiss to

my lips, and I just laughed, wiping my lip gloss off his face.

"You're a mess."

"Well, I'm your mess. So deal with it."

And with that, he slid me into the cab of his truck, and I fell that much more in love with Callum Ashford.

"I feel like I'm at an aquarium on the main stage."

My shoulders hunched as I tried not to laugh as Callum glared at anybody staring at us.

And they were staring.

Nearly every person we knew who walked by us nearly tripped over their feet, realizing that, yes, Felicity Carter and Callum Ashford were on a date. Shocking. I would've thought with the axe-throwing and us going out to coffee countless times that people would realize that we were dating, but apparently they hadn't believed it.

"Well, at least we're getting it over with here, right?"

He merely raised a brow at me before taking a sip of his beer.

"First off, no. That's not going to be how it is. They're always going to stare. Because it's what this town does."

I shook my head. "Maybe you're used to it with the way that your family's the center of attention here, but I don't know. The next big thing will happen, and people will forget about us."

"There's nothing forgettable about you, Felicity."

My cheeks heated, and somebody laughed beside me. I looked up, though, and couldn't help but grin. "Sterling, what are you doing out of the kitchen?"

"Yes, shouldn't you be cooking my food?" Callum growled.

Sterling Ashford, the youngest of all the Ashfords, merely smiled.

"I wanted to see what all the hubbub was about. You have my entire staff whispering in low voices about your salacious date."

He wiggled his brows, his eyebrow ring glinting underneath the low lights.

"Well, are you going to do something about it?" Callum asked.

"Why? You're hot gossip. And honestly, I'm sure Teagan and Finnian are glad that you're the center of attention these days rather than them."

I frowned. "What do you mean?"

"Well, everybody's always worried about Teagan because she's unmarried, God forbid. And well, Finnian's a poor single father, and it doesn't matter that he and Promise are friends. People like their gossip. And don't get me started on Bodhi."

I reached forward and squeezed Sterling's hand, ignoring Callum's glare.

"Okay, I get it. So I guess we're the center of attention for this moment."

"Here I was, trying to be nice by coming to your restaurant, and every person in this room is glaring."

Sterling clucked his tongue. "No, they aren't, but you just think they are. A couple of people will talk, and then they'll get over it. I'm sure one of us will do something worth talking about soon. Now, I realize you haven't ordered yet, and you don't get to."

I laughed. "No? Now we're getting kicked out?"

"Of course not. But you're getting the chef's choice. Because I know both of you. Though I didn't realize you two were dating, and now it's quite interesting. However, I know your tastes. So you get the chef's table tonight. Be happy. Others spend way more on this than you are."

"And how much am I spending?" Callum asked, deadpan.

"Exactly what you charged me at your house." He winked before whisking away without another word. Before I could say anything, however, two waiters came by, put two appetizers on the table, and went poof so quickly that I couldn't even tell that they had been there at all.

"Okay, I love this place already. And this service is impeccable."

"He's just trying to show off for you." Callum's lips twitched.

I shook my head. "No. I'm pretty sure he's trying to

show his big brother that he loves him. Because how much do you charge him?"

"Nothing. It's family dinner."

"Exactly. He just wants to show his big brother, the one who helped raise him, that he's good at what he does. Now, let's enjoy this meal. Because I'm being treated like a queen."

"Well, if this is going to get me laid later, why not?"

I snorted, ignoring the way one of the older women from my mom's church group glared at us.

"Now tell me what I'm eating," I whispered. "I'm not good at this whole fancy thing."

"And I am?" he asked.

"You lived in LA. You ate with celebrities. You went to the NFL playoffs. You know things."

"It's been a long time, Felicity."

"Tell me stories anyway."

He stared at me for a moment before nodding and pointing towards the puff pastry in front of me.

"That is a salmon puff, at least, I think."

I grinned and let Callum explain our food, course after course, and I sat back and talked about my time in Denver, and he told me everything about LA. Everything that we had missed when we had been apart, finding ourselves.

And with each passing moment and each course, it was easier to ignore everyone around us.

By the time we were done, I was so full I felt like I could roll out of there.

Sterling waved at us from the busy kitchen, and we headed back to Callum's truck.

"So, how was dinner?" Callum asked before lifting me into the cab of the truck once more.

"Didn't you notice I gained like one hundred pounds just then? All good pounds. Because that was the best food ever."

"It was pretty damn good. I guess I'll have to let Sterling know."

"If you don't, I will."

"Oh, no, you don't. I'm getting sexual favors for that food. My brother does not."

I threw my head back and laughed as he shut the door and came around the front of the truck.

I licked my lips as he turned over the engine and slowly began to dance my fingers along his thigh.

"You're playing with fire, girl."

"Am I?" I asked and slowly worked his belt.

"Do you want me to wreck?" he snapped, his voice tense.

"No. But I do want your cock in my mouth."

I'd only had a single glass of wine, so this was all him doing this to me. Nothing and no one else.

As I slowly slid my hand underneath his waistband, he groaned and gripped my wrist.

"You do that, and I'm going to pull over to fuck you in

this truck. And then one of our friends is going to catch us, or the sheriff will, and I'll have to deal with that. So you be a good girl and keep your hands to yourself."

I stuck out my lower lip and pouted, and he just shook his head.

"You're going to use that mouth later for something. Don't pout."

Grinning, I took my hand back and slid my fingers over my inner thigh.

"Well, if you're not going to let me touch you—"

"Felicity." He white knuckled the steering wheel as I slowly began to play with myself over my panties, just a stroke, a brush, a gasp.

But with each passing moment, I was afraid Callum was going to break the steering wheel right off.

"Thank God Ashford Creek is small," he snarled as he pulled into his driveway and turned off the engine.

Before I could blink, he was out of the truck and practically running around the side, opening the door.

Laughing, I slid my fingers deep into my pussy and gasped.

"Callum."

"Fuck," he ground out. He snatched my wrist and held my hand behind my back. "You're fucking wet." Then he licked my fingers clean, keeping his gaze on mine.

"Oh," I panted.

"You're in trouble for that, girl," he growled before he undid my seatbelt and carried me into the house.

I had no idea if our neighbors had seen anything, and I would be embarrassed later. But before I could do anything, he had the door closed, and I was bent over the back of the couch.

"Callum. What—"

Then he was on his knees behind me, and my panties were shoved to my ankles. He buried his face in my pussy, and he began to devour me. My toes curled as I gripped the edge of the couch, trying not to fall off. But he licked and sucked, spreading me before him. And when he used his tongue on my hole, spearing me slightly, I tensed, wanting more.

"You're going to come on my face and ride me. Do you get me?"

"Okay," I panted. "Please."

"Better keep begging, Felicity." Then he buried his face once more, sucking and licking and playing me with two fingers.

I came then, riding his face as he continued to lap at me.

I tried to arch my back, needing more, but then he was standing, the sound of his zipper going down, and before I could breathe, the tip of his cock was at my entrance, and he was shoving home.

We both groaned as my body stretched, trying to accommodate his length. His piercings rubbed me in just the right way so that I nearly came once again.

"You're perfect for me. So fucking tight and warm.

Your pussy just clenches around my cock, and I want to come so hard. I want to fill you up, so you're dripping with my cum as you walk back to the bedroom. Do you want to do that? Be filled with my cum, Felicity?"

"Just fuck me already," I panted, unable to think.

The hard smack on my ass was a surprise, yet the pleasure that came with it washed over me.

"Answer me. Do you want to be filled with my cum or covered in it?"

"Either. I just want you."

"That's a good girl."

And then he was fucking me hard, and I couldn't breathe, couldn't think. The couch moved with each thrust, and as he growled in frustration, he pulled out of me, flipped me over, and I whimpered. But then his hand was around my throat, and his mouth was crushed to mine, and I could only taste myself on him.

I reached between us, gripping his cock so I could work him, as his fingers went between my legs, finger fucking me so quickly that I came again on his hand, practically gushing into his palm. He lifted me by my thighs and moved my hand away before spearing me once more. I wrapped my arms around his shoulders, going on my tiptoes for the right angle, and so he picked me up the rest of the way by my thighs to the edge of the couch before pumping in and out of me.

"Look down. Look down between us," he whispered.

I did as he ordered and watched as his cock slid in and out of me, each time coming back wetter and wetter.

"This is all mine. You are all mine," he rasped before taking my mouth again. His thumb flipped over my clit, and then I was coming, my legs wrapped around his waist, keeping him close. He thrust into me over and over again, hard enough that both of us would have bruises, and then he was coming, filling me up, and I felt his warmth spread through me.

He bit my shoulder, groaning my name into my skin, marking me as his, and I couldn't catch my breath.

All I knew was that I had just been marked. And I knew I had done the same to him. "Well, that was one way to end a date."

Callum leaned back and just smirked. "Do you really think that was the end?" His cock hardened within me, and my eyes widened.

"Oh."

And then Callum carried me to the bedroom, and we finally finished our date, albeit hours later.

And I couldn't wait for our next.

CHAPTER 17

Felicity

"Y ou taste too good," Callum growled against my lips before he licked down my neck and over my breasts. I lay on the bed, arms above my head, arching for him.

"We're going to be late."

"I'll have to be quicker, then."

He nibbled down my body, licking at my thighs, before he spread me and sucked on my clit. I groaned, sharp waves of pain and pleasure sliding up my back and tightening my nipples as he continued to devour me.

"I can't, I can't."

Apparently, I couldn't even finish a sentence.

Because he continued to lick at me until all I could see were stars, and my thighs clamped around his head.

He groaned against me before he sat up and took me into his arms.

"We don't have that much longer. I have to get you dressed."

"You're the one who took my dress off," I growled the words, nipping at his lips before I pushed him back on the bed. He let out a laugh and slid his hands behind his head, staring up at me with those dark eyes as I wiggled down his body.

He had shown up at my house to pick me up for dinner, and with one look at the wrap dress I wore, he closed the door behind him and threw me over his shoulder in a fireman carry.

And that's how I found myself naked on my bed and now positioned between his legs.

I kneeled between his thighs and licked to the base of his cock.

"Baby, you do not have to do this. I want to come inside you."

"Maybe later. I really, really want you to come down my throat."

His eyes rolled to the back of his head as I licked up his shaft, careful of his piercings.

"We both know I'm not going to last long, especially with your tongue sliding along the slit right there."

I fluttered my eyelashes, trying to look as innocent as possible, as I licked up his length and opened my mouth wide in order to take him in. The salty taste coated my tongue, and I groaned, rubbing the tip of my tongue along the ridge of his cock.

He groaned again, sliding his fingers through my hair and tugging.

"Felicity, you're playing with fire."

"Well, I need my meal too."

And then I opened my mouth wider and swallowed him whole.

With the piercings, it was a little more difficult than a normal blow job, but then again, this was Callum Ashford.

There was nothing normal about him. I bobbed my head, continuing to hollow my cheeks as I sucked him down. He groaned, lifting his hips so he went even deeper down my throat, so I swallowed hard, letting the tip tap the back of my throat.

He froze, his whole body shaking as I breathed through my nose and took him even deeper.

"Fuck," he drawled out—the word a guttural moan.

I slid up again before taking him deeper, gagging slightly with my eyes watering as he tugged on my hair and buried my face closer to his hips.

"Your mouth is so fucking good. That's it, take my cock. Take it all."

I nodded, humming along his length as we angled so

he could slide his cock in and out of my mouth, deeper and deeper, until I was gagging, tears sliding down my cheeks, and he was fucking my face.

I loved every moment of it, every taste of him, and when he finally pulled out of me, I groaned, my lips swollen.

"You weren't done yet."

"I don't fucking care."

He crushed his mouth to mine, and before I could do anything, my ass was in the air, face pressed against the comforter as he stood at the edge of the bed and slammed deep inside me. We both froze, my knees shaking as the feeling of his piercings rubbed along the inside of me and made my toes curl.

"Callum."

"I'm so fucking deep this way. Am I hurting you?"

I shook my head against the comforter, my hands digging into the mattress.

"No. It feels so good. Fuck me. Please. I need to come again."

"We're going to be so fucking late," he growled. Then he slid out of me and licked up my spine before slamming home again.

He moved in and out of me, slowly at first, until there was nothing but groans and heat and pants. And when he slid his fingers over my clit, I came, my knees giving out so I lay face down on the bed while he continued to fuck me. Then his fingers were at my ass, slowly using my own juices to make it easier for him to slide one digit in. I froze, and he did the same, and I let out a breath.

"Callum."

"That's it. Just take one finger. Just like we practiced. You've got this, baby."

"I really don't think your cock is going to fit in there. I'm just saying."

"We've got time to practice."

And then he was working himself in and out of me, his finger in my ass, his cock in my pussy, and I just realized at this moment that I had never known it could be like this. Nor had I known I could even say the words that were currently escaping my mouth.

When I finally came again, Callum took both hands, gripped my hips, and slammed into me.

"Felicity," he growled, filling me with his cock, as he hovered over me, both of us wet, slick, and shaking.

My phone buzzed, and I looked down at the alarm next to my face, since my cell phone had bounced along the mattress, and let out a breath.

"We have twenty minutes to shower and get to my parents. They're going to know that you just fucked their daughter on her bed, aren't they?"

"I hope to hell not. Your brother is going to kick my ass."

"Be more afraid of my father," I teased.

337

Callum let out a breath and kissed my shoulder.

"Let's go get cleaned up and have dinner with your parents."

"Don't sound so scared," I said as I let him help me off the bed.

"Not scared. More worried this will be my last meal."

"My parents love you. You know that, right?"

He frowned at me as we made our way to the shower.

"They do. But I'm going to dinner as the person seeing their daughter. Not the person who's best friends with their son. It's a little different."

"Maybe. Or maybe not. Honestly, I don't think they're going to make it too weird. I mean, nothing's really changed, right?"

He stared at me then as he turned on the shower, and I knew I was losing my mind because, of course, things had changed. I didn't know where we were going or what would happen next, but I was about to have dinner with my parents and Callum. That meant something. I just didn't know what at this point.

How was I just supposed to tell him that I was falling in love with him? Or probably had already done so.

I hadn't meant to. I hadn't meant for any of this to happen, but there was no going back.

And frankly, I didn't want to go back. Nothing was like how I thought it would be when I had come home to Ashford Creek, but I wasn't sure what I could have ever hoped for. A man I was falling for? He treated me like I was special. Not spun glass, not so fragile that I would fracture with a heavy breath or deep kiss. But someone valued.

My job would be forever changed, and I didn't know what would happen next. Or how I was supposed to continue on as the sole owner of the accounting firm, but I was learning. And I would make it work. For Gregory's legacy and my own.

My family was here. I was making friends.

Even Fiona was treating me decently.

I had found my home in Ashford Creek, and I had found my home in Callum Ashford.

I just needed to figure out exactly what to do with that.

Thankfully, my hair had made it through our intense session, impromptu as it was. So I fluffed it out, redid part of my makeup, and we were in his truck and on our way to my parents' house, only a couple of blocks away, in a few minutes.

It was Ashford Creek, however, so everywhere was only a few blocks away.

"Why am I nervous? This is not my first time meeting your parents or going to a dinner where I'm meeting the parents of someone I'm seeing. And I'm fucking nervous."

"I don't know why that makes me so relaxed to hear, but it does."

"Are you a sadist and I didn't know?" he asked, raising a brow. "Maybe we should talk about that later."

I pressed my thighs together and glared at him. "Really? You're going to get me turned on before we head into my parents' house? Mean."

He looked down at my thighs, which he noticed were now pressed together, and smirked.

"At least you can hide your evidence." He looked down at his crotch, and I held back a laugh at where his cock strained against his dark jeans.

"Well, think about baseball. Or whatever it is you need to think about. Because if you go in there walking with a hard-on and limp, my dad will murder you."

"Thank you for that. I'm really glad that you're so helpful here."

He grumbled under his breath as he parked in front of my parents' house, and I bit my lip.

"Okay. We passed the gauntlet of our siblings already, so we can do this. I mean, my parents are totally okay, right?"

"I thought you were the one that was supposed to be making me relax," he said dryly as he undid my seatbelt and reached across the truck to unlock the door for me.

"Don't hop out. You're going to hurt yourself in those heels."

I had barely even begun to breathe again after inhaling his sandalwood scent from when he had leaned across from me, and I knew I had it bad.

There was just something about Callum, and it was probably a problem.

340

I shook my head, and I did indeed wait for him to come around the truck and help me down. There were runners, but I had nearly fallen on my face the day before, and now he was being a little overprotective.

I slid my hand into his for reassurance as we walked our way up the path to my parents' home, the home I had just recently lived in, and squeezed.

"We've got this."

"If you say so," he mumbled.

My lips twitched, and I didn't know what I was going to say before my dad opened the door and glared at us.

"You're late." He folded his arms over his wide chest, nearly as strong as he had been when he'd been the fire captain.

"My fault."

My dad gave me a look before nodding tightly at Callum. "Okay then. Let's go watch the game. Atlas is on the ice and in a pissy mood from what I can see."

"Wait. I thought the game wasn't until four. Am I wrong?"

"They moved it up for a scheduling conflict. I don't know, but the team looks to be out of sorts, and the fans are all grumpy because some of them are coming in late. It's a mess. The commissioner is pissing me off, and I don't even know the man."

"Are you grumbling at those two without even letting them walk inside?" Mom asked as she came forward and leaned down to kiss me on the cheek, then did the same with Callum.

"Come inside. And you did not have to bring wine, Callum."

"It felt right."

"Well, you're family." She paused and gave me a look. "Okay, well, our family's getting a little close in some aspects, but it's fine. Maybe I'll marry off one of the boys to Teagan and make it a full, interesting web."

"Mom."

Callum had frozen at the word marry, at least, I thought it was that word. Maybe it was the idea of Teagan with one of my brothers, but we weren't there yet. But hell, I wasn't even sure Callum wanted to get married again.

An odd feeling settled in, my stomach tightening at that. I didn't know what Callum wanted. He had already been married, but maybe he didn't want a future or children or anything like that. It was just one more thing we needed to speak about, but I was afraid I didn't want to know the answer.

After all, we had kept this thing to ourselves for so long that speaking of the future seemed farfetched. Perhaps not that farfetched.

"We both know that Teagan would eat your sons for breakfast. Just saying."

"I would take offense at that, but it's true," Dad said

with a laugh. "Come on, let's go watch Atlas kick some ass."

"Of course, he's going to kick ass. He's our son. And the best goalie in the NHL."

"As long as you stop saying that in front of him, we'll be fine," Rune said with a laugh. He lifted his chin up at Callum, and I figured that was a good thing. It was normal. He didn't punch him, at least.

Then, of course, Rune looked at me and narrowed his eyes. "Well, you're here."

"I'm going to sic Teagan on you," I said quickly.

"I might not be able to take Teagan, but she'd be on my side in this."

"And what side would that be?" Callum asked, an odd warning in his tone.

"Stop it. Both of you. Yes, this is different, but it's good." Mom looked between all of us, brows raised. "And if you fight in this house, I will ground you all. Including you," she said to her husband.

He held up both hands, attention on the game. "Excuse me, but I'm watching my son, a bright light of my life, stop pucks going far too fast. I'm not going to get into a fight with the others. Because Callum knows if he hurts my precious baby girl, we can bury him somewhere in the forest around here. This way, we can hide all of Felicity's suitors who wrong us."

"And how many suitors would that be?" Callum asked with a laugh.

"You guys are ridiculous," I said as I threw my hands in the air. "I'm going with Mom to help with dinner."

"Yes, a woman's place is in the kitchen," Rune said as he squeezed Callum's shoulder, none too lightly, and they headed into the living room.

"Aren't you the one who cooks dinner usually?" Callum asked.

"Gosh. Let's get the womenfolk out of here. Since you're dating my sister, now I can't even talk about certain things with you."

"And what things would those be?" I asked.

"Yes, son, what things would you be discussing about women that you can't say in front of us?" Mom asked, sing-songing.

"How we respect women, and we enjoy their company, and they are amazing?" Rune asked, fluttering his eyelashes.

"Ridiculous. All of you."

"If you think that's bad, just imagine how annoying it is when you have all of my siblings in one place," Callum said with a sigh.

"At least you only have these two in the house right now. It's worse when you add in all of mine."

"Well, we're just going to have to do that soon, aren't we?" Mom said with a shrug as we stood behind the kitchen island, still able to hear everything from the living room.

"What do you mean?" I asked, handing over a block of cheese so she could finish the cheeseboard.

"Well, you guys don't know it yet, but next week, we're going to be having an Ashford and Carter family dinner."

I froze. "What?"

"What do you mean, 'what'? We always used to do things like that. And ever since you moved back to town, and well, since the others have started their own businesses and you're all adults and moving on, we haven't had a good dinner with the whole group. So we're going to do it."

"How are we going to fit everybody in this house, Mom?" Rune asked with a shake of his head. "The Ashfords outnumber us more than two to one."

"You can have it at mine," Callum said with a shrug. He wasn't even looking towards us as he paid attention to Atlas on the ice, and I blinked.

"You'd do that?" I asked, confused.

"Of course. That's why I bought the big house. Not just to show off my football winnings but because I needed to fit the whole family in there. It's not like we'd go to Dad's."

There was an awkward silence as Callum went out of breath. "Sorry, I hate bringing him up. It just happened."

"No, your father's an asshole, and he deserves whatever's going to come to him next," Mom said simply, and Callum snorted as Rune and I just stared at each other.

"Well, that's just great. Having it at your house will make sure we can fit everybody, and I want to see the babies." She gave me a look. "At least somebody's giving me babies. Even though they're not my grandkids, I'm claiming them."

"Mom," I gasped as Callum nearly dropped his beer, an Ashford brew, of course.

Rune threw his head back and laughed. "Oh, this is going to be fun."

"Darling, you're older. I'm going to bother you about babies soon too. It's just what I do."

"Well then, I'm going to go hide in a closet with a bottle of wine," I said dryly.

"Callum, darling, do you think Briar is coming to town anytime soon?"

"No clue, but I'll ask. I want to see my niece. And we can try to make it work where it's the weekend that Finnian gets the twins."

"Well, if not, we can invite Promise as well. I love that girl. I'm sad that she and Finnian didn't work out, but they're so much better as friends, don't you think?"

I stood back and watched as my mother led us from conversation to conversation as if nothing had changed.

And I knew that she was doing it on purpose, showing everybody in this room, and then later the town, that nothing had changed. We were still the same, though irrevocably altered.

Or perhaps I was just looking too far into things.

By the time dinner was over and we had already planned the next meeting, Atlas had won, though he had let two goals in, as the starting forwards for the opposite team were some of the best in the NHL. I was going to have to text him later to make sure he knew that he was amazing. He took each goal harder than the last.

After we said our goodbyes, and were walking out the door, Callum said, "Hey, I need to head to the brewery real quick. I'm going to drop you off at the house, and then I'll be back, okay?" Callum kissed my temple, and I frowned.

"I can go with you if you want."

He shook his head. "I have to deal with some of the machinery, and you can't go back there."

"Oh, that makes sense. Okay. I'll just get some work done, and are we staying at my house or your house tonight?"

"Whatever you'd like, just know that you're not sleeping alone tonight."

"I kind of like how growly you got just then." I smiled.

"Oh, good. You decide where we're sleeping, but I need to go fix this."

"Is everything okay, really?"

"It should be. There's just a weird alarm going off."

He dropped me off at the front door, kissed me soundly until my knees went weak, and didn't drive off until I locked the door behind me.

That was it. I was in love with Callum Ashford, and there was no returning.

I moved towards the kitchen, turning on the light as I did.

And if I hadn't, I wouldn't have been able to duck out of the way in time. A shadow moved forward, and as I opened my mouth to scream, a hand went over my mouth from the side so I could see the man nearly in front of me.

Bradley smiled at me, that same look on his face from all those years ago.

"Hello, Felicity. It's been a long time."

CHAPTER 18

Felicity

My heart raced, palms damp, as I realized who exactly held me in place. The moment I saw his face, then heard his voice, everything came back to me.

A blind date I hadn't wanted to go on. A group event that had turned into a fun night of dancing and me running barefoot through the woods, screaming for help.

I had called Callum, hiding in a bush, hoping that Bradley wouldn't find me.

But here he was, over two years later, in my house.

He lowered his hand and took a step to the side so he could face me. I opened my mouth to scream, but he held up a knife. One from my own butcher block.

"No. Don't make a sound. We just need to talk it out."

"What are you doing here?" I asked.

Bradley's eyes narrowed as he stepped forward, knife in hand. "What part of don't make a fucking sound do you not understand? You're such an idiot." His arm slashed out, thankfully the one without the knife, and he backhanded me. My head hit the wall behind me, and I grasped for something to hold on to so I wouldn't fall. Blood trickled down my mouth, and I realized his ring had cut my lip.

"You know, I've been watching you these last few weeks. And you're just so boring."

Those moments where I had thought someone had been watching me, and I had thought it had been either Callum's dad, or one of the townspeople, wondering what I was doing with Callum, or just back in town. All those instances where the hair on the back of my neck had stood on end, and I had felt uneasy. All those instances I had told myself were nothing, and I was just losing my mind.

"No, don't speak. I'm not in the mood to kill you. I don't kill people. But I do make them regret things. Do you realize what you did two years ago?"

I opened my mouth to say something, but he waved the knife around.

"I don't actually want an answer. You're going to listen to me. Because all you did all those years ago was open your fucking mouth and ruin my life. My dad wouldn't take me in after college. I was supposed to go to law school, but he stopped me. Apparently, he didn't like what he had been hearing. Didn't like what my so-called friends told him about what happened that night. He wouldn't pay for fucking law school. He said I had to do it myself if I wanted to prove myself. Why do I need to prove myself?

I'm Bradley fucking McDonald of the McDonalds. I don't need to prove myself to anyone. But you decided to be a fucking cunt and lie to me. Then you lied to everyone else. I couldn't go to law school. I'm not going to get a fucking loan like some peasant. Like something you probably had to do to go to school. Though, what good was school for you if you're sitting at that little no-name building being a fucking accountant? How ridiculous is that? You are nothing. And you are ruining my life. All because you wouldn't open your legs like you promised me."

"I didn't promise you anything," I blurted. And when he lashed out again, I ducked to the side, chest heaving. "Please. You don't want to do this."

"I don't want to do what? Make you realize how wrong you have it? No, you're going to go to my father, and you're going to tell him that you made a mistake. That way, I can do what I was supposed to. I was supposed to be in the middle of law school right now, getting ready to join my dad's firm and, at the end of it, fulfill my legacy. Instead, you've ruined it. All because you're a fucking bitch who can't stop lying. The four Ls agree with me. When they came to visit? They told me how big of an idiot you are. Nobody wants to be with you. Well, I don't want to be with you, if that's what you're thinking, but I want you to tell the truth." He waved the knife around again, and I realized his pupils were so damn wide he had to be on something. What, I didn't know, but there was something wrong with him.

There had been something wrong with him two years ago, too, but it was worse now.

"Okay, I'll talk to your dad. I'll do whatever you want."

"You're such a liar. You're just afraid I'm not going to hurt you. Well, you're bleeding now, but I didn't stab you. So you don't get to tell anybody that I stabbed you. Don't keep lying to make yourself feel better. Oh, and your big old man that could probably be your daddy? That's gross, by the way. He's not going to come save you. There's a leak at the brewery, one by that small window that has a broken pane. Well, he's going to be dealing with that for a while. Probably with the fire station as well. So he's not going to come and save you."

So that was what had happened. The emergency. How long had Bradley been planning this?

"Don't worry. I'm not alone. I needed help. Not everybody in this town loves you. And most people hate the Ashfords. They just don't say it out loud. I mean, apparently, they lorded their wares or whatever over the town for too long, and now they're fighting back. Small-town lore is so fucking ridiculous, but I don't care. You're going to call my father, and you're going to fix this. Or I'm going to have to fix you."

He wavered on his feet then, and I scrambled forward without thinking. I shoved him, knocking the knife out of his hand before my fist collided with his jaw.

He let out a grunt, his head slamming into the counter as I punched him again.

I kicked the knife away before reaching for my phone.

"Bitch," he slurred as I realized blood trickled from the back of his head.

Bile coating my tongue, I grabbed my phone and scrambled out of the house.

I ran, not caring if he was following me or if people thought I was insane. I just dialed 911, ignoring the pain in my lip and hoping like hell that they would come soon.

Because I had a feeling once the adrenaline wore off, I'd throw up. Or pass out.

And I didn't want to be strong anymore.

"I can't believe I wasn't there," Callum snapped as he paced his kitchen, his hands running over his face.

My mother held me close as Rune and my father paced alongside Callum.

It had been twenty-four hours since the attack, and I

was pretty sure nobody had slept. I had tried to, but people kept coming over, making sure I was okay.

Word of the attack had spread through the small town far quicker than any gossip vine I had ever heard in my life.

Keely, Promise, Teagan, and the others had come to check on me. Even Bronwyn, a townie who kept to herself most days, came over for a few moments. Fiona had dropped off a pie, glared at me as she checked over the bruise on my face, and stomped out.

I didn't know what that meant, but she hadn't been the only one.

Nearly everybody in town had stopped by Callum's house, made sure I was okay, asked about Bradley, had a questioning glance about the fact that I was at Callum's house, and left.

Now I was with my family, with Atlas on the other side of the country, banned from coming here by every single person in this house since he had a game tonight, and all I wanted to do was go to sleep.

"I was fine. I handled it myself."

"Damn straight you did. Although, with the cut on your knuckles, we're going to have to work on your fist placement again," Rune mumbled.

"We have the punching bag in the garage. We'll work on it," Dad said as he made notes to himself on the phone. Apparently, me taking more self-defense classes and adding additional security to the house was only the tip of the iceberg when it came to my dad doing what he did best.

Planning my life so that he could keep his children safe.

"He broke a window and came through the house. That's how he got in. But you guys are going to put up a security system at the small house, and the owners understand, and everything is going to be okay. I'm fine. He didn't even cut me."

Mom's arms tightened. "Let's not talk about the knife when I feel like I'm going to throw up."

"Okay. Okay. But the good thing is I took care of myself."

"I should have been there."

I pulled away from my mother, ignoring her sound of protest, and stomped towards Callum.

"You should be sitting. Or lying down," he said.

"I will be lying down soon. When everybody leaves, I can go to bed. But Callum... He said he was working with somebody and found a way to mess with your brewery. He wanted you away from me. It's not your fault."

"I should have had one of my team members handle it."

"You're the boss. You wouldn't have let anyone else handle it. You made sure she was in the house. It's not your fault," Rune snapped.

I looked over at my brother and realized though he

was scared out of his wits, he was reassuring his best friend at the same time.

Maybe we weren't exactly figuring out how to deal with my dating Callum, but he was still Callum's best friend.

They were going to make this work.

Just like I was going to ensure that my family knew I was safe.

Before I could say anything, though, there was a knock on the door, and Rune went to answer it, even though it was Callum's house.

"Sorry I'm late," Bodhi said with a growl as he moved forward.

"Window's fixed, the house is safe. I have a friend who owns a security company down in Denver, and they'll be up tomorrow to fix everything up. Don't worry."

I sighed, then moved towards Bodhi. When I opened up my arms, hesitant that he would actually want to hug me back, he surprised me by pulling me tightly to him.

He kissed the top of my head and let out a sigh. "Let's not do that again, okay? I don't like to see my brother looking scared as shit."

"I'll try not to. Nearly getting kidnapped doesn't really sound like a fun thing."

"Maybe don't joke about that," Bodhi mumbled as Callum cursed under his breath and continued to pace.

With a sigh, I pulled away and realized that if I

wanted to get some sleep, I was just going to have to do it and ignore the others.

"Okay. I'm going to bed. I'm really okay. Yes, I'm going to be freaked out for a little while, but Bradley is behind bars, all the charges in the world will be pressed, and his father isn't going to try to get him out of it."

"His father tried to put his son on the right path before and failed," my dad corrected. "He's not going to fail this time."

"Well, you did threaten to bury me in the backyard somewhere, so we'll do that to him if I ever see his scrawny little neck again." Callum gave me a look.

My dad snarled. "Or if I see any of the four LS again."

I nodded tightly. "It might not have been all of them, but at least two of them were egging him on in this. I don't know what I did to annoy them other than just existing. But I'm done with them. I have my family here. I have my friends. I'm fine. I just want to go to bed."

"Now go to bed." My mother was there then and kissed my temple. "We're leaving, and you and Callum can go to bed, and he'll make sure you're fine. You sleep well, okay?"

"I don't know if I really want to just leave so that she's sleeping in Callum's bed," Rune mumbled.

"I don't want to think about that," Dad said with a sigh.

But Rune's lips twitched anyway, and then my family

was gone, taking Bodhi with them, and I stood there in front of Callum, just wanting to be in his arms.

"I'm really okay."

"It's going to take me a little while to get there. And Felicity? Somebody helped him. Somebody knew exactly what to do to fuck with my brewery. So you're going to have to bear with me for a little while until we find out what happened."

I nodded and wrapped my arms around his waist. It took a moment, and then he was holding me, and I could finally let myself relax in his embrace.

"Let's go to sleep, little flower. Because I'm never letting you go."

I kissed his chest and finally let myself just breathe.

If only for the moment.

"I wish you would just stay home. Maybe behind four alarms, where your family can watch you?" Callum posed it as a question, and I just shook my head.

"Really? You truly believe that I would be at home right now when you're having a huge bottle day event?"

Callum sighed and then kissed the top of my head. I ignored the odd looks from people who were either just now realizing Callum and I were seeing each other or still confused as to why we were.

"Hey, Callum, can you come over here for a minute? I

need to ask you a few questions thanks to the damn pump."

Callum pinched the bridge of his nose. "Just stay in sight of Rune and the others for the rest of the day. Okay? I know I sound like an asshole. But, well, your lip is still swollen, and I know it hurts whenever you kiss me. Okay?"

I smiled at him, trying to look reassuring, but instead, I just winced. His eyes narrowed, and I went on with a sigh. "I'll be good. I'll either be in your office or surrounded by people that we know and love the entire time. I promise. I'm not going to let any one of us get hurt, okay?

"Okay."

He kissed the other side of my mouth where the cut didn't hurt, and we both ignored the wolf-whistling before he went off to help one of his staff, and I went to Bodhi's side. The fact that Bodhi was here at all surprised me.

Another true crime documentary podcast had come out, and Bodhi's name had been thrown into the muck again. Now, people were remembering what they had thought about him all those years ago, and even strangers would come to town, knowing his name.

But it was Bodhi, and I wasn't going to let anyone hurt him either.

"Okay, where do you need me?" I asked.

Bodhi raised a brow. "Preferably behind some caged wall, so Callum stops freaking the fuck out."

I rolled my eyes. "Did you guys plan on saying nearly the same thing?"

"Maybe. He's just worried about you." Bodhi let out a breath. "Watching someone you love get hurt? Knowing you can't do anything about it and—"

He cut himself off, and I reached out without thinking and gripped his arm. The burn scars underneath my palm startled me for a moment, but I didn't let go. Instead, I just squeezed him reassuringly and looked up at the line forming.

"Let's get these beers out. People are going to love the red ale."

"Because it's yours," he mumbled. And I was grateful he seemed okay with my touch, even if for just that instant.

We sold out of the seasonal packs within an hour, apparently hitting a new record for Ashford Brews. I couldn't help but grin at how wonderful the company was doing. Callum was making a name for himself, and it had nothing to do with him being an NFL player. I was so damn proud of him.

By the time we went to work on the rest of the inventory, my feet hurt, and I was grinning so widely that the cut in my lip ached, not that I would tell anybody that. I just relished the fact that Callum was great at what he did.

Everybody seemed happy. Even if they didn't get exactly what they wanted, nobody left empty-handed. That just told me how organized the whole staff had been. Even with the unexpected issues, thanks to the break-in, they had fixed everything up, and it was as if nothing had happened.

Though if you had asked Callum, no one would ever forget what had happened. I wouldn't. I was still just excited to be here.

"Hey, Teagan, do you know where the extra boxes are?" Rune asked, a frown on his face.

Teagan looked up from her phone, where she had been texting rapidly, her eyes wide, and shook her head.

"What?"

"The boxes?

"Oh, they're in the back. I'm dealing with a stupid distributor issue. I'm sorry."

"I've got it," I said, since my hands were empty. "That corner, right?"

"Yes, but are you sure you should be going alone?" Teagan asked, and I narrowed my gaze.

"Not you, too."

"Just stay in sight of people, okay?"

"I will. I promise. I don't want that to happen again."

"Because it won't," Rune growled.

However, I was the only one with my hands free to actually go get the boxes. So I made my way down the hall, in clear view of everyone, and walked into the storage area.

I went to my tiptoes, angling for the boxes, wishing I knew where the damn step stool was, when the door snicked closed behind me.

Crap.

I leaned back down, looked at the closed door, and really hoped it would open from the inside. If it didn't, I was going to have to deal with the razzing from the rest of the group for far too long.

I moved forward, only a little worried that the door wouldn't open when I accidentally stepped on a piece of glass.

Frowning, I looked down and realized there was far more glass than I had thought.

And I looked up and realized the window had been broken. Again.

I opened my mouth to shout and ran towards the door.

But when a large body slammed into me, my head hit the concrete.

And then there was nothing.

CHAPTER 19

Callum

I nearly dropped the case of beer at Rune's words and narrowed my gaze at him.

"Are you serious right now?"

Rune just grinned. "No. Maybe. You guys look good. Settled. And the fact that I know that she's never truly alone and will be safe with you around helps me sleep better at night." He blinked at me before sighing. "She was an oops baby. If you ask Mom and Dad, that's what they say because it makes Felicity laugh. None of us were planned. We just showed up, surprised the hell out of our parents, and stayed."

I snorted. "You know that's the same with my folks."

Rune frowned. "You never talk about your mom. You know that, right?"

"I do with Felicity." I paused. "Maybe because it's Felicity and the fact that she has the same job my mom did. But I talk about her with Felicity. She's been gone for over two decades. And I still don't believe that she just fell. Nor do I believe that my stepmom just left town and never turned back."

"I hate your dad. More than anything. And that's saying something because a lot of people piss me off in this town."

"Well, I hope I'm not the one pissing you off anymore." I paused and set the case down. "I'm sorry. I'm sorry for lying and not telling you about me and Felicity."

"You didn't lie. You just didn't tell me. Which, I guess, is something different."

"Still, I should have at least told you. I don't want to say I should've asked for permission because I won't ask permission when it comes to her. I'm sorry."

"I think if you tried to ask permission, Felicity would kick us both in the balls."

"We'd deserve it."

My lips twitched even as I let out a breath.

"I love her."

Rune shook his head, even as I realized I hadn't truly said the words out loud before.

"I didn't mean to. Didn't mean to fall. But I'm there now. And I don't want to go back."

"Don't. I know we say things and warn each other about things like, if you hurt her, I'll kill you, but I don't think you will. You deserve happiness, Callum. After everything that happened with Georgia and with your dad and your family. With Malcolm..." He let his voice trail off as we each took a deep breath.

"It's hard for me to focus sometimes, knowing that I don't have a good answer for why I feel the way that I do. Or how I'm supposed to fix this shit."

"You don't have to fix everything. You know that, right?"

"Don't I? I'm the eldest. It's my job."

"Well, I can tell you that the more pressure you put on yourself as the eldest, the more likely you're going to fuck it up."

"That brings me so much joy," I said wryly.

"It's the truth. The fact that you talk to Felicity about your mom? That's huge. You only mention her to me when you're drunk or when you don't realize that you're saying it."

"I seriously miss my mom. I miss the way that she took care of us, even when I would hate her a little bit for not leaving. Which just makes me feel like an asshole."

"Your dad wasn't always bad. You know that."

I ran a hand over my chest, holding back a growl. "No. He wasn't. We had some good times when we were younger. That's why we ended up with so many siblings. But then he started drinking, and he didn't stop."

"I'll hate him forever for what he did to your family. But he doesn't matter. He can't matter. If you want to move on and try to find happiness here, albeit with my baby sister, you're going to have to push him from your mind."

"Easier said than done when he lurks around like a fucking weirdo."

"His liver has to give out sometime."

"I hear we're talking about Dad?" Bodhi said as he came forward, rubbing his shoulder where I knew the burn scars were the worst.

"Is it sad that you're right?" Teagan asked, barking a laugh. "What a family we make."

"I don't know. You let me be an asshole in the woods, and you only sometimes force me into family events like these. We're not all bad."

"I guess you're right." I ran my hand over my chest. "You ever miss Mom?" I blurted while Rune froze at my side.

Bodhi tilted his head, studying me. "Every damn day. I miss the way that she would take care of us and teach us to take care of ourselves. But it's been a long damn time, Callum. And we've gone through way worse hell since. Which is saying something."

"I didn't mean to bring her up. Damn it." I ran my hand over my face. "Sorry. It's just with that asshole coming at Felicity, it's just making me think about everything. You know?"

"Have you told that girl that you love her yet?" Bodhi asked.

"He hasn't. He's going to soon, though, because he just blurted it at me. So it'll come out eventually."

"I don't know if I should really be listening to romantic advice from either of you."

I realized I shouldn't have said that to Bodhi, but then my brother just smiled.

"You really shouldn't have. I have no idea what to do with women. I just got lucky the first time."

"And I'm not lucky at all. Though, why do I need to settle down, right? Are you ready to call it quits and settle down fully?" Rune asked, glaring at me.

"Can you give me a minute to just figure out what the hell Felicity and I want? We're still dealing with the glares of this small town."

"You're going to be dealing with those glares forever," Bodhi put in. "Trust me."

"It's a small town, and your name is Ashford. It comes with the territory." Rune shook his head. "Okay, I've got to get back to the bar and grill. You have everything taken care of here, though?"

I nodded. "Thanks for coming. Seriously. I don't think I could handle these big events without you or the rest of the family."

"Well, I am the linchpin for this friend group. Oh, Gray and Atlas should be back in town soon. You good with hosting something here? We always have it at Summit Grill, but it's time for you to take over the reins."

I let out a rough chuckle. "Sure. I'll throw them a

welcome party. Or maybe I'll make Felicity do it. She's better at that shit than me."

"I'm sure Teagan will like not having to plan something since you always make her do it. Though it kind of feels kind of sexist, doesn't it?" Bodhi asked.

I flipped them both off. "It's not sexist when they're the ones that actually know what they're doing. I mean, I'll get it done. But I'll earn a few favors out of Felicity along the way."

Rune threw his hand up in the air. "And on that note, I'm done."

"Hey, before you go, did Felicity come back with the boxes yet? That's what I was looking for when I came back here, and I didn't mean to get into this serious talk."

I stared at Bodhi, an uneasy feeling settling over me.

"She isn't with you?"

"What boxes?"

I was moving past them before they even finished speaking, my pace picking up with them on my tail.

Teagan sat at the front bar, helping with final orders, and she smiled at me.

"Hey." Her face drained of color as she stared at us. "What's wrong?"

"Where's Felicity?" I asked, my hands damp.

"She was just getting boxes. She hasn't come back yet?"

"Fuck."

"What's going on?" Thatcher asked as he came

through the front doors in uniform. "The sheriff wanted me to stop by. He had some news and wanted to tell us all. Why are you stressing?"

I couldn't think about that right now. Things were finally starting to click.

The fact that somebody had broken in once before. Damaged my truck. They knew my brewery despite me keeping them out. Somebody who had helped Bradley distract me, knowing exactly what to do.

"Fuck."

I ran to the back hall closet, threw open the door, and nearly fell to my knees at the sight of broken glass and blood on the floor.

"Call the cops. The sheriff. Everybody. I think Dad has her."

"What?" Rune asked, shoving me to the side. "Why the fuck would your dad have her?"

"Because he loves tormenting my family. And he doesn't like the fact that I keep trying to figure out what the hell he did with our moms."

"I'm calling now," Thatcher snapped as he started to give out orders. But I ignored them. Instead, I followed the blood trail, everyone going in different directions, searching for Felicity. All I could do was move towards the back, past the emergency exit door that was propped open, bile coating my tongue.

My father kept popping up around town, haunting me, and annoying the hell out of the rest of our siblings.

He kept talking trash about Felicity, his focus on her, and I had left her alone. Again. It didn't matter that she should have been safe. My dad had been a fucking locksmith. Of course, he had found a way in.

Yes, it could have been someone else. She could have fallen and been dizzy trying to find her way for help, but no, in the bottom of my gut, I knew it had to be someone else.

Footsteps sounded behind me, and Bodhi was at my side.

"Come on, you don't know tracking for shit."

"Where the hell would he take her?"

"This way."

My brother ducked his head, following the trail, and I let him lead, knowing that Bodhi could find anyone.

After all, he'd done things I wouldn't even dream of before the world had changed.

I swallowed hard, trying not to imagine exactly what was happening right now. Felicity had to be okay. I would kill the old man. I wouldn't even flinch at using the hands he had given me to strangle the life out of him.

"There. I think she's at the creek."

We ran, not caring about the sound we made, as the first scream echoed through the air.

I kept running, my pace increasing as I ignored each tree and limb slamming into me, the vines catching my shirt, leaving gouges on my arms.

And then I burst through the clearing as my dad stood

there at the creek side, knife in hand, and the blade pressing against Felicity's throat.

"Took you long enough."

"I'm fine, Callum. Don't do what he says." Felicity screamed as he dug the knife ever so deeper, and a thin line of blood welled.

"Get your fucking hands off her. You want to deal with me? You deal with me. You don't touch her."

"Why should you get everything you want? You're just a little know-nothing piece of shit who won't leave the past alone. Do you know that every time you get pissed off at me in town, the sheriff and all his little buddies question me? They won't let me just breathe. No, they have to blame every single fucking thing that happens in this town on me. Well, I didn't do it. I didn't hurt your precious Felicity, this little cunt, before. No, it was that little rich boy who wanted her. I just told him how to get her. It's not my fault."

I took a step forward, hands fisting, but Bodhi held me back. I wanted to swipe out, hating him at that moment, but with every step I moved, the closer to insanity my father became. And Felicity was already bleeding.

"Just let her go. I'll stop. Just let her go."

I'd do anything. Anything. But I had no idea what my father wanted. What the hell was he thinking? He wasn't going to get out of this. All I knew was that I was going to throw up if something didn't happen soon.

"Oh? You'll stop now? You always were a little bitch. I

just can't live my life in this town. We used to own this town. My father's father and all those before him—we owned this fucking town. And every time you harass me, or you treat me like shit, you just bring the Ashford name down again. No, I'm not the fucking murderer in this family. He is."

Bodhi froze at my side, and at that moment, I wanted to reach out and kill my father all over again for daring to hurt his son. I didn't care what he did to me. But this man continued to hurt my family. Those I loved. And it was over. It had to be.

"Let her go, Dad. This is between you and me."

"It's really not. Do you want to know the truth? Since you've already defamed me? I didn't kill your stepmom. That bitch ran away because she couldn't handle all of you. She thought she wanted to be a mommy, but Julie Ashford was *no one*. She couldn't handle it. And so I roughed her around a few times, but she deserved it. It's not my fault that she was going around the curve too quickly in her car. She was trying to take you away from me. All of you. She was trying to get custody, and she was nothing but a fucking whore who wasn't even good in bed. She killed herself by going off the road that day. How dare she try to take away my kids? Mine. Not hers."

Felicity's eyes widened as I tried to remember exactly what had happened nearly fourteen years ago.

Our stepmom had been trying to take us? To save us from this asshole?

I might've been an adult by then, but I wasn't old enough to raise those kids on my own. I tried, though. Teagan and I had tried so hard, and she hadn't left us. Our stepmom hadn't left us.

I would feel relief at that, and sorrow, but later. Right now, I could only stare at the man who called himself our father and wonder exactly when he had turned into a monster.

"Your mom, though? Here's a little secret. She was trying to go away too. Trying to leave me. Take our kids. But she didn't get to do that. She took my name, so I took her. Right around here, you know. This is where your mom died, where I shoved a little too hard." He let the knife fall slightly, gripping Felicity's shoulder as he shook her, and everything slammed into me at once.

I had been right. He'd killed our mom. He'd shoved her hard enough for her to hit her head on the rock, and she drowned. Only a couple of hundred feet from where we stood now.

Everything slowed to a crawl as the past consumed me.

My mom's laugh. The way she'd kiss the bruise on my knee when I fell off my bike. Or how she'd hold my siblings and sing to them so they'd fall asleep. Or the way she'd throw herself in front of us when Dad started to drink.

The blood drained from my face as I tried to come to

terms with what he was saying, even as it sounded as if Bodhi had been punched in the chest.

"Just let her go."

"Never." He waved the knife around, and everything happened at once.

Felicity shoved her elbows back, ramming them into my dad's gut, and as my dad tried to swing the knife, she ducked and rolled right into the creek.

"Felicity!"

I ran, ignoring the pain in my chest and the idea of what the hell had just happened, and just moved. At this point of the creek, it was more of a river than anything, just deep enough for her head to go under the water.

I tried to shove past my dad, but he didn't care. He pushed at me, his fist flying out. I ducked and slammed my fist into his shoulder. He growled, swiping his arm out, the knife nearly slicing into my flesh. I twisted to the side, trying for his arm, but he had a knife, and I had nothing but my hands and wits.

Fiery pain ricocheted up my arm as the blade slid along my forearm. I let out a hiss, shoving my arm into his chest. But then my father moved again, going for Felicity. I didn't think, didn't breathe. I just punched out, landing a blow on his chin. His head flew back, but he rotated quickly, his arm coming at me even as I shifted to the left. When he shoved the knife into my side, I gasped, taking him by the neck and shaking.

"Fuck you," I bit out, my vision going hazy.

"Bastard. Just like your mother."

I shoved my father, knocking him to the side, even as my knees began to give out. I cursed through the pain and leaned toward the horror that called himself an Ashford.

Felicity's head tore through the surface as she swam towards us, her eyes wide, even as blood trickled down her neck.

"Callum!"

Blood seeped down my side, but even as I went numb, I slammed my fist into my dad's face.

But then Felicity was coming towards me, and my dad's body was ripped from my arms. The knife glistened in the sunlight once again. But Bodhi was there, shoving my father out of the way as I fell back, and Felicity was at my side, bleeding, wet, and holding me.

"Callum. Callum. Oh my God. We need to call 911. You're bleeding."

"It's not that bad," I whispered, knowing it *was* probably that bad.

I pulled Felicity towards me, even as she tried to staunch the bleeding, and then there was silence, an eerie silence as my father stopped shouting.

And Bodhi stood there, blood on his arms, covering the burn scars, as our dad lay crumpled over his own knife, still in death, and no longer the ghost that haunted us with every waking moment.

"Oh my God. It's going to be okay. It's going to be

okay," she whispered as lights began to dim behind my eyelids, and I tried to say anything. Something.

"I love you," I whispered.

"No, you don't. You don't get to say you love me as you're bleeding out in my arms. Fuck that. I saved myself, you know. And I'm going to keep doing that in case this town decides to continue to come at me. But you don't get to leave me."

"I love you," I whispered, this time the words a little breathier.

"I love you, too, Callum Ashford. And you better be okay. Damn it. You better be okay."

Footsteps sounded behind us as sirens and other voices echoed throughout the trees, but I just kept my eyes on Felicity's, and I let out a breath.

And then there was nothing.

CHAPTER 20

Callum

"What do you mean, Fiona married a millionaire and moved out of town?" Rune practically screamed from the kitchen.

"Just what I was saying. Apparently, one of the regular tourists who comes in twice a month took a liking to her, and he didn't only like her pies," Mrs. Carter said as she finished plating yet another plate of vegetables, cheese, and other snacks for Felicity and me.

I lay on the Carter family couch, sore but not as bad off as everybody thought I would be and healing.

A few stitches and a minor bleed-out, but I was fine.

The knife hadn't even nicked an artery or an organ. Felicity's gash on her neck hadn't required stitches, and the one on her head had sealed up quite quickly. We both were a little tender and a little sore and weren't allowed to do anything other than sit on this couch for the next week.

That meant one day soon, I would be bending her over one of our couches and sliding deep into her because it had been too long.

All I wanted to do was hold her close, have her ride my cock, and both of us remember exactly why we were here.

Felicity, leaning against my chest while avoiding the stitches at my side, turned over her shoulder to glare at me. "Excuse me. I can feel exactly what you're thinking about."

I shifted slightly, my now rock-hard dick pressing into her lower back.

"I'm sorry. I can't help it. Your pussy is so close, and yet I'm not allowed to touch it."

"Freak," she whispered as she sighed, leaning against me. "Let me know if I hurt you."

"You could never hurt me, Felicity." I kissed her shoulder and held her close. "I love you."

"I love you too."

"Mom, they're doing it again," Atlas whined.

Atlas had taken off two games, and the backup goalie, the hotshot kid who continued to threaten to take Atlas's place, was doing a damn good job.

I had a feeling that if Atlas wasn't careful, it wasn't going to be the hotshot rookie breaking his heart, but Felicity breaking something on her brother's body if he didn't go back to Portland soon.

The hovering was getting a little ridiculous.

"So what's going to happen to the bakery?" Sterling asked.

The entire Ashford clan, including Briar and her husband and child, who'd flown in the day before, were inside the Carters' house.

My house was bigger, but the Carters wanted their baby and their practically adopted baby underneath their roof, and I wasn't going to complain.

Much.

For long.

I would be sleeping in my own bed tonight. Despite what they thought. And Felicity would be next to me. Even if I couldn't touch her. Dammit.

"Bronwyn bought it."

I blinked up at Teagan, confused. "What? How do you know that?"

"Because Bronwyn's a friend. She bought the whole building. I don't know how, but she did. And she's going to change the name and everything."

"Oh thank God, because telling people that Ashy Buns is a good bakery breaks my heart every time," Mrs. Carter said with a laugh.

"Well, I'm just glad that it seems like Fiona will no longer be bothering us." Finnian looked down at his phone and cursed. "Hey, big bro. I love you. I'm glad you're doing okay. You, too Felicity, but I need to go pick up the girls. Promise and Keely have a big event at the bed and breakfast today, and their grandparents can't watch them for long. I have to go do the whole dad thing."

"Go. Stop hovering. I'm fine," I said for probably the hundredth time.

"I'm fine too. Give those babies my love," Felicity said. Finnian leaned down, kissed Felicity on the cheek, and gave me a wink.

I held back a growl, only because I knew Finnian was fucking with me. But seriously, how annoying.

"I should head out too. I'm opening tonight." Sterling slid his phone into his back pocket, kissed Felicity on her other cheek, and flipped me off.

"Stop getting hurt. Both of you. My nerves can't handle it."

I shook my head and leaned back as Sterling and Finnian headed out.

Teagan and Briar left as well, with Briar's husband and baby in tow, after ensuring that we were all taken care of, and finally the noise started to die down. Yes, the Carters were loud as hell, but the Ashfords were a little louder.

Of course, there was one Ashford that wasn't here. But I didn't know how I was going to get him to come back unless I found a way to get off this couch and help my brother.

I needed to get healthy so I could do so, because it was killing me.

Because of all people in our family to have been part of that? Bodhi was the worst.

Because our father had fallen on his own knife. He had tripped and fallen while trying to kill us all and ended up burying the knife in his own chest.

Bodhi hadn't done it.

But that didn't stop the townsfolk from whispering. The same townsfolk who had whispered the same words about Bodhi's family.

As soon as I was able to, I was going to walk down the town street and glare at anybody who dared talk about my brother.

I already knew the rest of the Ashfords and the Carters were doing the same.

Because fuck anyone who blamed Bodhi for what happened.

No, all of this was on Matthew Ashford's shoulders.

May he never rest in peace.

The man was dead. We weren't mourning him. No, we were mourning what could have been.

Because now we all knew the truth. About both women who had tried their best to protect their children.

Both women who were no longer here.

And thankfully Matthew Ashford was now burning in hell.

"Okay, now, I want to make sure you all get enough fiber and protein. You're going to need it to heal."

"I'm fine Mom. I'm not even bruised," Felicity said.

"Make sure she eats enough protein," I warned Mrs. Carter and winked. "Because she never eats enough."

"I eat just fine, thank you." Felicity gave me a look that I had a feeling had nothing to do with food, and I was grateful that we had shifted so that way nobody could see my lap.

The woman that I loved was a menace, and I loved every moment with her.

"Don't worry, I'll have you both in tip-top shape soon. And then we can start planning the wedding."

I choked on a carrot and glared at the woman who thought I was just like a son to her. "Really? Really."

"What? I'm just putting it out there. I mean, it would be nice if I could at least get grandbabies at some point."

"Mom. Seriously?"

"I'm just kidding. I'm really just kidding."

Mr. Carter sighed and picked his wife up, carrying her like a newlywed.

"I'm kidnapping my wife. Rune, you go drive these two back over to his place. It's time they have space for themselves without us hovering."

"Have I ever told you how much I love you?" I said with a laugh.

"Oh, I'm sure you do. However, we all know that you're just going to go rest, because nothing is going to be happening underneath that roof. Do you hear me?" he snarled.

"I am loving this," Rune said with a grin. "Because the more they hover over you, the less they hover over me."

"We have enough hovering for the both of you." Mrs. Carter waved. "Actually, all of you get out. It's time for mommy and daddy time."

"And on that note, let's head out," Rune said quickly as I threw my head back and laughed, ignoring the twinge at my side.

By the time we got to my place, Rune left us with a two-finger salute, and I found myself standing in the entryway, albeit a little sore, with Felicity in my arms.

"Hi there."

"I can't believe they left us alone."

"Why are you whispering?" I asked, holding back a laugh.

"Because I feel like if I say that out loud, they're just going to show up at any moment. And then I'll never get rid of them."

"Your family is pretty amazing," I said after a moment.

"Your family is too."

I froze before pushing her hair back from her face. "My family tried to kill you."

"Your dad isn't family. Not to speak ill of the dead, but I hate that man. He was never your father. Not in the truest sense of the word. Your family is who you've created, and that includes the Carters, the siblings you've practically raised, and people like Gray and Kellan and Thatcher. Our friends. We're creating our own family in this small town of ours, and that's all that matters. Well, that and the fact that I love you."

"I love you so fucking much. I never expected you. I was afraid to even want you."

"I never thought you'd see me. Not that way. I'm so glad that you did."

"I blame the tiny shorts."

"Well if it helps, I'm wearing a long dress right now, but I forgot the tiny shorts underneath."

I froze before slowly running my hands up and down her ass.

"Are you not wearing panties right now?" I growled. "The doctor said I'm not allowed to touch you like that."

"No the doctor said you're not allowed to thrust or move or hurt yourself at all. So don't worry, I'll take care of myself, and then I'll be very gentle with you. I asked the doctor. I'm allowed to do that."

I closed my eyes and counted to ten. "Are you serious right now?"

"I'll be gentle. I promise. This is what happens when you're with a younger woman. I have tons of energy."

"Okay little brat. I'm not that old. I just have a slight knife wound."

That sobered her up and I wanted to kick myself.

"You saved me. Twice. I never want to be a damsel again."

"Baby, you saved yourself. More than once. All I did was come and clean up the pieces. You're so damn strong and I love you. But I never want you to be in a position where I have to do that again."

"Deal. I promise, I'll be safe and I'll be good and we're going to take this town by storm. And fuck what anyone else thinks."

"Exactly. My dad's gone." I ran my hand over my chest, confused. "He's gone forever. It's just us left. Finnian's girls and Briar's daughter are going to grow up in a world where they don't have to deal with the poison that is my dad."

"So if anything good could come out of the horrendousness of that memory, it's that. You can make your own legacy now. You don't need to worry about whatever that man would do or think."

"Brewing beer, taking care of this family, and loving you? It's a pretty damn good legacy. Nothing like I thought it would be."

"Life throws curveballs that change it all. But I'm so proud of you, Callum Ashford. And I cannot wait to see what happens next."

I leaned down and took her lips.

"As long as I allow myself to be with you? That's all that matters."

And I held her close, damning what the doctor said, and finally just let myself be.

I was never supposed to love Felicity Carter. Never supposed to crave her.

But she was mine and I was never letting her go. And I knew the town would just have to get over whatever they felt about it. And I had a feeling this was only the beginning.

CHAPTER 21

Bodhi

The hoppy brew slid down my tongue, and I swallowed, doing my best to hide in the shadows. It was where I needed to be, because if I stepped foot into that light once again, I'd catch the attention of others. I was done doing that. I didn't need the light of whatever harpy needed to stare at me.

I liked my brother's brewery. Hell, it was one of my favorite places to be. It was slightly out of the way, though sometimes a little too peopley for me. I much preferred my cabin in the woods. It took a four-wheel drive drunk to traverse the mountain roads, so I rarely had to deal with strangers. But the brewery wasn't that bad. After all, they needed to be near some form of civilization to actually get customers in for events like this.

Callum made damn fine beer, and with the way that he was practically beaming over at Felicity, he looked like a completely different man.

I ran my hand over my chest and took another sip of my beer. I knew that look. I knew it happened when you found that one person that was everything for you, and you knew that no matter what occurred or came at you, you would weather through it because you would have each other. And you'd face the future, waiting for whatever happened next.

But what happened when that person wasn't there anymore? What happened when the weathering took its toll, and took them along with it?

I downed the rest of the beer, put the bottle on one of the side tables, and reached for another one. I could have two, along with some water, and be fine to drive. But I wasn't sure I could handle this many people for long.

It might have been an event to celebrate Felicity and Callum making a go of it and finally being healthy after all the shit that had come at them recently, and while I knew nearly every single person in this building, it was still too much.

And how much of a wimp and a dick did that make me?

Disgusted with myself, I popped the top on the other beer bottle and took a big gulp.

I was a pussy, and everyone knew it.

Although what was that saying? Why was weakness called being a pussy. Because a pussy could take a pounding, and a dick was way too sensitive?

My lips twitched at the memory of the first time I had heard those words. The way she had practically growled them at me, leaving both of us in tears, laughing far too hard.

It bothered me that I couldn't get her off my mind. And it bothered me that she wasn't constantly there. But sometimes I had to close my eyes and drift off, letting those memories come back so I could still see her face. Still see their faces. Smiling up at me. Even when Callum had said it was just gas.

I knew when my kids smiled at me. A dad always knew.

I took another swig, wishing it was something a little harder. Why couldn't Callum distill something other than just beer. Then again, I'd probably end up like the old man, pickled and bitter and the murderer everybody thought I was.

I cursed under my breath, set the bottle down, and reached for my water. If I was going down that path, I needed more water. No good could come from the M-word.

Callum and Felicity laughed behind the bar, pulling drafts for family members as they milled about, and more town folk drifted along, some of them still judging. After all, the age gap between the two wasn't that small. In fact, the significance of it might've made other people raise their brows as much as they were. But our family was no stranger to being the talk of the town, or doing some shit that made people sneer.

My sister Briar getting married after she had gotten pregnant, well, that had just been the tip of the iceberg. My own twin died in a fiery crash that some still mumbled under their breath that it could have been drugs.

Stupid fucking people. Malcolm hadn't died of drugs. At least not on his end.

I rubbed my hand over my beard, wondering what I looked like underneath. After all, that's what Malcolm would look like. He always liked to be clean-shaven. And perhaps I'd been somewhat the same. She'd liked me with a beard and without.

But she was gone. And I was too tired to care about anyone else. I'd be the selfish asshole that people thought I was.

I ran my hand over my nose ring, twisting the hoop slightly. I always did that when I needed to get out of a certain situation, needed space. Teagan usually called me on it, but she was too busy laughing at something Finnian and Sterling were saying. Each of the twins had one of

Finnian's girls on their hips, bouncing them around and making the girls giggle.

It was like a cut straight to the heart. Bile coated my tongue.

I loved my nieces. All three of them. And when the rest of my siblings began to have kids, I would love them.

But seeing them hurt.

Because my kids were supposed to be here. My kids were supposed to be alive. And laughing and joking and giggling. My eldest was supposed to be the oldest cousin. Watching over Briar and Finnian's kids. And the baby wouldn't be a baby anymore.

I blinked away tears, pissed off that I let my mind go down that path. I needed to wall it up. To force myself to just breathe, because if I didn't, I would hurt those kids.

And I refused to do that.

"Wait. I know you." A stranger blinked at me, her bright red hair flowing around her face as she leaned into one of the townspeople that I couldn't name.

"Hmm?" I said, not bothering to do anything.

"Wait, you're not him. Because he's dead right? That drummer of that one band. But no, I know you." She snapped her fingers. "Oh, you're that guy. Who they thought killed his wife and kids? But they ended up being wrong. Right?"

The room went silent as the drunk girl teetered on her heels.

"Sorry man," the nameless townsperson muttered,

and I set my water down, letting the ice shiver down my spine. It was better than the flames that had once licked there. The scars on my body twitched, a stamped memory of my failures.

"What the fuck man?" Sterling whispered as he tugged the guy away, hopefully taking the girl with them.

And now here I was, the center of fucking attention, and all I wanted to do was get out of here. Why did people have to fucking be here?

"Bodhi," Teagan said as she came forward, hand outstretched.

I shook my head, drained my water, and turned on my heels. I knew where the back exit was. Hell, I always knew where the exits were.

I didn't need their pitying stares or their judgments. Because nearly every fucking person in that room who was not related to me by blood or by heart, had believed. They called me a murderer. They called me my father's name.

And they hadn't even for a second thought that maybe somebody else had done it.

I bumped into a hard wall of muscle as I turned the corner and looked into Thatcher's eyes. We were the same height, same build, and while Thatcher had a few scars, mine covered most of what was unseen beneath my clothes.

"Bodhi, let me walk you to your truck."

I shook my head. "I'm fine. I only had one beer and a couple sips of another. I did my peopling." I paused, a sourness filling my mouth. "Just let the others know I'm fine. Okay?"

"I'm not going to lie to them."

"Then tell them I'm shitty. I don't care. Your kids are in there. I know your parents brought them, so go hang out with them. You don't have enough time with your kids, Thatcher."

My friend winced but gave me a tight nod. After all, we used to be closer. Until he hadn't been fast enough to save my family. Just like I hadn't been.

Footsteps sounded behind me, and I knew exactly who they belonged to.

"Bodhi, son."

I just shook my head and stomped my way out the back exit.

Mr. Carter, Felicity's dad and the former fire captain, gave an audible sigh as Thatcher, the current fire captain, called after me.

But I ignored them, jumped into my truck, and headed up the mountain road where I'd find my solace.

The home I'd raised my babies in, that I'd made love to my wife in, no longer stood, but on another lot over, I'd built another cabin for myself. It wasn't large, but there was a place to sleep and a place to eat. And the barn in the back was large enough that I could do all of my work and store it. I had bought enough acreage that people wouldn't bother me, I could keep my bees, and just breathe the mountain air without having to deal with people. There were a couple other small cabins on the property, ones that I didn't use. But I guess if I ever felt like having company they could stay there. My lips twitched. Yeah, that wouldn't be happening.

I rolled down the windows and let that mountain air fill the truck cabin.

It was summer now, with the heat of a Colorado sunny day doing its thing. Though, when we were this far up in the mountains, summer wasn't exactly the same as it was down in the Mile High City.

But my bees were happy, even though keeping bees at this altitude was a technique all on its own, but I was learning.

And it was something I could do without dealing with people. It was really the best of all worlds.

I pulled into my driveway and frowned as I spotted a light off in the distance.

"What the fuck?" I mumbled under my breath.

There was a light on in the closest cabin to my place. Who the hell was squatting on my property?

I growled, jumped out of my truck, and went into my barn. I had a gun, but I wasn't going to use it. Instead, I pulled out my axe and figured I'd scare the teenager or whoever was using my cabin as a place to hook up. That had to be it. After all, the person that used to try to squat on my property was dead. And I didn't even miss the old man.

Hands fisted, I stomped my way towards the cabin. Without another word, I banged on the door, growling. "Whoever the fuck you are, get off my property."

No answer. I banged again and reached for the door handle. Unlocked. What a fucking idiot.

I slammed open the door, axe in hand, and blinked as the woman in front of me screamed bloody murder. She held up a bat, eyes wide, and when she finally quit screaming, she bared her teeth.

"A fucking axe murderer? Could you be any more cliche in the mountains?"

"Kiera?" I asked, aghast.

The light from the fire she had set even in the summer heat, not only filled the room but glinted off of her septum ring and her brow ring. She was covered in tattoos, from what skin she showed, and her eyes were swollen. So damn swollen, that I was afraid she'd not only been crying, but someone had hit her.

"What the hell are you doing here, Kiera?"

"So glad that you remembered my name." She dropped the bat, her chest heaving. "If you could maybe let go of the axe, that would be wonderful. Because you're starting to scare me."

I looked at the axe in my hand and let it fall to my side, careful of the blade. "You didn't answer my question. What the hell are you doing here?"

"Teagan said I could stay. I just need a moment. Can you let me stay?" she asked, her eyes filling with tears.

I didn't know Kiera well, but I'd never seen her cry. Not once.

And I had no idea why a world-famous, Grammy Award-winning artist, and drummer in one of the biggest rock bands in the world would be hiding in my cabin.

Yet all I could think, even with the fear on her face, was that she had taken my dead twin's place in the band.

And if my brother was alive, she wouldn't be here.

And I had no idea what the fuck I was supposed to do with that.

"Bodhi? Can I stay?"

And with no other good answer to that, I shook my head and sighed.

"Fine. But you want to tell me why you have that bruise?" I asked, my voice cutting.

And that's when Kiera West, the one woman who made my dick twitch after all these years, burst into tears.

What a great way to end this day from hell.

Don't miss the next Ashford Creek romance with Kiera & Bodhi in Crossroads.

AND IF YOU'D LIKE TO READ A BONUS SCENE, YOU CAN FIND IT **HERE.**

If you'd like to read the next Generation with the Montgomery Ink Legacy Series:
Bittersweet Promises

In the mood to read another family saga? Meet the Cage Family in The Forever Rule!

BONUS EPILOGUE

Callum

"Okay, boys. You know the rules. We have to be quiet. And we have to make sure that your mother and the others don't know where we are."

"You've got it, Dad."

I looked down at my youngest son and tried not to let my lips twitch. It was terribly difficult because seriously, Felicity and I made the best babies.

My back ached, my knees felt as if I had been kneeling in this position for far too long, but all that mattered was that I was going to win this game against the rest of the family.

My two sons were on my team, while the rest of my siblings and their families had all separated into different factions. I knew Felicity was mad as hell that she wasn't out on the field with us, but as somebody who was about to give birth any day now to our fourth, I wasn't about to let her out to play paintball.

Especially since the last time we had played, she had kicked my ass. Not that I would ever tell her that. No, it was for her health. Not because I hated losing. I had reasons. Reasons she could never know.

My lips twitched, and I nodded tightly before adjusting the hat on my second son's head. "You ready?"

"Yes, Daddy. And then can we have cake?"

I grinned and tried not to laugh, even though my shoulders shook. "Cake is always an option."

"As long as she doesn't get all of it."

I nearly rolled my eyes, because I knew who she was in this instance. They loved their little sister something fierce, but they were just as competitive as I had been with my siblings. Hell, they probably beat Felicity and her brothers in terms of competitiveness.

"Your little sister is not going to have all the cake. Your mom won't let that happen. Plus, your little sister loves you. She'll leave you a slice."

"A baby slice," my eldest said with a roll of his eyes.

I tried not to encourage their fighting, but sometimes they were just too damn cute.

"Okay, boys. Let's get going. Your Uncle Atlas wants to beat us, and we won't let him."

"Never give up," my eldest said.

"Never surrender," my second eldest added.

I rolled my eyes this time. Ever since their uncles had shown them that old movie, they couldn't stop quoting it. However, if it was going to help us beat the other Ashfords and Carters out there, we would make it work.

In the last few years, developers had created a soft pellet paint gun. Meaning even if it slapped you right against the chest, you could barely feel it. No longer would there be bruises, screaming, or crying once you got hit with the paintball. Just tons of mess. Hence why my kids were allowed to play today. They had the little goggles, helmets, and knee pads on. They looked ridiculously adorable, and I quickly snapped a few photos for Felicity. I knew she hated that she wasn't out on the field with us, but making babies took a lot out of you.

"And go," I whispered, and I watched as my two sons crawled along the ground, little butts in the air, and took a few more photos.

It was these memories that always came back to me and reminded me of all of the pain and issues we had gone through in order to get where we were.

I'd nearly lost Felicity more than once, but now we were proud parents of nearly four kids, and they were smart, well-adjusted, and rambunctious.

Perfect in every fucking way.

And completely wild.

Though in reality, all of the Ashford and Carter kids were. Not to mention the rest of our friends' kids. We were a jumbled array of infants to teenagers, and the connections had only strengthened over time.

There was a shout off in the distance, and I moved quickly, covering both kids, as Atlas came forward, paintball guns blazing.

Of course, I had to shoot him in the chest.

My best friend looked like he was ready to curse at me, until Rune tackled him to the ground and came at me.

There were shouts, giggles, and paintballs everywhere, but in the end, we lost.

Of course we lost.

Teagan grinned, lifting her chin, as she stared down at the carnage.

"Seriously?" I asked dryly.

"You act surprised. Of course I won. You should know your betters."

Bodhi leaned forward and shot her directly in the chest.

"Are you kidding me!" she called out before we all burst out laughing. I picked up both kids underneath my arms and carried them to where the rest of the family sat, food spread out everywhere.

"I see showers and baths and probably a dunk in the pool will be needed later," Felicity said dryly as I leaned forward and brushed my lips against hers.

"I can't help it. There was mud involved."

"I can see that." She looked over at our two sons and shook her head. "Wipe your faces off, please, and wash your hands. And then I have fried chicken, potato salad, and cake."

"Yay!" both boys called out as they ran over to wash their hands. I followed them, tiptoeing around my sleeping daughter as I helped each boy wash their hands and faces. They smiled up at me with little gap tooth smiles and chubby cheeks, and I still couldn't quite believe this with my life.

Honestly, I never thought I'd be a father. I never would have let myself become one. I may have started a little late in the game compared to some of my family, but Felicity had changed everything. For the better, of course.

They had strong grandparents with Felicity's parents, and enough aunts and uncles and honorary aunts and uncles to fill a football stadium. They would never know the terror of my childhood or ever wonder if they were loved. Because they would know deep down in their hearts that they were wanted, needed, and valued.

I kissed the tops of their muddy little heads and followed them back to the eating area.

Our daughter scrambled up into my lap, pressed her cute little mouth to my cheek, and then I kissed the top of her head.

"Good afternoon, pumpkin."

"Cake!" she called out, lifting both hands.

"Cake!" my boys added on, until they continued to chant the word. I looked over at Felicity as she leaned back against the tree trunk and rested her hand over her swollen belly.

"You're the one who started it."

"How is this my fault?" I asked, and she just laughed, pointing at the chicken.

"Get some protein in first, and then we can have cake."

"Cake!" my little girl squealed but did as she was told.

I moved to sit next to Felicity, and let her lean against me as we gorged ourselves on chicken, potato salad, vegetables, and indeed cake.

By the time we were full, and the rest of our family was all finished eating, we cleaned up everything and headed back to our respective homes.

We didn't always take time off like this where we could meet up in groups. As it was, not everybody had been able to come since some people had moved away from Ashford Creek, but others had come back in some cases. But in the end, we orbited each other. Because Ashford Creek was our touchstone, even if sometimes it didn't feel like it.

After I hosed down the boys, they got into their pajamas, even though it was still lunchtime, and they passed out for their naps. Our daughter joined them, never wanting to be left out, and that's how I found myself sitting on my couch, my wife's feet in my lap as I rubbed my thumbs into her arches.

"My God," she groaned, and my dick hardened.

"Keep groaning like that, and I'm going to bend you over this couch."

"I don't think I can bend that way anymore. And by the way, the last time you did that, that's how we ended up with this one." She pointed to her stomach and I just grinned.

"That was a fun afternoon."

"And evening and morning."

"Well, at least we're consistent." I shuffled her around a bit, so she now laid against me with my arm around her shoulders and over her belly.

"She's feisty today," I said as our second daughter kicked against my palm.

"She's giving me heartburn, and I think she's enjoying playing a melody on my ribs." My wife groaned and tried to rub the small of her back.

I frowned and looked down at her. "Are you in pain?"

"I've just been having back pains all day. It's been annoying, but just small ones. Nothing to worry about."

I narrowed my gaze and looked as her belly spasmed just a bit.

"That wasn't a kick. You're in labor!"

"I am not. There's no way. I've done this three other times. I wouldn't know if I was in labor."

I shook my head, knowing that we were both probably overreacting, but maybe not. I stood up quickly and brought her to her feet.

"I was just comfortable."

"Felicity, how long have you been having back pains?"

"Since last night?" she asked, her voice trailing.

Then she let out a sort of groan, and we looked down at our feet as liquid gushed between her legs.

"Your water just broke."

"Oh my God. I'm in labor."

"That's what I just said!" I called out.

"Oh my God. We're not ready. I mean, we're ready, but we're still a week early. Oh my God. What do I do?"

I cupped her face and pressed my lips hard to hers.

"We're having a baby."

She blinked up at me, eyes filling. "We're having a baby. Oh my God. Four kids? What were we thinking?"

"I'm not really thinking when I can't help but keep my hands on you."

"You're getting snipped. This is the last time."

"Anything you want," I said, knowing that while she had threatened that procedure last time, I had a feeling four would be enough for us, and I would indeed be getting snipped.

That hopefully would come later though. For now, I pressed my lips to Felicity's and sighed in to her.

"We're having a baby," I said softly.

She smiled, even as her eyes narrowed slightly in pain.

"A baby. I guess we should start the phone tree?"

"I think after all this time, we have that down."

So I called Teagan, my sister who could organize

anything, and after she finished screaming in joy, she handled the rest.

And so hours later, I found myself sitting next to my wife in her hospital bed, our daughter nestled against her in a tiny pink blanket, and feeling as if I had aged two full decades.

"That's it. No more. We are too old for this."

"Speak for yourself, old man," Felicity teased as she ran her finger along our daughter's cheek.

"I am an old man. Though you're not as spry as you used to be," I teased.

"If I hadn't just shoved an eight pound baby from my vagina, I would shift so I could kick you. Just know that kick is coming later."

I winced. "Sorry. But you're right, I am an old man."

"Our friends are on their way to becoming grandparents, and look at us with a new baby. I'm already exhausted."

"Tell me about it, but we'll get this down. I mean, we already have three perfect children. What's one more?"

She gave me a look that spoke volumes, and I threw my head back and laughed.

And that's how my siblings found me, our children amongst them, and their children with them as well.

Laughing, holding each other, and completely exhausted.

Because the woman that I had fallen for, the woman I

knew I shouldn't have, was my wife, and now the mother of our *four* children.

I hadn't been looking for a legacy, never looked for her. And yet, Felicity Carter Ashford had changed everything.

Exactly how it was meant to be.

And in accordance with our future, and the path that came forward, our youngest daughter opened her mouth and screamed, welcoming herself into the world exactly how she always intended.

Don't miss the next Ashford Creek romance with Kiera & Bodhi in Crossroads.

If you'd like to read the next Generation with the Montgomery Ink Legacy Series: Bittersweet Promises

In the mood to read another family saga? Meet the Cage Family in The Forever Rule!

A Note from Carrie Ann Ryan

Thank you so much for reading **LEGACY.**

The Ashford Creek series is quickly becoming one of my favorites. I truly cannot wait to dive deeper into this town and these families.

Yes, each Ashford is getting a book.

But they aren't all.

And yes...I have secrets too.

If you'd like to read Briar's story, you can find it in Pieces of Me!

Ashford Creek

Book 1: Legacy (Callum & Felicity)

Book 2: Crossroads (Bohdi & Keira)

Book 3: Westward (Atlas & Elizabeth)

Don't miss the next Ashford Creek romance with Kiera & Bodhi in Crossroads.

AND IF YOU'D LIKE TO READ A BONUS SCENE, YOU CAN FIND IT **HERE.**

If you want to make sure you know what's coming next from me, you can sign up for my newsletter at www. CarrieAnnRyan.com; follow me on twitter at @CarrieAnnRyan, or like my Facebook page. I also have a Facebook Fan Club where we have trivia, chats, and other goodies. You guys are the reason I get to do what I do and I thank you.

Make sure you're signed up for my MAILING LIST so you can know when the next releases are available as well as find giveaways and FREE READS.

Happy Reading!

FROM THE FOREVER RULE
ASTON

*The Cages are the most prestigious family
in Denver—at least according to the patriarch of
the Cage Family.
And the Cages have rules.
Rules only they know.*

I always knew that one day my father would die. I
hadn't realized that day would come so soon. Or that
the last words I would say to him would've been in anger.

I had been having one of the best nights of my life, a
beautiful woman in my arms, and a smile on my face
when I received the phone call that had changed my family's life.

The fact that I had been smiling had been a shock,

because according to my brothers, I didn't smile much. I was far too busy being *The Cage* of Cage Enterprises.

We were a dominant force in the city of Denver when it came to certain real estate ventures, as well as being one of the only ethical and environmentally friendly ones who tried to keep up with that. We had our hands in countless different pots around the world, but mostly we gravitated in the state of Colorado—our home.

I had not created the company, no, that honor had gone to my grandfather, and then my father. The Cage Enterprises were and would always be a family endeavor. And when my father had stepped away a few years ago, stating he had wanted to see the world, and also see if his sons could actually take up the mantle, I had stepped in— not that the man believed we could.

My brothers were in various roles within the company, at least those who had wanted to be part of it. But I was the face of Cage Enterprises.

So no, I hadn't smiled often. There wasn't time. We weren't billionaires with mega yachts. We worked seventy-hour weeks to make sure *all* our employees had a livable wage while wining and dining with those who looked down at us for not being on their level. And others thought we were the high and mighty anyway since they didn't understand us. So, I didn't smile.

But I had smiled that night.

It had been a gala for some charity, one I couldn't even remember off the top of my head. We had donated between the company and my own finances—we always did. But I couldn't even remember anything about why we were there.

Yet I could remember her smile. The heat in her eyes when she had looked up at me, the feel of her body pressed against mine as we had danced along the dance floor, and then when we ended up in the hallway, bodies pressed against one another, needing each other, wanting each other.

And I had put aside all my usual concepts of business and life to have this woman in my arms.

And then my mother had called and had shattered that illusion.

"Your father is dead."

She hadn't even braced me for the blow. A heart attack on a vacation on a beach in Majorca, and he was dead. She hadn't cried, hadn't said anything, just told me that I had to be the one to tell my brothers.

And so, I had, all six of them. Because of course Loren Cage would have seven sons. He couldn't do things just once, he had to make sure he left his legacy, his destiny.

And that was why we were here today, in a high-rise in Centennial, waiting on my father's lawyer to show up with the reading of the will.

"Hey, when is Winstone going to get here?" Dorian asked, his typical high energy playing on his face, and how he tapped his fingers along the hand-carved wooden table.

I stared at my brother, at those piercing blue eyes that matched my own, and frowned. He should be here soon. He did call us all here after all."

"I still don't know why we all had to be here for the reading of the will," Hudson whispered as he stared off into the distance. Neither Dorian nor Hudson worked for Cage Enterprises. They had stock with the company, and a few other connections because that's what family did, but they didn't work on the same floors as some of us and hadn't been elbow to elbow with our father before he had retired. Though dear old dad had worked in our small town more often than not in the end. In fact, Hudson didn't even live in Denver anymore. He had moved to the town we owned in the mountains.

Because of course we Cages owned a damned town. Part of me wasn't sure if the concept of having our name on everything within the town had been on purpose or had occurred organically. Though knowing my grandfather, perhaps it had been exactly what he'd wanted. He had bought up a few buildings, built a few more, and now we owned three-quarters of the town, including the major resort which brought in tourists and income.

And that was why we were here.

"You have to be here because you're evidently in the will," I said softly, trying not to get annoyed that we were waiting for our father's lawyer. Again.

"You would think he would be able to just send us a memo. I mean, it should be clear right? We all know what stakes we have in, we should just be able to do things evenly," Theo said, his gaze off into the distance. My younger brother also didn't work for the company, instead he had decided to go to culinary school, something my father had hated. But you couldn't control a Cage, that was sort of our deal.

"Why would you be cut out of the will?" I asked, honestly curious.

"Because I married a man and a woman," he drawled out. "You know he hasn't spoken to me since before the wedding," Ford said, and I saw the hurt in his gaze even though I knew he was probably trying to hide it.

"Well, he was an asshole, what do you expect?" James asked.

I looked behind Ford to see my brother and co-chair of Cage Enterprises standing with his hands in his pockets, staring out the window.

With Flynn, our vice president, standing beside him, they looked like the heads of businesses they were. While they wore suits and so did I, we were the only ones.

Dorian and Hudson were both in jeans, Hudson's having a hole at the knee. And probably not as a fashion statement, most likely because it had torn at some point, and he hadn't bothered to buy another pair. Theo was in slacks, but a Henley with his sleeves pushed up, tapping his finger just like Hudson, clearly wanting to get out of here as well. Ford had on cargo pants, and a tight black T-shirt, and looked like he had just gotten off his shift. He owned a security company with his husband and a few other friends, and did security for the Cages when he could, though I knew he didn't like to work with family often. And I knew it wasn't because of us. No, it was Father—even if he had officially *retired*. It was always Father.

And he was gone.

"Can't believe the asshole's gone," I whispered.

Ford's brows rose. "Look at that, you calling him an asshole. I'm proud."

"You should show him respect," Mother said as she came inside the room, her high heels tapping against the marble floors. I didn't bother standing up like I normally would have, because Melanie Cage looked to be in a *mood*.

She didn't look sad that Dad was gone, more like angry that he would dare go against their plans. What plans? I didn't know, but that was my mother.

She came right up to Dorian and leaned down to kiss his cheek. She didn't even bother to look at the rest of us. Dorian was Mother's favorite. Which I knew Dorian resented, but I didn't have to deal with mommy issues at this moment.

No, we had to deal with father issues at this point.

"I'm going to go get him," Flynn replied, turning toward the door. "I'm really not in the mood to wait any longer, especially since he's being so secretive about this meeting."

As I had been thinking just the same, I nodded at

Flynn though he didn't need my permission. However, just then, the door opened, and I frowned when it wasn't just Mr. Winstone walking into the conference room.

I stared as an older woman walked through the door following Mr. Winstone, and four women and another man with messy hair and tattered cut-up jeans that matched Hudson's walked behind them.

The guy looked familiar, as if I'd seen him somewhere, or maybe it was just his eyes.

Where had I seen those eyes before?

"Phoebe? What are you doing here?" Ford asked as he moved forward and gripped the hands of one of the women.

"I was going to ask the same question," Phoebe asked as she looked at Ford, then around the room.

Those of us sitting stood up, confused about why this other family—because they were clearly a family—had decided to enter the room.

"We're here to meet the lawyer about my father's death, Ford. Why would you and the Cages be here?" she asked, and I wondered how the hell Mr. Winstone had fucked up so badly? Why the hell was he letting another family that clearly seemed to be in shock come into our room? This wasn't how he normally handled things.

Ford was the one who answered though—thankfully —because I had no idea what the hell was going on.

"Phoebe, we're here for my dad's will reading. What

the hell is going on?" he asked. Phoebe looked around, as well as the others.

I stared at them, at the tall willowy one with wide eyes, at the smaller one with tears still in her eyes as if she was the only one truly mourning, and at the woman who seemed to be in charge, not the mother. Instead she had shrewd eyes and was glaring at all of us. The man stood back, hands in pockets, and looked just as shell-shocked as Ford.

But before Mr. Winstone or anyone else could say anything, my mother spoke in such a crisp, icy tone that I froze.

"I don't know why you're acting so dramatic. You knew your father was an asshole. He just liked creating drama," she snapped.

As I tried to catch up with her words, the older woman answered. "Melanie, stop."

This couldn't be happening. Because things started to click into place. The fact that the man at the other end of this table had our eyes, and that everybody looked so fucking shocked. I didn't know how Ford knew this Phoebe, and I would be getting answers.

"We had a deal," my mother continued, as it seemed that the rest of us were just now catching on. "You would keep your family away from mine. We would share Loren, but I got the name, I got the family. You got whatever else. But now it looks like Loren decided to be an asshole again."

"What are you talking about?" the shrewd sister asked as she came forward, her hands fisted at her side.

"Excuse me," I said, clearing my throat. I was going to be damned if I let anyone else handle this meeting. I was The Cage now. "Will someone please explain?"

"Well, I wasn't quite sure how this was going to work out," Mr. Winstone began, and we all quieted, while I wanted to strangle the man. What did he mean how *the hell this would work out*? What was this?

This seemed like a big fucking mistake.

"Loren Cage had certain provisions in his will for both of his families. And one of the many requirements that I will go over today is that this meeting must take place." He paused and I hoped it wasn't for effect, because I was going to throttle him if it was. "Loren Cage had two families. Seven sons with his wife Melanie, and four daughters and a son with his mistress, Constance."

"We went by partner," the other mother corrected.

I blinked, counting the adults in the room. "Twelve?" I asked, my voice slightly high-pitched.

"Busy fucking man," Dorian whispered.

Hudson snorted, while we just stood and stared at each other.

This could not be happening. A secret family? No, we were not that cliché.

"I can't do this," Phoebe blurted, her eyes wide.

"Oh, stop overreacting," my mother scorned.

"Do not talk to my daughter that way." The other mother glared.

"It was always going to be an issue," Mother continued. "All the secrets and the lies. And now the kids will have to deal with it. Because God forbid Loren ever deal with anything other than his own dick."

"That's enough," I snapped.

"Don't you dare talk to us like that," the shrewd sister snapped right back.

"I will talk however I damn well please. I am going to need to know exactly how this happened," I shouted over everyone else's words.

Out of the corner of my eye I saw Phoebe run through the door. Ford followed and then the tall willowy one joined.

"Shit," I snapped.

"Language," Mother bit out.

I laughed. "Really? You are going to talk to me about language."

I looked over at James, who shrugged, before he put two fingers in his mouth and whistled that high-pitched whistle that only he could do.

Everyone froze as Theo rubbed his ear and glared at me.

"Winstone," I said through gritted teeth. "I take it we all have to be here in order for this to happen?"

He cleared his throat. "At least a majority. But you all had to at least step into the room."

"Excuse me then," I said.

"You're just going to leave? Just like that?" my mother asked.

I whirled on her. "I'm going to go see if my apparent *family* is okay. Then I'm going to come back and we're going to get answers. Because there is no way that I'm going to leave here without them."

I stormed out the door, and thankfully nobody followed me.

Of course, though, I shouldn't have been too swift with that, as the woman who had to be the eldest sister practically ran to my side, her heels tapping against the marble.

"I'm coming with you."

"That's just fine." I paused, knowing that I wasn't angry at these people. No, my father and apparently our mothers were the ones that had to deal with this. I looked over at the woman who Mr. Winstone and the mothers had claimed was my sister and cleared my throat.

"I'm Aston."

"Is this really the time for introductions?" she asked.

"I'm about to go see your sister and my brother to make sure that they're fine, so sure. I would like to know the name of the woman that is running next to me right now."

"I'm running, you're walking quickly because you have such long legs."

I snorted, surprised I could even do that.

"I'm Isabella," she replied after a moment.

"I would say nice to meet you Isabella..." I let my voice trail off.

She let out a sharp laugh before shaking her head. "I'm going to need a moment to wrap my head around this, but not now."

"Same."

We stormed out of the building, and I lagged behind since Ford was standing in front of Phoebe who was in the arms of another man with dark hair and everybody seemed to be talking all at once.

"I just. I can't deal with this right now," Phoebe said, and I realized that something else must have been going on with her right then. She looked tired, and far more emotional than the rest of us.

I looked over at the man holding her and blinked. "Kane?" I asked.

Kane stared at me and let out a breath. "Wow," he said with a laugh.

"We'll handle it," Isabella put in, completely ignoring us. "And if we need to meet again later, we will." Then she looked over at Ford and I, with such menace in her gaze, I nearly took a step back. "Is that a problem?"

I raised my chin, glaring right back at her. "Not at all. However I want answers, so I'd rather not have the meeting canceled right now. But I'm also not going to force any of my," I paused, realization hitting far too hard, "*family* to stay if they don't want to."

And with that, I turned on my heel and went back into the building, with Isabella and Ford following me. Everyone was still yelling in the interim, and I cleared my throat. As Isabella had done it at the same time, everyone paused to look at me.

"Read the damn will. Because we need answers," I ordered Winstone, and he shook like a leaf before nodding.

"Okay. We can do that." He cleared his throat, then he began going over trusts and incomes and buildings and things that I would care about soon, but what I wanted to know was what the hell our father had been thinking about.

"Here's the tricky part," Winstone began, as we all leaned forward, eager to hear what the hell he had to say.

"The family money, not of the business, not of each of your inheritance from other family members, but the bulk of Loren Cage's assets will be split between all twelve kids."

"Are you kidding me?" Isabella asked. "What money? We weren't exactly poor, but we were solidly middle class."

"We did just fine," the other mother pleaded.

My mother snorted, clearly not believing the words.

I glared at the woman who raised me, willing her to say *anything*. She would probably be pushed out of the window at that point. Not by me, by someone else, but she probably would've earned it.

The lawyer continued. "However to retain the majority of current assets and to keep Cage Lake and all of its subsidiaries you will have to meet as a family once a month for three years. If this does not happen, Cage Enterprises will be broken into multiple parts and sold." He went on into the legalese that I ignored as I tried to hear over the blood pounding in my ears.

"You own a town?" the other man asked.

I looked over at the one man in the room I didn't know the name of. "Not exactly."

"Kyler," Isabella whispered.

In that moment, I realized that I had a brother named Kyler—if this was all to be believed.

"This can't be legal right?" the tall willowy person said.

"Yes Sophia, it can," their mother put in.

Oh good, another sister named Sophia.

Only one name to go. What the hell was wrong with me?

I forced my jaw to relax. "Are you telling us that we need to have all twelve of us at dinner once a month for three years in order to keep what is rightly inherited to us? To keep people in business and keep their jobs?"

"We don't need the money, but everyone else in our employ does," James snapped. "As do those we work with."

"Damn straight," Dorian growled.

"How are we supposed to believe this?" I asked, asking the obvious question.

"First, only five must attend, and two must be of a different family." The lawyer continued as if I hadn't spoken. "Of course you are *all* family..."

"Again, how are we supposed to believe this?" I asked.

"Here are the DNA tests already done."

"Are you fucking kidding me?" Isabella asked.

I looked at her, as she had literally taken the words out of my mouth.

"Isn't that sort of like a violation?" Kyler asked, his face pale.

"We need to get our own lawyers on this," James whispered.

I nodded tightly, knowing we had much more to say on this.

"There's no way this is legal," the youngest said, and I looked over at her.

"What's your name?" I asked.

"Emily. Emily Cage Dixon," she said softly, and we all froze.

"Your middle name is Cage?" I asked, biting out the words.

"All of our middle names are Cage," Sophia said, shaking her head. "I hated it but Dad wanted to be cute because our father's name was Cage Dixon, or maybe it wasn't. Is he also a bigamist?" she asked.

Her mother lifted her chin. "We never married. And no, your father's name was not Dixon, that was my maiden name."

"What?" Sophia asked. "All this time...are our grandparents even dead?"

"Yes, my parents are dead. The same with Loren's." The other mother's eyes filled with tears. "I'm sorry we lied."

"We'll get to that later," Isabella put in, and I was grateful.

I let out a breath. "In order to keep our assets, in order to keep the family name intact, we need to have *dinner*. For three years."

The small lawyer nodded, his glasses falling down his nose. "At least five of you. And it can start three months after the funeral, which we can plan after this."

"This is ridiculous," Hudson murmured under his breath, before he got up and walked out.

I watched him go, knowing he had his own demons, and tried to understand what the hell was going on. "Why did he do this?" I asked, more to myself than anyone else.

"I never really knew the man, but apparently none of us did," Isabella said, staring off into the distance.

"Leave the paperwork and go," I ordered Winstone, and he didn't even mutter a peep. Instead, he practically ran out of the room. James and Flynn immediately went to the paperwork, and I knew they were scouring it. But from the way that their jaws tightened, I had a feeling that my father had found a way to make this legal. Because we would always have a choice to lose everything. That was the man.

"It's true," my mother put in. "You all share the same father. That was the deal when we got married, and when he decided to bring this other woman into our lives."

"I'm pretty sure you were the other woman," the other mom said.

I pinched the bridge of my nose.

"Stop. All of you." I stared at the group and realized that I was probably the eldest Cage here, other than the moms. I would deal with this. We didn't have a choice. "Whatever happens, we'll deal with it."

"You're in charge now?" Isabella asked, but Sophia shushed her.

I was grateful for that, because I had a feeling Isabella and I were going to butt heads more often than not.

I shrugged, trying to act as if my world hadn't been rocked. "I would say welcome to the Cages, because DNA evidence seems to point that way, however perhaps you were already one of us all along."

Kyler muttered something under his breath I couldn't hear before speaking up. "You have my eyes," he said.

I nodded. "Noticed that too."

The other man tilted his head. "So what, we do dinners and we make nice?"

I sighed. "We don't have to be adversaries."

"You say that as if you're the one in charge," Isabella said again.

"Because he is," Theo said, and they all stared at him.

I tried to tamp down the pride swelling at those words—along with the overwhelming pressure.

Theo continued. "He's the eldest. He's the one that takes care of us. And he's the CEO of Cage Enterprises. He's going to be the one that deals with the paperwork fallout."

"Because family is just paperwork?" Emily asked, her voice lost.

I shook my head. "No, family is insane, and apparently, it's been secret all along. And it looks like we have a few introductions to make, and a few tests to redo. But if it turns out it's true, we're Cages, and we don't back down."

"And what does that mean?" Isabella asked, her tone far too careful.

Theo was the one who finally answered. "It means we're going to have to figure shit out."

And for just an instant, the thought of that beautiful woman with that gorgeous smile came to mind, and I pushed those thoughts away. My family was breaking, or perhaps breaking open. And I didn't have time to worry about things like a woman who had made me smile.

The Cages needed me and after today's meeting there would be no going back to sanity.

Ever.

In the mood to read another family saga? Meet the Cage Family in The Forever Rule!

FROM ONE WAY BACK TO ME

ELI

When my morning begins with me standing ankle-deep in a basement full of water, I know I probably should have stayed in bed. Only, I was the boss, and I didn't get that choice.

"Hold on. I'm looking for it." East cursed underneath his breath as my younger brother bent down around the pipe, trying his best to turn off the valve. I sighed, waded through the muck in my work boots, and moved to help him. "I said I've got it," East snapped, but I ignored him.

I narrowed my eyes at the evil pipe. "It's old and rusted, and even though it passed an inspection over a year ago, we knew this was going to be a problem."

"And I'm the fucking handyman of this company. I've got this."

"And as a handyman, you need a hand."

"You're hilarious. Seriously. I don't know how I could

ever manage without your wit and humor." The dryness in his tone made my lips twitch even as I did my best to ignore the smell of whatever water we stood in.

"Fuck you," I growled.

"No thanks. I'm a little too busy for that."

With a grunt, East shut off the water, and we both stood back, hands on our hips as we stared at the mess of this basement.

East let out a sigh. "I'm not going to have to turn the water off for the whole property, but I'm glad that we don't have tenants in this particular cabin."

I nodded tightly and held back a sigh. "This is probably why there aren't basements in Texas. Because everything seems to go wrong in these things."

"I'm pretty sure this is a storm shelter, or at least a tornado one. Not quite sure as it's one of the only basements in the area."

"It was probably the only one that they had the energy to make back in the day. Considering this whole place is built over clay and limestone."

East nodded, looked around. "I'll start the cleanup with this water, and we'll look to see what we can do with the pipes."

I pinched the bridge of my nose. "I don't want to have to replace the plumbing for this whole place."

"At least it's not the villa itself, or the farmhouse, or the winery. Just a single cabin."

I glared at my younger brother, then reached out and

knocked on a wooden pillar. "Shut your mouth. Don't say things like that to me. We are just now getting our feet under us."

East shrugged. "It's the truth, though. However much you weigh it, it could have been worse."

I pinched the bridge of my nose. "Jesus Christ. You were in the military for how long? A Wilder your entire life, and you say things like that? When the hell did you lose that superstition bone?"

"About the time that my Humvee was blown up, and when Evan's was, Everett's too. Hell, about the time that you almost fell out of the sky in your plane. Or when Elliot was nearly shot to death trying to help one of his men. So, yes, I pretty much lost all superstition when trying to toe the line ended up in near death and maiming."

I met my brother's gaze, that familiar pang thinking about all that we had lost and almost lost over the past few years.

East muttered under his breath, shaking his head. "And I sound more and more like Evan these days rather than myself."

I squeezed his shoulder and let out a breath, thinking of our brother who grunted more than spoke these days. "It's okay. We've been through a lot. But we're here."

Somehow, we were here. I wasn't quite sure if we had made the right decision about two years ago when we had formed this plan, or rather *I* had formed this plan, but there was no going back. We were in it, and we were going to have to find a way to make it work, flooded former tornado shelters and all.

East sighed. "I'll work on this now. Then I'll head on over to the main house. I have a few things to work on there."

"You know, we can hire you help. I know we had all the contractors and everything to work with us for some of the rebuilds and rehabs, but we can hire someone else for you on a day-to-day basis."

My brother shook his head. "We may be able to afford it, but I'd rather save that for a rainy day. Because when it rains, it pours here, and flash flooding is a major threat in this part of Texas." He winked as he said it, mixing his metaphors, and I just shook my head.

"You just let me know if you need it."

"You're the CEO, brother of mine, not the CFO. That's Everett."

"True, but we did talk about it so we can work on it." I paused, thinking about what other expenses might show up. "And what do you need to do with the villa?"

The villa was the main house where most things happened on the property. It contained the lobby, library, and atrium. My apartment was also on the top floor, so I could be there for emergencies. Our innkeeper lived on the other side of the house, but I was in the main loft because this was my project, my baby.

My other brothers, all five of them, lived in cabins on the property. We lived together, worked together, ate together, and fought together. We were the Wilder brothers. It was what we did.

I had left to join the Air Force at seventeen, having graduated early, leaving behind my kid brothers and sister. After nearly twenty years of doing what we needed to in order to survive, we hadn't spent as much time with one another as I would have liked. We hadn't been stationed together, so we hadn't seen one another for longer than holidays or in passing.

But now we were together. At least most of us. So I was going to make this work, even if it killed me.

East finally answered my question. "I just have to fix a door that's a little too squeaky in one of the guestrooms. Not a big deal."

I raised a brow. "That's it?"

"It's one of the many things on my list. Thankfully, this place is big enough that I always have something to do. It's an unending list. And that the winery has its own team to work on all of that shit, because I'm not in the mood to learn to deal with any of the complicated machinery that comes with that world."

I snorted. "Honestly, same. I'm glad there are people that know what the fuck they're doing when it comes to wine making so that didn't have to be the two of us."

I left my brother to this job, knowing he liked time on his own, just like the rest of us did, and went to dry my boots. I was working by myself for most of the day, in interviews and other "boss business," as Elliot called it, so I had to focus and get clean.

I wasn't in the mood to deal with interviews, but it was part of my job. We had to fill positions that hadn't been working out over the past year, some more than others.

Wilder Retreat was a place that hadn't been even a spark in my mind my entire life. No, I had been too busy being a career military man—getting in my twenty, moving up the ranks, and ending up as a Lieutenant Colonel before I got out. I had been a commander of a squadron, and yet, it felt like I didn't know how to command where I was now.

When my sister Eliza had lost her husband when he was on deployment, it had been the last domino to fall in the Wilder brothers' military career. I had been ready to get out with twenty years in, knowing I needed a career outside of being a Lieutenant Colonel. I wasn't even forty yet, and the term retirement was a misnomer, but that's what happened when it came to my former job.

East had been getting out around that time for reasons of his own, and then Evan had been forced to. I rubbed my hand over my chest, that familiar pain, remembering the phone call from one of Evan's commanders when Evan had been hurt.

I thought I'd lost my baby brother then, and we nearly had. Everett had gotten hurt too, and Elijah and Elliot had needed out for their own reasons. Losing our baby sister's husband had just pushed us forward.

Finding out that Eliza's husband had been a cheating asshole had just cemented the fact that we needed to spend more time together as a family so we could be there for one another.

In retrospect, it would have been nice if Eliza would have been able to come down to Texas with us, to our suburb outside of San Antonio. Only, she had fallen in love again, with a man with a big family and a good heart up in Fort Collins, Colorado. She was still up there and traveled down enough that we actually got to get to know our sister again.

It was weird to think that, after so many years of always seeing each other in passing or through video calls, most of us were here, opening up a business. And all because I had been losing my mind.

Wilder Retreat and Winery was a villa and wedding venue outside of San Antonio. We were in hill country, at least what passed for hill country in South Texas, and the place had been owned by a former Air Force General who had wanted to retire and sell the place, since his kid didn't want it.

It was a large spread that used to be a ranch back in the day, nearly one hundred acres that the original owners had taken from a working ranch, and instead of making it a dude ranch or something similar, like others did around here, they'd added a winery using local help. We were close enough to Fredericksburg that it made sense in terms of the soil and weather. They had been able to add on additions, so it wasn't just the winery. Someone could come for the day for a winery tour or even a retreat tour, but most people came for the weekend or for a whole week. There were cabins and a farmhouse where we held weddings, dances, or other events. We had some chickens and ducks that gave us eggs, and goats that seemed to have a mind of their own and provided milk for cheese. Then there was the main annex, which housed all the equipment for the retreat villa.

The winery had its own section of buildings, and it was far bigger than anything I would have ever thought that we could handle. But, between the six of us, we did.

And the only reason we could even afford it, because one didn't afford something like this on a military salary, even with a decent retirement plan, was because of our uncles.

Our uncles, Edward and Edmond Wilder, had owned Wilder Wines down in Napa, California, for years. They had done well for themselves, and when we had been kids, we had gone out to visit. Evan had been the one that had clung to it and had been interested in wine making before he had changed his mind and gone into the military like the rest of us.

That was why Evan was in charge of the winery itself

now. Because he knew what he was doing, even if he'd growled and said he didn't. Either way though, the place was huge, had multiple working parts at all times, and we had a staff that needed us. But when the uncles had died, they had left the money from the sale of the winery to us in equal parts. Eliza had taken hers to invest for her future children, and the rest of us had pooled our money together to buy this place and make it ours. A lot of the staff from the old owner had stayed, but some had left as well. Because they didn't want new owners who had no idea what they were doing, or they just retired. Either way, we were over a year in and doing okay.

Except for two positions that made me want to groan.

I had an interview with who would be our third wedding planner since we started this. The main component of the retreat was to have an actual wedding venue. To be able to host parties, and not just wine tours. Elliot was our major event planner that helped with our yearly and seasonal minute details, but he didn't want anything to do with the actual weddings. That was a whole other skill set, and so we wanted a wedding planner. We had gone through two wedding planners now, and we needed to hire a third. The first one had lied on her résumé, had given references that were her friends who had lied and had even created websites that were all fabrication, all so she could get into the business. Which, I understood, getting into the business is one thing. However, lying was another. Plus, we needed someone with actual experience because we didn't have any ourselves. We were going out on a limb here with this whole retreat business, and it was all because I had the harebrained idea of getting our family to work together, get along, and get to know one another. I wanted us to have a future, to be our own bosses.

And it was so far over my head that I knew that if I didn't get reliable help, we were going to fail.

Later, I had a meeting with that potential wedding planner. But first, I had to see what the fuck that smell was coming from the main kitchen in the villa.

The second wedding planner we hired was a guy with great and *true* references, one who was good at his job but hated everything to do with my brothers and me. He had hated the idea of the retreat and how rustic it was, even though we were in fucking South Texas. Yes, the buildings look slightly European because that was the theme that the original owners had gone for. Still, the guy had hated us, hadn't listened to us, and had called us white trash before he had walked away, jumped into his convertible, and sped off down the road, leaving us without help. He had been rude to our guests, and now Elliot was the one having to plan weddings for the past three weeks. My brother was going to strangle me soon if we didn't hire someone. And this person was going to be our last hope. As soon as she showed up, that was.

I looked down on my watch and tried to plan the rest of my day. I had thirty minutes to figure out what the hell was going on in the kitchen, and then I had to go to the meeting.

I nodded at a few guests who were sipping wine and eating a cheese plate and then at our innkeeper, Naomi. Naomi's honey-brown hair was cut in an angled bob that lit her face, and she grinned at me.

"Hello there, Boss Man," she whispered. "You might need to go to the kitchen."

"Do I want to know?" I asked with a grumble.

"I'm not sure. But I am going to go check in our next guest, and then Elliott needs to meet with the Henderson couple."

"He'll be there." I didn't say that Elliot would rather chew off his own arm rather than deal with this, considering we had a family event coming in, one that Elliot was on target with planning. The wedding for next year was an important one, so we needed to work on it.

Naomi was a fantastic innkeeper, far more organized than any of us—and that was saying something since my brothers and I knew our way around schedules, to-do lists, and spreadsheets. Naomi was personable, smiled, and kept us on our toes.

Without her, I knew we wouldn't be able to do this. Hell, without Amos, our vineyard manager, I knew that Evan and Elijah wouldn't be able to handle the winery as they did. Naomi and Amos had come with the place when we had bought it, and I would be forever grateful that they had decided to stay on.

I gave Naomi another nod, then headed back to the kitchen and nearly walked right back out.

Tony stood there, a scowl on his face and his hands on his hips. "I don't understand what the fuck is wrong with this oven."

"What's going on?" I asked as Everett stood by Tony. Everett was my quiet brother with usually a small smile on his face, only right then it looked like he was ready to scream.

I didn't know why Everett was even there since he was part responsible for the financials side of the company and usually worked with Elliot these days. Maybe he had come to the kitchen after the smell of burning as I had after Naomi's prodding.

Tony threw his hands in the air. "What's going on? This stove is a piece of shit. All of it is a piece of shit. I'm tired of this rustic place. I thought I would be coming to a Michelin star restaurant. To be my own chef. Instead, I have to make English breakfasts and pancakes with bananas. I might as well be at a bed and breakfast."

I pinched the bridge of my nose. "We're an inn, not a bed and breakfast."

"But I serve breakfast. That's all I do these days. That and cheese platters. Nobody comes for dinner. Nobody comes for lunch."

That was a lie. Tony worked for the winery and the

retreat itself and served all the meals. But Tony wanted to go crazy with the menu, to try new and fantastical items that just weren't going to work here.

And I had a feeling I was going to throw up if I wasn't careful.

"I quit," Tony snapped, and I knew right then, it was done for. I was done.

"You can't quit," I growled while Everett held back a sigh.

"Yes, I can. I'm done. I'm done with you and this ranch. You're not cowboys. You're not even Texans. You're just people moving in on our territory." And with that, Tony stomped away, throwing his chef's apron on the ground.

I was thankful that the kitchen was on the other side of the library and front area, where most of the guests were if they weren't out on one of the tours of the area and city that Elliott had arranged for them. That was the whole point of this retreat. They could come visit, and could relax, or we could set them up on a tour of downtown San Antonio, or Canyon Lake, or any of the other places that were nearby.

And yet, Tony had just thrown a wrench into all of that. I didn't know what was worse, the smell of burning, Tony leaving, the water in the basement that wasn't truly a basement, or the fact that I was going to smell like charred food and wet jeans when I went to go meet this wedding planner.

"You're going to need to hire a new cook," Everett whispered.

I looked at my brother, at the man who did his best to make sure we didn't go bankrupt, and I wanted to just grumble. "I figured."

"I can help for now, but you know I'm only part-time. I can't stay away from my twins for too long," Sandy said as she came forward to take the pan off the stove. "I wish I could do full time, but this is all I can do for now."

Sandy had come back from maternity leave after we had already opened the retreat. She had been on with the former owners and was brilliant. But she had a right to be a mom and not want to work full time. I understood that, and I knew that Sandy didn't want to handle a whole kitchen by herself. She liked her position as a sous chef.

I was going to have to figure out what to do. Again.

"I'll get it done," I said while rubbing my temples.

"You know what we need to do," Everett whispered, and I shook my head.

"He'll kill us."

"Maybe, but it'll be worth it in the end. And speaking of, don't you have that interview soon? Or do you want me to take it?" His gaze tracked to my jeans.

I shook my head. "No, help Sandy."

Everett winced. "Just because I know how to slice an onion, it doesn't mean I'm good at cooking."

"I'm sorry, did you just say you could slice an onion?

Get to it," Sandy put in with a smile, pointing at the sink. "Wash those hands."

"I cannot believe I just said that out loud. I just stepped right into it," Everett said with a sigh. "Go to the interview. You know what to ask."

"I do. And I hope we don't get screwed this time."

"You know, if we're lucky, we'll get someone as good as Roy's wedding planner, or at least that woman that we met. You know who she is." Everett grinned like a cat with the canary.

I narrowed my eyes. "Don't bring her up."

"Oh, I can't help it. A single dance, and you were drawn to her."

"What dance? You know what? No, I don't have time. We have to work on lunch and dinner. Tell me while you work," Sandy added with a wink.

Everett leaned toward her as he washed his hands. "Well, you see, there was this dance, and he met the perfect woman, and then she got engaged."

Sandy's eyes widened. "Engaged? How did that happen? She was dating someone else?" she asked as she looked at me.

I pinched the bridge of my nose. "It was at Roy's place when we were looking at the venue to see if we wanted to buy the retreat here." I sighed, I knew if I just let it all out, she would move on from this conversation, and I would never have to deal with it again. "Somehow, I ended up at a wedding there, caught the garter. This woman caught the bouquet, and she happened to be the wedding planner. We danced, we laughed, and as she walked away, her boyfriend got down on one knee and proposed."

"No way!" She leaned forward with a fierce look on her face, her eyes bright. "What did she say?"

"I have no clue. I left." I ignored whatever feeling might want to show up at that thought. Everett gave me a glance, and I shook my head. "Enough of that. Yes, the wedding that she did was great, but I honestly have no idea who she is, and she has a job. She doesn't need to work here." And I didn't know what I would do if I saw her again or had to work with her. There had been such an intense connection that I knew it would be awkward as hell. But thankfully, she had her own business and wasn't going to come to the Wilder Retreat for a job.

I left Sandy and Everett on their own, knowing that they were capable, at least for now. And I knew who we would have to hire if she said yes, and if my other brother didn't kill me first.

I washed my hands in the sink on the way out, grateful that at least I looked somewhat decent, if not a little disheveled, and made my way out front, hoping that the wedding planner who came in through the doors would be the one that would stick. Because we needed some good luck. After the day we've had, we needed some good luck.

I turned the corner and nearly tripped over my feet.

Because, of course, fate was this way.

It was her.

Of all the wedding planners from all the wedding venues, it was her.

In the mood to read another family saga? Meet the Wilder Brothers in One Way Back to Me!

FROM BITTERSWEET PROMISES
LEIF

"Not only did you convince me to somehow go on a blind date, it became a double date. How on earth did you work this magic on me, cousin?" I asked Lake as she leaned against the pillar just inside the restaurant.

Lake grinned at me, her dark hair pulled away from her face. She had on this swingy black dress and looked as if she were excited, anxious, nervous, and happy all at the same time. Considering she was bouncing on her toes when usually Lake was calm, cool, and collected, was saying something. "I asked, and you said yes. Because you love me."

"I might love you because we're family, but I still think we're making a mistake." I shook my head and pulled at my shirt sleeves. Lake had somehow convinced me to wear a button-up shirt tucked into gray pants, I even had on shiny shoes. I looked like a damn banker. But if that's what Lake wanted, that's what I would do.

Lake might technically be my cousin, even though we weren't blood-related, but we were more like brother and sister than any of my other cousins.

I had siblings, as did Lake, but with the generational gap, we were at least a decade older than all of our other cousins. That meant, despite the fact that we had lived over an hour apart for most of our lives, we'd grown up more like siblings.

I loved my three younger siblings and talked to them daily. Unlike some blended families, they *were* my brothers and sister and not like strangers or distant family members. I didn't feel a disconnect from the three of them, but Lake was still closer to me.

Probably because we were either heading into our thirties or already there, where most of our other cousins were either just now in their early twenties or still teenagers in high school. With how big we Montgomerys were as a family, it made sense that there would be such a widespread age group. That meant that Lake and I were best friends, cousins, practically siblings, and sometimes the banes of each other's existences.

We were also business owners and partners and saw each other too often these days. That was probably why she convinced me to go on a blind double date. But she had been out with Zach before. I, however, had never met May. Lake had some connection with her that I wasn't sure about, and for some reason Lake's date had said yes to this double date.

And, in the complicated way of family, I had agreed to it. I must have been tired. Or perhaps I'd had too many beers. Because I didn't do blind dates, and recently, I didn't do dates at all.

Lake scanned her phone, then looked up at me, all innocence in her smart gaze. "You shouldn't have told me you wanted to settle down in your old age."

I narrowed my eyes. "I'm still in my early thirties, jerk. Stop calling me old."

"I shouldn't call you old since you're only a few years older than me." She fluttered her eyelashes and I flipped her off, ignoring the stare from the older woman next to me. Though I was a tattoo artist, I didn't have many visible tattoos. Most of mine were on my back and legs, hidden from the world unless I wanted to show them. I hadn't figured out what I wanted on my arms beyond a few small pieces on my wrists and upper shoulders. And since tattoos were permanent, I was taking my time. If a client needed to see my skin with ink to feel comfortable, I'd show them my back. My body was a canvas, so I did what I could to set people at ease.

But I still had the eyebrow piercing and had recently taken out my nose ring. I didn't look too scary for most people. But apparently, flipping off a woman, growling, and cursing a time or two in front of strangers probably made me appear too close to the dark side.

"Yes, I want to settle down, but this will be awkward, won't it? Where the two of us are strangers, and the two of you aren't?" I wanted a life, a future, and yeah, one day to settle down with someone. I just didn't know why I'd mentioned it to Lake in the first place.

"If it helps, May doesn't know Zach, either. So it's a group of strangers, except I know everybody." She clapped her hands together and did her version of an evil laugh, and I just shook my head.

"Considering what you do for a living and how you like to manipulate things in your way, this makes sense. Are you going to be adding a matchmaking company to your conglomerate?"

Lake just fluttered her eyelashes again and laughed. Lake owned a small tech company that made a shit ton of money over the past couple of years. And because she was brilliant at what she did, innovative, and liked pushing money towards women-owned businesses, she owned more than one company at this point and was an investor in mine. I wouldn't be surprised if she found a way to open up a women-owned matchmaking company right here in town.

"It might be fun. I can call it Montgomery Links." Her eyes went wide. "Oh, my God. I have to write that down." She pulled out her phone, began to take notes, and I pinched the bridge of my nose.

"You know I trust you with my actual life, but I don't know if I trust you with my dating life."

Lake tossed her hair behind her shoulder as she continued to type. "Shut up. You love me. And once I finish setting you up, the rest of the family's next."

"Oh, really? You're going to get Daisy and Noah next?" I asked, speaking of two more of our cousins.

"Maybe. Of course, Sebastian's the only one of the younger group that seems to have a serious girlfriend."

I nodded, speaking of our other familial business partner. Sebastian was still a teenager, though in college. He had wanted to open up Montgomery Ink Legacy with me, the full title of our company. There was a legacy to it, and Sebastian had wanted in. So, though he didn't work there full-time, he was putting his future towards us. And in the ways of young love, he and his girlfriend had been together since middle school. The fact that my younger cousin was better at relationships than I was didn't make me feel great. But I was going to ignore that.

"You're not going to start up a matchmaking service, are you? Or maybe an app?"

"Dating apps are ridiculous these days, they practically want you to invest in coins to bid on dates, and that's not something I'm in the mood for. But maybe there's something I can try. I'll add it to my list."

Lake's list of inventions and tech was notorious, and knowing the brilliance of my cousin, she would one day rule the world and might eventually cross everything off that list.

"Oh, here's Zach." Lake's face brightened immediately, and she smiled up at a man with dark hair, piercing gray eyes, and an actual dimple on his cheek.

Tonight was not only about my blind date, but me getting the lay of the land when it came to Zach. I was the first step into meeting the family. Oh, if Zach passed my gauntlet, he would meet the rest of the Montgomerys, and we were mighty. All one hundred of us.

"Zach, you're here." Lake's voice went soft, and she went on her tiptoes even in her high heels as Zach pressed a soft kiss to her lips.

"Of course, I'm here. And you're early, as usual."

Lake blushed and ducked her head. "Well, you know me. I like to be early because being on time is late," she said at the same time I did, mumbling under my breath. It was a familiar refrain when it came to us.

"Zach, good to meet you," I said, holding out my hand.

The other man gripped it firmly and shook. "Nice to meet you too, Leif. I know you might be the one on a blind date soon, but I'm nervous."

I chuckled, shaking my head. "Yeah, I'm pretty nervous too. Though I'm grateful that Lake's trying to look out for me."

My cousin laughed softly. "You totally were not saying that a few minutes ago, but be suave and sophisticated now. Or just be yourself, May's on her way."

I met Zach's gaze and we both rolled our eyes. When I turned toward the door, I saw a woman of average height, with black straight hair, green eyes, and a sweet smile. I didn't know much about May, other than Lake knew her and liked her. If I was going to start dating again after taking time off to get the rest of my life together, I might as well start with someone that one of my best friends liked.

"May, I'm so glad that you're here," Lake said as she hugged the other woman tightly.

As Lake began to bounce on her heels, I realized that my cousin's cool, calm, and collected exterior was only for work. She was bouncing and happy when it came to her friends or when she was nervous. I knew that, of course, but I had forgotten how she had turned into the mogul that she was. It was good to see her relaxed and happy.

Now I just needed to figure out how to do that for myself.

May stood in front of me, and I felt like I was starting middle school all over again. A new school, a new life, and a past that didn't make much sense to anyone else.

I swallowed hard and nodded, not putting out my hand to shake, thinking that would be weird, but I also didn't want to hug her. I didn't even know this woman. Why was everything so awkward? Instead, I lifted my chin. "Hello, May. It's nice to meet you. Lake says only good things."

There, smooth. Not really. Zach began to move out of frame, with Lake at his side as the two went to speak to the hostess, leaving May and me alone.

453

This wasn't going to be awkward at all.

The woman just smiled at me, her eyes wide. "It's nice to meet you, too. And Lake does speak highly of you. Also, this is very awkward, so I'm so sorry if I say something stupid. I know that your cousin said that I should be set up with you which is great but I'm not great at blind dates and apparently this is a double date and now I'm going to stop talking." She said the words so quickly they all ran into one breath.

I shook my head and laughed. "We're on the same page there."

"Okay, good. It's nice to meet you, Leif Montgomery."

"And it's nice to meet you too, May."

We made our way to Lake and Zach, who had gotten our table, and we all sat down, talking about work and other things. May was in child life development, taught online classes, and was also a nanny.

"I'm actually about to start with a new family soon. I'm excited. I know that being a nanny isn't something that most people strive for, or at least that's what they tell you, but I love being able to work with children and be the person that is there when a single parent or even both parents are out in the workforce, trying to do everything."

I nodded, taking a sip of my beer. "I get you completely. With how my parents worked, I was lucky that they were able to get childcare within the buildings. Since they each owned their own businesses, they made it work. But my family worked long hours, and that's why I ended up being the babysitter a lot of the times when childcare wasn't an option." I cleared my throat. "I'm a lot older than a lot of my cousins," I added.

"Both of us are, but I'm glad that you only said yourself," Lake said, grinning. She leaned into Zach as she spoke, the four of us in a horseshoe-shaped booth. That gave May and me space since this was a first date and still awkward as hell, and so Lake and Zach could cuddle. Not that that was something I needed to be a part of.

"Oh, I'm glad that you didn't judge. The last few dates that I've been on they always gave me weird looks because I think they expected a nanny to be this old crone or someone that's looking for a different job." She shrugged and continued. "When I eventually get married and maybe even start a family, I want to continue my job. I like being there to help another family achieve their goals. And I can't believe I just said start a family on my first date. And that I mentioned that I've been on a few other dates." She let out a breath. "I'm notoriously bad at dating. Like, the worst. Just warning you."

I laughed, shaking my head. "I'm rusty at it, so don't worry." And even though I said that, I had a feeling that May felt no spark towards me, and I didn't feel anything towards her. She was nice and pleasant, and I could probably consider her a friend one day. But there wasn't any spark. May's eyes weren't dancing. She wasn't leaning forward, trying to touch my hand across the table. We were just sitting there casually, enjoying a really good steak, as Lake and Zach enjoyed their date.

By the end of dinner, I didn't want dessert, and neither did May, so we said goodbye to the other couple, who decided to stay. I walked May to her car, ignoring Lake's warning look, but I didn't know what exactly she was warning me about.

"Thanks for dinner," May said. "I could have paid. I know this is a blind date and all that, but you didn't have to pay."

I shook my head. "I paid for the four of us because I wanted to be nice. I'll make Lake pay next time."

May beamed. "Yes, I like that. You guys are a good family."

"Anyway," I said, clearing my throat as I stuck my hands in my pockets. "I guess I'll see you around."

May just looked at me, threw her head back, and laughed. "You're right. You are rusty at this."

"Sorry." Heat flushed my skin, and I resisted the urge to tug on my eyebrow ring.

"It's okay. No spark. I'm used to it. I don't spark well."

"May, I'm sorry." I cringed. "It's not you."

"Oh, God, please don't say that. 'It's not you. It's me. You're working on yourself. You're just so busy with work.' I've heard it all."

"Seriously?" I asked. May was hot. Nice, but there just wasn't a spark.

She shrugged. "It's okay. I'll probably see you around

sometime because I am friends with Lake. However, I am perfectly fine having this be our one and only. You'll find your person. It's okay that it's not me." And with that, she got in the car and left, leaving me standing there.

Well then. Tonight wasn't horrible, but it wasn't great. I got in my car, and instead of heading home where I'd be alone, watching something on some streaming service while I drank a beer and pretended that I knew what I was doing with my life, I headed into Montgomery Ink Legacy.

We were the third branch of the company and the first owned by our generation. Montgomery Ink was the tattoo shop in downtown Denver. While there were open spots for some walk-ins and special circumstances, my father, aunt, and their team had years' worth of waiting lists. They worked their asses off and made sure to get in everybody that they could, but people wanted Austin Montgomery's art. Same with my aunt, Maya.

There was another tattoo shop down in Colorado Springs, owned by my parents' cousins, who I just called aunt and uncle because we were close enough that using real titles for everybody got confusing. Montgomery Ink Too was thriving down there, and they had waiting lists as well. My family could have opened more shops and gone nationwide, even global if they wanted to, but they liked keeping it how it was, in the family and those connected.

We were a branch, but our own in the making. I had

gone into business with Lake, of course, and Sebastian, when he was ready, as well as Nick. Nick was my best friend. I had known him for ages, and he had wanted to be part of something as well. He might not be a Montgomery by name, but he had eaten over at my family's house enough times throughout the years that he was practically a Montgomery. And he had invested in the company as well, and so now we were nearly a year into owning the shop and trying not to fail.

I pulled into the parking lot, grateful it was still open since we didn't close until nine most nights, and greeted Nick, who was still working.

Sebastian was in the back, going over sketches with a client, and I nodded at him. He might be eighteen, but he was still in training, an apprentice, and was working his ass off to learn.

"Date sucked then?" Sebastian asked, and Nick just rolled his eyes and went back to work on a client's wrist.

"I don't want to talk about it," I groaned.

The rest of the staff was off since Nick would close up on his own. Sebastian was just there since he didn't have homework or a date with Marley.

"Was she hot at least?" Sebastian asked, and the client, a woman in her sixties, bopped him on the head with her bag gently.

"Sebastian Montgomery. Be nice."

Sebastian blushed. "Sorry, Mrs. Anderson."

I looked over at the woman and grinned. "Hi, Mrs. Anderson. It's nice to see you out of the classroom."

She narrowed her eyes at me, even though they filled with laughter. "I needed my next Jane Austen tattoo, thank you very much," the older woman said as she went back to working with Sebastian. She had been my and then Sebastian's English teacher. The fact that she was on her fifth tattoo with some literary quote told me that I had been damn lucky in most of my teachers growing up.

She was kick-ass, and I had a feeling that she would let Sebastian do the tattoo for her rather than just have him work on the design with me as we did for most of the people who came in. He had learned under my father and was working under me now. It was strange to think that he wasn't a little kid anymore. But he was in a long-term relationship, kicking ass in college, and knew what he wanted to do with his life.

I might know what I want to do with my work life, but everything else seemed a little off.

"So it didn't work out?" Nick asked as he walked up to the front desk with the clients after going over aftercare.

"Not really," I said, looking down at my phone.

The client, a woman in her mid-twenties with bright pink hair, a lip ring, and kind eyes, leaned over the desk to look at me.

"You'll find someone, Leif. Don't worry."

I looked at our regular and shook my head. "Thanks, Kim. Too bad that you don't swing this way."

I winked as I said it, a familiar refrain from both of us.

Kim was married to a woman named Sonya, and the two of them were happy and working on in vitro with donated sperm for their first kid.

"Hey, I'm sorry too that I'm a lesbian. I'll never know what it means to have Leif Montgomery. Or any Montgomery, since I found my love far too quickly. I mean, what am I ever going to do not knowing the love of a Montgomery?"

Mrs. Anderson chuckled from her chair, Sebastian held back a snort, and I just looked at Nick, who rolled his eyes and helped Kim out of the place.

I was tired, but it was okay. The date wasn't all bad. May was nice. But it felt like I didn't have much right then.

And then Nick sat in front of me, scowled, and I realized that I did have something. I had my friends and my family. I didn't need much more.

"So, you and May didn't work out?"

I raised a brow. "You knew her name? Did I tell you that?"

Nick shook his head. "Lake did."

That made sense, considering the two of them spoke as much as we did. "So, was it your idea to set me up on a blind date?"

"Fuck no. That was all Lake. I just do what she says. Like we all do."

I sighed and went through my appointments for the

next day. "We're busy for the next month. That's good, right?" I asked.

"You're the business genius here. I just play with ink. But yes, that's good. Now, don't let your cousin set you up any more dates. Find them for yourself. You know what you're doing."

"So says the man who dates less than me."

"That's what you think. I'm more private about it. As it should be." I flipped him off as he stood up, then he gestured towards a stack of bills in the corner. "You have a few personal things that made their way here. Don't want you to miss out on them before you head home."

"Thanks, bro."

"No problem. I'm going to help Sebastian with his consult, and then I'll clean up. You should head home. Though you're doing it alone, so I feel sorry for you."

"Fuck you," I called out.

"Fuck you, too."

"Boys," Mrs. Anderson said, in that familiar English teacher refrain, and both Nick and I cringed before saying, "Sorry," simultaneously.

Sebastian snickered, then went back to work, and I headed towards the edge of the counter, picking up the stack of papers. Most were bills, some were random papers that needed to be filed or looked over. Some were just junk mail. But there was one letter, written in block print that didn't look familiar. Chills went up my spine and I opened it, wondering what the fuck this was. Maybe it was someone asking to buy my house. I got a lot of handwritten letters for that, but I didn't think this was going to be that. I swallowed hard, slid open the paper, and froze.

"I'll find you, boy. Oops. Looks like I already did. Be waiting. I know you miss me."

I let the paper hit the top of the counter and swallowed hard, trying to remain cool so I didn't worry anyone else.

I didn't know exactly who that was from, but I had a horrible feeling that they wouldn't wait long to tell me.

Read the rest in Bittersweet Promises! OUT NOW!

ALSO FROM CARRIE ANN RYAN

The Montgomery Ink Legacy Series:

Book 1: Bittersweet Promises (Leif & Brooke)

Book 2: At First Meet (Nick & Lake)

Book 2.5: Happily Ever Never (May & Leo)

Book 3: Longtime Crush (Sebastian & Raven)

Book 4: Best Friend Temptation (Noah, Ford, and Greer)

Book 4.5: Happily Ever Maybe (Jennifer & Gus)

Book 5: Last First Kiss (Daisy & Hugh)

Book 6: His Second Chance (Kane & Phoebe)

Book 7: One Night with You (Kingston & Claire)

Book 8: Accidentally Forever (Crew & Aria)

Book 9: Last Chance Seduction (Lexington & Mercy)

Book 10: Kiss Me Forever (Brooklyn & Reece)

Book 11: His Guilty Pleasure (Dash & Aly)

ALSO FROM CARRIE ANN RYAN

The Cage Family

Book 1: The Forever Rule (Aston & Blakely)

Book 2: An Unexpected Everything (Isabella & Weston)

Book 3: If You Were Mine (Dorian & Harper)

Book 4: One Quick Obsession (Hudson & Scarlett)

Book 5: Pretend it's Forever (???? & ????)

Ashford Creek

Book 1: Legacy (Callum & Felicity)

Book 2: Crossroads (Bohdi & Keira)

Book 3: Westward (Atlas & Elizabeth)

Clover Lake

Book 1: Always a Fake Bridesmaid (Livvy & Ewan)

Book 2: Accidental Runaway Groom (Jamie & Sharp)

The Wilder Brothers Series:

Book 1: One Way Back to Me (Eli & Alexis)

Book 2: Always the One for Me (Evan & Kendall)

Book 3: The Path to You (Everett & Bethany)

Book 4: Coming Home for Us (Elijah & Maddie)

Book 5: Stay Here With Me (East & Lark)

Book 6: Finding the Road to Us (Elliot, Trace, and Sidney)

Book 7: Moments for You (Ridge & Aurora)

Book 7.5: A Wilder Wedding (Amos & Naomi)

Book 8: Forever For Us (Wyatt & Ava)

Book 9: Pieces of Me (Gabriel & Briar)

Book 10: Endlessly Yours (Brooks & Rory)

The Falling for the Cassidy Brothers Series:

Book 1: Good Time Boyfriend (Heath & Devney)

Book 2: Last Minute Fiancé (Luca & Addison)

Book 3: Second Chance Husband (August & Paisley)

Montgomery Ink Denver:

Book 0.5: Ink Inspired (Shep & Shea)

Book 0.6: Ink Reunited (Sassy, Rare, and Ian)

Book 1: Delicate Ink (Austin & Sierra)

Book 1.5: Forever Ink (Callie & Morgan)

Book 2: Tempting Boundaries (Decker and Miranda)

Book 3: Harder than Words (Meghan & Luc)

Book 3.5: Finally Found You (Mason & Presley)

Book 4: Written in Ink (Griffin & Autumn)

Book 4.5: Hidden Ink (Hailey & Sloane)

Book 5: Ink Enduring (Maya, Jake, and Border)

Book 6: Ink Exposed (Alex & Tabby)

Book 6.5: Adoring Ink (Holly & Brody)

Book 6.6: Love, Honor, & Ink (Arianna & Harper)

Book 7: Inked Expressions (Storm & Everly)

Book 7.3: Dropout (Grayson & Kate)

Book 7.5: Executive Ink (Jax & Ashlynn)

Book 8: Inked Memories (Wes & Jillian)

Book 8.5: Inked Nights (Derek & Olivia)

Book 8.7: Second Chance Ink (Brandon & Lauren)

Book 8.5: Montgomery Midnight Kisses (Alex & Tabby Bonus(

Bonus: Inked Kingdom (Stone & Sarina)

Montgomery Ink: Colorado Springs

Book 1: Fallen Ink (Adrienne & Mace)

Book 2: Restless Ink (Thea & Dimitri)

Book 2.5: Ashes to Ink (Abby & Ryan)

Book 3: Jagged Ink (Roxie & Carter)

Book 3.5: Ink by Numbers (Landon & Kaylee)

The Montgomery Ink: Boulder Series:

Book 1: Wrapped in Ink (Liam & Arden)

Book 2: Sated in Ink (Ethan, Lincoln, and Holland)

Book 3: Embraced in Ink (Bristol & Marcus)

Book 3: Moments in Ink (Zia & Meredith)

Book 4: Seduced in Ink (Aaron & Madison)

Book 4.5: Captured in Ink (Julia, Ronin, & Kincaid)

Book 4.7: Inked Fantasy (Secret ??)

Book 4.8: A Very Montgomery Christmas (The Entire Boulder Family)

The Montgomery Ink: Fort Collins Series:

Book 1: Inked Persuasion (Jacob & Annabelle)

Book 2: Inked Obsession (Beckett & Eliza)

Book 3: Inked Devotion (Benjamin & Brenna)

Book 3.5: Nothing But Ink (Clay & Riggs)

Book 4: Inked Craving (Lee & Paige)

Book 5: Inked Temptation (Archer & Killian)

The Promise Me Series:

Book 1: Forever Only Once (Cross & Hazel)

Book 2: From That Moment (Prior & Paris)

Book 3: Far From Destined (Macon & Dakota)

Book 4: From Our First (Nate & Myra)

The Whiskey and Lies Series:

Book 1: <u>Whiskey Secrets</u> (Dare & Kenzie)

Book 2: <u>Whiskey Reveals</u> (Fox & Melody)

Book 3: <u>Whiskey Undone</u> (Loch & Ainsley)

The Gallagher Brothers Series:

Book 1: <u>Love Restored</u> (Graham & Blake)

Book 2: <u>Passion Restored</u> (Owen & Liz)

Book 3: <u>Hope Restored</u> (Murphy & Tessa)

The Less Than Series:

Book 1: Breathless With Her (Devin & Erin)

Book 2: Reckless With You (Tucker & Amelia)

Book 3: Shameless With Him (Caleb & Zoey)

The Fractured Connections Series:

Book 1: Breaking Without You (Cameron & Violet)

Book 2: Shouldn't Have You (Brendon & Harmony)

Book 3: Falling With You (Aiden & Sienna)

Book 4: Taken With You (Beckham & Meadow)

ALSO FROM CARRIE ANN RYAN

The On My Own Series:
Book 0.5: My First Glance
Book 1: My One Night (Dillon & Elise)
Book 2: My Rebound (Pacey & Mackenzie)
Book 3: My Next Play (Miles & Nessa)
Book 4: My Bad Decisions (Tanner & Natalie)

The Ravenwood Coven Series:
Book 1: Dawn Unearthed
Book 2: Dusk Unveiled
Book 3: Evernight Unleashed

The Aspen Pack Series:
Book 1: Etched in Honor
Book 2: Hunted in Darkness
Book 3: Mated in Chaos
Book 4: Harbored in Silence
Book 5: Marked in Flames

The Talon Pack:
Book 1: Tattered Loyalties
Book 2: An Alpha's Choice
Book 3: Mated in Mist
Book 4: Wolf Betrayed
Book 5: Fractured Silence
Book 6: Destiny Disgraced
Book 7: Eternal Mourning
Book 8: Strength Enduring

468

Book 9: <u>Forever Broken</u>
Book 10: Mated in Darkness
Book 11: Fated in Winter

Redwood Pack Series:
Book 0.5: <u>An Alpha's Path</u>
Book 1: <u>A Taste for a Mate</u>
Book 2: <u>Trinity Bound</u>
Book 2.5: <u>A Night Away</u>
Book 3: <u>Enforcer's Redemption</u>
Book 3.5: <u>Blurred Expectations</u>
Book 3.7: <u>Forgiveness</u>
Book 4: <u>Shattered Emotions</u>
Book 5: <u>Hidden Destiny</u>
Book 5.5: <u>A Beta's Haven</u>
Book 6: <u>Fighting Fate</u>
Book 6.5: <u>Loving the Omega</u>
Book 6.7: <u>The Hunted Heart</u>
Book 7: <u>Wicked Wolf</u>

The Elements of Five Series:
Book 1: From Breath and Ruin
Book 2: From Flame and Ash
Book 3: From Spirit and Binding
Book 4: From Shadow and Silence

Dante's Circle Series:
Book 1: <u>Dust of My Wings</u>

Book 2: <u>Her Warriors' Three Wishes</u>

Book 3: <u>An Unlucky Moon</u>

Book 3.5: <u>His Choice</u>

Book 4: <u>Tangled Innocence</u>

Book 5: <u>Fierce Enchantment</u>

Book 6: <u>An Immortal's Song</u>

Book 7: <u>Prowled Darkness</u>

Book 8: Dante's Circle Reborn

Holiday, Montana Series:

Book 1: <u>Charmed Spirits</u>

Book 2: <u>Santa's Executive</u>

Book 3: <u>Finding Abigail</u>

Book 4: <u>Her Lucky Love</u>

Book 5: Dreams of Ivory

The Branded Pack Series:

(Written with Alexandra Ivy)

Book 1: <u>Stolen and Forgiven</u>

Book 2: <u>Abandoned and Unseen</u>

Book 3: <u>Buried and Shadowed</u>

ABOUT THE AUTHOR

Carrie Ann Ryan is the New York Times and USA Today bestselling author of contemporary, paranormal, and young adult romance. Her works include the Montgomery Ink, Redwood Pack, Fractured Connections, and Elements of Five series, which have sold over 3.0 million books worldwide. She started writing while in graduate school for her advanced degree in chemistry and hasn't stopped since. Carrie Ann has written over seventy-five novels and novellas with more in the works. When she's not losing herself in her emotional and action-packed worlds, she's reading as much as she can while wrangling her clowder of cats who have more followers than she does.

www.CarrieAnnRyan.com

www.ingramcontent.com/pod-product-compliance
Lightning Source LLC
Chambersburg PA
CBHW021345130726
47899CB00019B/3111